I0725540

CHILD OF WRATH

CHILD OF WRATH

JB Biggs

© 2019 Beacon Publishing Group.

All rights reserved.

No portion of this book may be reproduced in whole or in part, by any means whatsoever, except for brief passages excerpted for the purpose of review, without permission of the publisher.

For information, or to order additional copies, please contact:

Beacon Publishing Group
132 West, 31 Street, 15th Floor
New York, NY 10001

800.817.8480 / beaconpublishinggroup.com

ISBN-13: 978-1-949472-84-4

ISBN-10: 1-949472-84-1

Publisher's catalog available upon request.

Printed in the USA.

"One of the greatest gifts you can get as a writer is to be born into an unhappy family."
-Pat Conroy

Foreword

At the age of seven and a half, I have a clear memory. The wide, grassy field of the elementary school had wisps of fog rising up from the ground as the morning sun cut through the chill of a wet California autumn. Red maple leaves cluttered the sides of the road outside the fence. It had been raining in the night and would drizzle in the day, but for a moment, it was clear and bright and cold under a perfect, high, blue Pacific sky.

I wore the cowboy boots that my mom had bought me. They were too small and hurt my feet and I'd worn them so smooth on the bottom that I looked like a cartoon character trying to get traction when I tried to run in them. I loved those shoes for some reason.

Walking around the schoolyard with hands in the pockets of my jacket, I was working on a problem. I had memories. Many, many memories, but they were all jumbled up. Looking back, I could clearly picture at least six different places that had been "home" at one time or another. There had been the house in Greenville (which I'd called "Greenland") with the Brahma Bulls grazing on the hill behind our house. There had been the apartment with the pomegranate tree behind it in Los Angeles. There had been several others … I could not understand why or how, but I felt that I was on the edge of losing something important. My history-where I had come from, what "home" was, it was all slipping into a jumbled pile of snapshots in my mind. It occurred to me that if I let it happen, this moment with the mist rising up out of the field would flutter full of color and die like one of the red leaves soaked by rain waiting to decompose in the gutter.

Being a little over seven years old, I decided to solve my problem by use of a game. I pretended that my jacket was a "computer jacket" which had keyboards in the pockets. I could see whatever I typed in my vision like a heads-up-display. I typed out a long letter to myself, first visualizing, then memorizing every letter as if it were hanging in the monochrome blackness of a computer screen. I forced myself to visualize and remember, so that I would never lose what I saw, where I was, where I came from. Who I was. I could remember that letter verbatim for years afterward. I remember snatches of it even now.

I like to think that I started writing in the yard of an elementary school at seven and a half, on a cold autumn day in California. To me, writing is about observation. Good writers are not thinkers or performers or instructors. Good writers are observers, rememberers, visualizers.

The idea of novelizing one's own childhood has always seemed to be so narcissistic as to be masturbatory in my mind. To do it properly, you have to put yourself in the head of your characters, which in this case are siblings, parents, and relatives. It is incredibly easy to rewrite things to make you look better, and it is so self-regarding to put that much effort into examining one's own life that I never wanted to even bother. It has occurred to me recently that my upbringing and life are so completely different from the norm that it is worth recounting just so people can understand something so alien. It has also occurred to me that it cannot "keep" forever in the imperfect film-reel I keep always in my head-snatches of video and pictures spanning the decades. Eventually even the letter I so painstakingly wrote to my future-self had faded in detail, and so must memories that are not written down.

As to the novelization, that will be understandable as you read. In going back to these memories, one must feel again what one felt at the time, smell the smells, see the colors, hear the sounds. To do that when one had a childhood as I had, one invites pain. It really helps to be able to fictionalize, create a third person character to whom it happens, not yourself.

I write for many reasons, but one of the most compelling is the sense that it isn't enough to train yourself to observe and memorize. Eventually everything decays, moments pass, and with them lessons, stories, and people. Some things need to be remembered.

Prologue

Pacific Ocean, 2000

The call came amid the haze of nausea and exhaustion that hung over everything like a fog. It was Laura shaking Jonah's shoulder, begging him to get up. Curled on his side like a dying animal turned into roadkill, Jonah managed a groan and tried to push his mother away. Suddenly he raised his head, realizing that if she was shaking him awake, there could be nobody at the wheel.

The boat hit a big wave and tipped up, then down and sideways in the sickening side-rolling motion it had started as soon as they hit open ocean and never stopped. Jonah was battling to get to his feet as Laura braced herself in the doorway against the violent rocking motion.

"Jonah! Jonah I can't do it. You have to take the wheel." Laura was pale. She looked like she was about to collapse. She was barely holding herself upright. In the darkness of the cabin, her eyes were pits of darkness with an earnest gleam in their depths.

Jonah nodded, fighting his legs underneath him, clutching the hand holds in the cabin, walking with his arms across the miserable few feet to the brass ship's wheel as they careened up and down and sideways and back like an out of control seesaw set on a merry go round mounted to a ferris wheel.

Jonah's inner ear was spinning. His vision was blurry. He had no earthly idea what time it was. It was just dark. Time didn't exist out here, just the endless beating of the waves.

Laura was on her knees, one hand on the rail to the cabin below decks. "Keep the compass pointed north. You have to keep it pointed north or we are going to die."

Jonah nodded. So this was how it would happen. Of course. He held the wheel, looking at the marks on the big compass set on the wooden dash behind it. The light under the compass was the only illumination he could see. Even their faint running lights seemed to have been swallowed in the all-consuming darkness of the storm.

Behind and below his feet, Jonah could hear the steady chugging of the big diesel engine. It was slightly comforting that the old thing somehow hadn't quit.

Jonah blinked a few times, trying to see anything whatsoever in the dark spray and haze beyond the cockpit windows. He knew about the waves by the feel of the ship. Every time they crested a wave, the bow would dip and they would swoop downward into the trough like a skateboard going down a halfpipe. Then they would turn up and up as the face of the next wave caught them, tilting the entire boat back like they were going up a steep ramp. Every time they did this, Jonah winced. He could feel the boat creaking, he was anticipating the wave that would smash into the bow like an avalanche, blasting over the front of the boat in an explosion of noise and water. Every time this happened, Jonah thanked God that they hadn't split a seam somewhere and started taking on water.

Why the hell am I here?

Jonah clutched the wheel as another wave of nausea overcame him. He clenched his jaw shut so he wouldn't retch in the middle of the cockpit, not that it would make a difference. He had spent the last four or five hours emptying his body of *anything* it might possibly contain over the side of the boat. There was nothing left inside him but dry heaves. The hobbyhorse forward and back motion of the big waves was something he could deal with. What had killed them all was the endless, unceasing, almost violent back and forth side to side bobbing this damn crate had started the minute they got out of San Diego Harbor.

Naturally, Walter had had the wheel long enough to get them out of the smooth harbor, had insisted that they would get out of the rough seas soon, and had been among the first to collapse below deck in a heap when it got really rough. Once again, here was Jonah being the dad, taking care of his family because nobody else would.

Why the unholy fuck am I here? How the hell do I do this to myself? What the fuck is wrong with me?

Walter and Laura wanted to have "one last family vacation" in the small window of time left before Jonah was called up to the Israeli army. They had been planning something, and after more than two years working in high end construction in the uber rich enclaves of Sausalito and Tiburon California, they had actual money and (apparently) an actual plan. Just that proved that at least some things really *had* changed. He had to believe that they were reaching out, trying to reconnect with their only son before they lost him forever.

Jonah had been loath to return, even with no work available in Israel. He had cross-examined his sisters carefully, listening for holes in the story his parents had given him. They assured him that yes, Walter was making very good money now. Yes, so was Laura. Yes, they had been planning out a whole trip and it seemed legit.

Walter had purchased a boat in San Diego and he wanted to bring it up the coast to San Francisco. He and Laura thought this would be a great opportunity to have a nice vacation. It would be a leisurely cruise up the California coast, from the idyllic, warm beauty of

Southern California to the whale-cruising waters of the north. Jonah found the plan encouraging for several reasons. The fact that his father had bought a boat made him think they really *were* doing well. He knew that Walter was a competent navigator and sailor. They had spent many days on his sailboat in the San Francisco Bay back in the "good days" of Jonah's childhood. If Walter knew anything well, it had to be boats. They had been an obsession of his since he was a young man. Still, Jonah had been unsettled. He had known for a very long time that he had to triple check *anything* his parents told him. Unfortunately, he still didn't know how to really be on his own with no support system at all, no close friends, no family, and no idea of what "normal" looked like. It had been loneliness that finally pushed him to listen to the voices over the phone telling him how different everything was now. He still had a need for a family even if his family didn't know what to do with him. Some part of Jonah wanted to believe that his parents could change and could become "real" parents. He knew the way he had left had been traumatic for them, and he hoped that it had jarred them into some self-reflection.

The boat sort of tipped over the top of a big wave and slid sideways with a sickening lurch. They seemed to be getting some kind of cross-chop, like one set of waves was coming one way and another was cutting through at an angle. Every time they hit one that wasn't square on the nose, the boat rolled sideways so far that Jonah worried they were going to just go completely over like a sailboat getting "knocked down."

He clutched the wheel so hard his knuckles were white, desperately praying that the boat not open up a seam along the line of dry rot he had seen below the water line.

Pay attention to this shit, you moron. This is a perfect example of what is wrong with you.

The voice of himself in his head wasn't letting up. Jonah forced himself to stay at the wheel, locking his knees to prevent his body from just collapsing, clenching his jaw against the dry heaves, holding himself upright with his arms clutching the wheel. He exerted the same willpower mentally, carefully and systematically examining every circumstance, every event that had led to him being here, in the dark, in a storm, miles off the coast in the largest body of water on the planet, standing on a rotting hulk that should never have been taken out of its berth, much less into the deep ocean.

This is you. This is what you let yourself get into. You have nobody to blame but yourself.

Jonah closed his eyes for a second as the worst of the sideways rolling abated like an inflatable punching bag toy bobbing its way back upright. Yes, this boat had a very appropriate nickname: The Puker. That was what the old fisherman had called it… That had been the first red flag. Jonah and Walter had been coming back from the store where they bought all the supplies for the trip. They had been walking back down the pier loaded down with shopping bags. As they passed the big fishing boat two berths down from Walter's new purchase, a middle aged guy with a beard had stepped off the fishing boat and started talking to them.

"Hey, I heard you're going to buy that boat…"

Walter had nodded, not wanting to slow down.

"Don't buy it. I used to crew for the owner back before they built that whole mess on the back of it." He gestured to the big extended cabin that now took up most of what had once been a working deck on the old fishing boat. "We had a name for it. We called her The Puker. Believe me, *you don't want that boat!*"

Walter had brushed him off. When Jonah asked him about it later, Walter had claimed the man was "jealous" and wanted the boat for himself.

No, Jonah, that was not the first red flag! Don't delude yourself!

Jonah swallowed against a dry throat as the boat tipped sideways, the deck undulating up and down, side to side, back and forth, never stopping the constant movement. He was developing a feel for the way she hit the waves. He could tell when a hit was too harsh for the old tub. In his mind's eye he was seeing that line of dry rot along the inside of the hull that the former owner had pointed out to Walter as they discussed the terms of sale. The guy had probably wanted to get rid of The Puker with a clear conscience. If that dry rotted section of hull got hit too hard with a wave, it could open up and they would be on the bottom of the Pacific Ocean in about five minutes. Jonah was trying to hit the waves in a way that minimized the shock on the old wooden hull.

He remembered the harbormaster coming out and telling them point blank not to go up the coast today. There was a storm out there, he'd said. Wait until tomorrow. Walter had insisted. He only had a couple days off from work. He had to get the boat up north during that window. Waiting out the storm wasn't an option. But no, that wasn't the first red flag either…

The first red flag? Probably the airport. Walter and Laura had arranged a flight down to San Diego to pick up the boat. They had arrived at a tiny little municipal airport that looked like it was straight out of the 1930s. Everything had seemed to be going great. Walter and Laura had obviously planned some things out this time, the trip had been easy, they were actually excited about the idea of a relaxing cruise vacation. Jonah had let down his guard.

They had come out of the airport terminal and Walter was having some kind of issue with the line of taxis waiting there. He was going to just grab a cab, but there were five of them plus luggage, and none of the taxis were vans. Walter and Laura had not arranged for transport to the boat, obviously. In a moment, Walter and Laura had jumped into the first cab in the line, yelling back to Jonah and his sisters to get in the second one and follow them.

Obviously, things didn't just work like they did in movies, and in moments, the second cab had lost sight of the first one in the chaos around the airport. Jonah was shocked to realize that neither of his sisters had the address of the marina they were going to, nor did either of them have a cell phone except him, but his cell was Israeli, and would not work in the USA.

They pulled over at a pay phone, Jonah found Laura's cell number in his phone's memory, and he had called her to get an address. They had finally arrived almost a half hour after their parents, to find an empty boardwalk and no sign of either of them. Eventually, Laura had come down from one of the docks looking for them, but Walter was too caught up in the excitement of buying his boat to bother. That had been quite a shit show.

Close. You are doing better. Don't pretend you didn't know this would be a fucking disaster before you ever got on the plane to come back to the States though Jonah.

Jonah sighed, the overpowering smell of brine, mildew, and vomit making the air feel thick like soup. He blinked to keep his eyes functioning. He thought he could see bright running lights somewhere out there in the endless, vast expanse of massive waves that must have extended for hundreds of miles. He knew there were big container ships out here that moved fast. It was very possible to get hit by one if you weren't paying attention. It went without saying that the bucket of shit Walter had bought didn't have radar.

Jonah knew he should never have trusted his parents as soon as they started saying things like "Everything is different now." He never should have come back. He should have stayed put and toughed it out until he was called up by the army. It was just so hard to find a job over there…

No, it wasn't just that.

Jonah had been lonely. He had wanted to have a family. He had wanted parents who were normal so much he had talked himself into believing them even when he knew better. It wasn't mere loneliness either. It was the black depression he'd lived with since he could remember.

It was hard to describe. There was a darkness always ready at hand, which stood ready like a shadowy watchman. It hovered there, and when the time was right, extended a smoky finger, plunging Jonah's soul into black despair. He lived in the hole he dug in his own heart, pounding on the walls in silent screaming. A tunnel led to a pinpoint of light and at the top, faces peered down in pity and scorn. In that pit, dark things slithered and seethed and drunk the blood that pumped from his veins as he waited and watched for the storm to pass.

That was what it was like. It was like there was no light, no life anywhere, no hope, no point, and he had no value. Hell, he'd known for an absolute fact that he had no value since he could walk. He had been taught that he was worthless from a young age. He just hadn't wanted to be *alone* with that blackness. Filling in activity and motion and busyness only kept the blackness at bay for so long. He knew it was coming and he knew he couldn't be alone with that.

Jonah should never have trusted Walter and Laura again after Papua New Guinea.

Don't fool yourself. You aren't that fucking stupid, Jonah. You should never have trusted them since you were ten years old!

Jonah closed his eyes again for a second, just moving with the boat as it bucked like a horse. It was true. He was a fucking codependent. There was something in him that was bent, broken, non-functional.

Something that had to do with self-esteem and trusting people you shouldn't. He was physically healthy, but somewhere in his soul he was like a man recovering from a nearly fatal accident. His soul was learning to walk again.

As the dark hours dragged on, Jonah let the memories come. One after another, every little thing he had hid from himself out of habit, every uncomfortable, almost unbearable to remember minute of his childhood. He made himself stand there and remember them all, not hide from any of them, just as he had to stand at that wheel and keep the boat on course or they would all die. He opened himself to the black storm within him as the black storm raged outside. Every humiliating moment he had wanted to put away and never look at again, every despicable thing he had lived through, every moment of suffering he had experienced, every time he had blatantly, willfully, willingly, intentionally, stupidly pushed it all aside and believed in his parents despite everything they had ever done.

You fucking loser. You are the reason you are here. You deserve to die here like a goddamn moron. You know that bowsprit is rotted out. If that opens up, this boat will be on the bottom in a minute flat and you will deserve everything you get! You did this to your fucking self, Jonah!

And he fought. He fought the waves. He fought the nausea, he fought the exhaustion. He fought the weakness within him that had led him to this point where he was a hair's breadth away from death *yet again.* Jonah fought, because he had to. It was the only thing he knew. Whatever else he may or may not be able to do with his life, even if it was only a few minutes longer, he had to get mad and he had to fight.

1

SATURDAY

Vallejo, California 1987

The light streamed in through the windows on the front of the yellow semi-Victorian house, filling the second story bedroom with dust particle beams of holographic glory. That bedroom was the best one in the house, according to Jonah, because it had two front facing windows with nice roof pop outs that overlooked the wide porch at the front of the house and delivered a view of the big, intimidating, cathedral-like church across the street.

Jonah often wished that he had that bedroom, but since there were two girls, and only one boy, he had been allocated a strange sort of cupboard-like room with no door on the back side of the house. He only had one very small window with a sill just big enough to set a broken set of binoculars on that he used to pretend to look at the sky at night.

The house creaked as the kids moved around upstairs. Century-old redwood studs shifted under the weight of the three of them as they played. It was the weekend and they were goofing off and enjoying not being in school. The backyard of the tall, narrow yellow house was large and had a lot of potential on such a sunny California day, but it also had a chain link fence between it and the alley behind the property which provided no protection from the roving gangs of black kids who had declared that block of Kentucky Street to be their "territory." Playing in the backyard might entail an encounter with armed kids who worked as drug peddlers for the local gangs. It was safer to stay upstairs, or at least that is what Jonah thought.

The kids were outcasts in this ghetto neighborhood. At school, they were the small minority who were not minorities, and were at times bullied by the majority minority kids who outnumbered them 5 to 1. They knew they were different, and while the random hatred of strangers based on skin color sometimes made them sad, they were mostly too young to really understand what it was all about.

Jonah was happy. He was feeling good. It might have been the California sun, or the gentle breeze that floated in through the old-fashioned screens in their heavy wood framed windows bearing the smell of the Pacific Ocean. He knew that not being in school helped his mood immensely. Things had begun to go bad at school and he didn't completely know why. Being ten, he tried to think of matters like visits to the assistant principal's office as little as possible.

It was one of those days in California that made you ache at the beauty of it all. The immensity of the blue sky strung across with "horsetail" clouds from the Pacific Ocean, the warm perfection of the climate, the light that had drawn filmmakers from across the country to settle on that coast so they could shoot their movies during the golden hour near sunset. During summertime, that little yellow house would get quite hot as the San Joaquin Valley got into triple digits and bubblegum would readily melt on the sidewalk as the kids took turns in front of a fan blowing air across a hunk of ice from the freezer in lieu of an air conditioner in their antique house, but it was not that time of year yet. Today, everything was perfect.

Hayden and Amy sat in the window seats under the big windows with the beams of glowing dust catching sunlight. They were watching in bemusement as Jonah did his 10 year old best to "gross out" the girls. Hayden was two years older than he was. A serious looking, pale-faced girl about as straight and thin as a broomstick. She was usually the leader of whatever activity the three engaged in during the blessed peace when their parents weren't home. She had once turned an old cassette recorder into an object of endless entertainment, first by recording the top 10 hits off the radio, and then by recording their own radio show complete with music, improv comedy acts, and interviews with outlandish characters of the kids' invention. They had become proficient at stuffing little wads of paper into the holes in the tops of cassettes to allow them to be recordable, and several of their grandfather's missionary sermon tapes had been repurposed in this way.

Amy was a chubby blond child with a ready laugh. She was always willing to be amused by the antics of her older siblings, and Jonah knew he could get a rise out of her. Amy would vary between being a fat-cheeked cherub and being a fat-cheeked imp, depending on whether or not there was any risk to her. The other two knew that she would sell them out to Mom and Dad at the drop of a hat. She was giggling in anticipation of the next part of the show, for when Jonah and Hayden got going, they could keep up their own version of a "Muppet Show" with their toys for hours.

Today Jonah was being mischievous. He wanted to do something to "gross out" the girls, so, being a ten year old boy, he went for bodily functions. Jonah was sitting down next to Amy's closet where an assortment of ridiculously cute stuffed bunnies, ponies, and glittery things were carefully arranged in the open closet doorway. With a wicked grin on his angular face, he picked up a stuffed bear and a barbie doll and began making them "talk."

Amy looked suspicious at first. She knew that Jonah considered her toys "stupid" and "girly" (which were pretty much synonymous for him). She dropped her guard after a minute as he knew she would, and he went in for the kill. Suddenly, the bear developed a bad case of the shits and, she being called "honey bear" (a bear that obviously excretes honey), the shits proved delicious to the barbie doll.

Jonah was amused by his own cleverness and didn't notice that the room had gone dead quiet at first. He looked up, wondering why he hadn't heard the inevitable "EEEWW!" and had several toys hurled at his head yet. Then he saw that neither of the girls were looking at him.

They were looking with ashen-faced horror at the doorway.

Jonah knew what had happened even as his mind fought to understand how. It was inexplicable. Dad never came up here … certainly not on a weekend. It just didn't make sense. How long had he been standing there?

There was no time for sound, only flashes of sight like stop motion film.

He came around the corner from the doorway like a charging animal. His highly angular, almost stylized looking face was twisted into something resembling a caricature of Satan. Long, pointed nose, extreme, angled eyebrows, narrow face, pointed chin. There was a twinkle in his dark eyes that told Jonah an entire story at a glance. It was like nothing he had ever seen in any other human's eyes. It was a mixture of blind rage and blind terror. It was the final stage of the Wrath.

Jonah sucked in his breath, knowing what would come. Normally, there were warning signals. Usually, the Wrath came after several stages had been met. Today there was nothing. No time to prepare. He decided to stand. The best thing he could do was try to stand up. He didn't even try to explain or speak as the toys dropped from his hands.

The powerful man was lean and wiry, with a strength borne of a lifetime of hard, outdoor work. He snatched Jonah off his feet like a ragdoll and held him up by his shirt, literally spitting in his face as he howled.

"FUCKING SHIT! YOU PIECE OF SHIT!!! FUCK!" And with something unintelligible, he had tucked the ten year old under an arm and charged back out the doorway.

Jonah was at a weird angle, his head lower than his legs, he tried to shield his face as his dad slammed his way through the doorway to the bedroom, feeling his head bounce off the side of the doorway as they went. He felt them traveling at improbable speed down the creaky, carpet-covered stairs and prayed that his Dad wouldn't drop him. At this angle he would surely break his neck.

They were through the kitchen on the first floor and into Dad's lair- the living room. Here, one did not go unless one was willing to risk the Wrath. If one HAD to go in the living room on a weekend, one brought Dad a beer or something from the kitchen on direct request from Mom and then got the hell out of there as soon as possible. Usually, he was fine, amusing himself with the TV, unless the beat up old hand-me-down TV wasn't working properly, in which case the house would be full of the sounds of fury and howling and the kids would be outside, as far away as possible.

Jonah hit the couch face first. He knew what was coming. It was almost a relief to know that there would be no anticipation, no time to dwell in terror or wonder when the shit would hit the fan. He assumed the position, knowing without even looking that his Dad had retrieved the huge buckled, wide leather belt from the bedroom next to the living room that the kids had learned to dread. It was wide enough to almost not fit through normal belt loops, had a massive square buckle with an ornate Levi Strauss cowboy picture on it, and it hurt like a motherfucker.

Dad wasn't wasting time today. He looped the belt over and brought it down across Jonah's lower back like a whip. There was a sharp cracking sound and a flash of pain. Jonah didn't move an inch though. He was like a log. Four, five more lashes on the butt, lower back, upper legs … nothing. The boy was a stone.

Jonah had learned long ago that his father fed off of others. He reacted to things. He and his Mom would get one another worked up until he would fly into a Wrath. You did not give him feedback. You didn't react, you didn't speak, you didn't make a sound. He had taken plenty of spankings with that belt. He knew what it would do. At ten, he had become a very tough boy who played rough outside and lived outdoors whenever possible. Jonah had been toughened by experience, so he stoically took the beating like an ox pulling a cart, barely acknowledging the man hitting it to make it go faster.

Dad was never quiet though, he never stopped yelling through the whole thing. "NEVER. FUCKING. DO. THAT. AGAIN. YOU. FUCKING. PIECE. OF. SHIT!" Each word was punctuated by the belt, as if his arm was motivated by the force of his howling voice.

Suddenly Dad went quiet and stopped. He stood there with that inexplicable gleam in his eyes, making no sound, unmoving. He seemed to have realized that he was tiring himself out with the belt and having remarkably little effect on the boy, despite all the noise it made. Jonah hadn't let out so much as a whimper.

Dad's eyes glided around the room and finally came to rest next to the front door. He dropped the belt and walked that way.

Jonah felt a cold horror. Dad was going for his hammer.

Dad's hammer was a "holy instrument." It was a symbol of divine rulership and a measure of manhood.

There wasn't just *one* hammer either. Like any carpenter of his generation, Jonah's dad took considerable pride in his hammers and would not use just any old hardware store "girl hammer." He had a custom-made, 32 oz. framing hammer leaning against the wall next to the front door. That was the in-home security system. He loved to tell a story about coming home from a job site in Los Angeles and being followed by a biker. The guy followed him right off the freeway (probably because Dad had cut him off) and into the parking lot of a Burger King. He'd gotten off his bike and walked over to Dad's beat up orange work truck, apparently planning to teach the carpenter some manners. Dad had thought like a cornered rat - he had grabbed his custom made, red handled 32 oz framer (the one that would let him sink a 16-penny nail with one stroke every time), leaned out of the door of his truck, and aimed for the first thing that came around the corner of his vehicle - the biker's knee. It had folded back like a broken twig and Dad had driven off. He always kept a hammer under his seat for emergencies and another near the door of the house, and he liked to say that in the hands of a skilled carpenter, it was more lethal than a gun.

Dad grabbed his framing hammer.

He came back to where the 10-year-old boy was lying face down on the couch, doing his best to remain utterly still and quiet. The boy glanced back up at him over his shoulder, no fear in his eyes, just calculation. Jonah was calculating physical survival, just like an animal.

Dad stood for a moment, unmoving, as if thinking about whether to put the hammer through his son's skull or do something else. There was no indication in those eyes of any intelligent thought. Nothing but that fanatical, terrified gleam. He flipped the huge framing hammer backward, holding it by the metal head, and suddenly brought the wooden handle down across Jonah's legs with the force of a lifetime of swinging tools in the hot sun.

Jonah saw a bright flash for a second and let out a bit of the air he had sucked in at the beginning of the Wrath. He didn't feel the full pain for a while. It was delayed, but it felt like a crowbar coming down on his legs and butt again and again. He remembered later thinking that if only Dad had started with that, he would have been fine, but he'd used up some resistance with the belt.

Actually, the hammer was doing so much damage that the pain was not registering, which was enabling Jonah to remain silent. He was starting to worry that there was going to be some permanent damage to his numb legs. He suddenly realized that he and his father were in some kind of contest of wills. Whatever one did, one did *not* get in a contest of wills with Dad. He mentally kicked himself for not realizing sooner that his father was waiting for him to cry.

Crying was not easy or natural for Jonah, but he did his best under the circumstances. It was not his best performance by any means, and it was interrupted by exhalations of breath caused by the hammer's blows. Still, it did seem to do the trick. At last Dad stopped.

"GET THE FUCK OUT!" Jonah was grabbed by the back of the shirt and hauled to his feet.

He didn't need to be told twice. His feet were already moving before he hit the floor. He would have darted from the room like a cat, but inexplicably his legs weren't working right and he actually stumbled to the ground in a pile before jumping back to his feet and running awkwardly up the stairs like a three legged dog. His legs would be stiff for days.

It was the sound that would haunt him later. Not the words, not the crack of the belt, but the weird, inhuman pitch of his dad's voice. It rose almost an octave, like a man screaming in desperation. Spit would fly from his mouth. His eyes would register nothing human, no intelligence or compassion, just the weird gleam of terror-rage. The voice was so loud it beat against your eardrums and carried for city blocks. If a full grown man were literally screaming out words as he watched a vision of utter mortal horror materialize in front of him, it might sound like that. Dad's voice would make the kid's blood pressure spike. They would go rigid and their eyes would roll up in their heads like a horse about to bolt. It had a physically taxing effect all by itself. Jonah wished that he could just endure a quiet beating without having to hear it.

Jonah spent a bit of time thinking after that. He knew that he must not let that happen again. The problem was that he wasn't really sure what had set his dad off. Being gross with Amy's toys? Not enough to go right into full Wrath mode. Whatever it was, he must not ever do it again.

In fact, it took years for him to piece together that his Dad had probably thought that he'd managed to find his porno stash and was recreating some scene for his sisters. The fact that a ten year old would be suspected of this didn't improve his opinion of the man.

2

SUNDAY

The living room of the one-story brick house was stained yellow from decades of smoking. The ceiling had a strange pattern of ivory, yellow, orange, and brown in roiling waves that echoed the placement of the more comfortable chairs in the room over the years.

Uncle Matt sat in his big reclining chair as always, quietly watching the world through dark eyes. He seemed to have receded from the world at large. First behind a big, bushy beard, then under a trucker hat that he usually wore, and finally behind rolls of fat that had turned him into a mountainous captive of gravity. He was affixed to that chair most of the day, huge feet with cracked, long yellow toenails raggedly jutting out angled to keep the world as far from his childlike, fear-filled dark eyes as possible.

Jonah eyed Uncle Matt warily as he absently wandered the living room looking for something resembling candy. Matt was harmless, but almost to the point where the harmlessness itself was more terrifying, if that were possible. He seemed like a gigantic version of a child trapped in a monstrous body, unable to move, unwilling to speak. For a moment, the boy and the man met one another's eyes and it seemed to Jonah as if there was some hidden understanding there of something that he didn't know. Almost as if Matt was like him in some way and knew it, but remained silent. He was always silent when Dad was in the house…

Jonah turned away, scowling. He didn't want Uncle Matt to "understand" anything about him. He didn't want to be anything like Matt. Uncle Matt smelled bad. He was disgusting and weighed so much that he had flattened his recliner chair into a caricature of itself and rubbed the fake cloth surface until it was black from old sweat and polished to a sheen from constant use. Uncle Matt didn't cut his fingernails and his hands were yellow from the cigarettes that were ever burning in them. Jonah was embarrassed to be related to him.

Eventually, the brown-haired boy turned to the old crystal jar that Grandma kept on the mantelpiece. It was always there. It had once been placed on the mantelpiece no doubt to "fancy up" the very lower-middle class living room with its red shag rug. At some point, a bag of carob chips had been dumped inside to provide something to offer guests. As if this house EVER had guests. Since nobody liked carob chips, they had remained in that crystal jar for years. Jonah remembered that same jar being there several Christmases ago and it had been just as dusty then.

The ten-year-old shrugged to himself, lifted the lid and grabbed a small handful of the old, waxy non-chocolate chips. He remembered how Grandpa used to take them to the corner store to get ice cream and candy when he was little. He'd been a lively man of indeterminate late middle age. His hair had been the steel color of a once blonde head gone grey. An energetic, short man with sparkling blue eyes, Grandpa had always been charming. Everyone around here had known him, and some of those who had ample reason to hate him had liked him anyway.

Grandpa had been born a cowboy (on a real ranch) and had migrated to Hollywood after World War II. He had eventually ended up as a welder, a chain smoker, and an alcoholic. Whatever he had been like as a young man had left Uncle Matt as a shell of a human being, their older son estranged, and Mother just claimed not to remember. In any event, he'd been a violent drunk. Sometime around when Jonah was born, the man had tried to change it seemed, and had stopped drinking, started going to church, and taken an interest in his grandchildren that he had never shown his real kids. At least that was the story Jonah had heard. He just remembered that Dad had hated Grandpa and hadn't wanted them around too much, and whenever they had come, Grandpa had gone out of his way to dote on him and Hayden.

Now, with Grandpa gone, the old house Mother had grown up in seemed sad, empty, relieved, and haunted. Every dark corner seemed like a place with lurking secrets to tell of the bad memories that still hung like black ghosts in the shadows. Grandma used to have a little dog, and there were small, black turds tangled into the ruin of long, red shag carpeting behind every large piece of furniture like the physical manifestation of the psychological gloom that hung over the place. The smell of ancient, stale nicotine was almost sickly sweet, like rotting fruit, and the yellow and orange smoke residue literally dripped down the walls like wax from a candle.

Bizarrely, Jonah found respite in that place. He knew Dad hated to visit. He knew Dad had hated Grandpa when he was alive, and liked Grandma little more. Every time Mother managed to cry and sob like a preteen girl enough to get Dad to agree to come down here, Dad would yell and scream, but most of the way back would be quiet, and while they were here, Dad would be lurking somewhere, hiding from that ruined place left in the aftermath of a man's drunken life and the broken remnants of his family. That gave Jonah hours of peace. He could explore like a spaceman investigating a disgusting alien hulk drifting through space. He could play in the backyard in peace. He could lower his guard for once and actually be a kid for a little while.

Ironically, that house was a refuge- stale, dusty carob chips and all.

9 Years Later -California, 1996, Sunday

Jonah walked down the narrow hallway of the apartment. The walls always felt damp, as if they were slowly bleeding the humid, salty air of Marin County in through the concrete. The place was cluttered with the detritus of endless moves. Cardboard boxes turned into "permanent" furniture by a family that had given up even unpacking. Like a ship, every tiny little inch of the place was claimed. There were invisible lines of territory crisscrossing that dimly lit apartment like the war-fought borders of old Europe where battles had delineated every curve of every line between ancient neighbors.

At the end of the hall were two bedrooms. To their left was a large closet conformed to fit under the bottom of the apartment stairs that ended on this level. The door to the closet had been covered with pieces of paper, most of which had little colored pencil sketches on them. Fantastic characters or creatures like a collage of clippings from an alien news magazine.

Jonah knocked, then waited. As ever, there was no response from inside. There never was anymore. He grew irritated. He was the only one who ever knocked anymore … he was the only one who ever even *checked* anymore as far as he knew.

The wide-shouldered young man with eyes and a full beard too old for his youthful frame scowled at the door, then grabbed the handle and pulled it open with a jerk.

Hayden sat on her chair no more than four inches beyond the closet doorway facing away from him. A solitary light bulb hanging from the ceiling of the nearly triangular space had been supplemented with

Christmas lights that had been strung up all over, giving the tiny space a strangely cheerful glow. Eucalyptus leaves, lichen, and other bits and pieces of nature had been strung up here and there, along with hundreds of little sketches, pages full of carefully inked notes, bits of maps, and photographs clipped from magazines or newspapers. Literally every inch of that cupboard-like space was covered in something.

Hayden didn't move. She was slouched forward, peering at some papers she had stacked up on the TV tray in front of her. She looked skinny to the point of being unhealthy. The knobs of her spine were clearly visible jutting out of her back as she slouched. The young woman had hair that was starting to go silver early. Lately, a solitary white streak had appeared and begun to gain ground in her straight, split and frayed looking mane.

Her skin was paper white, with blue veins visible in her wrists and hands. The contrast with Jonah was extreme. The young man had spent a good deal of time outdoors lately, working very hard. His hands were calloused and his body just filling out into the full strength of manhood. He thought to himself how strange it was that Hayden and he had once been so alike that some people had thought them twins.

"It's a nice day out there. I might go up the trail…" Jonah said it just to prod Hayden into action. He didn't really feel like climbing the trail today, even though the sun was out.

She moved like someone under water, slowly reaching for something on the table where crumpled, half-eaten bits of food remained from days before. Her wraithlike hand found a huge, heavy mug with several tea bags steeping in it and brought it up toward her lips. Her eyes still hadn't moved to look at her brother. They were staring ahead, into the distance beyond the wall that was only three feet in front of her face.

"So go."

Jonah clenched a wide fist. He hated that particular tone of voice she used that sounded like she was underwater or calling up from a deep well. It spoke of giving up. He hated anything resembling giving up with an instinctive violence. His voice was calm, belying the inner turmoil. "Have you been down to the store lately?"

Hayden had been working at a local art store as a way to get some money. It seemed that she had given up, despite the owner appreciating her work there. Instead of saving cash to Escape, she had been converting all her earnings into discounted art supplies anyway, so it hadn't served much purpose except to get her out of that damn closet.

Hayden shook her head like someone who was stoned or maybe very drunk. Jonah decided that she must have been up all night again.

"Look, Hayden, you have to get out! Just go outside and feel the sun or something! How long have you been in here? A *week*? *Two*?"

Hayden smiled slowly, looking *vastly* older than just barely to drinking age. She turned her head toward him with a sloth-like movement and finally, for the first time, met his eyes.

"I've been speaking to them! The angels! They showed me things … so many things …" Now there was some small animation to her, a little spark in her eyes, a gleam that seemed to have set her limbs to some kind of jerky motion. Jonah looked away from those eyes. They were the eyes of a fanatic.

"I've been speaking to the Prince of Light …"

At that moment, a memory triggered in his mind. Something, many, many ages ago, before so many things, so many long, difficult times. As if across many lifetimes, Jonah remembered being in Grandma's filthy house looking for something to eat. He had seen Uncle Matt, and for a moment their eyes had met. Matt had looked like a child trapped in a huge body. A scared child terrified of life. Broken, hiding inside himself from terrors only he could see. Something had happened to him that had remained in front of those eyes forever and he had given up on life completely. After Grandma had come to live with them, he had died only a short time later, just giving up on everything. He'd only been 34.

Hayden had that look in her eyes now.

Jonah was filled with rage. He had tried, he had cajoled, he had bullied, he had pleaded. He could not pry Hayden from her closet and her spiral of hopelessness. He could only do so much! At some point HE had to Escape! Even walking back into this apartment made his skin crawl. He hated every second that he was here. It was like jumping into quicksand to grab a drowning person. He needed them to try to get out too, or they would just both get sucked down. At some point, he had to look to himself and pull his own ass out of this!

At that moment, Jonah made the final decision. He was leaving. He was getting out of there before there was nothing left of *any* of them. He didn't care if he died, he would live in the attempt. He would not go like Uncle Matt.

1987

Jonah was in the backyard of the filthy, haunted old brick house when the call came. It was the inevitably angry voice of his father. "Get the kids in the car!" The tone broached no argument.

Mother was saying goodbye to her own sick mother. Grandma was taking a turn for the worse, which was why Dad had relented enough for them to come visit. Mother would probably sniffle tonight. There was something wrong with Grandma which the children didn't yet understand. She was a strangely brusque, hard-faced woman who had the look of a survivor. After living with a violent alcoholic for decades, it was understandable. Still, Mom crying about her mother's sickness was normal and comprehensible. What was not was her blind, blank-eyed cheerfulness.

"Jonah!" The tone was melodic and cheerful to the point of being insipid. "Come on! Time to go!" In Mother's mind, the kids had not heard Dad yell just a moment ago. In her mind, everything was always normal and good. In her mind, a song in the heart made up for a world of ills.

Looking back at the house on Fifth Street as they pulled out, the kids could see a house that seemed to be a physical incarnation of some great old darkness that had been allowed to grow and grow until it overshadowed everything, begging to be mentioned. There was a tree in the front yard. It was Uncle Matt's tree. He had brought it home from school as a kid and planted it, and in some strange way, it seemed to be tied with him. Matt had been told that it would not grow very big, so it had been planted close to the house, but it was a species of pine very rare in California. Something monstrous. In the perfect California climate, it had grown and grown and become darker and darker until it literally towered over every single thing in the entire neighborhood. It was a vast, unruly dark blot that could be spotted from across town. The tree had to be over a hundred feet high. It was some kind of freak of nature. In growing, its roots had burrowed under the house until they were starting to lift the slab foundation and it had totally covered the house in about a foot of old orange pine needles. There was nothing but a tiny fringe of grass left in the front yard, the rest had been choked of the sun by the great, dark tree or the acid of its pine-scented blood had poisoned the ground.

Jonah would watch that vast tree as they drove down the long, tree-lined street to downtown Fairfield. He could keep his eye on it all the way up the freeway onramp blocks away. It was like a beacon to navigate by as the land slid past the windows of their car. A dark, tumor-like beacon that blotted out the very sky. Something that had grown and grown and grown in plain sight and never been addressed until it dominated everything for miles around. To him, that tree and that house and Uncle Matt were all connected in a way a ten-year-old was not equipped to understand.

3

THE PATRIARCH

Since the family was packed up in the car anyway, Walter made the decision to swing by *his* parents' house, which was only a short hop up the freeway from the house on Fifth Street.

In those days, Fairfield was just starting to become a big town. It had not yet transformed into a proper city, but all the signs were there. A once quiet and dusty place spread across fields and orchards between Travis Air Force Base and the freeway, Fairfield had grown inexorably until it now spread for miles with new suburbs, old suburbs, an old downtown, and a new mall all jumbled up together. Depending on what block you were on, it had the quaint charm of an old style Western small town or the soulless, generic character of a mass-produced Southern California housing development.

Fairfield was the closest thing the kids had to home. Both of their parents had grown up there. Both sets of grandparents lived there. Their earliest memories were from there. Strangely though, they rode through the town now like indifferent visitors. All three merely watched the town roll past the windows impassively like strangers in a somewhat familiar place. They were like a regular commuter who passes through the same town every day on the way to work but never stops. He feels that he knows the town, at least in a way. He thinks to himself as he rolls past "oh, look, they have demolished the old gas station" or "how long has that stupid old sign been up anyway?" Really, if he were ever to actually stop, he would realize that there

were thousands of people he did not know going about
lives totally unconnected with his own who knew every
inch of that place. To them, it was *home*.

The kids hadn't really grown up in Fairfield, but
they had grown up there more than anywhere else.
Jonah and Hayden both hated to explain where they
were "from" when they came to a new school. It was
always arduous to try to explain all the moving, all the
different places. Even at ten and twelve, they had a hard
time remembering all the places they had lived. They
were twentieth century nomads. Worst of all, none of
them really knew why.

It was possible that Walter knew why. One did
not simply question Dad, however. One lived with
certain mysteries unless one wanted to deal with the
Wrath.

Grandpa and Grandma Franklin lived in a neat
looking suburban house that was a few years newer
than the one on Fifth Street. It had a strange looking
front yard. Grandpa was always interested in trendy
experimentation and trying to make things more
efficient. He had eliminated grass entirely by turning
the front yard into a big stone "rock garden" of sorts in
order to save the water bill. Of course, what he saved
by not watering grass out front he more than spent in
extra water that he was obliged to put into the fish pond
he had in the backyard. He'd also bought a solar water
heater system. One of the only "solar panel" like
objects to be found in the entire town. Jonah thought it
looked "high-tech."

The mood in the car altered radically as they
turned into the cul-de-sac where Grandpa and Grandma
Franklin lived. Jonah, Hayden and Amy felt less on
edge. They were no longer worried about setting Dad
off with a wrong sound or word. The heavy, oppressive
silence from the three abated and they began to stir and
chatter almost like normal children.

In the front, Mom's incessant heavy sighs had abated as well and she had apparently placed the dark thoughts about her sick mother in the corner of her mind where bad things went. She visibly perked up and even hummed a few bars of one of her "Christian rock" tunes. Mom was receding and Laura was coming out.

This was all in reaction to Dad of course. The visible tension in the lean muscled shoulders that was always there and the smoldering rage that lived just under the surface every second that he was not at work lifted away. As the sullen tension in the man evaporated, the four passengers in the car relaxed, for they had grown so accustomed to always watching every single flick of an eyelash, every twitch of a muscle in his face, every subtle change in tone or gleam of the eyes, that they lived in a continual state of always reading his mood, always holding very still and being very quiet so as not to set him off.

As they approached the house itself, taking a wide, lazy turn in front of the driveway, Dad seemed to fade completely and Walter returned.

"That stupid solar water heater ..." he seemed bemused. "Damn thing never worked!" As ever, he directed this to Laura as if they were the only two in the car. The three pairs of eyes in the back watched in silence.

Walter's tone was mildly gruff but almost jovial.

Laura smiled and shook her head. "I know." Again, it was as if nobody else was in the car and they had just picked up a conversation started moments before instead of one begun probably a year ago.

Hearing anything other than Wrath or brooding anger from the driver's seat put the three kids in a fine mood. They were ready to spring out the doors of the car the second it slowed enough for their running legs to keep up. It was as if there was time for being children that desperately needed to be caught up on.

The chiding "Jonah! *Hayden*! Stay in the car until we stop! What's *wrong* with you?" from Laura in the passenger seat was as fake and abnormal as the interaction of the Brady Bunch on TV, and it was given a similar amount of respect.

The kids rushed up the driveway at a run, but they did not go immediately to the front door that was now opening. Instead, like wild dogs let off a leash, they simply ran full tilt around the side of the house, up the top of the driveway, around an old, rusted truck that was parked there, and back down like a wave breaking on the rocks. They knew the protocol. Ancient hierarchies had to be maintained. They would greet Grandma and Grandpa at the proper time.

First, the purpose of the visit had to be taken care of.

Grandpa Franklin came out of the house bouncing on the balls of his feet with suppressed energy as usual. He read as a tallish man, though at most he was a hair over six feet. It was his ramrod straight posture that probably made him seem to be tall. That and the way he would tilt his head back slightly and look down his thin, straight nose at someone when they were talking, never losing eye contact for a second. He always wore a smile, which is not to say that he was a happy man, or that he had a sunny disposition, for that isn't right at all, despite his continual attempts at very bad puns. He *wore* a smile exactly the way a politician or a used car salesman wore one. As if he had a rack full of smiles in the closet and he placed one on his face in the morning. His eyes behind that 1950s car grille of a grin were usually calculating, not in sync with the facade at all.

The transformation that came over Walter as he ambled up the walk from the street was both awesome and somewhat terrifying. At step one, he was a hardened man used to rough work outdoors and barely holding back a coiled rage like a cobra that could lash out at any second. By the fifth step, his gait had changed. He had started to slouch just a little, throw his arms out just a touch as he walked. His posture and bearing metamorphosed until one would not expect to see a silver haired man with glasses, but perhaps a teenager in Birkenstocks and long hair slouching up to his dad in a perpetual show of teenage rebellion. He came up to the other man, both almost identical in height, but it seemed almost like the old, balding man in the 1970s-era button down shirt was taller. Like a puppy dog touching it's nose to its master, Walter sort of dipped his head just slightly in greeting. Like an officer receiving a salute, Grandpa grinned harder and nodded back.

Homage had been paid. Now, the kids could go greet Grandma.

Visits to Grandma and Grandpa Franklin were more than just stopping by to say hello. They were homage. They were a re-initiation into the mysteries of The Family. Grandpa and Grandma's house was not a home, it was an institution.

Grandpa and Grandma Franklin lived in Suisun City. It had once been a bustling port town in the Old West. The railway from Sacramento had ended abruptly in the Suisun marsh here where flat-bottomed schooners had once carried the railway cargo on to San Francisco. To Jonah, Suisun was permanently associated with the smells of licorice and tar. Licorice plants grew everywhere around the marsh, even creeping up through cracks in the old sidewalks of downtown Suisun. These bushy, vividly green plants scented the air through the long California summertime. For some reason, the telephone poles of the town had been dipped in tar, probably to protect from the wet, marshy climate, and during hot summers, they would slowly ooze tar out, adding a spicy smell to the sleepy little town. Pluff mud was the other smell that was always associated with Suisun. Californians don't usually call it pluff mud though, Jonah just called it "marsh mud." The uniquely slippery, sometimes incredibly deep type of mud only found in marshes and swamps had a smell that wasn't bad per-se, but it was unmistakable. At low tide, the pluff mud smell overpowered even the licorice.

Suisun had become an appendage of Fairfield in more recent years. There was now no way to clearly tell where Fairfield ended and Suisun began, except perhaps by the smell of the marsh and the cattails that grew in the golden fields alongside the roads.

The Franklins were nestled in a newer suburb closer to Fairfield proper than to downtown Suisun. It was not the house where Walter and his brother and sisters had grown up, so to Dad, it didn't have the same kinds of memories associated with it as it did to his children, but to Jonah, Amy, and Hayden, that house meant Christmastime.

Jonah could remember many Christmases spent at Grandma and Grandpa Franklin's house. Those were always happy memories. They would decorate their house, light a fire in the fireplace, and always have a great big tree. For once, usually stingy Grandpa Franklin would discover some generosity and there was always lots of food. Grandma would always be baking something and the house would literally fill up with the seven Franklin kids, their spouses and children, until herds of them came and went from every corner. The kids would swarm and flock out through the sliding doors into the wide, grassy backyard, and the adults would camp out in the living room and talk. Jonah remembered how his Dad would be the center of the "bad boys club" every year. Uncle Danny and Uncle Oscar would flank him on one of the couches and they would all talk and laugh uproariously. Uncle Danny was a scummy looking man with a thin moustache that looked like it had been taped onto his lip and watery, fearful eyes. He never spoke over a low mumble and never opened his mouth enough to speak clearly when he did. There was something slimy feeling about him and the kids shied away from him. He had once brought an obviously stolen bike to one of Jonah's birthdays and Dad had been forced to ask him to "take it back."

Uncle Oscar was a man of uncertain background. Just dark enough to be Hispanic, but with little clear indication otherwise. He always wore a "Kangal style" hat, long before that became trendy, and sometimes looked like he'd dressed in the remnants of the costume van for the filming of "Saturday Night Fever." He had bright green eyes and an almost hyperactive disposition. He was way too ready to smile and laugh, way too eager to poke or touch the kids, and gave off a different sort of creepy vibe. He liked to get the kids to dress up in frilly, doll-looking outfits and take lots of pictures.

There would be Dad right in the middle of those two, ever the "bad boy" teenager whenever he was in his father's house. Jonah didn't know until many years later that Uncle Danny was beating his Dad's sister senseless every night and would keep doing it for the next 15 years. He was also a petty thief. Uncle Oscar had him beat though … he was a pedophile.

Those were Jonah's happy memories of Christmas: his Dad sandwiched between a kid diddler and a wife beater, laughing and carrying on.

Today wasn't Christmas. It was just another weekend. Grandma was making a pot roast, but had emerged from the kitchen with a big smile and open arms and her habitual "Come in! Come in! Oh! You are so big!" to all three of the grandkids as if it had been a year since they had seen her instead of two weeks. Once they had escaped her hug, and in Jonah's case received the barest hint of a nod from Grandpa (he was a male child, and thus worthy of slight recognition, though children in general were beneath notice most of the time), they were free to charge into the kitchen looking for cookies (if they were lucky) or whatever else might be available to consume.

Grandpa and Dad would stay in the front room while the inevitable confrontation happened. Grandpa would pointedly ask whether Dad had "found a church" to attend. Dad would demur and say they hadn't. Grandpa would look down his nose with disappointment. Many times there would be some discussion of money. Dad had often been forced to ask for a loan from Grandpa in the past, and Grandpa kept track of every penny.

While that conversation went on, everyone else would move past them into the wood paneled living room, and in Jonah's case, out through the sliding glass doors into the backyard. He loved being outside. He loved feeling the sun on him and hearing the wind in the trees. Grandpa had a fish pond that he had dug out one year. He kept it going as best he could, and had seeded it with goldfish. Cattails had grown up all by themselves that close to the Suisun Slough, and frogs had arrived in great numbers. Grandpa had taken one of Dad's old "projects" that had been left derelict in his backyard for a long time (a gold panning sluice Dad had made before he and his brother had taken off into the northern woods to find gold one year) and converted it into a little bridge over part of the pond. Jonah loved that spot. He could hide behind the cattails on the side of the pond next to the fence and pretend that he was somewhere else, very far away. He would look up at the jet aircraft flying ever so high on their tracks to the West and wonder where they were heading. If they were that high and going west, were they going out over the Pacific? Were they going to Japan? Jonah would have given anything to be on one of those planes. To just get on, fly, and walk off into a new world was his fondest dream.

Walter and Laura sat at the table just inside the sliding glass doors, looking at one another as if they were high school sweethearts again. Walter's transformation upon the arrival at his dad's house allowed the two to forget the responsibilities of children and work and remember being hippie kids sitting in the back of an old beat up RV on its way to a Bible Camp youth retreat, strumming on a guitar and singing songs. Walter believed that he had "heard the Voice of God" asking if he would like to marry Laura the first time he'd ever seen her. He'd persisted until she said yes, and Laura had been his "blessing" ever since.

Laura was more than just Walter's wife. She was his only real friend and almost an appendage. Walter and Laura were like trees that had been planted too close together and had become dependent on one another for support. The moment they had decided to get married had been the moment they had stopped really growing up. The two were now 18-year-olds trapped in middle-aged bodies. Laura was Walter's servant, audience, verbal sparring partner, and (to appearances) mommy when necessary. In return, she had the comfortable fit of a relationship she had been bent and broken for by an alcoholic father and a codependent mom.

Walter watched the people around him with keen intelligence. As always, he was alert, on the lookout for a hint that he was no longer the center of attention. Whenever he sensed the conversation turning away from a focus on him, he would say something to get the eyes back on him. It didn't have to be controversial, though that worked too.

Walter wasn't reflective. He lived in the now for the most part. He didn't think consciously about the need to attract attention; it was nothing more or less than a conditioned behavior that he'd learned as one of seven siblings desperately trying to get any kind of attention from a mother who let them run like wild animals while she lost herself in a novel and a father who spent every living second striving, working, pushing, driving toward his goal of fulfilling "The Mission" that he had set for his life as a student in a Christian college in the 1940s. It wasn't necessary that the attention be *good*, just that people be looking at *him*. Not his siblings, not his children, *him*.

Walter suddenly realized that his mother was out in the backyard with his kids and his father was looking out back as they ran around her like three little hooligans. Everyone was paying more attention to them than to his elaboration of a fine point of theology that he'd been toying with and now wanted to expound upon to an audience. He decided it was time to go home.

"Come on!" Walter was on his feet with a sudden surge of restless energy. "We're going home!"

Walter should've been happy building in a place where people wanted to spend vast amounts of money on houses, but the L.A. heat, the smog, the High End Designer, and the Beverly Hills Housewife were wearing him down and there continued to be this restless search in his life for True Truth. Truth and the search for truth didn't belong in Beverly Hills where the only thing that seemed to be true was that everything was fake. So Walter Franklin took his young family and through a series of small building adventures ended up back in the hills of his youth in Northern California. Walter wanted to build meaningful things and he wanted to resolve this conflict of the Spiritual Life versus the Earthly Life. He began talking to his father about the missionary life, or since he was a builder, the support of the missionary life. Walter's father had some connections with the Wycliffe Bible Translators and soon Walter was connected with Wycliffe's school in Texas where a building project was getting underway... Walter sold everything but his tools

and bought a small travel trailer to tow behind his work truck, loaded up his kids, and took off for Texas.

-The Carpenter Chronicles by Walter Franklin, p. 34

4

THE ELECTRIC SPIDER

It loomed in the dim light that filtered through the cheap blinds into the tiny room from the city. It sat, hunched over Jonah's bed like a malformed alien life of some kind, one unblinking eye watching him, always watching. Arms spread out from the central body mass, traveling down, down, under Jonah himself as if the thing were attached to him somehow… as if it were drawing life out of him.

It was an electric monster. It was Jonah's nightly companion. It was his secret that he would never, ever tell anyone. It was a reminder of everything about him that was bad, wrong, malformed, like it's hulking, bizarre shape in the darkness.

Jonah lay still, staring up at the single, unblinking electric eye that watched him in the darkness. Self-loathing seemed to overwhelm him as he lay on the thin mattress placed directly on the floor of the tiny cupboard-room. He felt as if he had to rip off his covers in order to breathe. He also felt as if something dark and evil waited in the darkness for any opening in the covers to appear in order to leap at him. He imagined the sinister thing in the darkness looked like a spider … a huge spider … crouched over him with one, bright eye unblinking, staring …

Jonah turned over to put his back to the electric thing. It had become the latest thing in his life that tormented him. It had all started when things at work started getting stressful for Dad. When that happened, things got worse for the kids at home. Dad would come in the door in the evenings looking for a fight. The kids learned to hide and make no sound, but sometimes it wasn't enough. All the anger, all the frustration, all the viciousness that Dad must have kept hidden all day at work came pouring out like a flood on his children. He screamed, he ranted, he chased them around the house. Life became a strange, flashing series of still images of terror and nonsensical situations for the kids. Dad would say things that didn't actually make any sense, his eyes wild, spittle flying out of his mouth as he screamed. He reminded Jonah of the stories of King Saul and David, where Saul would suddenly jump up for no reason and throw a spear at David while he was playing a harp for him. Whatever was going on in Dad's mind must have been torture, because he poured out the torture on his family every single moment that he was home. They prayed for the beautiful, precious hours when he was at work and dreaded the ominous hour between 6 and 7 PM when he would return.

Sometime in the midst of this, things had gone badly for Jonah as well. He couldn't explain why, but his body had started to betray him suddenly. He would wake up after an evening of terror, his bed completely soaked with urine. He hadn't wet the bed in years, but now, right at the moment when it was *most* important that Dad take no notice of him, he had started again.

Nothing had helped. Mom and Dad had tried not letting him have water before bed. They had made him promise to wake up. His mom had tried teaching him mind tricks to wake himself up when he needed to go. Nothing worked. Night after night, after the nightmare of screaming and sometimes violence in the living room after Dad got home, Jonah would go to bed and wake up covered in piss.

Something about it made his skin crawl. There was nothing at all in the world like waking up soaked in cold urine. Jonah's toes curled at the thought. It made him want to scrub his skin until he had scrubbed it right off. Worse, again and again he would awaken to see Mom and Dad looming over him, that look of pitch-black anger in Dad's eyes, that look of mindless panic in Mom's. When she had that look, she would work herself up into near hysterics, very much like an eight-year-old child, crying about some problem (which could be anything from an unpaid phone bill to a son who suddenly started to wet his bed). When she did this, Dad would get more and more worked up as well. It was like a performance theater when both of them really got going in the living room, shouting back and forth about how they "DON'T KNOW WHAT TO DO ABOUT IT!" until Dad would be wound up to the point that he would fly into a Wrath, stalk through the house until some kid crossed his path, and take it all out on them one way or another.

Jonah hated being a problem. He hated being noticed. He hated that the more hysterical Mom and Dad got about him, the worse things got. He hated hearing the massive voice of Dad fill up the house from where he was screaming in the living room: "WE'LL PUT HIM BACK IN FUCKING DIAPERS!" It made him want to disappear forever and never show his face again.

They took him to a doctor. They had sat in on the exam as the doctor worked to determine that there was nothing physically wrong with him. Nobody had ever told Jonah what a prostate exam entailed. He was simply told to take down his pants, bend over a table, and let the doctor stick a finger in his butt. He had never been so mortified or humiliated in his life, and to make matters worse, there was Dad, looking on. Jonah had no idea that a person could feel such shame and terror.

Finally, they had brought in a man. He had a little mustache and a furtive air. His clothes were supposed to be professional but were rumpled around the edges. He seemed very much like one of those old fashioned door to door salesmen who always seemed just a little bit seedy, but also desperate, unlike their more prosperous used car salesman cousins. Bizarrely, the man tried to combine this door to door salesman persona with some sort of medical air, as if he were some kind of specialist. Jonah shrunk away when he was brought down to say hi while the man sat on the couch.

Jonah knew that while company was present, his parents would do whatever was necessary to maintain the image of a happy, normal household, but if he did not comply now, the moment the man was gone, Dad was liable to go into a Wrath. He sat and listened and kept his mouth closed while the adults discussed him as if he wasn't there.

That was where the electronic spider had come from. It was a pretty simple machine when you boiled it down. There was a metal mesh about two foot square that went under the sheets of the child's bed. It was uncomfortable to lay on, but Jonah was sleeping on a thin mattress with no bed right on the floor. He was used to a little discomfort. He'd had to do much worse during the First Missionary Trip. This electric mesh was connected to two cables that came out of the box-body of the machine. The cables were part of an electric circuit which would be completed if any moisture got on the metal mesh. At that instant, an alarm, much like the fire alarm bells in school would ring with the most incredibly loud sound Jonah had ever heard. Theoretically, the machine would not electrocute a kid by accident, though looking back years later, Jonah wasn't sure how the adults were so sure of its safety.

The unblinking eye was an electric light that flickered steadily with the wavering current from the old wall sockets. There was a metal switch on the front that was supposed to reset the machine, but it didn't always work. Sometimes, once the metallic wail had started, nothing could shut the thing up except yanking the cord out of the wall.

Now it sat there, looking down on Jonah, waiting for him to make a mistake so it could scream it out to the entire neighborhood and Mom and Dad could scramble blearily up the stairs to stand over him and start working themselves into a frenzy.

Jonah had once read a poem by Edgar Allen Poe. There had been a man in a room and a pendulum, and the pendulum went down bit by bit every swing, and eventually it was going to come down and slice off the man's head, or something like that. (Jonah was always picking up stuff more advanced than a ten-year-old would normally read.) The poem reminded him of the Electric Spider and the way it watched him every night, waiting for him to close his eyes. He would try to stay awake. He would listen to the sounds of the police sirens in the city … a horrible far away sound that might be a backyard dogfight … a neighbor woman screaming at her man as he stormed out of their rental … a baby crying. He would stand up in the tiny room, point the broken binoculars that he'd rescued from a junk heap somewhere out through the blinds and pretend that his little room was the prow of a ship and he was a captain looking out with his spyglass, and he were going somewhere … somewhere far away from here … anywhere.

Eventually sleep would take him, and as soon as his eyes fluttered closed, Jonah would be jolted upright by the buzzing, clattering sound of the Electric Spider. The sound was answered by a loud curse from the lower story of the house and a massive thumping coming up the stairs like a steam train…

5

MONDAY

Jonah's school was literally a cage. It was built on a flat concrete slab that had been made perfectly level, which made it appear to jut up because the street next to it sloped downward. At the low end of the natural slope, the concrete pad of the school was around six feet above the level of the sidewalk, forming an imposing concrete wall. Topping this pad, the urban school had thrown up a 25 foot chain link fence all the way around the city block which was the school grounds. This gave the entire block the aspect of a gigantic animal cage, which Jonah found ironically apropos, even at ten years old. It was completely graffiti covered concrete, with not even a single blade of grass to be seen.

To get to the great animal cage, Jonah had pedaled his knock off BMX bike past the neighborhood crack house (everyone knew it to be a crack house and it was generally referred to that way, not that Jonah knew what that meant, other than that there was always a very bad smell in the air around it). He'd crossed two extremely busy streets, swung wide around an ongoing drug bust taking place on the broken sidewalk, and pedaled up the hill to the imposing chain link edifice of the school.

When the doors opened for recess, the concrete yard was flooded with hyperactive kids who had no outlet and not enough room in the overcrowded facility. It closely resembled a prison yard.

Like a prison in California, white kids were a small minority of the school's population. They either hung out together, or were picked on by the much larger groups of black kids. In that neighborhood, many of the boys would shortly graduate from that elementary school to jobs as runners for drug gangs. A very high percentage of them would eventually end up in a very similar looking institution with very similar fences and bells and gates as adults, where they would act in a similar manner. They came from broken homes without fathers, they came from divorce, domestic abuse, even foster homes. They had parents in jail in some cases, older brothers in gangs, and in the very worst cases moms turning tricks to get high. A lot of those kids were not bad, but in so many ways, they had nowhere to go, nothing to do but turn on one another like the fighting dogs kept in the backyards of that ghetto.

There was a particularly large boy named Tyrone who was always surrounded by at least four cronies. He was connected somewhere in an important way (which is to say his older brother was in a real gang). He was loud, he was mean, and he was at least a full foot taller than most of the kids in that school. It is possible that he had been held back a year due to bad grades, though Jonah had no idea of such things. All he knew was that Tyrone was the biggest kid in the entire school.

Because Tyrone had connections on the outside, he knew that he could get away with a lot, and he did. If he wanted something, he took it. If he didn't want to do something or go somewhere, he didn't. In a city where every block was one or another gang's "territory" and there was a growing epidemic of drive-by shootings, Tyrone's kind of pull seemed to give him a lot of slack with the school administrators.

Jonah didn't care much about Tyrone one way or another. He didn't hang out with the white kids

either, nor try to pander to the black kid groups like
some of his peers. He mostly just played alone. He
loved tetherball. It was one of the very few bright spots
in his day to go out to the line of metal poles sunk into
the concrete of their play yard and hit a ball so hard that
it spun right over the head of a taller kid and went
around and around until he won. Everyone knew that if
Jonah started with the ball, the game was as good as
over because he had an enormous, powerful swing that
most kids had no chance of catching. When Jonah
wasn't playing tetherball, he was in line for one of the
courts where kids remained for as long as they could
keep winning, losers always replaced by someone else
from the line. That's where he was when it happened.

Tyrone had just left one of the courts after being
beat and didn't look too happy. He stepped out of the
court and walked over to one of the lines. Barely
slowing down, he saw that a little girl was in front of
him in line, so he simply grabbed her and shoved her
aside, taking her place at the front of the line.

Jonah looked up from where he stood just in
time to see the little girl, who looked only half as big as
Tyrone, fall on her butt with a scared and shocked look.
He saw fear in her eyes. An expression of shock and
pain. That expression registered something within
Jonah that was vast, all-encompassing. A rage swept
over him, boiling right up out of his toes and sweeping
up his body like an electric current. It was total fury. It
came in an instant, with no warning to bystanders. One
second Jonah was standing, waiting his turn in one line,
the next, he had locked eyes on Tyrone and started
toward him like a pit bull.

Jonah didn't understand it, but he could not
tolerate picking on someone smaller, someone weaker.
His vision centered on the much larger black kid who
was at least six inches taller than him. His arms and
legs tingled and his vision seemed to literally go red.

"Leave her alone!" Screamed out the small voice of the little white boy. He was next to Tyrone in a flash and his right hand whipped out twice, a balled fist catching the big kid on the side of the head with a tetherball swing. Tyrone was turning, stunned. He hadn't had time to react.

Jonah knew Tyrone's four followers would be all over him any second, so he just went all out as fast as he could. At that moment, all he knew was unutterable rage at the injustice of a big, powerful kid pushing around a small one. There was no room for anything but Tyrone's shocked face in his vision.

Jonah reached up to grab the bigger kid around the back of his neck, taking advantage of the fact that he was totally stunned. He grasped Tyrone's neck, then turned where he stood, just as he would if he were winding up a very powerful "serve" with a tetherball. Rotating his hips, Jonah unknowingly performed a Judo throw that flipped Tyrone completely upside down and left him flat on his back and gasping for air.

Jonah leapt onto the larger kid, straddling him and pounding at him with his fists, screaming "Leave her alone!" over and over. He didn't realize it, but he began to verbalize as he beat him, curses hissing out of his mouth in time with the flying fists, exactly the way his Dad cursed him as he was beat.

"Don't. You. Fucking. Ever. Do. That. Again. You. Piece. Of. Shit!" Every word was punctuated by a fist to the face.

Jonah didn't realize that there was some flurry of activity around him until he was lifted bodily from behind. He had no idea who was trying to grab him, but he was pretty sure it was Tyrone's minions coming to his defense. He fought like a wildcat, twisting out of their grasp and hitting someone in the face with his fist. As soon as they let go, he was off like a shot.

The fat, middle-aged yard duty woman reeled from the punch the fifth grader had just landed. She grabbed her nose and screamed for someone to catch that little punk.

Jonah didn't know what was going on, but he came out of his blind rage in time to realize that every yard duty and teacher in the entire school were running out of doors, blowing whistles, and trying to grab him. The school yard erupted in cheers, chaos, and movement as the kids sensed the firm grasp of authority losing its hold. Whistles were blown as adults desperately tried to herd the little monsters back inside. The recess bell blasted ten minutes prematurely and Jonah's newfound fame turned to infamy as a hundred other kids blamed him for stealing their precious outside time. The prison yard was on the verge of a riot; it was time for a lockdown.

Meanwhile, Jonah had not stopped moving. He had run toward the front of the school, making for his bike and sure escape, but he'd been cut off by the Vice Principal bounding out of the front door of the building, forcing him to turn and run back into the "yard." The yard duties were fat and slow and hampered by dozens of berserk kids, but the recess yard was a dead end. There would be no escape. Jonah thought fast, dodged a teacher, and made for the chain link fence. He leapt and caught the fence as high as he could, then he started up like a frightened monkey, his little Converse shoes just small enough to fit in the holes in the fence.

The fence was about 25 feet high. Jonah just kept going up until he got to the very top, then he swung a leg over, precariously balanced over a busy street and a drop onto hard concrete. He had planned to get over the fence and to the outside of the school and make a run for it, but it had taken him enough time to climb that the adults had gotten the other kids corralled and had sent out two yard duties to the sidewalk below him, so he was now treed like a cat. The adults couldn't possibly climb the fence, and he had nowhere to go.

The more they yelled for him to come down, the less he wanted to.

At last the Vice Principal came out to play police negotiator. He told the still furious yard duties to back away and walked down to the sidewalk below Jonah. He was a young looking man in his early thirties. He had an athletic demeanor and usually wore short sleeved polo-type shirts and jeans, unlike the much more formal looking Principal types. Jonah had been genuinely scared by the look in the eyes of the yard duty, and had not had any intention of coming down, but the calm manner of the Vice Principal calmed him down a lot.

"Jonah! If you don't come down, we are going to have to call your parents!"

Jonah shook his head, feeling a wash of despair come over him. He had nowhere to go. He would get in trouble. There would be a Wrath. No matter what he did at this point, he was too much in trouble to get out of it. He just wanted to go home. Whatever happened, Dad must *not* find out.

"No! *Don't call Dad!* Don't! Call my mom!" Something about this terrified plea struck the Vice Principal. He frowned, looking troubled.

"Jonah! You aren't going to leave me any choice! Come on down and I won't call your dad, but if you stay up there…"

"Don't call him!"

What Jonah didn't realize and the Vice Principal didn't know was that Dad worked for the school district. He knew the Principal because he was in charge of the maintenance department for Vallejo Unified School District. He had his own office somewhere and was "Important," and when the incident had gotten out of hand, some totally pissed off yard duty had told the Principal, and someone had called Dad's office and told him that his son had gone crazy,

beat up a yard duty, and climbed to the top of a fence
like a monkey.

Before the Vice Principal had gotten very far
with negotiating him back down to earth, a white sedan
had pulled up next to the school and out of nowhere,
Walter was walking across the street.

Jonah was shocked. He hadn't seen Dad's truck.
Walter had had to borrow a car from someone else at
the office to drive down to the school. One moment
there was no sign of him, the next, Dad was striding
across the street like an enraged mountain lion, his eyes
locked on Jonah the whole way. He brushed right past
the Vice Principal.

"Get. Down. Right. Now." The words were
clipped, taut with suppressed rage. They seemed to
come out of him like steam from a boiler about to blow
up. He was trying to keep a lid on his Wrath.

Walter wore those big lens, almost frameless
glasses that were popular with professional "smart"
people in the 1980s. In the sunlight, they were
polarized (a very expensive feature at the time), and
with his severe face, the top of the glasses cut across his
eyes like a single, overhanging brow. Somehow, it
made him look even more angry, almost like a
caricature of rage itself. He wasn't funny though, he
was deadly serious.

Jonah might have actually wet himself right
then and there if he had had anything in his bladder. As
it was, he instantly lowered his head and rapidly made
his way down the fence with the agility of a cat. He
stepped down onto the sidewalk and physically drooped
like a dog that knows it is about to be kicked. He didn't
dare make eye contact with Dad.

"Get in the car." Dad was calm, but the words
were heavy with malice.

Jonah knew his father. More than anything, he
hated to be embarrassed in public. There was no hope
that this would go well. He climbed into the passenger

seat of the strange sedan, looking longingly out the window. He wanted to be away … somewhere.

On the short ride home, Walter explained in painstakingly clear terms that he had been forced to interrupt his *important* work because he got a call that his son was "climbing a wall like a *fucking* monkey!" This was *not* over, and there was going to be a reckoning that night.

Jonah stared out the window of the car the entire ride, imaging what it might be like to live in the places they saw as they passed. He liked to pretend that he was a tiny person, the size of one of his GI-Joes, like four inches, and he could hide in the attic of one of the houses, or sneak into one of the big buildings, and live on popcorn and stuff he might steal out of the vending machine. He would hide away and nobody would be able to find him because he was so small…

6

FIRST FLIGHT

It was Monday evening. The sky over the city was turning from an amazing Pacific sunset into a city night sky glowing with reflected colors from thousands of lights below and thousands of stars above. The air was sweet with the smell of roses and lemon trees and a tinge of salt from the ocean. California's huge valley was still warm even after the dying of the sun. The heat would slowly rise up out of the streets and sidewalks for half the night negating, any chill until the early morning hours. The night had a freshness and clarity that made Jonah pause as he stood in the front yard of the little semi-Victorian house.

It was long after 6 PM. In fact, it was much closer to 7! Dad and Mom were late coming home. It was insanity to be standing out in front of the house where they walked up before even opening the door. There was no hiding here. Jonah hadn't come out to hide though, he had come out to try to do something proactive. It was a child's plan. He knew that Dad always started his anger when the front door opened, so maybe if he got out here to talk to them *before* that …

Jonah knew it was useless and stupid, but he didn't know what else to do. If only he didn't have to be here for this … if only he had somewhere to go … If only he could go away.

Jonah glanced sideways at the knock-off BMX bike his dad had arranged for someone from the school to bring to the house. It had been set on its side on the big concrete porch. Jonah loved that bike. He could go anywhere. He could hop curbs, zoom up and down the blocks of the city as fast as a car in the tight confines of the neighborhood. It was freedom.

Slowly, the ten-year-old turned in a circle, taking in everything very carefully. He looked hard at the lemon tree in the yard, the fig around the side, the little picket fence his mom had loved so much… the house had once been very nice, back in the days when this neighborhood wasn't rotted and dying. Jonah wanted to take a picture of everything, to keep it, remember it, save it. He had just decided that he didn't mean to ever come back.

Jonah jogged to the porch, grabbed the bike and ran it out the front gate. Once on the cracked sidewalk, he lifted himself effortlessly onto the pedals and immediately accelerated with an ease born of practice and a natural athleticism. For a brief moment, he was terrified. They could come swinging into this street at any moment, and if they caught him out this late, it would compound his trouble … He counted the heartbeats until he was down the long city block and made the first corner going downhill toward the waterfront.

He was away.

The hills of downtown Vallejo slope abruptly toward the marina area. In the old days when Vallejo was a bustling satellite port of San Francisco, this was the hub of the city. Even later, after the entire economy of the city revolved around the massive Navy Yard that overhauled submarines on Mare Island (which really wasn't an island, but was called that) across the straight from Vallejo, the Marina area was the gateway to jobs and prosperity.

Now, things had begun to go bad for the old town. Much like the semi-Victorian house with the sagging floors, the city itself was rotting. The Navy Yard was being throttled year by year until it was to shut down completely in the wash of base shutdowns under Clinton. The old neighborhoods had gone bad. Drugs and gangs had moved in and middle class business owners had moved out. The Marina was something of a monument to the elegance that the old port town had once had, a memorial to the importance it had enjoyed during World War II and the height of the Cold War. Now, there wasn't much there but miles of walks along the waterway and old propellers and anchors from great ships turned into monuments in cradles of concrete.

Jonah found himself at the Marina almost inevitably after pedaling around the city for a while. He had come to realize already that he was not a good planner. He wasn't tired yet, but he knew he would be, and he didn't have any solid ideas about rest. He also didn't have good ideas about food or money either. His primary concern had been avoiding Dad, now that he had done so, he didn't know what to do. He had no relatives within biking distance, he had no longtime friends (because his family moved almost every year). Really, he didn't have a lot of options. Jonah began to think that his best bet was just to see if he could last the night and then maybe sneak back home to find food.

Jonah may have been ten, but he wasn't a fool. He kept moving, knowing that there were bad people out and about at night. There were bums camped out in some of the dark corners here at the marina (one of the things that had occurred to him was that if *they* could find food and some place to sleep, maybe he could too) but being there at night, he now realized that he had no chance of defending himself or his own particular dark corner against someone who wanted to take it or him. His best bet was to stay mobile, stay on the bike, and keep on rolling. He didn't know where to go.

Jonah knew that there were spots under the freeway overpasses, shelves up the sides of the embankments on each side where a person could climb up and hide. He had thought of finding one of those places until he had set out, but he didn't know how to get to a freeway on-ramp and he hadn't thought of how he would make his way along one until he got to an overpass. There were no on-ramps anywhere close to downtown. Looking out at the city from a car window, it had always seemed that there were innumerable places to hide out, but being on the street, things didn't seem so easy at all.

Jonah had read a short story in school about a boy who had lived in a subway station in New York. He had found an abandoned station down a little tunnel he could reach from the main station, and he had hidden there, coming back to find food. It had seemed easy enough for a kid to survive on the street in the story, but that was just a story. Downtown Vallejo at night was fairly terrifying.

Jonah stopped at the end of the long, long walk that ran along the Vallejo side of the waterway. It was bordered with massive heavy anchor chains from a ship that had been turned into the railing for the walkway. Here, it ended abruptly at a point where on a clear night, you might catch a glimpse of lights out across the Bay and wonder if they were San Francisco. He looked around. There was nobody nearby. The waterfront was dead at this time of night. He considered sheltering under one of the big ship propellers set up as civic art … Nothing about that seemed comfortable or practical, nor would it hide him from the eyes of bad people passing by.

The ten-year-old scanned the marina area. There was a yacht club and a restaurant. The yellow glow from the restaurant's windows lent a cheery glow against the cold blue of the water and the night. Yuppies were in there eating expensive food right next to the waterfront. Nothing there looked too promising. He wasn't yet at the level of desperation where he'd be willing to dig through restaurant garbage for dinner, and he didn't have enough faith in humanity to ask for help from one of the customers.

He looked past the restaurant at the yacht club itself. There was a marina there. Boats, which he knew could probably be broken into and slept in … *if* you could get onto the marina docks. Most people only came out to their yacht on the weekends at most. There would be plenty of time to find a place to shelter and scout the least used boat … some people even kept canned food and things on their boats for when they slept aboard. He decided it was the best plan available and headed toward the forest of bobbing sailboat masts.

It was then that Jonah found the real flaw in his plan. The marina was closed off from the sidewalk by a heavy duty metal door and a section of chain link fencing. There were lights all the way down the walk. He knew he could get over the fence pretty quickly and probably not be noticed, but there was no way he could get his bike over it. Leaving it on this side would guarantee that it would be stolen before morning, and he would have lost his only transportation. Even if Jonah could muscle the bike over the chain link fence, it would take him enough time that he would be spotted from the yacht club for sure, and he had no way to explain himself … Somebody might call the cops, the cops had probably been called by his parents by now … Jonah realized that he'd been unmoving for too long and there were suspicious shapes moving down the walk in the darkness. He had to make a decision. He might be able to get over that gate without anyone noticing. If he did get out into the marina, he could surely find somewhere to hide among all those boats, even if he couldn't break into one. Some of them had covers over their decks like tents which he could hide under overnight.

Jonah sighed. There was absolutely nowhere to put his bike here and he didn't have the lock, not that that would make any difference anyway. Bike thieves in the 1980s had it pretty easy; they just carried bolt cutters and walked away with a bike in about ten seconds flat even *if* you used a chain. If Jonah went out there, some jerk would have enough money to get high or drunk tonight and he would be reduced to getting around on foot and not being able to outrun grownups who might want to hurt him.

Jonah put his feet back on the pedals and started back up the marina walk. He was running out of options and out of ideas. His ten-year-old knowledge of this city was now exhausted, and the night was getting late enough that a kid on a bike out on the street was starting to draw attention.

After cruising around a few more blocks and getting both cold and tired, he decided to admit defeat and head back home to face the inevitable. He just didn't have anywhere to go and didn't have any way to survive out here by himself. He was still less terrified of the ghetto streets at night than he was of Dad (mostly because he could see trouble coming and could run for it), but he knew that people his size could get killed or kidnapped out here. He wasn't stupid. He was taking a big risk and it was starting to look like it was a dead end. Getting beat again would be better than what could happen to him out in the street.

Jonah didn't know what time it was when he slowly pedaled his way back home. He dreaded his homecoming every moment of that long, painful trip back up the hill. He wracked his brain trying to think of another option, but nothing came. If he had had more time to plan, he could have made a clean getaway. If he were setting out from Grandma and Grandpa's house in Fairfield, he would be very confident and could even find a hiding place in the marsh around Suisun. Here, now, this late, he just had nowhere to go.

At last, Jonah rolled back up to the house. He stopped on the sidewalk in defeat. The truck was parked out front and the porch light was on. They were awake inside. He had no doubt that Mom and Dad had worked themselves into a panic. They had had plenty of time to get worked up by now … Dad would be crazy … Jonah had done too much wrong, there was no going back. He didn't want to think of what would up the ante from the *hammer*…

The ten-year-old wearily opened the fence gate and rolled his bike inside. He dropped it on the front porch and prepared to open the front door with a heavy sigh.

The door flew open suddenly and Jonah was shocked to realize that it wasn't Dad but Mom standing there. She had been crying (as usual). She flung herself at him and grabbed him, lifting him off his feet in a hug. This was not what Jonah had expected or braced himself for.

"Where were you?" Mom was sobbing.
Jonah said nothing.

"We were so worried! We called the police! Don't you *ever* do that again!" She was shaking him for emphasis as she spoke.

Jonah was looking over her shoulder for his father. So far, there was no sign of him. Dad had remained in the living room.

"Where did you go?" She repeated.

"I … just … rode down to the marina." Jonah was still looking around for Dad. He didn't trust this.

Mom was crying. Jonah didn't like it when she cried. She did it way too much, and nothing positive ever came of it. It was like her way of not dealing with things.

"Why did you run away?"

Jonah knew he could not answer. There was no possible answer he could give that would not get him in more trouble than he already was. If she could not understand why his life was a living hell by virtue of her own two eyes, nothing he could say would change that.

Jonah gave a child's answer.

"I … don't know." He knew. She knew. He knew she knew.

"Were you …" She was having a hard time controlling her voice. A sob was trying to break through. "... were you *that* unhappy here?" Her question ended in a series of sobs.

"Yes."

Laura stood there, her arms wrapped around her ten year old son, sobbing like that for several minutes. "Please promise me you won't ever do that again!"

"Okay."

Jonah didn't understand by what mysterious power Dad had been held at bay. He didn't know what must have been the conversation between Laura and Walter when they realized that he'd run away from home. Whatever it was, something had changed. He was in trouble, but there would be no Wrath tonight. Walter sat brooding on the couch, not making eye contact with anyone. Jonah had no curiosity about this whatsoever. The last thing he wanted to do was ask why Dad wasn't giving him a whipping.

"When Walter came to the Vallejo School District the schools were critically overcrowded and literally falling apart. Walter found seriously dangerous conditions, a lack of fire safety, poor heating and leaking roofs with buckets everywhere catching the rain. The teachers would walk around ringing little bells they held in their hands to signal a fire drill. There were very few intercoms working, and the boilers were literally ready to blow up and take out half the school. ... When Walter left the Vallejo School District eight years later, it was being represented by the State as a model district."

-The Carpenter Chronicles by Walter Franklin, p.37

7

COUNSELING

They all sat at the table in the small office, shifting uncomfortably. Laura, Walter, Hayden, Amy and Jonah. They were dressed up, the way other families might get dressed up to go to church. Jonah had been forced to even allow his mother to hold him down long enough to comb his wild, curly hair.

The table was very stark. The office was almost bare. There was nothing there but a clock on one wall and a window with the mini blinds closed. The clock tick-tocked to fill the heavy silence, the counterpoint of the ticking only making the lack of human words thicker.

The man sitting opposite the Franklin family wore Birkenstocks. He had a funny looking sweater and frameless glasses that made him look "smart." He exuded the silky false confidence of a politician.

"Now, I'd like to ask *you* something, Jonah." The man directed his slightly *too* measured and reassuring tone at the sweating ten-year-old right in the middle of the Franklins across the table.

"Is everything okay at home? In your opinion? Are you happy?"

Jonah could barely make out the words. His face was white. His ears were ringing. The smoldering eyes of Dad were boring into the back of his skull. He didn't need to turn to see them.

"Um. Uh huh. Sure … yeah."

"Are you *sure*?"

Jonah glanced at Mom. She sat extremely stiff and upright, looking very uncomfortable. She was trying *way* too hard to seem relaxed, which only made her look more unnatural.

"Sure? Um, yep … I'm happy. Uh … *really* happy. Um …" Jonah glanced around in desperation for the attention of all the adults to be on something other than him. "Are *you* guys happy?" He tried to indicate the two girls and his mom to his right. He never turned even a degree to the left where his Dad stared at him with a gaze like a magnifying glass burning an ant.

"Yeah, yeah. We're all happy!" Mom had picked up the limp thread. She glanced nervously at Dad, then abruptly shut up and tried to paint a smile on her face. She looked like someone who had just swallowed a bug but is trying not to throw up in public.

"Mmm hmm." Said the man, writing something in his notebook.

Five sets of eyes were glued to that notebook in silent panic. What was being written in there? What could happen to them if it were bad? They had been told (in preparation for this meeting) that they had better be on their best behavior because if the man reported the wrong thing, Dad might lose his job and they would all be out on the street. They didn't want to be out on the street.

Mr. Birkenstocks leaned back in his chair with a creak. He looked like he was pretending to be very thoughtful in order to hide the fact that nothing much was going on upstairs. Jonah had long ago decided that he didn't like him.

The man now turned to Hayden and the entire family seemed to let out a collective sigh of relief as the focus left Jonah.

Hayden tried to smile and hide behind her thin hair at the same time.

It had probably started with the Vice Principal at Jonah's school. After the "monkey on the fence" incident, Jonah had been the subject of concern by some of the staff there. Anyone who had seen the way he had reacted to his father must have been certain that something was wrong. Someone in the school district had suggested that the family sit for "counseling" because something seemed wrong at home. It must have been someone important, because Walter went through with it (rather in the manner of a cat going through with being put in a bathtub to get washed) and seemed genuinely worried about losing his job (which made him bitterly angry at Jonah, who had brought all this on).

The session with Mr. Birkenstocks didn't turn into anything. Whatever he wrote in his notebook, it would never matter because they never came back and nothing more came of it. Dad's job was safe for now.

In the meantime, the Vice Principal at Jonah's school wasn't done with him. He reached out to Jonah's mom and his teachers. He sat down with some of the teachers at the school who realized that Jonah wasn't "engaged" in class and was "acting out." Jonah got in a lot of fights that year. It was a regular occurrence for him to be spending time outside the Principal's office that he should have been in class. He was even suspended more than once for fighting. Every time, it was always the same story: Jonah saw some bigger kid picking on some smaller one and reacted violently. After he became known as a "troublemaker" (and especially after the yard duty got hit in the face) he was a "bad kid" and he bore the brunt of the blame every time after that.

Jonah was very advanced for his age. He spent time in the school library, voraciously consuming every book available to him. He was often bored in the huge, crowded, public school classrooms that went at the pace of the slowest kid there. It was decided that he wasn't learning, so Jonah was taken out of the regular class. There was no program for advanced students available though; the only program the school had was for the "special" kids who had no hope of ever catching up to their peers. So, Jonah was placed in the "special" kids' room for much of his school day. He had regular visits with a school counselor, and he didn't do recess at the normal times with the rest of the school, but with the special kids, which meant that he would not be able to play tetherball anymore. Recess left him utterly isolated, bouncing a rubber ball against a concrete wall of the building by himself, unable to really connect to the very nice but *very* slow kids he was now surrounded with.

It was during this time that Jonah decided that he hated "counselors."

Things at home did begin to get better now. Not much, but enough to make things sort of tolerable at least. Many years later, Hayden would say that Laura had spoken to her, not as a mom, but as a friend, and confided in her during this time. She claimed that Laura had thought seriously about leaving Walter. She'd been stopped by the knowledge that there was nowhere to go and she couldn't make enough money to support them. Grown-up Jonah had been skeptical. He hadn't remembered anything along those lines, and he couldn't understand why both grandparents' houses were out of the question. In any case, it was pointless to speculate about what had been thought of by whom when nothing had been done.

The rest of that school year was ever so slightly easier for Jonah than the beginning. He remembered how his "save the whales" obsessed science teacher went out of his way to personally shuttle Jonah to a school outing he wanted to go to because the first day of the outing overlapped with the last day of a suspension he'd received for fighting. The man had driven him in his own car so he could go out to Point Reyes with his class.

Hayden had once told Jonah that they were "latch key kids." He didn't really know what that meant, but he knew that they were pretty good at taking care of themselves. Laura was managing a store full time, Dad was waging a "Crusade" of some kind at the School District, so that left them to their own devices, which they had come to prefer anyway.

During the First Missionary Trip, Hayden and Jonah had been homeschooled. Mom had managed to use a home school course to keep them on or ahead of their grade levels while the nomadic family crossed half the continent in a little travel trailer towed behind Dad's work truck. There were still some homeschool books lying around and when Amy had had some trouble in school, Jonah had decided to try to tutor her using the old homeschool books. He painstakingly erased the answers on each page of the workbook, set up an old school desk that had been in the house when they came there, and played school with Amy. Jonah would go through the exercises with her, trying to teach her what she needed to know thanks to his four year head start. Amy had quickly gotten bored though and announced to Jonah that "I know all this." When Amy threw the book aside, for some reason he could not explain, Jonah had felt a pang of sadness. He hadn't been eager to "play school" so much because Amy needed help, he realized. He'd been eager to go through the old homeschool workbooks because they were a tangible connection to something before the all-consuming blur that was sweeping away his past moment by moment. Before the continual state of emergency that was life now.

8

THE HOUSE ON 5th STREET

Fairfield, California, 1987-88

Jonah looked out at the freeway complacently from the shaking, noisy cockpit of the old work truck. Dad's truck had been retrofitted with big, swiveling cup holders that he had screwed to the dash to hold his ever present cups of coffee. He had also bolted in a compass, rather like what might be found in the cockpit of a sailboat during the long trip across country on the First Missionary Trip. All of this and the ever present work tools gave the place a certain sense of importance to a ten-year-old mind, as if this were the bridge of a spaceship or the control tower of an aircraft carrier.

Dad always had his dented stainless steel thermos full of hot coffee with him. The lid had been broken at one point by some rough use and remained halfway intact, but still capable of closing off the top of the metal cylinder. Dad had once bragged about using the thing during a fight with a bigger man on a job site. Jonah liked to look at the exterior and wonder which of the dents in it came from the man's head.

It was early. Cold. The wind from the freeway crept up under the firewall from the engine compartment of the old 1970s pickup truck and tried to chill Jonah's legs where he sat. Outside, mist was creeping up from the fields of golden grass that stretched between Vallejo and Fairfield, along miles and miles of Interstate 80.

Jonah had the plastic cup-shaped outer lid of the thermos in his hand half full of black coffee. He held it gingerly, trying not to spill despite the undulations of the freeway. Dad had stopped at Burger King for an egg and cheese breakfast sandwich for each of them, and Jonah was still feeling the afterglow of such a wonderful breakfast.

He was used to foraging for whatever was available in the empty house while his parents were away. He remembered the time that some cousin's birthday cake had ended up parked on the counter for a week, with Mom telling them all that it was too old to eat, but the kids had been so hungry after school that they had slowly picked apart the frosting on the cake day by day even while it turned green. Jonah remembered the penicillin taste of that rotting birthday cake.

Dad always had good things. If Dad wanted a bag of chips, he bought them and ate them. He always had expensive, imported German beer in the refrigerator that was bare of snacks or lunch meat. Traveling with Dad had some major perks, such as the fact that he would just splurge on junk food because that was what he wanted and you happened to be with him.

Walter had taken a minor interest in teaching Jonah to drink black coffee out of the thermos lid cup, and that moment of interest was like a rain in the desert to the boy, who still wanted to be able to have a relationship with a dad that was like the kids on TV, where it wasn't just fear, where he could have someone to look up to. At ten years old, Jonah really wanted to believe that his father could be his hero.

Walter was preoccupied with bigger, more important things. They had been obliged to take in Laura's mother, whose health was slowly deteriorating. Walter had rigged up a temporary partition in the living room of the house in Vallejo, which had been a challenge complicated by the fact that they were renting and he was not allowed to modify the walls or interior in a permanent way. He had ingeniously built a temporary wall partition with a doorway that abutted the intact sheetrock of the living room and could be removed without damaging anything.

Things had progressed rapidly after that. Laura's brother, Matt had died suddenly of heart failure. Nobody was that surprised, considering how obese he had been. There had been funeral arrangements to make, a grandmother to care for, and the unending stress of work where the bureaucracy seemed to be punishing him for the crime of actually accomplishing things.

Walter had been able to attend a seminar on estimating paid for by the school district, and that had led to his being able to estimate replacement costs of schools, which turned out to be the missing link in the school district applying for grant money. Now he was singlehandedly funding the entire maintenance department for the district by submitting cost estimates to the government.

Walter was a man who had always been aware of his own importance and capability. When he was in elementary school, he had started earning money as a paperboy even though he was too young to work for the paper. He'd earned his spot by working for an older boy who had not wanted the job, but had qualified, and he'd been so good, he had become the star paperboy of the entire town. His life, to hear him tell it, had been a succession of similar experiences. He claimed that he had to constantly take care of less capable people around him. Walter's youth had been defined by the fact that his father was a pastor and would-be missionary. Every summer, he had spent time at a Christian campground first as a camper, and then as staff. He had once been his father's one-man work crew for building projects that needed to be done at the camp, and that was how he had begun to learn his trade as a builder.

Now, Laura's mother had agreed to let them take out a bank loan on the home that she and her alcoholic husband had paid off years ago. With the loan money, Walter was going to build a large addition on the house. His kids and his mother-in-law would all be able to live there. He was going to take care of everything. He was going to take care of them all, as he always did.

Walter had once built a spec-house with money left to him by an uncle. His father the pastor had had to be pulled in because the project went over budget and they needed new financing to keep it going until they could turn around and sell it. At the end of the whole thing, they had had a chance to take a deal that gave them back exactly the money they had put in to the spec house, or they could use it as collateral and get a loan that would have allowed them to build a bigger commercial project that might have paid off a lot better. Walter's dad had made the final call because his name was on the deed. He had said they needed to get out and walk away. Walter had disagreed. He thought his dad was so caught up with his biblical precepts that he was unable to grasp the real world. In the *real world*, you make money by borrowing money. That was what Walter understood about business.

So they were remodeling the house Laura had grown up in. It was a place where she had lived years of her life that she didn't remember at all. She swore it was just a blank. The most awful times of her childhood just didn't exist anymore. They were lost in the fog of a memory selectively wiped in order not to have to deal with its contents. Now, Walter was going to fix that too. He was going to renovate that house, change it so much that it was unrecognizable. He was going to rip out all the walls, all the carpets, all the things which might remind her of the past she had tried to bury, so that it would never come back up again. He would spend anything and do anything and work as hard as necessary to keep that abusive past dead. Walter was going to save everybody.

Jonah looked up at his dad, stunned by the fact that they were actually going somewhere together, doing something together, *working* together. He had never known the mysterious and so important details of *work* which was so awesome that it made he and Hayden and Amy nothing in comparison to its mysterious grandeur. He knew that *work* was the thing which his Dad cared about above anything, and he knew that it was work that he was really mad at when he took it out on the kids, so it stood to reason that *work* must be some incredibly momentous, important, mystical thing which was beyond the understanding of a ten-year-old boy, or … or it wouldn't be worth it … or … it would be inconceivable to choose it over one's own children over and over again. It simply *must* be important. Now, he had the chance to actually *go with* his Dad and see the kind of *work* he did. He could barely contain himself. It must be *so* great, to merit the kinds of terror that had been rained down on them over it. He could barely wait.

Jonah had reason to be happy. The Electric Spider had finally begun to malfunction more than it actually worked. The metal mesh under the sheet had begun to rust, and the contraption had become useless, simply going off whenever it was plugged in. Finally, in a moment of triumph for the boy, he had watched as Mother grabbed the rusted, bent hunk of metal mesh the way someone might hold a snake, and carried it gingerly to the trash can behind the house. To Jonah it was as if a symphony were playing in the background as he watched the machine being dismantled. Perhaps surprisingly to his parents, Jonah suddenly began to sleep like a normal boy his age almost as soon as the machine was thrown away.

During the weekends and then the long days of summer, they spent many hours gutting that house. They brought in a construction dumpster and filled it with all the carpets in the house, all the yellowed sheetrock that had been so stained by nicotine as to look like lemon pudding.

Dad brought in someone to scale that massive, dark pine tree in the front yard with a chainsaw. That tree which could be seen for miles around -the tallest tree in the entire town- came down in gigantic chunks of pine and sawdust that filled the yard with pungent, sticky pine blood for months.

Jonah was sad when he saw it. For some reason, the speed with which Uncle Matt's tree was removed disturbed him. The gaping hole it left in the yard disturbed him too. It was like the thing which had grown out of control, the dark, invisible thing nobody noticed that came to loom over them was gone ... but it wasn't. Now, it had been swept under the rug in a flurry of pine scented sawdust.

They toiled and the house was transformed, day by day. They knocked out the front wall and built a bay window because Mom wanted one. They bought the most expensive front door in the home repair store because Dad wanted it. They added an entire second story and a massive master bedroom, with an apartment below it behind the main house. The yard that Jonah had once played in was reduced to a small fringe around the huge mass of the house.

The day came when they moved in. They were in a hurry to get out of the house in Vallejo. Dad was yelling, Mom was bustling. The perpetual chaos of modern nomads had turned into the special, panic-tinged chaos of a looming deadline. They rushed out of the house, clinging to whatever possessions they had been able to keep. Hayden spent much of the ride complaining that she had left behind her most treasured toy, one she had had since she'd been very little. It was a knit frog. They drove on. Hayden continued to complain that it must have been left behind. Dad said it was probably in some box.

Years later, Hayden still brought up that trip and the loss of that toy. Rather than turn around, they had charged blindly onward, leaving a trail of memories behind like a snail's path. Jonah didn't understand Hayden's pain. To him, she had displayed weakness by not clutching her most valuable possessions when a sudden move uprooted the family, as it always did. Did she expect the inevitable chaos to stop for *her*? What he didn't realize then was that old keepsakes from her childhood were Hayden's way of holding onto something else. She didn't have Jonah's mind. She lacked the ability to record moments in time for posterity, so amid the chaos, she tried to hold little scraps of this and that, little bits of things as reminders of the past that died a little more after every move to every new town. Jonah didn't realize that Hayden tried to hold on to her own past for the same reasons he did. Unfortunately, she could never manage to keep enough of it from slipping through her fingers.

Jonah was happy that he got a door and a bed with a mattress. He had been sleeping on the floor in a converted closet with a curtain for a door for the last two years. Anything seemed like an improvement, even though they gave him Uncle Matt's old room.

If any house had ever been haunted, it must have been that house on the tree-lined street in Fairfield California. Uncle Matt had died there, *somewhere* in that house. They didn't tell Jonah exactly where, but he was sure it was in Matt's room- the one he was given to sleep in.

Some of Matt's things were still on the top shelf in the closet when Jonah came there. The desk he would use for his homework was scarred almost as if it had been chewed on by a large animal- it was from Matt's belt buckle cutting into it as he got up and sat down. The wall under the window was completely stained- it looked as if some slow leak had been eating away at the sheetrock of the wall for years until it was melted. The studs could be seen in the dark hole left by the melted wall like blackened, rotted teeth in a skull fully three feet wide. The leak had come from *inside*, not outside, and when the builder who had seen everything looked at it even Walter was puzzled. They realized that Matt must have been urinating where he sat at that desk under that window when he couldn't make it to the bathroom. The piss had literally eaten away the wall.

The first night Jonah slept in that room he felt as if something was watching him from the open closet, but his eyes kept going back to that awful gap in the wall under the window. The bare studs showing through the rotted hole, like a gigantic cavity in the wall of the house, desperately in need of a root-canal. In the darkness, the hole was so black that nothing could be seen within. It seemed to Jonah that there was something oozing out of it, some small, chittering, shiny black things in that pitch black gap like a boiling swarm of black ants coming out of an ant mound … or worse … it was like spiders. Pitch black, swarming *spiders*.

Jonah felt some kind of connection between the urine that had eaten away that wall and the shame of the Electric Spider that he had slept with. He sat horrified, staring at the gap in the wall until exhaustion took him that first night in the house. Possibly it came from a connection with a warning his mother had given him about the Black Widow spiders that might be found under the house or in the *walls*, but somehow, out of this soup of shame, terror, and revulsion, an unreasoning horror of spiders settled into Jonah's mind. It would stay with him for the rest of his life.

That was the beginning of the best part of Jonah's childhood.

10

HOME

Fairfield, California 1988

"We are never going to have to move again!"
It was Laura's cheerful voice, telling the kids that they
had finally reached the end of their eternal migration.
The nomads were going to stay here forever. They were
home.

They had been driving to the house on Fifth
Street during one of the endless shuttle trips between
the rented house in Vallejo and there. She had been
happy, talking with Dad about what they would do,
how they wanted to replace the vinyl siding on the
place on Fifth Street. How she wanted a white picket
fence. She had announced to the kids that this was it.
They were going to have a home. Everything was going
to be good now.

They believed her.

Laura and Walter were born to the tail end of
the Most Selfish Generation. Those a little older than
them had rebelled against the draft and started
communes. Those a little younger than them had
rebelled against the communes and embraced
conspicuous consumption. For the very last of the baby
boomers coming of age in the roiling, tumultuous 70s,
the excesses of the first wave of hippies with their LSD
and "free love" seemed both decadent and wrong. They
were young enough to see the beginnings of the human
husks-the walking ruins begging in the street left by the
hippie pursuit of … whatever the hippies were

pursuing. The last of the boomers were more practical. They turned their generation's need to rebel and overturn institutions to directions closer to home. For two kids who came out of the church, the siren call that led them to chase the spirit was the Jesus Freaks.

Laura had clung to the church the way a castaway clings to a hunk of floating debris. Her home life was a ruin of alcoholism and codependence. Walter had grown up as the "pastor's son," paraded in innumerable churches as a "leader" (or trained monkey) and "example" while his father served as a guest pastor. He had never had a family life outside of the church. Walter had literally been born on the tail end of one of his father's missionary trips. Even when they were at home, Grandpa Franklin had invited missionaries or had people from one church or another staying with the family. The Franklin house was almost a public institution. In some ways, Walter and Laura were both orphans, and for both of them, the only home they had ever known was the church.

The young couple had sought the perfect Christian community the same way their hippie forbears had sought the perfect human community. They had gone to live in "Christian houses" in much the same way that hippies of a decade earlier had founded communes. Inevitably, they had faced the same problems except with perhaps a more toxic mix of theology and idealism. This was the era that led to the Children of God. It led to Jim Jones, it led to many strange cults with many bad outcomes scattered in the wilds of the American West. Walter and Laura had barely escaped several of these burgeoning cults in fact. It was only the grace of God and a weak sense of practicality that had spared their children from growing up in one of them.

In the late 70s, it seemed that there was something in the wind. It seemed that a "real" Christian community was just around some corner. It seemed as

if exciting new ideas were blowing through the world
and they just had to catch up … and then, just after
Walter and Laura were married, it seemed as if they
had missed the boat.

10 years of insanity had finally caught up with a
critical mass of people and the excitement Walter
sought began to dissipate just when he was old enough
and independent enough to pursue it full time. He
remembered as a youth missing out on watching the
Apollo moon landing because he was walking in the
woods of a Bible camp with some hippies, talking
about new and exciting ideas. Laura wanted what
Walter wanted. Which was to say that she *made* herself
want the excitement he craved. If pressed, she might
get a far off look and talk about always longing for a
real home. To her, this place was a little yellow house
in the country somewhere with a white picket fence,
where she could have a vegetable garden. It was more
of a mythical symbol of "home" than a real place, and
she forgot it (or told herself she did) whenever Walter
grew excited about some "Great Thing" around a new
corner.

Seeking this "Great Thing" had led Walter to
pack up his wife and firstborn child in a converted
school bus to go to Mt. Shasta in search of a Christian
Community called "Narnia." This had been a financial
bust, of course, and Walter had managed to work his
way back down the length of California until he was
building expensive mansions for millionaires in
Beverly Hills.

He could have stayed and earned a good living,
but again, the wind blew him to sell everything he had,
pack up three children in a travel trailer towed behind
his work truck, and make a pilgrimage across the
Western United States to go live on a mission support
base and build dormitories for missionaries in training
in Texas. The kids had grown brown in the sun chasing
tarantulas and scorpions around the RV camp where

they lived while Walter toiled. Again, there had been no money and no way to raise three kids in a travel trailer, and again Walter had had to compromise with reality and limp home, working odd jobs to pay for repairs along the way.

Now, it seemed that Walter was roped in. He had been anchored at last. Three children needed a home, he had to take care of an ailing mother-in-law, and the school district he worked for had rules of tenure and a good salary. Once he'd been there a certain time, he literally *could not be fired.* All the pieces and parts of a normal, suburban life began to accrue, but the restless spirit did not abate, and it only seemed to increase the roiling torment apparent within the man every time his Wrath overcame him, his eyes became dead like a shark, and all the frustration he had bottled up for years came out at the things that had chained down his free spirit; usually the kids.

They had moved from the rented house in Vallejo to Laura's mother's house in Fairfield. If Laura suffered moving into the home where so many bad memories lingered for her, she usually kept it hidden. She was a master at hiding things, even from herself. She had committed herself to working very hard while they were in Vallejo. She had become a manager at a major department store and then moved into better management positions at a specialty manufacturing concern. Despite never finishing college, she was very smart, very reliable, and almost fanatically dedicated to whatever office she worked for. She adopted the spirit of the time, starved herself on a diet of mostly lettuce and Diet Coke, and cut her hair severely short in a style that eerily resembled her son. Laura had become a Professional Woman of the 80s.

Things bothered her. She was troubled by the memories that her mind kept from herself. She was troubled by the way Walter ran the household, but she kept it to herself. She was troubled by her mother slowly dying before her eyes and her brother's sudden death. She decided to start going to therapy. Now, once a week, she would return home regaling Walter with the things she had been able to remember and how much better she felt getting it all off her chest, and he would return home haranguing her for wasting her time talking to a stranger about personal things. It had always bothered Walter when Laura had friends other than himself, had social activities other than what he did, or worst of all had people to talk to other than him.

All of this professional development and personal development for Walter and Laura left the kids a lot of time to themselves. Mom and Dad both worked full time. After work, they started doing things like joining the Vallejo yacht club (ironically right next to where Jonah ended up when he ran away) for sailing boat races on a boat owned by one of Walter's co-workers. The kids fended for themselves, but now, they were in a more normal suburban neighborhood without gangs and crack houses, and they had their own rooms.

Now, there were often snacks in the house for them, and they could ride their bikes to the county library a few blocks away, or even down to the mall. Grandma did basically nothing but stay in her room, but once in a while she would get a social security check and she'd fire up the huge, blue land yacht Oldsmobile she called "Jezebel" and drive them to the Dairy Queen for dipped cones. Every now and again, she would slip them money too, so it was almost like having an allowance.

For Jonah, school was a major challenge. Getting used to a new school was routine for him by now, but this time he was a small 7th grader in a rough middle school where some of the kids being held back in 8th grade a second time were almost the size of full grown adults. Biology betrayed him, and he went from being a lean, wiry 6th grader to suddenly filling out in all directions in preparation for a growth spurt that seemed to be taking its sweet time. He'd never been "the fat kid" before, so it was surprising to realize that he was right on the border now. Worse, the hormones of adolescence were beginning to kick in just to make things awkward. Still, even with all of that, life was better than it had been. There was a glint of normalcy that seemed to be in the air. Stability seemed to have arrived. The kids forgot about the ever present need to be ready to move at a moment's notice. They started to think of Fifth Street as just "home."

When Grandma died, Laura seemed to fade away for a while. Even though they were literally living in the home she had grown up in, the cords of memory that tied her to her own past seemed to be disappearing, almost like the keepsakes Hayden clung to to remember where she had been. Laura had always been a fragile soul. She had always tried to cling to people. She had never forgiven her elder brother for disappearing from her life when he basically cut off all contact with his family. She couldn't stand to lose people, and the loss of her mother came hard.

Walter was restless. The spirit that always drove him hadn't stopped blowing. He needed an outlet. He tried to write stories. He bought a sailboat. He bought a new car. He didn't finish the house remodel. Nothing he did seemed to fill that void left in the absence of the total freedom of being on the road. Meanwhile, the bills were piling up. Even with two good salaries, the family was swimming in debt. Walter wanted to be in charge of the money, but he was no good at tracking all the little details and balancing the books for the family. He could make good money, but he spent it as fast as he made it. Payments were always being missed. Money was always a strain.

It must have been one of these missed bills that led to the tirade one day in spring. Walter came home already worked into a frenzy. He demanded the attendance of the kids (who, by longstanding habit and immutable tradition had all disappeared into their rooms before Dad and Mom came in the door). He berated everyone in the family for "hiding" his mail in tones which would make a headbanging rocker cover his ears. Walter screamed at the idiocy, ineptitude, mendacity, dishonesty, and foolhardiness of his family as he herded them systematically through the house for at least an hour, searching high and low for some hidden piece of paper lost in the inevitable clutter of nomads who have camped in one place too long.

The kids stood like statues. It was impossible not to hear the screaming voice, to see the unhinged spectacle of spittle forming in the corners of Dad's mouth, and see the level of total rage he had achieved without being affected at least a little. Still, they were old pros. They had been the subjects of such rants for years. As much as it was possible, such things rolled off them now. After the curses and slamming of furniture, and the theatrical tantrum subsided, they went back to their rooms. It wouldn't even occur to them to think about the event again.

The next day was a weekend. The sun was bright, the air was sweet, and Jonah was in the little remnant of a backyard relaxing when he heard the neighbor kids over the fence playing in their own yard. It seemed that they had developed a new game. Either they were playing some kind of hopscotch or jump rope, but they had a sing-song chant that went with it.

"I'm a MEAN MAN; Give me MY MAIL! I'm a MEAN MAN; Give me MY MAIL!" They went on and on, hopping or jump roping or whatever they were doing. Jonah couldn't quite suppress a snicker, even though he saw Mom coming toward the back door from the kitchen. She opened the door, looked around for a moment as if she were about to call out to Jonah, then stopped, hearing the chant from next door.

"I'm a MEAN MAN; Give me MY MAIL!"
Mom disappeared back inside the house.

Jonah was laughing by the time Dad came ambling toward the back of the house. He was in a reasonable mood. He looked as if he had been starting to putter around with his tools in preparation for a continuation of the endless construction project that they all lived in.

Jonah didn't wait around for the inevitable. He knew how Dad hated to be embarrassed and he didn't want to be within eyeshot when it came. He ran around the outside of the addition to the side door to the mother-in-law suite and thus inside, slipping back into the safety of the central house without Dad seeing him.

Jonah did pause to look back and see Mom and Dad in the kitchen talking. Dad looked bewildered and slightly angry. Mom was trying not to laugh.

Jonah slipped out the front, got on his bike and was halfway across the neighborhood before anyone could call him.

*... But Walter's ... habit of getting things done was
performed in a Bureaucracy. And in a Bureaucracy it is
something of an unforgivable sin to get things done. ...
So, while Walter was getting things done, he was also
making Bureaucratic enemies. Enemies who waited for
opportunity, and when it came they acted and Walter
found himself laid off. Laid off even though he was in a
Bureaucracy which had rules that after five years of
tenure you could not be fired. ... Walter's enemies
found something they could put before the Board, and
the Board approved the removal of Walter. Five
thousand nine hundred and forty nine years into Gods
Inherit the Earth project, God was once again moving
his carpenter and preparing another long hard road
with a long hard lesson."*

-The Carpenter Chronicles by Walter Franklin, p. 39

11

BROKEN BY MY MASTER

Oroville, California 1992

They had to move again.

It came very suddenly in a storm of chaos, paperwork from bill collectors, Dad screaming, Mom crying, and fear. The kids didn't know what was going on. They were not filled in, but it was pretty clear that some series of things had happened that amounted to disaster.

When he looked back on it later, it seemed to Jonah that the first thing to go had been Dad's sailboat. He'd bought it from someone he worked with and it had served the family well enough. That boat had provided a nice getaway on several weekends when they sailed it out through the salt marsh and into the vast San Francisco Bay to anchor off Angel Island where they camped out in sleeping bags. Jonah even had a very positive memory of his father on that boat.

They had been exploring the islands of floating vegetation in the salt marsh of the Suisun Slough. Walter, always in a much better mood when they were out on the water, had let them pull up alongside one of the floating islands, and the kids were bouncing on the masses of spongy vegetation and grass. Jonah had been coming back onto the sailboat and just at the moment he stepped up, the boat and the island bobbed in opposite directions. Jonah had plummeted, finding himself underwater before he knew what was happening. The speed with which Dad moved was amazing. One moment, he was in the cockpit of the boat near the tiller, the next, he had leapt across the boat after Jonah.

There had been no real danger of course. Jonah wasn't an expert swimmer, but he would have had no trouble getting back to the boat. The salt marshes of California are nearly devoid of anything more harmful than pluff mud and small snapping turtles. Still, the alacrity of Dad's reaction sent a message to Jonah that ran counter to the beating rhythm of most of his childhood experiences: that his Dad did actually care about his welfare. That, perhaps, he was more than an afterthought, baggage, a burden to him. The dim flame of hope that had been kindled by moments like going to work on the house together had been fed once more, even amid the continual barrage of fear that his Dad rained down on the family every night after work.

They locked the sailboat when the Franklins stopped paying the marina fees. Walter toyed with the notion of getting it out, but eventually it was abandoned.

Like dominos, the things which the family had come to depend on began to fall one by one. The major blow was the house. It had been paid off, but the loan they had taken out with the bank in order to build the addition on and renovate it meant that when they stopped paying, the bank seized it. The family was left without a home once more.

Walter *swore* that none of it was his fault. He said that getting fired by the school district was unprecedented since he had tenure, and once he'd been fired, everything was inevitable. He said they had taken out the loan and bought the car and the boat and all the other things because he knew he could *not* lose the job. He seemed to believe that he was the object of persecution at work. It was impossible to say for sure, but based on the gist of the endless complaints Dad had brought home every night, grumbling about this or that individual, he did seem to have some personal issues with some of the people at the school district. It was not for the family to judge. Walter had held on there longer than any other job he'd ever had. If there was blame, it was the way they had racked up debts and spent money so freely during the good times.

This was a time of chaos. Even more so than the move from Vallejo. Jonah would remember a series of flashes as the family scrambled to collect whatever it could and be ready to move. For some reason, despite having moved so often, this one was a shock for them. They had let themselves believe that they finally had a permanent home that they would never have to leave.

Walter's older sister owned some property way up north in the endless forests of Northern California. She had a strange relationship with her husband, a Los Angeles police officer of many years and Vietnam vet. He lived in Los Angeles where his work was. Despite their being together literally since they were sweethearts in high school, the couple had drifted ever further apart and that divide had seemed to physically manifest itself into actual distance. Aunt Mary now lived practically as far away from Los Angeles as you could possibly go and still be in the same state.

To non-Westerners, the size of the states out West is often hard to imagine. If you had grown up in a state that you could drive out of in the matter of two hours or less on a highway, California's size is hard to grasp.

Los Angeles lies in the south of the state, but not all the way south. There are still hundreds of miles of desert below it before one hits Mexico. Going north from LA, it usually takes about eight hours by freeway to get to somewhere in the San Francisco Bay Area, which is called "Northern California" but is actually almost at the halfway point up the length of the state. From there, it usually takes about that much time again to get to the far northern end, where the mountains and endless, virgin pine forests roll over the border into Oregon.

Aunt Mary lived in a place called Paradise, California. It was a small town high in the mountains completely buried in pine forest and far closer to the Oregon border than to San Francisco. Her husband lived more than ten hours by freeway to the south, and would drive the entire length of California in his gigantic, four door pickup truck at almost a hundred miles an hour, flashing his badge at any cops who tried to pull him over at least once or twice a week, so he could see his wife and daughter.

Jonah always liked Uncle Boone. The man seemed preternaturally calm, a trait he may have gained as a Marine in the jungles of Vietnam, and which he undoubtedly had perfected as a cop on the streets of LA. Considering that his home was anything *but* calm, Jonah was always attracted to the even-tempered, blunt, soft spoken man. He was content to just sit and listen as Uncle Boone cooked chicken on the grill, telling stories of busts and crazies he'd dealt with over the years. Uncle Boone would teach Jonah to shoot a gun, a skill that would come in handy for him much later.

Aunt Mary speculated in real-estate. This was one of her various business schemes. She had attempted to set up a business as a literary agent, had bought and sold (modern parlance would call it "flipping") several houses, and now operated a little business appraising houses in the area (which no doubt helped out with the house flipping). She had managed to buy a massive monstrosity of a place that resembled a pile of geometric shapes covered in wood siding and pine needles, which served as her base of operations.

Aunt Mary offered to help out the Franklins as everything began to fall apart for them. She had a rental property way out in Oroville. It wasn't much; a mobile home on eight acres of steep hillsides covered in pine forest. Still, it was a place to land, which was what they needed.

Mom still had a good job as a manager, but Dad had never liked her having that job. He had never liked her having friends from work or attending Christmas parties or pretty much anything resembling having her own life. He'd been pressuring her to leave that job for some time. Whether that played into it or whether it was a simple matter of there being absolutely no practical way to commute all the way from Oroville to the San Francisco Bay area every day was hard to tell, but she left amid the chaos of the move north. Mary had actually been able to get her appraisal business going enough that she could bring in a second appraiser to help out, and she got Laura set up working with her.

Mary became Laura's boss *and* the family's landlord, which suited her just fine. She had always been the kind of person who dearly loved having sycophants to boss around.

Walter took the move hard. He retreated into depression for a while, neither looking very hard nor finding work. He took to being an out of work dependent rather well in fact, starting a string of projects each more improbable than the last. At one point he tried to start a literary magazine called the "Franklin Flyer," with collections of essays and poems from himself and the kids (Jonah had shown a certain talent for writing, receiving a scholarship to attend an art college summer program). At another time, he investigated the theoretical possibility of a time machine, staying up all hours of the night, pouring over his designs and notes, and sleeping during the day. Each project flared up as an all-consuming passion, then burned out suddenly to be replaced by the next "Big Thing."

Meanwhile, Laura worked, the kids found themselves in yet *another* new school, and they were all very poor.

Jonah knew that the way he was growing up wasn't normal. He didn't know what normal actually *was* though. It is one thing to realize every time you have to explain to a new set of classmates the entire litany of moves you have made in your life, that the other kids can't understand living as a nomad. It was quite another to know what a normal family actually did, how they actually acted, dealt with one another, and lived their lives. It didn't help that Jonah and Hayden had never had a chance to fit in with a group of peers. Moving so often taught them to be self-reliant and not get too attached to anyone outside the family, because such relationships always went away. They were both smart kids, and the sheer weight of their experiences and their childish reactions to them made them peculiar to the other kids at school. They had no way to define normalcy, so as they grew, they grew ever stranger to their peers, which contributed to the natural instinct of kids to try to bully outsiders.

Jonah had done reasonably well in Fairfield. He'd embraced the reputation he had begun in Vallejo as a "bad kid," and struck up friendships with some local reprobate kids who mostly came from broken or dysfunctional homes. They had grown rat tails or mullets, collected knives, raided one of their elder brother's room (the brother being a biker gang member) to find his porno stash, and generally acted like the California version of redneck boys. Jonah would have been happy to continue down this path, but again, they had moved, and he had lost connection with all his friends.

In retrospect, Jonah would consider it a blessing in disguise that he'd been removed from that group of friends just as they were getting to be old enough to get into *real* trouble.

Hayden was always more socially awkward. She had had her brief spell of having friends back in Vallejo, where she'd begun the awkward stage of self-reinvention a girl often begins at the onset of puberty. Back in those days, she'd actually had friends close enough to have sleepovers. Jonah remembered once being shooed away to his little closet-room so Hayden and her friends could have the run of the house for a birthday party. Naturally, he had resented having to go to sleep early while Hayden and her pals got to stay up late, so he'd crept down the stairs to the living room to see what was going on.

Shockingly, he had seen Dad, sitting at a table playing a board game with the girls. No trace of the smoldering Wrath could be seen. He was like a different person, making jokes and small talk, eyes bright as he entertained the girls.

Jonah had been troubled, partly by the transformation and partly by Dad's demeanor. Hayden would later complain that he had monopolized the entire evening that was supposed to be *her* party, and her friends didn't want to come over to her house anymore.

In the years since, Hayden had retreated into her own world more and more. Her one outlet now was an art college summer program that she had received a scholarship to attend for visual arts. It involved a full month away from home during the summer, and Jonah had been terribly jealous the first year she attended. The second, he had submitted an entry for writing and been accepted as well, much to Hayden's dismay.

She had some friends she had made there, and even a boyfriend for a little while. The pimple-faced, gangly youth even managed to talk his dad into driving him all the way up to Oroville from the Bay Area to visit her.

Jonah adapted well to the wild country of Northern California. He had always been physically active and basically fearless. He and Amy both took to tromping all around the 8 acre property; up and down steep trails Dad had cut through the woods, learning how to track raccoons, coyotes and even Mountain Lions by their droppings.

Uncle Boone had taught Jonah how to shoot on a hunting trip with him and his father, and Dad had started keeping a .22 long rifle around the house that had come down from Laura's father. Jonah would go tromping off into the woods with the .22 to shoot cans he'd set up on rocks out in the ravine, feeling like a pioneer boy from the days of covered wagons when his family had first come to California.

To him, the outdoors was always preferable to anything that school might offer, particularly since he now seemed permanently marked as an outsider in the high school he had just begun to attend.

Dad had good days and bad days. One day he emerged from the room where he spent most days sleeping quite suddenly in a rage. It seemed that a stray cat had had a litter of kittens right under his room in the trailer. He swore he was done with that damn cat this time and grabbed the .22.

Suddenly, he turned and asked Jonah to come with him. He wanted help hunting down that cat.

Jonah felt strangely ill as he halfheartedly looked around the huge property for the little animal. He liked cats. He'd once had a giant tomcat that had almost been like his dog and had let him lay on it as a young boy. He didn't like what they were doing, but he made no effort to talk his Dad out of it, not that Dad could really be talked out of something when he was in such a mood.

Walter spotted what he thought was the cat in the bushes and asked Jonah to spot it with his younger eyes and tell him if he had it. Jonah glanced, saw what was probably the cat, but merely shrugged. "I don't know what it is."

Dad raised the rifle, sighting down its length. Jonah looked away.

There was a crack as the trigger was pulled.

Jonah glanced, seeing something scurry away in the bushes. He could not be certain, but he thought Dad might have missed. It was long range for him.

"I think I got it. I saw white… it might have been its skull."

Jonah blinked, heading back up the crunching gravel drive toward the trailer. It was probably the white spot of fur on the animal's chest, but he didn't say anything. The image of a white, gleaming skull remained with him. The whole incident just seemed disturbing.

They got a dog. It was a golden retriever that came from an old couple who lived nearby. Something had happened to one of them and they could no longer take care of the dog, and had sought a home for it. For whatever reason, Dad had agreed. He was being "country Walter" at that time, hiking on the trails and cutting branches with his bow saw. Perhaps a dog fit his image of what a country man should have.

Walter had always hated dogs. His entire life, no dog could ever stand him, and the feeling was mutual. If he visited someone with a dog, he was uncomfortable the entire time. He would never relax, and the dog would never stop barking. It didn't matter how nice or well-trained the dog was, whenever they encountered Walter, the mutual animosity was instant.

It took perhaps a week at most. Walter would start into one of his screaming tirades. His kids would sit around the kitchen table, dumb as stones, deaf as stones after so many years. Laura would say nothing. The dog couldn't handle it. It grew more and more nervous, reacting to Walter worse and worse every time it saw him until it literally could not control itself and simply pissed wherever it was, whenever it saw him. Ears back, hunched in fear, it would urinate in terror at the mere sight of Walter walking into a room.

Jonah remembered sitting at the little table in that trailer kitchen. The family had been trying to have meals together as a "thing." Even Walter had been on somewhat better behavior as he tried to have a family meal. The dog had been in the kitchen next to its bowl, staying quiet and still so as not to be noticed.

Suddenly Walter said something loud. Not a scream of Wrath, nor even a yell, just somewhat louder than normal. Jonah and the dog both jumped just a little bit at the same moment. He locked eyes with it as it bent where it stood and instantly began to urinate all over the kitchen floor. This made Dad angry of course, and he got louder, which made it worse.

Jonah sat there, his fork poised over the plate of spaghetti, watching the dog watching him. He felt a massive wave of self-loathing wash over him.

That's me. Jonah's voice seemed to say in his own head. *That, right there, is me reacting to my dad.* He remembered the Electric Spider, wetting his bed out of … what? Fear? He was literally just a beat dog pissing on the floor. That was what he would always be.

Walter got rid of the dog a few days later. They found a better home among one of the redneckish "neighbors" (neighbor being a relative term in a place where every plot of land is several acres) who already had two Labs and who loved Golden Retrievers. He was a real dog person, and Jonah was glad to know that the old dog had found a decent home. It gave him hope somehow.

Another move, more small projects, Laura providing much of the support of the family in those days. Living very poorly in Oroville, California ... The Northridge earthquake in Los Angeles provided a meager opportunity for Walter to be part of the recovery effort and he found himself living alone in his uncle's motor home in Los Angeles with his family four hundred miles away. ... He felt like there was a curse upon him, yet he struggled to do right.... Laura struggled in Oroville working as an appraiser to provide food for the children and keep the house in order. With Walter not able to provide steady work since the School District, and now struggling in Los Angeles, she considered that maybe they should split up.

-The Carpenter Chronicles by Walter Franklin, p. 40

12

EARTHQUAKE

Dad hadn't worked for a while when the Northridge earthquake struck the state of California. Jonah remembered the big quake in '89 that had leveled the Embarcadero freeway in San Francisco. He remembered standing in his living room watching what looked like rippling waves move right through the floor, like waves across a waterbed mattress. The roll would come right to him and he'd feel it lift him up, then it would roll on. They hadn't really been touched by that quake, and the Northridge earthquake was so far away that they only saw it on the news. To Jonah, Northridge was a curious event. To Walter, it represented an opportunity.

Laura had been increasingly unhappy. Walter hadn't had work for a long time. His projects seemed to drift farther and farther from anything that could ever be practical enough to pay the bills. She was under considerable pressure to keep the family fed and rent paid.

Hushed earnest discussions at odd times of the night were evidence of some seismic shift going on between Walter and Laura, though as always, a front of total solidarity would always be kept up, even to the children, just as the family kept up a front of total, happy "normalcy" to outsiders.

The pressure to go seek construction work in the wake of the earthquake probably came from Laura. She had heard from Uncle Boone about how a wave of small time contractors had swept down upon the damaged suburbs in a feeding frenzy of repair contracts. Money was to be had if you knew how to build and you could hustle. Walter could do both.

One day, Dad was just gone. He packed up his truck and drove off. Mom didn't explain very much to the kids and they knew better than to ask.

After a couple of weeks, the news trickled back that Dad was in L.A. trying to find work. He was staying with *his* uncle in Simi Valley, a vast suburb of Los Angeles that crept up into the golden hills of Orange County.

When school ended, for some reason he couldn't later understand, Mom thought it would be a good idea for Jonah to go down and help out Dad. Dad had undoubtedly asked for him to come down. He had served as laborer and apprentice carpenter during the long, unfinished building project with his Dad on the house in Fairfield, and it was likely that Dad thought he might be useful. It was also likely that his dad hated to be alone, since he had never spent any time alone in his entire life.

In any case, Jonah decided that Los Angeles sounded more interesting than the trailer all summer and went along with the plan. He knew his Dad, and Walter out on an "adventure" was much easier to be around than Walter stuck in any kind of routine.

Jonah had forgotten how much he missed a big city. Simi Valley was a sprawl of leafy suburbs, perfectly maintained streets, and golden hills that shimmered with the peculiar, gold colored wild straw grass found only in California. Uncle Jared (not *his* uncle actually, Jared was his grandmother's brother) was a peculiar old man, brilliant, but quirky. He had snow white hair that he kept combed straight back from his forehead and a matching beard that gave him a slight resemblance to Santa Claus. He always wore big, thick framed glasses and carried a calculator in his pocket protector. Jared had been an aerospace engineer for many years. He'd once worked for Lockheed

Martin, and he was extremely smart. He never deviated from his daily routine, only ever ate salami and potato salad every meal, and was incapable of keeping his house in order. He reminded Jonah of a stereotype of a "genius" who might be so caught up solving a problem of quantum physics that he forgets to put on pants before walking out of the house.

Jared had been pretty successful as an engineer, and he had owned several houses at different times (he considered houses to be a better way to invest money than the stock market). His final residence was a very comfortable house with a backyard almost completely covered in stone pavers except for a "secret garden" on the side full of overgrown exotic plants once maintained by his wife before she died. He had let Walter stay in his RV in the driveway, because a room here was kept for Uncle Boone when he was in L.A.

Boone lived more or less like a bachelor most of the time, and with the loss of his wife, Uncle Jared had been happy to have someone around, so they had worked out a simple arrangement that gave Boone a place to stay in return for a small rent.

To Jonah, Uncle Jared's house was wonderful. He'd become accustomed to making do with a cramped trailer or whatever accommodation was available. His best years growing up had been in a house which at least had enough room for the family, but had never actually been finished, so they had lived with framed-in walls with no sheetrock in some places, a bare concrete floor in the living room, and walls that didn't match one another. It had been comfortable enough, but Jonah had only ever lived in a real *house* after the family had returned from the First Missionary Trip when he was very young and stayed with Grandpa and Grandma Franklin for a while. Coming down to stay with uncle Jared felt like a vacation stay in a nice hotel for him, even though he had to crash on a couch in the study.

Dad was doing things, but what *exactly* that was became unclear to Jonah. Walter had licensed a new business, gotten the paperwork filed, and taken out an ad in the newspaper. He had worked out a process for repairing cracked masonry and concrete using a new type of high strength epoxy that looked promising. There were literally hundreds of miles of masonry retaining walls, privacy fences, and innumerable other constructions in the area, and a lot of it had been cracked in the recent earthquake. Walter's process would be much cheaper than the traditional way to repair all those things. There seemed to be a good market. Walter even had stationary with a letterhead and a logo for his new business.

Shortly after Jonah came, Walter took him to his single customer, probably a friend of Uncle Boone, who had a cracked slab foundation that Walter had been working on. Through a process of drilling, injecting epoxy, and then grinding off the residue after it hardened, it looked like Walter had come up with a way to save the foundation of the house and save the homeowner a lot of money.

Walter was very enthusiastic about his venture. He seemed happy to have someone to talk to, and spent hours going on about how many people needed this kind of service, how few people could currently do it, or even knew about this new material technology, and how profitable it was going to be. He took Jonah on a long drive to a county building for some paperwork, talking the entire time.

"It's going to be great! Once I have a couple crews going, we can branch out across the L.A. basin…"

Jonah nodded. He was still bemused by the fact that Dad was smiling, talking in excited tones, and even cracking jokes. Walter seemed like a completely different person. Undoubtedly, this was the Walter that people who worked with him would recognize. This was the public Walter, not the one that emerged at home. He couldn't remember his father *ever* talking to him this much. Jonah was a *kid*, and was used to being told to "get in the car" by way of explanation that the family was going somewhere. He was used to Laura and Walter having conversations about things as if he wasn't there. He was used to avoiding drawing his Dad's attention at all costs for fear of becoming the subject of a Wrath. Being talked to like an adult by a personable and optimistic Walter was pretty revolutionary.

"You see that?" The lean-faced man with the glittering eyes was pointing out the window of the truck at a new model of minivan that had just come out that year. "I'll get a few of those. We will paint them up as fleet vehicles and put the company logo on the side. That will be our trademark fleet van."

Jonah nodded. It all sounded great.

Walter drove him way out to an industrial park and they walked around the buildings there. Walter talked excitedly about what he was going to do. "This one here. We'll lease this place and it will be our headquarters. It's located right in the middle of our market area. We will send out crews from here. We can manufacture our own material right here…"

Jonah looked up at the massive building with the loading dock made for big trucks. The entire place was brand new. The industrial park was still being worked on at the far end. It smelled like new paint and gleamed in the Hollywood sunlight. The big "For Lease" sign seemed to radiate optimism.

On the way back, they swung by a drive-through Chinese place for dinner with some of the cash Dad had made on that first job. Jonah had never seen a drive-through *Chinese* place before. He loved how in Los Angeles you could find drive-through *anything*. It was a city of people who never got out of their cars.

It was dark by the time they returned to Uncle Jared's house. The night smelled like flowers from someone's garden and the warm-grass smell of the California hills. Jonah felt as if a new chapter was about to open. All the hard, dark, awful parts were past. They were finally going to settle down and be a normal family and have a house and he would go to high school and maybe try out for the football team and date a cheerleader and…

Suddenly it occurred to Jonah that they had spent the *entire day* mostly driving around to look at stuff and get one piece of paperwork filed. Something in his gut felt wrong. If they were going to make this company work, they should have been out getting another customer. That uneasy feeling stayed with him over the next several days.

Jonah couldn't help it. He had never had any particular attention paid to him by his Dad. He was like a stray alley cat given food. It didn't matter what his gut told him, visions of what Walter said would happen began to float in his mind as if all he had to do was reach out and grasp them.

"You see that?" Walter pointed at one of the new convertible cars that had become an overnight fad the previous year. Jonah loved the ridiculous little Miatas and envied the happy people he saw driving them around L.A. with the Pacific breeze in their hair and Ray Ban's on their face.

Jonah nodded.

"I'll buy you one of those so you can drive it to school."

Jonah blinked. He looked out at the freeway stretching endlessly before them, the golden sunlight made famous in hundreds of Hollywood movies, the big, fancy houses and BMWs driven by happy yuppies all around them. For a second, he actually saw himself; a few years older, a bit taller, more filled out, curly brown hair the same, wearing a letter jacket, pulling up to a SoCal high school in a convertible with a girl in the passenger seat. It was the most glorious vision of his entire life.

The days passed, they printed up some flyers. They mailed some, others remained in a box on the floor of Uncle Jared's living room. The phone didn't ring.

Mom came down. She had to talk to Dad. Something was going on between them and as with all such things, nobody mentioned what it was or what they were talking about to "the kids." Jonah didn't know what was going on with Hayden or Amy, but as for his own sake, he actually felt a pang of resentment when he was utterly and completely ignored by Dad the moment Mom arrived. He was back to being told to "get in the car." He'd have to infer what had been talked about and what the hell was going on while it was already underway.

Dad took them out to a new housing development where they had model homes open for walkthroughs. Jonah felt oddly like a criminal somehow as they walked through the model home, Dad telling them about how Hayden would get *this* room and he would get *this* one… Mom looked like a child being given a piece of candy.

That night, Mom and Dad went for a long drive to talk stuff out. They stayed out late and probably talked through the night. Whatever they discussed, the outcome would change Jonah's life forever.

Some couples go to therapy, some go to third world countries. Different strokes…

"...She decided splitting up wasn't wise and took a trip to Los Angeles to talk everything through with Walter. The outcome of the discussions was to return to their first assumptions when they were married. They had wanted to work in a Christian House for God. They still wanted to try to make this happen ... So they contacted organizations that put Christians together with Ministries in need of help and support ... Once again Walter and Laura sold or gave away everything they had except the old work truck and Walter's tools. A few precious memories were stored in a shed behind his father's house and they prepared to leave family and friends."

-The Carpenter Chronicles by Walter Franklin, p. 40

13

THE FAMILY MEETING

For the *second* time in his life, Walter turned his back on making money in Los Angeles and decided to go on a Missionary Trip.

Everything happened very fast. Jonah and his parents drove back up to the trailer in Oroville. There seemed to be some new closeness between Laura and Walter that Jonah hadn't seen in a long time. Laura suddenly seemed very happy. She would break out with humming a song now and then, placidly watching the countryside go by out the windows like a contented child.

Neither of them told Jonah what had been discussed, nor was it explained to him why his father suddenly dropped everything to do with his business, packed up the truck, and took them north. He knew only that something momentous had occurred and that they were to have a family meeting when they got back.

The family meeting was unprecedented. It was also bewildering. The Franklins were not the sort of family that held "meetings" to decide things. That kind of thing might happen on TV sitcoms, but in real life (at least in Jonah's life) Dad told them to "get in the damn car!" and they hopped-to immediately, learning where they were going on the way. Mom and Dad talked things through on their own and you found out what was going to happen when it did. Now, after all these years, they were going to have a family meeting?

The kids lined up with all the enthusiasm of inmates shuffling out for inspection. Whatever the hell was going on could *not* be good.

Mom took the lead with the air of a kindergarten teacher explaining a wonderful new game to her class. Her pubescent offspring blinked at her in astonishment.

They were being asked if they agreed to Work for God.

It would only be on a trial basis. They would go that summer to volunteer at a Bible camp as staff. If God wanted them to continue, He would provide the way for them to continue working for Him. If He did not, they would come back.

The kids looked at one another in bewilderment.

"Just for the summer?" One of them said.

"Yes. Just for the summer. We are going to try it out. It will be so much fun! There will be horses and hiking trails and I think they have a tennis court..."

Jonah was confused. He remained under the impression for some time afterward that they would be able to come back to the place in Oroville.

"So, what do you say?"

Hayden frowned. "What if we say no?"

"You can ..." Mom and Dad looked at one another, "... probably stay with Grandma and Grandpa..."

Grandma and Grandpa had recently moved to Paradise, California (partly because Aunt Mary was there). They had sold their home in Suisun and bought a trailer way out in something of a retirement community in the woods. Their trailer had exactly one "spare" room about the size of the curtained closet Jonah had called a bedroom back in Vallejo. As the parents of seven children, most of which had children of their own, and as lifelong church community leaders, there was always *someone* staying with Grandma and Grandpa Franklin for one reason or another.

"...or Aunt Mary... we can find something..."

None of the kids liked Aunt Mary. She was the most domineering, overbearing person they had ever known.

Jonah frowned. "But… it's just for the *summer*, right?"

Mom and Dad nodded. "Yeah, just for the summer. It'll be so much *fun!*"

They all nodded assent. There didn't seem to be much else to do.

There was a flurry of activity. Everything they owned had to be boxed up yet again. Walter got Grandpa and Grandma Franklin to offer the use of a small metal shed behind their trailer to store anything that wouldn't fit in the truck with them. Jonah remembered looking incredulously at that beat-up, leaky shed that looked as if it were going to fall down a hill into the forest and disappear at any moment.

Everything seemed to be in a haze. Nothing really made sense to him anymore. He was excited about the prospect of the campground, but the rest of it all just seemed like he was trapped in a strange dream that he couldn't wake up from.

Just before they took the last load of their earthly possessions out of the trailer in Oroville, Jonah stopped and looked at the side of the pump house.

Back in Fairfield, he had begun collecting cactuses. He liked how they looked and how different they all were and they were easy to grow. He had somehow managed to hang on to his collection in little pots during the chaos of the move from Fairfield. They had continued to grow, and he had finally taken the leap of building an elaborate cactus garden for them and planting them in it. He'd scoured the countryside for miles and brought back the most interesting looking rocks of all sizes, carefully fitted them together into a retaining wall that backed up to the pump house, and mixed sand and potting soil to fill it in. He'd obsessed over the care of his cactus garden, knowing that the climate of Northern California is not ideal for desert plants. Somehow, they had thrived.

"Hey, Dad…" Jonah was standing more or less on the spot where the repo men had once come in the middle of the night to take away the new car Dad had bought when he worked at the school district.

"What?" Dad was in a hurry. He was trying to get everything loaded up and didn't want to be bothered.

"Who is going to water my cactus garden? I don't want them to die before I get back."

"Jonah, we aren't coming back."

Something struck Jonah like a blow and he stopped perfectly still for a moment, looking down at his black Converse shoes. Why had he thought they would come back *here* after the summer? Why was he surprised they weren't? Why did everyone else seem to know what was going on? Maybe Amy and Hayden had paid attention better at the family meeting. He felt totally lost.

Jonah watched that cactus garden as the truck pulled away. He kept his head looking until he couldn't see it any more. He felt dumb for not realizing that he had to pot up those plants and take them, he felt childish for being so hurt over *stupid plants*. He felt cheated after spending so much time to make *one* nice, beautiful thing in that ugly, gravel covered yard in front of that ugly trailer, knowing that in a week under the beating sun it would be totally dried out, covered in dust from the road, and all the cactuses would eventually wither away and die.

14

MT. PROMISE

The Sierra Nevada mountains are the steepest in North America. They aren't as high as the Rockies, but they are sharp and jagged and form an impassable wall between the lush California coastline and the barren moonscape of the Nevada desert. It was this wall that stopped the Donner Party in its tracks as they tried to reach California. Toward the southern end, the Yosemite Valley opens up with a grandeur unequaled in the world, and the most massive forms of life on the planet - Giant Sequoia trees - grow in only one place alone. The beauty of the cliffs, granite peaks, and endless pine and fir forests is hard to describe. It was in the midst of this range that an organization associated with grandpa Franklin had come to buy land and carve a campground out of the virgin forest.

Mt. Promise was the name given to the bible camp they had established about halfway up the Sierra Nevada range. One of the amazing things about California is that city kids can grow up in some of the biggest concrete sprawls ever built, hardly seeing any more nature than the grass of a school field, board a bus with a church group, and with about a two hour drive emerge in the most rugged and almost untouched mountains in the country. This reasonable driving range eastward from the big cities of the San Francisco Bay area made Mt. Promise quite popular with several large churches who always booked the camp right through the summer.

The campground was lovely. It sprawled across several acres of gently rolling hills in a valley between two steep mountains. There was a cold, clear lake nearby, and a series of meandering paths through the pines that gave the impression of eternity, as if this place had been unchanging forever and would go on when the frantic crush of the cities ground to a halt in the dim future.

Mt. Promise was the destination chosen by Jonah's parents to try out their "working for God" experiment. Jonah, his sisters Hayden and Amy, and mom and Dad would live on the grounds as staff for the summer. While normal high schoolers were spending the summer going to parties, Jonah was moving into a Christian Compound full time.

Jonah was not completely happy, but he genuinely enjoyed the campground. He was given a cabin for boy staff, apart from Hayden and Amy (and thankfully his parents). It had a kitchenette and even a stereo, thanks to the boy he would be sharing it with.

Darryl was almost exactly Jonah's age, and he had a little sister almost exactly the same age as Amy, which they both thought was kind of funny. He was a valley boy, growing up directly in the middle of California's huge valley in Sacramento. Darryl was blond, very quiet, and had a self-effacing attitude about him. Jonah liked him immediately.

The boys found an old refrigerator left over from the 1950s behind one of the buildings. They recharged it, cleaned it out, and set it up in their staff-cabin. As camp workers, they received a paycheck, and while it wasn't a lot, when combined with the steep discounts they got at the camp store, they were easily able to completely fill that ice cold little refrigerator with Mountain Dew, Dr. Pepper, and Cherry Coke.

Darryl was a Rocker. He was obsessed with Megadeth, Metallica, Slayer, and a lot of bands Jonah had hardly even heard of. His greatest wish in life was to be a drummer in a rock band, and with his long, blond hair, doc marten boots, and too frequent use of the word "dude," he seemed perfect for the part. They would crank up Darryl's stereo to heavy metal, get brain freeze from icy-cold cans of caffeine and sugar, and bounce around the cabin like hyperactive animals, or just lounge around and talk about what they wanted to do someday. For teenage boys, you could do a hell of a lot worse.

Between episodes of Beavis And Butthead, Jonah learned that Darryl's father was very much like grandpa Franklin. He was totally committed to his church, worked tirelessly and incessantly on Mission-Related Things, and even had missionaries over to stay all the time. Meanwhile, his family lived at basically poverty levels in a neighborhood of Sacramento that was slowly turning from quiet suburb to gang-infested ghetto. Darryl had been working at Mt. Promise every summer since he was 13, and he liked getting away from his hyper controlling dad. His dad didn't approve of rock music (it was "of the devil"), nor the way Darryl had grown his hair long, nor his black Doc Martens, and that just increased the appeal of his lifelong ambition to play with Megadeth someday.

Darryl had even saved up his own money working odd jobs to buy himself a drum set, which he moved into the cabin before the end of the summer, much to Jonah's entertainment. As far as Jonah was concerned, Darryl was probably the best roommate you could possibly have.

Amy and Hayden had to share staff cabins with some of the other girl staff, including some pretty humorless Hard Core Believers who were fairly miserable to be around, so they would come over to the "cool cabin" whenever they could to hang out with the boys. Mom and Dad had their own cabin-house with a kitchen in it and for most of the summer, Jonah only had to see them when they were working together, which made everything go a lot smoother.

Work was hard. They pulled long hours cleaning up the campground, repairing cabins, painting fences, repairing vehicles, and worst of all; helping in the kitchen. The kitchen at Mt Promise was designed to handle about 200 campers. Some of their biggest groups were more than three times that size. They had to split them into groups who ate lunch at different times, so that when one group finished, the other group would be starting. The cleanup was a miasma of huge plastic garbage cans in the hot sun full of half-eaten camp food. They could be pulling duty in the kitchen and by the time they got lunch finally cleaned up, dinner would be starting, and they would have to just go on working until late at night. When the biggest groups were in, it was every hand on deck and everybody on staff helping in the kitchen.

When the largest groups weren't in, they did most of the outdoor work, cutting a pad and a new road on part of the property, helping out in the stables, and always and ever repainting. The camp had a lot of buildings and by the time they had painted the last one, the first one needed to be painted again, so between all the cabins, the railings, the fences, and the outbuildings, it was a constant effort.

Jonah didn't mind hard work, he enjoyed the outdoors, and he had almost immediately become friends with his roommate. In general, things were going pretty well. He could buy candy and some junk food from the camp "bookstore" with a staff discount, swim in the pool when he was done with work, and even drive the work trucks around the grounds once in a while. All in all, life was pretty good.

Walter didn't seem to be enjoying his time at Mt Promise nearly as much. He seemed to have begun to disagree with "leadership" almost immediately.

"Leadership" in this case, was a short, slightly pudgy man with a mustache who ran the camp and lived on the property in a nice house with his family.

Mr. Anderson was a bit stern, and a little bit tyrannical, but in general, he ran Mt. Promise as a business which had to do things a certain way and on a strict schedule in order to function. There was no way to pump 700 campers through a two-week camp without running things with some military efficiency.

The precise nature of Walter's disagreements with Mr. Anderson were never totally clear to Jonah. They undoubtedly involved important theological concepts which Walter could expound upon at great length, but for which Mr. Anderson probably didn't have time. Walter had grown up as the pastor's son, more educated in high theological concepts than those around him. It seemed that he believed that in a proper Christian community, the most theologically erudite man should be running things.

Walter became more and more stressed as he carried out the orders of the man he disliked. He complained about his pay, his treatment, and Mr. Anderson's lack of understanding of great concepts with Laura. Jonah and the kids didn't understand exactly why he was dissatisfied, but since (other than Laura) they didn't have to actually *live* with him, it wasn't a big problem for them.

By the end of the summer, it was apparent that Walter wanted to go somewhere else.

The family had another Meeting, except this time, it was more of an announcement of what was going to happen than a request for assent. Walter had talked to his father about Christian organizations that had paid staff positions, and grandpa Franklin had tapped his nation-wide network of contacts and come back with a place. There was a "boy's ranch" in Missouri that had paid staff positions. Mom and Dad had seen pictures and said it was nice.

"It will be like here."

Mom and Dad were happy too because unlike Mt Promise, the whole family could stay together. They had staff housing that were real apartments. Jonah didn't consider that to be a perk, but he wasn't really being asked his opinion this time. Nobody brought up or seemed to remember the "only for the summer" line from the first family meeting.

Jonah had thought that his parents meant to sit down, vote on continuing with this "working for God" stuff, and determine if it was really working out, but it seemed they had already been making arrangements. This was more of a longer, more elaborate version of "get in the car."

So, they got in the car.

"When they took Walter's old truck to Texas with the travel trailer, Walter had built a false floor into the bed of the truck and installed a camper shell. The tools fit under the false bed and the kids played on top. Now the kids were either teenagers or turning into teenagers and too big for both kids and tools to fit in the truck, So Walter ... made the bed of the truck and the camper shell into travel seats. Then Walter, Laura, and three teenagers took off for Missouri and the Boy's Ranch. A trip across country in an old truck in not without adventure, but Walter and family survived hurricanes, flooding, and travel hardships to arrive at the Boy's Ranch in Lampe, Missouri."

-The Carpenter Chronicles by Walter Franklin, p. 40

15

IN DAD'S TRUCK

The morning was cold and wet. It had rained the day before, complicating Dad's efforts to get the trailer loaded and the tarp bungeed down properly. Like an ancient covered wagon, the old beat up orange truck and the work trailer behind it now represented an entire household with everything most dear to them.

The truck was parked in the cul-de-sac that led to Grandpa and Grandma Franklin's house. The trailer had been an offering, or donation, or perhaps a tithe. Once Walter had transitioned to *working for God*, he qualified as the proper recipient of the 10% of all earnings that a true believer must tithe to God Things. Perhaps it was in that spirit that Uncle Boone had donated the trailer. Boone had an ambivalent relationship with the Franklin family and their deep religiosity. He himself was not devout. He didn't bother with church, and he spent time in cop bars with his buddies from the LAPD drinking and playing darts, which his wife, the eldest of the Franklin children, considered blasphemously awful. She even hated how he openly drank beer when he was grilling in the yard.

Still, Boone seemed to think of Christianity as "above his pay grade" in a sense. He tipped his hat to God and periodically did things in the same way that an atheist who is about to line up to board an airplane he will jump out of suddenly finds it very valuable to have a book of Psalms on him. Boone said they could consider the big metal work trailer a tithe, so that was how it happened that the family had a way to haul everything they owned with them to Missouri.

Jonah sat in the kitchen of his grandparent's little trailer home, looking out the window at the grey, chill world outside dripping from the recent rain and feeling cold. He didn't feel cold physically. It was as if the sky and his mood were reflecting one another somehow. He clutched the solidity of the coffee cup his Grandmother had given him, sipping the black coffee he'd learned to drink from his dad, feeling as if he must remember this place and this moment, because it was the last he would see of anything familiar.

Something just felt wrong. Mom and Dad were excited about the boy's ranch, but every time they talked about it, something in Jonah's gut bothered him. He was sure that Hayden felt the same. Some brooding portent of disaster seemed to loom like the grey clouds hanging over the place. He wanted to ask to stay with Grandma and Grandpa, but he couldn't imagine leaving the only friends he'd been allowed to *keep*; his two sisters, and there was nowhere to go here and nothing for him to do. Anyway, it was too late now. Every single thing he owned that he hadn't been willing to trust to the weather in that leaky shed behind their grandparent's house was hitched to that truck.

Grandpa prayed while they all stood in a circle. This was the greatest thing he could hope for his son to do to carry on his lifetime's work. Grandpa Franklin had sacrificed his time, his money, his children's home, and their formative years, to his "Great Work for God." Walter had been born on the tail end of a trip to a jungle camp to train to-be missionaries. If anything Walter had ever done in his life would gain the blessing of his father, *this* would be it.

Jonah glanced at Dad from under eyelashes as he prayed. He was wondering what Walter was thinking at that moment. Somehow, Grandpa Franklin's benediction seemed underwhelming. It was exactly the same kind of prayer he would offer on a normal Sunday after criticizing Walter's secular ways and seeming to cluck his tongue in disappointment at him. Had Walter expected something special? Was this good enough? Jonah didn't know. He later guessed that perhaps it wasn't.

The prayer circle broke up and the Franklin family climbed into the work truck. It was wet and climbing over the trailer hitch to get over the tailgate into the back of the truck took some agility. The space in the bed of the truck under the shell had been lined with carpeting and improvised seats gave the kids somewhere to sit more or less. A few throw pillows had been brought in by Hayden, who loved lots of pillows and blankets around her. Jonah instantly felt a sense of claustrophobia kick in as he ducked low to get under the shell and settle in behind the cab of the pickup.

The truck was a 1970s step-side pickup, which meant that the bed was narrower than standard. It had one bench seat in the front which three people could sit on with reasonable comfort, but which now had a bundle of necessities taking up the middle of the seat. To fit everyone, the kids had to sit with their backs against the sides of the shell, crouched in the bed of the truck, alternating the direction they sat, so their legs could have somewhere to go. One kid, whoever was closest to the tailgate, got the big window of the shell's door. The other two had to make do with small, narrow slit windows in the aluminum which could be cranked open manually about five inches.

Jonah felt a creeping panic as Hayden started throwing all her stupid pillows in on top of him.

"Get them off! Get them off! I can't breathe back here!"

Hayden glared at Jonah.

"I want something to sit on! I can't just lean against the metal wall of the truck! It'll kill my back!"

The siblings grumbled at one another, dividing up the tiny space they were to share down to the millimeter.

Through the opening that had been left when Dad removed the back window of the truck so as to have a pass-through to the shell, a voice bellowed.

"Shut up and sit down back there!"

And they began to move.

Amy made a face at the back of Dad's head from her perch right toward the back near the tailgate.

Jonah glanced at the 12-year-old disapprovingly.

"Don't get him mad, Amy." He said dryly. She had claimed the best spot, right near the tailgate with the view out the back because she'd claimed she was too claustrophobic to sit anywhere else. Jonah had fought back the sense of panic and feeling as if he couldn't breathe because he was a boy and boys didn't admit such things. He could tough it out. Plus, Jonah would rather die than beg Mom and Dad for favors by claiming weakness.

Mom put on a tape in the stereo she had up front on the bench seat with her. It was her favorite Christian rock musician. Jonah had never liked it, but Mom had put together a special, inspirational mix tape to go with their expedition. She was in a fine mood. The kids didn't complain, because if they did, she was liable to pull out her guitar and that would lead to demands that *they* sing along with her "Jesus Freak" songs.

Mom and Dad seemed to be having a good time. They were reliving their youth, listening to Larry Norman and putting all their cares in God's hands.

Jonah tried to keep his eyes fixed on the slit of landscape he was able to see going by out the little side windows as they took a series of deep, switchback curves in the mountains. He felt like he was going to throw up.

"Give me some space, Hayden!"

Hayden didn't look up from the notebook she was scribbling in. "Shut up."

"I think I'm going to puke."

"Don't you dare get any on *me*!" Hayden inched her pillow nest a little bit away from Jonah.

The music continued from the cab of the truck, muffled by the sounds of the road coming up from the bed underneath them. Jonah could smell a distinct odor of car exhaust. It was definitely contributing to the car sick feeling.

"Oh God…" The fifteen-year-old stuck his face in the slit window, trying to breathe clean air, his eyes closed. He felt like an animal in a cage.

The nausea never completely went away over the next four days and nights. It did get better though, or perhaps Jonah became so numb, hypnotized by the endlessly receding road always flowing away, away, away out behind the truck that he didn't notice so much.

They drove over the mountains and down into Nevada like a 1990s remake of the Grapes of Wrath. The road became an endless, straight line through the nothingness of open desert, going on forever to the horizon. Dad navigated by map and compass like a man from another century. They had bought a big book of roadmaps of every state in preparation for the journey, and now they steered the rolling caravan as if it were a ship at sea, setting a course south by east.

Mom and Dad had decided to see a few of the "Wonders of America" since they were going across country anyway. This lengthened their trip, but gave them the opportunity to see the miraculous stone arches of Utah and the Grand Canyon.

Jonah remembered the Grand Canyon from his childhood. They had stopped to see it on the way to or from Texas (he couldn't remember which) during the First Missionary Trip. The sight had struck him as beautiful, alien and somehow wonderful at the same time. From the top where they had stopped at an overlook, it seemed so high that heights stopped being scary. It was like being in an airplane looking down at a desert painted in stripes of vivid red and orange and pink. Jonah had a picture from that trip. It was himself, sitting on a rock ledge, looking slightly nervous. The ledge looked as if it were a tiny little shelf of rock hanging over a vast chasm. The boy in the picture was only a foot or two from the edge, hanging out over space, surrounded by nothing but air, with the tiniest finger of rock supporting him.

Jonah remembered that Dad had wanted to get that picture and Hayden had demurred. Amy was too small, and he had agreed in order to not show that he was scared. He remembered the nothingness, the wind beneath his shoes, hanging in space.

Now, looking at the Grand Canyon again, that picture came to his mind unbidden. There was something sad in that boy's eyes, out there on that tiny ledge over nothing. It haunted Jonah, so he pushed the thought away.

They drove until Dad was exhausted, usually all day and most of the night. They would find RV rest stops and pitch a little camping tent. Mom and Dad would sleep in the back of the truck where the kids sat during the day. The kids would sleep in sleeping bags in the tent because Dad's back couldn't take sleeping on the ground.

Mom and Dad seemed happy. They looked and acted like different people from the ones Jonah had known his whole life. Mom always had a song ready to burst forth. Dad was grouchy and tired, but reasonably well behaved. He spoke to Laura as if they were high school sweethearts. He growled to the kids to get their stuff loaded and get ready to go as if they were baggage.

In the haze of endless movement, of never stopping, of being nowhere, of never arriving, time became meaningless. It was day, it was night. It was hot, it was cold. They ate, they tried to sleep, they stared at the two lines of yellow highway paint receding to a point on the horizon with the stripes going away, always away, rolling, rolling, rolling from them like the world was a huge scroll of a picture being let out and they were falling backwards into nowhere.

For years afterward, Jonah could close his eyes and see the road going away, away, moving from him as he stared out the back of a truck.

It took over a week to get to Lampe, Missouri. Jonah was never sure exactly how long it had been. He felt as if he had been lying sick, in the hold of a ship bearing human cargo for months.

When they emerged now and again to stretch their legs, the kids looked and felt like the walking dead. Even when standing on firm ground, they never lost the sensation of movement, as if they had been at sea for days. The ground under their feet seemed to sway like a truck going down the freeway.

Many years later, Hayden would tell Jonah about a dream she had. She said the three of them had been "in the back of Dad's truck." By the way she said those words, Jonah had understood everything. She'd said that in her dream, Jonah had escaped somehow. He had jumped out and was heading to some destination and gotten himself his own car. She and Amy were left in the truck, and she knew that Dad was going down the roughest, most impossibly winding little back roads to get to their destination, bouncing around in the back of Dad's truck with a bunch of tools. The dream had clearly affected Hayden deeply.

Jonah had listened on the other end of the line, feeling the warm nighttime breeze of the Middle East as the voice on the chunky Nokia phone beamed its way to his ear from California ...all the way across the world.

"You said you were in the back of dad's truck... Why didn't you jump out?"

Hayden hadn't been able to answer.

The weather never seemed to give them a break. When they were going through Texas, they crossed paths with an incoming hurricane. They spotted a couple of tornados spinning off near the highway and ended up trying to roll through a town that was flooding so bad the water came up over the tops of the wheels of the truck. Dad frantically kept the truck moving, knowing that the only thing keeping the water from running up the tailpipe of the truck and flooding the engine was the exhaust coming out as he kept his foot down on the gas. It was almost as if someone didn't want them to get where they were going.

Missouri was brown, flat, and ugly. At least that was Jonah's impression of the place. The grass was the color of shit in the winter time and a slightly off bright green in the summer. The hills seemed to terminate in lumpish piles of earth as if the land itself were unsure whether it should be hilly or flat. The little scraggly trees stood here and there neither big enough to make shade nor numerous enough to be ornament for the hills nor few enough to allow the land to be easily worked. The mud was a pale clay that oozed into slippery grease in the rain and was hard as granite when the world froze in wintertime. The roads were all gravel as far as the eye could see, rutted and turned into washboard ripples by the broken pickup trucks urged down them way too fast.

Little clusters of misery huddled at the crossroads of the few paved highways, buildings that resembled unpainted sheds thrown up in another century renovated for human life by generations of people unwilling to just tear the lumpen masses down and start over. Rusted out vehicles ornamented the yards like the carcasses of pack animals forced to go too long, beaten one too many times.

Every place had a church. Even places that weren't places at all had churches. Jonah counted at least eight different offshoots of "Baptist" denominations. They made a game of trying to guess at the strange names and what they meant. The "Military Baptist" denomination gave them the most amusement.

Most of the churches were old, sagging buildings that looked as if the will to live had been sucked out of them by too many Sundays. Not a single sign of ornamentation could be seen anywhere. No house was painted in bright colors, nobody had tried to brighten up a public place with a mural nor a city put flowers next to their roads or a statue in their square. No church had stained glass windows. Every single thing that could be seen was as ugly and functional and desperately poor as Jonah had ever imagined. The sight of this corner of Missouri made him long for the dusty gravel and old trailers of Oroville.

By the time the family turned to the long, long gravel drive that led to the boy's ranch, even Mom and Dad's mood had been dampened. Nobody said anything as they rolled past lonely, badly kept up pig farms apparently devoid of human life. Jonah hadn't seen one window box with flowers, or a brightly painted door, or a hammock or flowering tree in someone's yard in the entire state. It was like the land that hated cheer.

Suddenly there was a high bank of earth almost like a wall to their right, and the road had a branch. There was a small, dusty sign and a big electric gate. The fence had barbed wire on top. That gate stood out in a place where houses looked like they were falling down, and old cars grew grass up through raised hoods. It represented more money than most families around there would make in a year. There were men at the gate. They had apparently been expecting the Franklins, because they barely acknowledged them, but opened the gate from the inside. They had a hard look, like prison guards.

What was this place supposed to be again? Jonah thought. His parents had said it would be like Mt. Promise, but this was about as far from that as he could imagine. He recalled it being some kind of place where parents could send boys who were too young to go to real prison and too violent to be anywhere else. They were "reformed" with a little "tough love" and Christian teachings.

As the gate rolled closed on its electric motors behind them, Jonah felt a sense of doom. Something about that place was just wrong. It was *very* wrong, and now they were all locked inside.

16

THE HALLS OF MADNESS

Lampe, Missouri 1994

The boy's ranch was a sprawling compound encompassing probably a hundred acres or more. The main cluster of buildings stood on a little hill which had been covered in gravel and turned into something resembling an ancient village square. The largest building of the cluster was a huge, cabin-style hall, which had a wide porch and log-cabin style trim. It was placed in a way which gave a clear view of most of the property from the porch. A large bell had been affixed to a post next to this porch, and the combination gave something of the air of a quarterdeck of an old sailing ship, where the captain might stand and order floggings for wayward sailors.

The second they pulled in, Jonah felt eyes on him. It was as if every corner of every building and every dark gap in some fence had eyes, and they bored into the back of his skull. He felt the hair on his arms and neck stand out.

It was clear that people were here. In fact, the place had an extremely lived-in feel, with rutted dirt tracks worn by feet everywhere and dozens of buildings of all sizes. The presence of people seemed to hang in the air like coming upon the warm remains of a campfire, but there wasn't a soul to be seen. Years later, Jonah would see the same phenomenon in Arab villages, where nobody wanted to be seen in the street, not even men and absolutely *never* women, but you could tell they were all there, lurking in the shadows watching out of every dark window.

The Franklins looked at one another in silence. Nobody wanted to get out of the car.

Finally, a lanky man appeared, stuffing a pair of work gloves in the back pocket of his jeans. He was perhaps a year or two younger than Dad, with similar dark hair (at least the dark hair Dad had once had before it started going silver). He was lean and walked with the efficiency of someone who knew how to cover ground. He had a dark mustache and dark curls to match that came out from under his faded John Deere hat.

Dad stepped out of the truck and the man introduced himself as Steve. He was the head rancher for the facility. He was in charge of taking care of all the various animals at the ranch. Something about the intensity of his eyes and his demeanor reminded Jonah instantly of Dad.

Steve let them know where to go. The ranch had set up an apartment for the family. He told them how to get there. He said that the Head of the ranch would see them at dinner, and they could meet everyone then. Until then, "the boys" were out in the field working, and the Franklins could go ahead and get themselves set up in their new place.

Steve seemed genuinely friendly, but also totally uncurious about the peculiar looking, ragged caravan. He looked like a man who had literally seen it all.

In a few minutes, they had (gratefully) driven away from the invisible eyes that seemed to watch them every second from that little hill, down a rutted dirt road past a truly enormous metal barn (more like a warehouse, in Jonah's opinion), past a small, malodorous pigpen, and to another little cluster of buildings that looked strangely out of place. They were three little condominium-type buildings, each divided into two condos, like some small apartment house development in a city. The first dusty door on the left side was theirs.

The kids emerged from the truck, stretching out legs that had forgotten how to walk. Amy just went over to some grass and sat down for about 15 minutes, unmoving and mute to anything her parents said. Hayden looked around hopefully. She seemed to like the fact that they had a real apartment (she'd complained a lot about "roughing it" in the cabins of Mt. Promise). Mom and Dad were a little quiet. They had obviously felt the oppressive doom that had lowered itself over them the second they came through the gate, but Mom was working very hard to be chipper and started bustling around, investigating the kitchen and making a lot of happy sounds.

Jonah stood there, watching as Dad started unpacking the truck and beginning the long task of unloading the trailer. He helped when asked, so as not to incur a Wrath, but he felt as if a motor had stopped within him. The act of unloading all of their earthly possessions here felt so wrong he could barely do more than carry boxes. He wanted nothing to do with this place. He barely looked at the room they had decided to give him. It was roughly the size as the little one he had had back in Vallejo, but at least had a door and a little window. It was almost completely taken up with a single twin mattress that smelled of astringent cleaner.

Jonah didn't want to see the inside of the apartment. He escaped the unloading operation after a little while and sat out front in the sun. The apartment made this real. Unpacking their things made this somehow permanent, or as close to permanent as the Franklins ever got.

He sat, looking up at the impassive blue sky, feeling totally lost. He heard Hayden mention that there was no television in the place. No radio either. No cable connection.

Jonah smiled grimly. "Of course not." They might as well have been in another country.

Dinner was a big deal on the Ranch. The big bell next to the porch was rung at precisely 6 PM. Everyone, wherever they were, dropped whatever they were doing, and made their way up the hill to the main hall. The way they came in was regimented. The boys were broken up into groups by some internal logic of the Ranch, and the groups would work and eat together. Each of these would come in with the staff member who was overseeing their activity. Then, after the boys had been brought in and seated, the staff would come up, more senior staff first, junior staff later. Mr. Dan stood on the porch watching them come up the stairs like an emperor watching his troops march by for inspection. He was a tallish man with a broad forehead and icy blue eyes who had looked as if he had never smiled once in his entire life. Discipline was the watchword by which he ran the camp, and likely the reason it was as big and successful as it was, and somewhere under that discipline was a leering enjoyment, like a cat toying with mice, as he silently accepted the homage of all those he owned.

Walking past Mr. Dan, Jonah felt the cold blue eyes on him. He felt like a piece of meat being walked into a butcher shop. Walter didn't seem to notice. He introduced himself and the two made fake make-nice conversation for about ten seconds before Mr. Dan cut it off and ordered the staff to sit down.

Inside the hall, the building seemed like the banquet hall of an old, cheap hotel. Faded, stuffed chairs were lined up with military precision next to long wooden tables that didn't match. The carpet looked like something repurposed from an old movie theater, and every inch of every surface had a lingering scent of grease and rotting food.

The peculiar rotting food smell, Jonah would learn, was a feature of the Hall, and he would realize its source before long.

As they entered and lined up to follow their parents to the staff tables, the Franklin kids were at first awed by the sight of what was laid out on the tables. It looked like a feast out of a movie set. Cakes, pastries, donuts, roast chicken, ham, and an amazing variety of foodstuffs were all laid out along the vast length of the wooden tables. Jonah saw staff walking by as if they didn't even notice the delicacies piled high at every table. It took him a little while to realize why.

It seemed that Mr. Dan had made arrangements with several supermarkets in this part of the state. Items that had not been sold by their expiration date, but which were "still good" were picked up in vans sent out by the Ranch and brought here for dinner. Cakes from the bakery that could no longer be sold stood next to chicken that hadn't been thrown out, but brought here instead. The supermarket managers no doubt felt they were doing something for God instead of throwing out all this stuff. Mr. Dan, for his part, could receive $50 a day per kid of upkeep, and get most of their food for free. It was a win-win. Jonah's experience would later cause him to suspect that the Ranch had not made clear the nature of the use of the food to those donating it, however. Considering that the Ranch raised a lot of pigs, they may have led the donors to believe that the food was going to be used as pig slop.

The scene, with Mr. Dan presiding over the long tables full of sullen, angry young men and boys, with the long tables arrayed with a sample wedding cake and absurdly overdone looking, worthless "food" reminded Jonah of something from Alice In Wonderland. It was like a bizarre fairy tale where the guests think they are at a royal banquet until they bite into the dirt that has been magicked to look like a roast.

Mr. Dan took ceremony seriously, and they were all treated to a long, terse lecture in the guise of a prayer before being allowed to dig in. There was a respite from the hard silence of the Hall, and the boys all started making noise enough for Jonah to feel almost like a real human living in a real place again. He looked around on the table for something to eat; he was hungry.

Hayden glanced at her brother as he hesitantly reached for a piece of something.

"Don't eat that, Jonah."

"Why not?"

Hayden turned the plate so he could see the other side. There were maggots crawling out.

Jonah contented himself with some stale bread rolls.

There were other staff at the Ranch who sat in the staff section of the big hall. Only one of those staff members had a family like Walter. The others were mostly middle aged "empty nest" Christian couples helping out with a Ministry or older people from the surrounding area.

Steve, the dark haired rancher they had met first of all, had come into the hall with a plain looking woman who had the personality of wall paint and looked almost as if her features, her clothes, and her entire spirit had been sort of bleached out in the sun until there was nothing left but the faintest outline of eyes and a mouth. Behind the two had come a line of kids like ducklings, walking ramrod straight and in line behind their parents the way staff kids were expected to. (Jonah now understood that he'd made a faux pas by walking up to the porch *alongside* his Dad). The two in the back were boys, one a little younger than Jonah, the other right around Amy's age. Jonah wasn't looking at them though, he was watching the leader of the three kids who followed Steve.

She was the same age as Jonah, but she stood very straight and acted very proper, so she almost came off as older (Jonah, for his part had no manners then, having basically grown up wild). She had honey colored hair that curled just a bit where it was cut at her shoulders, the curls going out to the sides, and giving her a somewhat triangular look. She had the bluest eyes Jonah had ever seen and a hint of freckles. She wore Wrangler jeans like everyone in her family, and a flannel shirt like she had just come in from work, and for some reason, Jonah was immediately smitten.

As they sat down, the girl's eyes had come to rest on Jonah and lingered for a moment. She kept her head down virtually the entire time she was in the hall, so as not to make eye contact with the rowdy, leering boys, but had actually looked up when she saw someone who looked more like he fit in with *them* than the people at the staff table.

Jonah found himself smiling just a bit in greeting. He hadn't smiled once since he'd come into this state.

Steve instructed his family to introduce themselves to the Franklins, and they did. The only name that stuck with Jonah that day was Laney.

Steve and his family had come from Wyoming, where ranches were the norm and cities the exception. All of them came across as tough country kids, but they also had an eerie similarity to the Franklins. Like them, Steve and his wife had decided to join the staff here because they wanted to "Work for God." They were from a similar generation, and they had lived through many "adventures" and hardships too. Over the next few months, they and the Franklin kids would get to know one another and become more or less the only possible friends the others could have. Except for Jonah and Laney who didn't appear to be friends at first, at least to the adults. Laney was very careful to show a cool indifference to the California boy.

Living on the Ranch was hard for everyone. Staff kids like the Franklins were expected to be "examples" of good Christian living to the boys, which made life unbearable for the very few of them that lived there. They had to be out and waiting for the bus that came special to the Ranch to take the boys to school early. Jonah's mom made sure the kids were out early enough to be standing by the tiny, decrepit, dusty little sign near the front gate of the ranch for at least fifteen minutes before the bus came.

They were not allowed to mix socially with "the boys," which was for the best, as several of them were there because they had committed crimes that would have had them sent to prison for serious terms if they had been adults. As it was, being minors, there were sentencing agreements that let some of them come to places like the Ranch instead of serving hard time in an adult prison. Others were hard core addicts. Even at age 13 or 15, some of them had been hopelessly addicted to heroin or meth, and were at the Ranch for "rehabilitation," sent by parents with no other, better ideas. Generally, there were "ranch boys" who one could look at and know they were trouble, and there were "ranch boys" one could look at and know they were *very dangerous*. Those were pretty much the only categories. All of them were obviously very curious about Laney and Jonah's two sisters, which made the trip to school and back oppressive for them.

The problem with not mixing socially with the "ranch boys" was that it went right out the window the second the bus they all had to ride on arrived at Blue Eye High School. Every one of them, staff kids and ranch boys both, attended the same classes at the same local high school together. This naturally made life very complicated for the staff kids.

Jonah was so far out of his depth the second he walked into Blue Eye High that he gave up even trying to make sense of anything. The kids here spoke as if they had marbles in their mouths. He literally had a hard time understanding what they said. The boys all wore Wrangler jeans with a "Skoal ring" in the pocket, because *the coolest thing* was to chew tobacco. Jonah was completely bewildered. To him, "cool" was long haired rocker dudes, skateboards, and heavy metal. He wore Converse All Star sneakers. The entire school wore boots. He was the *only* kid in the entire school who came wearing sunglasses during his first week. He decided not to do *that* again. They looked at him as if he was from Mars. The kids from Blue Eye Missouri were nice enough, but to them, a weird looking kid from California or wherever arriving with unconventional clothes on and coming on the *Ranch Bus* could only mean one thing. Jonah must obviously be a "ranch boy" and a very, very bad kid, who they must not talk to.

Jonah found himself totally isolated immediately. Even worse, the ranch boys stuck together at the high school. They at least had one another to hang out with. He had literally nobody. The ranch boys knew he wasn't one of them and the regular kids thought he was a ranch boy. There was little he could do to even try to make friends. At least Steve's kids blended in better in Missouri and Hayden and Amy were not singled out because there were no *girls* at the boy's ranch.

Why Laney thought Jonah was interesting was not clear to Jonah at the time. He was a good-looking boy, he was strong, quite tough after all the experiences he'd been through, but he wasn't a country boy. He looked "rebellious" in black T-shirts and sunglasses, but he wasn't just a city kid who was hopeless out in the real world. Jonah had a physical competence born of years living in the wild forests of Northern California and working hard outdoors. He took on challenges fearlessly and acquitted himself well.

Nevertheless, he was, to appearances, the antithesis of the kind of "Christian rancher" culture her father represented. Undoubtedly it all lent Jonah a certain mystery and allure that he was completely unaware of at the time. He didn't seek out to be known as a "bad boy," certainly not in a place chock full of people who should have been in a real prison, but the reputation seemed to stick to him and it must have helped.

For his part, Jonah was smitten by Laney's calm, Western "cowgirl" way. She was from a place where everyone pulled their weight, where a girl like her learned to keep control over an angry 1,200 pound animal as a matter of course by the time they are 12, and where people said *exactly* what they thought, without complicated bullshit and lots of pretense. She was "proper" and kept herself in a way he found fascinating. He'd never known a 16-year-old girl who seemed like a man when she was out in the field and a *lady* when she wasn't. She used "Ma'am" and "Sir," and seemed to come from another century-maybe a *better* century. Unlike the local Blue Eye kids, she wasn't ignorant or totally lacking in curiosity about the world outside of Blue Eye, MO. Laney was a Westerner, who had *traveled*, seen the soaring sky over the Rocky Mountains, heard the roar of a crowd at a rodeo, and longed to see the ocean someday.

At one point, Laney came up to Jonah while they were waiting for the dreaded bus, before the troop of ranch boys arrived. She seemed oddly elated, despite her permanently buttoned-down demeanor.

"Hey, they're having a barn-swing near here this weekend. We're all going. It might be fun."

Jonah blinked. He definitely liked the idea of going somewhere that she was going, but ... was a barn swing a thing one put up in a barn or was it some kind of event?

"Yeah … cool … um, what's a barn swing?" The just-turned 16-year-old tried to sound more confident than he was.

Laney laughed. "You've never been to a barn swing before?"

Jonah shook his head, mystified. "Uh … no. Is that like a swing ... in a barn?" He was trying to picture how on God's green earth this could *possibly* lead to anything fun, except he was willing to try any event that Laney was going to be at.

"It's cool. They put all kinds of things in a barn for you to do. It's kind of a kid thing, but it should be *kind* of fun." She adopted the aloof demeanor of a teen girl. "My brothers are *all excited* … but, it could be fun anyway, *you know*."

This explanation didn't help Jonah at all, but he didn't care. He said he would love to come to this "barn swing," whatever the hell it was.

The night of the barn swing, Jonah's parents had arranged for him to be transferred over to Steve's family for the transport. Unfortunately, since two sets of parents were involved in the logistics, it inevitably became a "Oh, there's this fun thing going on." "Why that sounds nice, maybe Amy and Hayden would like to go too!" sort of night.

By the time the logistics of a ride were sorted out, they were packed into an old Toyota minivan with Laney's two younger brothers plus Amy (Hayden had thankfully declined), all looking excited, with Steve and his wife up front. Jonah and Laney stole glances at one another in the darkness of the van as they trundled over rutted gravel roads, up and down hills, and finally to a neighboring county town where the big event was going on.

The barn swing turned out to be fun after all. Jonah had no idea what these kinds of things were or where the idea had gotten started, but basically someone's very large barn had been temporarily fitted out as a three-dimensional fun house/obstacle course with all kinds of activities from slides to zip lines running up, down, inside and out of the place. Walks, stairs, and ladders had been set up to let visitors climb to different levels, and the entire place had either crazy colored lights, black lights, or glow in the dark strips, or a combination of all these, plus loud music blaring from hidden speakers everywhere.

Jonah did his best to hang around with Laney, but the entire place seemed to be self-organized into groups of guys and groups of girls. He had some fun running through some obstacles, climbing some things, and trying out the zip line that stood in the center of the place. Once again, Laney stood to one side with a group of girls, watching, gauging, and being coolly satisfied when the boy launched himself fearlessly from the third story of the barn.

Later, he caught her in the darkness near one of the entrances to the place. He was sweaty from running and climbing like a crazy animal. She was dry and cool. They found one another's hands in the darkness where her parents couldn't see them. Jonah felt the thin, soft hand grasping his own and felt a surge of power and greatness and wonder he had not known, and he ducked in toward her to steal a kiss. Their lips brushed and fumbled in the darkness, and it was over before it had begun, but somehow, Jonah had had his first real kiss there in the dark outside the frenetic light and chaos of the barn swing, in *someplace* Missouri (he never did learn the name of the town, or even if it *was* a town).

The music they were playing was upbeat modern country, but many years later, the song that brought it back to him was "Joey" by Concrete Blonde. Jonah couldn't understand then, but like the heroin addict in the song, one of them would never be able to give up the religious poison that was killing them both. There could only be one ending to that love story.

But if I seem to be confused
I didn't mean to be with you…
…And if you're somewhere out there
Passed out on the floor
Oh Joey, I'm not angry anymore

After that, Jonah and Laney tried to find ways to hang around. It was pretty difficult, since every moment of life on the Ranch was regimented. Jonah made friends with her younger brothers (which wasn't hard since they automatically thought of him as "cool" by virtue of his being an older boy) so he'd have an excuse to visit. Amy actually helped him out, being friendly with the brother who was her age and coordinating a visit with Jonah.

Steve had been *somewhat* careful about bringing a 16-year-old girl to a ranch full of dangerous delinquent boys. He had negotiated accommodations *off* of the main compound. It helped that he was the primary staffer responsible for the care of the animals on the ranch, because the ranch owned what had once been a small pig farm with a house directly across the road from the gate. This was where many of the pigs owned by the ranch actually were most of the time, though they also had pigpens on the Ranch grounds itself.

Jonah and Amy found themselves in a very bare room in the farmhouse entertaining the rambunctious boys while Jonah tried to get away and talk with Laney alone. Amy was able to run interference enough for the two to hang around on the porch and talk for a while.

They talked about where they had grown up, what had happened to them on their respective family's odysseys, how annoying their siblings were, and life in general for 16-year-olds. Jonah found her to be a dead end when he tried to explain how isolated he was in the high school. Laney wasn't from Missouri, but she was far closer to the culture here and hadn't had much trouble adjusting. Also, as a girl, she wasn't tainted with the lingering suspicion in all the other kids' minds that she had to ride the Ranch Bus because she was a sociopath or an addict.

Laney had grown up as a sheltered Christian girl in Wyoming. Her parents were obviously devout, or they would not have been there in the first place. There wasn't a lot of pop culture they could talk about that they both had been exposed to. They totally disagreed on music; she was a fan of Billy Ray Cyrus and Jonah disliked most pop country. He loved Metallica and she had never even been exposed to them (they being "of the devil" obviously).

Coming from a ranching background had made her oddly blasé about things that made Jonah wince. She tried to make conversation by talking about how it was so cold in the winter in Wyoming that one of their farm cats had taken to crawling up into the engine block of her dad's truck between the radiator fan and the block. One morning, her dad hadn't checked before he started it and the cat had tried to get out through the fan … instant cat puree under the hood of that pickup.

She'd tried to sort of laugh and shrug at the same time, but Jonah just felt a bit ill. Actually, that was another thing they had in common; when either of them tried to tell stories of how they had grown up, they never knew what the reaction of the listener was going to be. Neither of them had a real compass of "normalcy," so the stories they took for granted as just "stuff that happens to people growing up" were always at risk of merely horrifying the listener, which made kids their age think that it must be something *they* had done wrong.

Steve wasn't stupid. He also had a peculiar restless energy and bright-eyed temper that Jonah recognized from his Dad. Eventually there came a day when he "invited" Jonah to go with him to go "see something" on the farm.

Jonah actually felt relieved. It was a normal thing to him that a dad would want to have a talk with the boy who was obviously interested in his daughter. He expected some version of the ancient and much celebrated "shotgun talk." He wasn't concerned.

Unfortunately, on this occasion, Walter was there, and he managed to insert himself, wanting to come along as if he didn't understand the meaning of the talk. This instantly made everything awkward for Jonah (and probably Steve too). Jonah wondered if Walter knew something he didn't. Walter and Steve both worked together on the staff, they had both participated in the mysterious, wild, terrifying "takedowns" of wild boys who had managed to find a patch of hallucinogenic mushrooms on the grounds and tried to get knives out of the kitchen to slash the staff with. Maybe Walter knew something Jonah didn't know? Maybe there was some danger here that he didn't understand? Did Jonah actually *need* to be chaperoned to go talk with the father of the girl he was trying to go out with? Surely, for the love of all things holy, even Walter could not be so clueless that he didn't understand what was going on.

The three walked across the rough fields in awkward "conversation." Steve was sullenly offering insights into the function of various things around the pig farm while giving Walter a hard side eye now and again. He looked like he was trying to figure out what Walter was up to and whether or not he should go ahead with his original intention for the "talk." Walter walked on, nodding with professorial interest at the machinery or outbuildings Steve pointed out, with an air of a kid on a school outing. Jonah walked along next to Walter, staring at the dirty toes of his shoes, feeling utterly mortified. Something that would have been completely comprehensible to him had now become something that could *only* end in humiliation one way or another.

After meandering around the fields in a halfhearted attempt to talk about enough random stuff to satisfy Walter's curiosity, they got to the point.

"I want you to see something." Steve said by way of explanation as they arrived at a pig pen. He was addressing Jonah as if Walter wasn't there.

Jonah met his eyes, as if to say, "I know why you want to talk to me." He didn't have anything to be ashamed about.

Wyoming ranchers are not known to be verbose as a general thing. Steve's idea of a "lecture" was more of a *demonstration*.

Steve jumped the fence of the pig pen with the lithe ease of a bull rider. He was in and among the piglets in a second and darted out his gloved hand to snatch a squealing young pig from among the group. With a practiced ease, he flipped out a knife he carried in his back pocket and wiped it on a handkerchief while still holding the squealing, squirming piglet upside down in the other hand. Then, very systematically, he locked eyes with Jonah and then slit the pig's stomach right between the hind legs. The squealing went up an octave.

Steve found the piglet's testacles and popped them off like grapes, with a careful move borne of long practice, he neutered the animal, then set it back down to run away, its back legs jerking spasmodically as it ran away in pain.

Jonah realized that what to him looked like something from a horror movie was actually a relatively normal procedure for a pig farm. These piglets were being neutered. They had reached the right age, and now their nuts had to be cut off. It was a nice, simple, blunt kind of message worthy of a pig farmer who had a 16-year-old daughter. He could see that the pigs were not being *irreparably* damaged. Steve had obviously done this hundreds of times.

Steve kept looking up at Jonah to see if he were getting queasy or showing weakness as he went through piglet after piglet, flipping them on their backs, wiping his knife, and popping out their testicles one by one. Jonah forced himself to watch steadily, impassively. The blood and the little organs on the ground that the other pigs were nosing at hungrily … he forced himself not to see that … He stood there, steady, knowing that Steve was a man like Dad, and like Dad, showing weakness would only prolong it.

To his left, Walter prattled on about what was going on like a science teacher leading a field trip. He had turned a little as if explaining "interesting things" to Jonah, so he wasn't *quite* facing the pigpen. Jonah ignored him. He stood there, watching the slicing of the glittering blade, letting Steve see that he had not turned away, listening to the crescendo of pig squeals rising, joining with one another, almost like the sound of shrieking women, but somehow more terrible in their expression of mindless pain.

Steve almost seemed frustrated that Jonah was standing as solid as a stone, showing not even the tiniest flicker of emotion or reaction as he went through the entire herd. His hand darted out one last time and grabbed a rather small piglet that squealed even more shrilly than the others. He frowned, grunting with effort as he cut and probed … and probed … the piglet continued to squeal and twist in a desperate effort to get away. It was taking a lot longer than the others… something was wrong.

Finally, Steve removed the tiny balls from the pig and set it down.

"Oh shit, that was one of the *young* ones … No wonder I had such a hard time finding 'em." He was wiping his blade on the handkerchief and then his jeans as he strode back toward Jonah.

Only at that last piglet had Jonah winced. It was just the smallest movement of his eye, but it had been enough. Steve seemed happier. Jonah wasn't really listening. He was watching the piglet dance around the pen, kicking out it's legs again and again, trying to walk but jerking in pain. He was seeing an image of a ten-year-old boy landing on the floor of the living room, stumbling … trying to walk, finding that his legs wouldn't move right … jerking his way up the stairs…

Jonah turned away, not even acknowledging anything Steve said. He just started walking back to the farmhouse as if neither of the men were even there.

"The Boy's Ranch in Missouri was a place where people paid to have their troubled teenagers, some serious criminals, taken care of until they reached eighteen ... Walter found himself in the middle of the night talking down a kid with two butcher knives who wanted to cut up all the staff. Or, nose to nose restraining a kid who was violently possessed with a demon ... who then threatened Walter and his entire family forever. And the confrontation with evil did not stop with the boys, but also affected the staff until Walter ... was truly concerned for the safety of his little family, but Walter found that God continued protecting him and kept him and his family safe. Walter had brought to the Boy's Ranch a true knowledge of God and True Truth. With this background Walter was ... aligned with those on the staff who were part of God's Chosen People, and alienated from those who were not. He was quickly targeted by those forces that wish to take this world by force since he was ... recognized as one of God's Chosen with the ability to recognize Truth."
- The Carpenter Chronicles by Walter Franklin, p. 41

17

ESCAPE

Everything went to the pigs, eventually. The food that was heaped upon the feasting tables in the Hall would be picked over each meal perhaps once or twice, and then it would all get loaded up by the ranch boys and driven out to the pigpens. Everyone knew they were eating food that was one small step away from pig slop, and the smell of the small pigpen near the Franklins apartment was a constant reminder, because there was some quality to it that matched the sickly-sweet smell of the dining Hall.

They had something on the Ranch called "consequences." It happened pretty regularly that the ranch boys would "act out" and then they would "have consequences." Staffers would say things like "Oh, Jared isn't here, he's in Consequences right now."

Consequences varied. Most often it was something to do with the pigs, logically enough. The ranch boys would carry the slop on their backs in big plastic garbage cans. Or they would be set to running the grounds. Those who didn't run were "helped" to run by staff members holding their arms. The staff men also informally trained with one another to perform "takedowns." Walter found his high school wrestling experience useful here, though the physical demands of life on the Ranch were clearly taxing him greatly.

Whatever the agreement was that Walter and Laura had made when they came to the Ranch, it wasn't just for them to work while the kids went to school. Staff kids were expected to pitch in too, particularly Jonah, who was a strong teenage boy. They were given assignments related to the ostensible God Work that had brought them there (building things, since that was what Walter did). Hayden and Amy usually had projects like painting the interior rooms of a new building, Jonah was given work more suited to a rugged boy, but a step above the labor that served as "Consequences." The ranch boys leered at Jonah as he pushed a wheelbarrow just like one of them. They had singled him out for a special antipathy because he was right about the same age as most of them, he clearly didn't belong there, but he lived on the grounds and he worked at the same sorts of jobs they usually did (when they weren't serving Consequences at least). It seemed like a provocation. Even worse, he sat up in the front of the school bus with the staff kids and girls, but he was in classes with several of the ranch boys at the high school. They knew for a fact that he didn't have any group of friends to watch his back at Blue Eye High, and he didn't seem to have anyone to watch his back at the Ranch either.

There probably would have been less resentment if he had done work they couldn't or didn't do, or worked off the grounds, or lived off the grounds, but *he* wasn't the carpenter. He was a teenage boy without specialized trade skills. In fact, some of the boys who were learning trades like welding or woodworking in the Ranch's training shops had more valuable work skills than Jonah did.

Jonah began to be aware of the steady hatred. A sense of boiling and ever rising violence barely suppressed. The ranch boys stopped talking when he walked by somewhere. They all turned to watch him in unison whenever they were in eyeshot. They stopped working in a field to openly lean on shovels and stare at him while he worked nearby. He knew they were waiting and watching for a good moment. He wasn't stupid. He had lived in a ghetto surrounded by gang kids. He avoided good places for an ambush. He kept to places where he was in eyeshot of staff. He worked when possible in places away from the bigger groups of boys.

Still, avoiding gangs on the street where there is plenty of room to run is one thing. In the enclosed compound, there were only so many places to go, and the ranch boys knew every inch of that place better than Jonah did. It was just a matter of time before they managed to ambush him and they knew it.

There would be calls in the middle of the night. Sometimes 2 or 3 AM, the phone in the apartment would ring. It could only ever be one person on the other end of the line, and Dad jumped up to get it. Mr. Dan would be calling about something that had happened… some boys had been huffing gasoline until they lost consciousness and needed to be driven to the hospital and they needed staff to cover, or some boys had gotten high on something and needed to be restrained, or something had happened in the Hall and they needed all the staff there to keep the boys under control.

Dad would disappear into the night, to return in the early morning exhausted, with a dark look in his eyes. That dark look settled there and after a while, it never lifted for as long as they were at the Ranch.

Jonah was unsettled. The look on his Dad's face was the shark-eye look he got during a Wrath. Now, it was just there all the time, and he didn't seem to have the energy for a Wrath, he just went about his work with the grim determination of a man barely holding on. He barely spoke to the kids, and only spoke to Laura in hushed tones at night when they were in their bedroom.

Amy had struck up a very unlikely friendship during this time. She was almost the same age as the very youngest of all the ranch boys currently staying there. He was an obnoxious little punk of a kid that Jonah didn't like. He had a big mouth and a bigger swagger to make up for his size, but he was not one of the really *dangerous* ones. The kid had likely been sent to the Ranch because he was a bad boy who acted out too much and his parents didn't know what to do with him. Despite posing like a "gangsta," he hadn't ever done anything *really* bad.

Amy was mildly annoyed with the kid too, but he followed her like a puppy when the kids were lined up to get onto the school bus. There was a window of a few minutes when he could creep over to the staff kid side of the area the ranch boys stood, and if she was on his side of the staff kids, he could talk to her. He would always get the seat as close to the front of the bus as the ranch boys were allowed to go, and he'd spend the ride doing his best to get any kind of attention, good *or* bad from Amy.

Jonah had seen him get a bit too close to the staff kid side of the bus stop once and suddenly started toward him, walking up to the kid until he was towering down at him like a 16-year-old bull. The kid had backed off fast, and Amy had told him he was harmless, and not to "go crazy." Over the weeks, he realized that while the kid was an annoying big mouth, he really *was* harmless and even seemed to act kind of protective toward Amy. What exactly he wanted was not clear, but he was desperate for any sort of attention.

Amy used her "inside contact" to get *intel*. She would let the kid spill the beans on whatever was going on among the boys, since he was incapable of *not* talking, then she would fill in Jonah and Hayden later about all the goings on among the ranch boys. This allowed her to be a useful source of information to Jonah. Several times, Amy knew about planned escape attempts, inter-ranch boy feuds, and illicit drug stashes before any of the staff did.

The Franklin kids had naturally just accepted that they were in the sort of world where survival *was* in question and they absolutely had to stick together and protect one another however they could.

The thought of escape had bubbled up, unspoken and unbidden in Jonah's mind. Like the slowly rising heat of hatred he sensed from the ranch boys, it would never stop simmering in the back of his mind as long as he was there. He found Amy's intel reports very valuable, because they included details of the "3AM emergencies" that involved ranch boys trying to run away.

There was a pretty well-oiled machine in place for retrieving runaways. The staff operated like prison guards and it was "all hands on deck" until they got the runaway. They knew all the places the boys had thought of to try and hide in the nearby town over the years (that was *if* they could get across several miles of open country to the town in the first place). Steve was located in a strategic position outside the gates and could control the entire length of the gravel road to town at a moment's notice. Going the back way through the "woods" meant miles of rough country before the Arkansas border, and Mr. Dan knew every inch of that land. The ranch boys had been making regular escape attempts for years and very few had succeeded.

Even worse, the ranch boys at least got out of the gates in work crews doing cleanup or landscaping and could scout out the town. Jonah didn't even get that. He worked exclusively inside the gates. The only time he was out was when he was at school, but the school had a close relationship with the local police department because of the presence of the boys and they were on the lookout for escapees. Jonah had already rejected the notion of trying to smuggle what he might need into a book bag and taking off from the high school. The cops in Blue Eye would be handing him over to Mr. Dan and his Dad in about twenty minutes, tops.

Literally the *only* time they got off the compound was church on Sundays, and Mr. Dan wanted all the staff to go to the same church that he was visiting that week, with his people all around them. All the boys were usually there. He basically packed up the entire facility, and Steve and the men herded everyone like sheepdogs into and out of one of the rickety, desperately poverty-stricken little churches that he pumped for donations every Sunday like an old world circuit judge working a route. Dad had started lobbying Mr. Dan to take his family to a *different* church, but that had caused friction. The amount of control over every moment of their lives undoubtedly rankled Walter.

Amy would have been up for an escape attempt, but she was only 12 and would be basically useless, plus she still thought escape was some kind of "adventure." Jonah didn't think she completely grasped the reality of the situation. Even worse, she might just go to Dad and rat on him if he brought her in on a plan. He couldn't be completely sure. She seemed to be toying with the idea of escape, but she also tended to go to Dad with her hot tips of ranch boy activity with an air of someone who still expected Dad to "fix things."

That left Hayden or going all by himself. Jonah found a rare opportunity when his parents weren't there, but the kids were, to knock on the door of the room Hayden had taken to hiding in one night. There wasn't a lot that needed to be said, the looks on both of their faces told him they were on the same page.

"We need to *get out* of here." Jonah had kept the door to Hayden's room a little open so he could see if Amy was trying to listen. She might be taking her "Harriet the Spy" routine a little too far and try to turn them in to Dad "for their own good." He casually watched the door to the apartment (which Mom and Dad might come through at any moment) through the slightly open bedroom door, keeping his voice low.

Hayden looked like she had known this conversation was coming. "We *can't!*" The pale faced teenager sat on her bed, looking hopeless. "Do you have any idea where we even *are*? I mean, *really*? We don't know anything about what's out there. We don't have anywhere to go. We are across the *entire country* from anybody we know. What do you think you are going to do, just start walking? Hitchhike across country?" Hayden looked horrified.

Jonah shrugged. "But we *have to*."

"Don't you dare! They will catch you. Do you have any idea how many boys have tried to escape in the last month? They know the area, some of them are even *from* Misery." Hayden and Jonah had taken to intentionally mispronouncing Missouri as "misery" when they talked to one another. "What makes you think *you* can do it?"

Jonah shook his head. "I don't know. I just… can't… stay." There was something inside Jonah that was like a river of lava. It was like a steady rage of overwhelming intensity that waited in the background and might come up to the surface at any moment. He knew as certain as he knew that he was breathing that he *could not live* as a prisoner. He would rather *die* than give up.

"You're going to get yourself *hurt*! Don't do it!" Hayden's eyes softened as if she hated to say what she was saying. "If you try, I'll… turn you in."

Jonah nodded. So that was how it stood. If he went, he left behind the only good friend he'd ever been able to keep. He shrugged as if the entire conversation had been casual and walked back to his room.

The gigantic warehouse/barn next to the Franklins apartment was actually used to store Mr. Dan's automobiles. Jared found himself in there during the course of after school work one time. He was absolutely blown away by the place.

The entire interior of the huge metal building was taken up with at least a hundred cars, probably more. There were old classic corvettes, muscle cars, hot rods, historical cars including a totally restored Ford Model A. Jonah walked between the rows of cars in awe. He'd never seen anything like this collection in his life.

It seemed that the Ranch, as a charitable institution, received a lot of donations in the form of someone donating a car, or an estate actually being left to it, in addition to all the support it received from the local churches. Still, considering just how desperately poor that section of Missouri was, Jonah found it mind boggling to see this collection, in pristine condition *here*, literally right next to a pigpen.

Apparently donated cars were in ready supply on the Ranch. Mr. Dan just kept the best ones for himself. He liked the fact that he didn't have to pay for upkeep for the boys or staff, feeding them donated pig slop food, receiving money from the state to pay for them, having no building codes apply to his facility since it was a charitable institution, selling the pigs fed with donated food at a profit, using the labor of the boys for profit (he even farmed out teams of boys to local communities to do work here and there by way of a favor) and accepting the tithes sent by churches from all over the state. Mr. Dan definitely had a pretty good thing going. He was something like a feudal lord or an old plantation owner, taking his cut of everything right off the top. It was always clear to Jonah that Mr. Dan *really* liked his money.

Something about the cars had struck Walter. He felt that if he were being asked to get up at all hours of the night to respond to emergencies and drive all over creation to do things, the Ranch should provide him with a car so he didn't destroy his old work truck on the rutted gravel roads and hauling Ranch equipment around. The old beast had managed to get them across the entire country, but not too much could really be asked of it now. Also (Jonah was never sure) it seemed that *some* staff had been allowed to use a car or a pickup and some (like Walter himself) were using their own truck to do a lot of heavy work that would literally beat the vehicle to death. Considering that Mr. Dan had an entire warehouse full of cars, how hard would it be to let Walter use one?

Jonah wasn't there for the conversation. Like most everything Walter did, it was only revealed to his family after the fact - if they happened to overhear him complaining to Laura. As with anything requested of Mr. Dan, the conversation apparently hadn't gone that well.

Mr. Dan grudgingly handed over the keys to an old Dodge Aspen. It was blue, and about the same year as Dad's truck. It had been some old person's car before being donated by the estate to the Ranch, so it had been garaged its entire life and was in pristine condition. Jonah immediately liked it. He dreamed about owning a 1974 Dodge Charger someday, and even if the Aspen wasn't a Charger, it had some similarities to his dream car, being the same year and the same brand.

Seeing as how Jonah was now 16, Dad took the opportunity to do some formal driving lessons with him. He took him out to a field on the Ranch one day and they spent a little time with Jonah showing Dad that he could do proper driving maneuvers, practicing parallel parking, and other stuff that normal dads do with normal kids.

Jonah had already gotten in some experience driving with the work trucks at Mt. Promise. Even before that, Uncle Boone had once towed a VW Rabbit with a blown engine all the way up to their trailer in Oroville from Los Angeles. Boone had told Dad that it had been abandoned and seized by the city, and basically been handed over for a dollar at an auction somewhere in L.A. The driver had blown the engine getting up one of the few big hills in L.A. and left it. That car was otherwise in perfect shape. Boone said you could get a Rabbit engine dirt cheap and change them out yourself, so basically it was a working car (if you bought an engine) for a dollar. He had thought maybe Jonah could drive it when he got his permit.

Dad had assented. Obviously, they had never got around to buying the new engine for it. Jonah thought it might have been $200 for a rebuilt Rabbit engine at that time. Dad had taken each of the kids into the stranded car in turn and had run them through drills with the manual transmission. "You are going up a hill now, downshift… use the clutch… you ground the gears…" It was sort of like a flight simulator -except kind of sad. As far as Jonah knew, that Rabbit never left the property in Oroville again.

So, by the time Dad decided to "teach Jonah to drive" at the Ranch, he already knew how to drive pretty much, or at least he felt reasonably confident doing so. The Aspen was pretty similar to one of the pickups from Mt. Promise, just a regular automatic.

In between the lessons, Dad would talk. Jonah didn't always listen anymore.

"We're going to get to go to our own church on Sundays … and things are going to get better."

Jonah turned the car with a precise move, going through the motions of parallel parking as if two hay bales were the corners of cars in an imaginary city. He was focused on what he was doing with a laser like intensity.

"… Mr. Dan is coming around. Things will get better. I'll get him to let me use a truck … a real work truck ... And maybe we can give you *this car* to use so you don't have to take the bus to school."

Jonah stopped. He was dead silent for a second. His head turned to face Dad. He said nothing, but just looked at him for a moment. In Jonah's mind, he remembered a moment on a freeway in Los Angeles, Dad pointing to a new Miata … Then he turned back to what he was doing.

Maybe they actually will "give me" this car … just not how they think...

Jonah knew where Dad kept his keys. If he could get this car, he could get *hundreds* of miles away from here before anyone could stop him.

"... See, I was talking to Mr. Dan, and I think he can see reason…"

It will have to be at night, obviously...

"... He's just stubborn … I think I can teach him proper management practices…"

I just have to get past that damn gate...

"... You'll see, we'll start going to our own church and you'll like it."

How the fuck do I get this thing past that gate?

"... We're working on some exciting projects. We have some big plans…"

Maybe daytime? No, everyone would see who was driving. Wait, there's a gap to the left of the fence where we wait for the bus, I could probably just drive this thing right through the little fence there.

".. .Jonah, I know you've been unhappy here…"

I have to make damn sure I can drive this thing … concentrate on the lesson. Get this down. You are going to need it later.

"Very good job, you are really doing good."

"Thanks Dad."

Maybe Walter recognized the look in the eyes of his son. The same look he'd once had as a wild animal of a child climbing twenty-foot chain link fences and running away from home in Vallejo.

Perhaps that was why he felt the need to spend a little time with him now. Jonah didn't know, he didn't inquire. He was no longer interested.

18

RUNNING IN THE NIGHT

It had probably started with Walter complaining about something Mr. Dan asked him to do. Jonah later figured it must have been something along the lines of "I can't take *that* out to the South Field, you only gave me a car to use! It isn't a pickup truck!"

Jonah never knew exactly what it was on that particular day, but it was clear that there was some kind of considerable tension between Walter and Mr. Dan. The Lord of the Ranch stood on the porch as the staff filed past on their way to dinner, glaring malevolently at the Franklins. It was the look he had before he ordered one of the boys to "consequences" like running the ranch grounds until he collapsed, sweat pouring from him, filthy from falling and being picked up by staff, body totally spent as he bent at the bottom of the stairs to the Hall to vomit … like the boy who had tried to escape that week.

Jonah walked past Mr. Dan with very much the same demeanor as Laney, eyes in front, not looking at anyone, sort of keeping his shoes in focus, staying behind his Dad like a duckling.

Mr. Dan gave a prayer that made it clear that *some people* really need to think about how they are "backsliding" (universal Christian lingo for going bad). They ate in sullen near silence. The whole place felt like a beat dog, too tired to bite, just watching for the next kick.

Jonah glanced over at Laney. It had been hard to see her very much, but he had managed a couple of visits, even with the busy work schedule they had him on. Her dad's "demonstration" hadn't stopped Jonah obviously (though it had made him dislike a man who would hurt animals in order to hurt *him*). Actually, their relationship had cooled down of its own accord as the teens had realized that they had very little in common other than being fellow castaways learning to deal with teenage hormones. They probably would have made reasonably good friends eventually, but they didn't share a common language and once they had run out of things to talk about (and lacking any opportunity to do much else than talk) things had sort of fizzled.

Jonah felt like a man on a ship going down in the ocean. Laney had been an exotic drink available at the ship bar. Sure, it was sweet and wonderful and made you feel good, but he just didn't have time to hang around the bar … he had bigger things to think about, like how he was going to get off the ship.

After the dinner of high-grade pig slop they lined up in dejected silence, filing back out of the hall. As usual, the ranch boys began to make a lot of noise as they energetically swept everything from the tables into huge plastic garbage cans. Something was different today. Mr. Dan stood on the deck with a glint in his eye. The boys looked excited, like dogs in a pack chasing a lone cat. They energetically threw the food from the tables into the cans, pieces and bits of this and that flying in every direction as they jubilantly worked.

Dad was standing on the porch next to Mr. Dan. They were looking down at something. Dad was utterly silent. He stood very still, sort of rigid. Jonah looked down and started to say something along the lines of "No! Don't!" but Dad's hand went out and he said nothing. The three of them stood there, watching.

Dad had driven the Aspen to the dining hall and the Franklins had all walked up the stairs to dinner, leaving the blue sedan parked on the gravel. Now, one of the older ranch boys was behind the wheel and every piece of food from the tables was being systematically dumped into the car through the open windows until the interior was literally flooded with slop right up to the tops of the doors. The ranch boys were jubilant as they performed the act of vandalism.

They were going to drive the slop to the pig pens. The car would never be used for a normal purpose again.

Jonah glanced at the two men next to him. It was almost as if Mr. Dan was saying "what did you say about not being able to haul something in the car *I* gave you to use? What were you saying about what can and cannot happen on *my* ranch again?" There was a gleam of pleasure in his eyes.

Mr. Dan and the ranch boys had the same look. They *knew* he wanted them to punish a member of the staff, and they got to do so rarely. They *loved* this.

Jonah found himself wondering who were the prison guards and who were the inmates here.
After that, things kept going downhill.

It was clear the ranch boys were gunning for Jonah. They whispered as he came by, huddled in groups and watched him, and smiled with a patient leer as if to say "Any day now." They were going to jump him. It was going to happen sooner or later.

Amy heard from her informant on the bus ride home that the word had officially gone out. That day, as the Franklin kids walked from the gate of the compound back to their apartment after school, she was frantic.

"But Jonah, the word went out! They are going to *jump you!* It's going to happen probably tomorrow!"

Jonah scowled as they marched along the dirt path in the hot sun, clusters of ranch boys leering their way from behind outbuildings here and there.

"Fine." He found himself saying. He met the gaze of one of the boys, letting his entire depth of fury pour into that look. "Let them come! They'll all get to know me better!" If they were a pack of dogs trained to fight, he was a cornered bear. He would do some *damage*. Jonah wasn't afraid. He actually looked forward to having some outlet for the molten rage boiling up inside him.

"You don't understand! They will use *weapons*, it won't be a *fair fight!*"

"So will I." Jonah set his jaw grimly. He could use work tools and rocks pretty damn well himself. Still, a faint fear told him that Amy was probably right. This would be like a *prison* fight. They knew what they were doing. He wouldn't have a real chance, even being smart, even carrying something … it was likely he'd be seriously hurt at best.

Jonah shrugged off the girlish clucking of Hayden and Amy as they got to the apartment. The girls were both worried about him. They knew his mood. They knew he would only be pushed so far, then he'd recoil like a spring. They yelled at him. He yelled back.

"I don't care! Let them come!" and he slammed his door like a child. There was nothing for any of them to do until Mom and Dad came home.

When they walked in, Amy and Hayden went to them immediately and ratted Jonah out.

"Dad! He said it was okay if the boys jumped him because it would let them all know each other better!" Amy had a particularly annoying way of twisting meaning when tattling on her elder siblings.

"That's not what I said."

"Yes it is."

Jonah sighed deeply. Mom now joined in with the general hysteria as Hayden and Amy and they *all* railed at Jonah at once about how foolish it was to do anything like fighting with the boys and how he had to let staff know whatever was happening immediately and…

Jonah stood there, facing the full assault of female hysterics in the little apartment kitchen. For once, it wasn't Dad filling the world with the sound of insanity … Dad was actually quiet. He looked kind of deflated, just standing there, trying to work up enough energy to get angry and failing.

Dad finally told the girls to shut up (and for once, Jonah was grateful for that). He took Jonah aside and said. "Promise me you won't fight them, you just stay away from those boys and let me know the second anything happens."

Jonah found this so absurd he could barely contain himself. What the *hell* was he supposed to do to stop them from picking a place and a time and beating the living shit out of him?

"Sure Dad, I promise." He didn't mean a word of it. Jonah's survival instinct had told him that maybe if he gave a good accounting of himself, they would stop targeting him so much. Maybe that would save his life, since bringing up issues *after the fact* with Dad certainly wasn't going to. With the Aspen FUBAR (Fucked Up Beyond All Repair), he was back to square one as far as getting out of here. He had vague ideas about using some other vehicle, but he didn't know where the keys to any of them were kept and (unlike some of the ranch boys), he had no idea how to hotwire a car.

It seemed as if Walter intended to do something about the impending crisis surrounding Jonah. He seemed to think this was connected to his issues with "leadership", which, if true, meant that Mr. Dan did indeed use the ranch boys as attack dogs to pressure staff when necessary. Jonah didn't know what Walter was thinking, but in any case, Walter's issues with Mr. Dan were overtaking other events.

Walter had been working on Mr. Dan's new residence. It was going to be a nice house. In fact, it was enormous.

After the first falling out with Mr. Dan, Walter had been called because there was an "emergency" regarding the house project. Apparently, when the storm cellar had been dug, it had not been properly coated on the outside to keep out moisture. There had been water seeping through the concrete walls of the basement and into the house. Mr. Dan had called out Walter and most of the ranch boys at 10 PM, and they had toiled all night long, digging out the basement all the way around the house, through the impenetrable Missouri clay to a depth of 8 feet. Then, they had coated the outside of the concrete basement wall with thick tar, ruining their clothes in the process of handling the stuff. By the time Walter had stumbled home at dawn, he was so exhausted he could barely stand. Mr. Dan had probably explained it to Walter as "Consequences" for a group of boys who had misbehaved, but it was more likely that the entire exercise had been "Consequences" for Walter.

Now, there was another call. Mr. Dan's wife was upset about the house, which meant that Mr. Dan was upset about the house. The ranch boys had messed up badly in an effort to paint the interior. The entire house had to be repainted *tonight*. The Franklins would have to do it.

Walter got them all corralled and drove them out to the huge mansion he had been toiling on for Mr. Dan. It was made clear to them that (just like boys who were receiving "consequences") they could not leave until the *entire* interior was totally painted. Every wall, every square foot of the ceiling…

Walter organized his family into a work crew. Hayden and Amy had done a lot of interior painting at the Ranch, so they were given the more careful work of cutting in around doors and dealing with trim. Jonah was a strong boy, so he was given the roller on the long pole and shown how to do the ceiling. Mom and Dad each took up rollers and attacked different areas.

Within an hour, the entire world was a vast sea of white paint. It coated every inch of Jonah's forearms and hands and much of his face. His back and arms burned from the effort of rolling endlessly on the high ceiling. Life was reduced to a simple misery of trips to fill up the paint tins, wash the rollers, move on to the next room, keep on going…

It was sometime in the middle of the night when Jonah kind of snapped. He just stopped giving a shit about what they were doing. "They want the entire ceiling done? Fine!" He dipped the entire roller in a bucket of paint, so that it was dribbling with it, then slapped it to the ceiling and ran it down the hall so fast white droplets sprayed in every direction. "There! Look, I just did an 8-foot strip!"

Hayden poked her head out of the room she was working on. "Don't make a mess, Jonah!"

Jonah shot her a glare, loaded the roller up the way a ranch boy would do one more time and did it again. He started almost throwing the paint up any which way. He finished that hallway in about twenty minutes.

They got out of there after midnight, exhausted, barely able to move. The entire house was painted, but it looked as if someone had loosed 80 rabid cats dipped in white paint in there and then let in a dog to chase them around for a while. Jonah thought it was a very *good* paint job considering the circumstances. He was sort of proud of it. It made a certain *statement*…

"Mr. Dan isn't going to like it!" Hayden whispered to Jonah as they got in the car.

"Fuck Mr. Dan."

Mom and Dad were too tired to do more than drive them home in silence.

The family told Jonah to call in sick to school the next day. He wasn't really given a choice. His mom did the calling, and she stayed home from work too, still trying to recover after the "consequences" session of the night before. It was clear to Jonah (even if it wasn't clear to her) that they were being treated exactly the way the ranch boys were and being given consequences because Walter was (obviously) giving lip to Mr. Bossman. The same tactic was being used; they were simply being worked to exhaustion until they were too beat down to resist.

Walter suffered that day. Mr. Dan made sure of it. Hayden and Amy were escorted back from the bus by Mom. Jonah was told to stay in the apartment all day. He asked if he should go to work during the normal work time after class. Mom said no.

Dinner was incredibly awkward. The Franklins made their way up the steps to the dining hall, past Mr. Dan, and made their way to the table they had been assigned. Nobody asked Jonah if he was "feeling better." Apparently, they had bigger fish to fry. Walter and Mr. Dan were clearly not happy with one another. Steve had managed to have his family not be there. It was just him.

Mr. Dan didn't say anything to the Franklins, and they skulked back down the steps.

"I'm not going back there again." Jonah heard his Mom saying to Walter.

Walter looked grim.

That evening, Walter and Laura worked furiously. They got on the phone and called Grandpa Franklin in California. The exact nature of the call wasn't completely clear to the kids (they used the phone in their bedroom), but they were able to overhear such things as "No … TONIGHT!"

They knew something was up. Walter began throwing boxes in the truck. He got the trailer hitched up to the old beast. Thankfully, they had only halfway unloaded the big work trailer when they arrived at the Ranch. It took surprisingly little time to get it loaded again.

Once direction had come from Grandpa Franklin (plus whomever else they called that night), Walter perked up. He worked himself into a pretty fine flow and Jonah heard him complaining bitterly to Laura as they worked (as if Jonah wasn't there).

"He told me I couldn't take communion! He said he was my spiritual leader as head of a community of believers and as such, until I got right with him, I wasn't allowed to take communion at a church!"

Laura shook her head at the effrontery.

"What is he, some kind of damn *Catholic*?"

Jonah was actively helping get the truck packed up. He shook his head in confused disbelief at what it was that outraged his parents. After everything else, the thing you couldn't take was this guy telling you that you aren't allowed to take communion? *Really*?

The kids had never really unpacked. They had spent the entire time at the Ranch living out of boxes. It spoke to the feeling they had had the second they came through the gates. Only Laura really lost some things in the scramble to get out of there. She had a few kitchen items and things that went missing in the little apartment kitchen.

The night was losing the last tinges of a sunset as the heavily loaded truck pulled the trailer down the dusty gravel road to the gates. Dad said something to the staffer at the gates like "Going out to get some supplies…" Which Jonah didn't hear. Whatever it was, Walter was staff, and as such, he was allowed to drive places so long as it was official business. The guy at the gates mentioned they weren't supposed to go out at night, but he opened them and the old truck painfully sped up out the driveway and down the long gravel road toward Blue Eye, MO. Maybe the guy couldn't see what was in the trailer in the dark and thought there were ranch boys in the back. Maybe he was used to Walter running special errands for Mr. Dan's house project. Whatever the reason, once they got to the town, they found the highway and sped up, not looking back.

The night was darker than any night Jonah remembered. The landscape flashed past the window slits of the truck's shell in amorphous black shapelessness. No city or town lights could be seen wherever they were, no other cars lit the highway, street lights seemed like something from another world. It was like being on a ship in a dark sea heading nowhere, surrounded by nothing, with a hostile shore behind, uncertainty ahead, and sharks all around.

Suddenly, something popped into Jonah's head as he lay in total exhaustion in the back of Dad's truck. *"They shall flee, though none pursue them."* It was a paraphrase of Proverbs 28.1, referring to the wicked. Jonah didn't know why that struck him so much at that moment. He didn't have the energy to think about it. He collapsed into the black oblivion of total exhaustion.

***

In 2013, two boys from the ranch who had been sent out on work crews in the local community escaped. They went back to some of the residential areas they had been working, broke into the house of an elderly couple and stabbed and beat them to death. The Ranch never called the police after the escape.

"The situation became intense but while Walter felt like he was in the Lion's den, he recognized that the Lions could not eat him. ...one night Walter received an unexpected phone call from an old friend ... "Hey your Dad said you were in Missouri so I called to say that you should come over here to work with these folks." "Where are you, what folks?" "I'm here at FNTM in Mansfield, Missouri. These are some really good people supporting missionaries all around the world and they could use someone like you." God was five thousand nine hundred and fifty one years into his Inherit the Earth project and he decided it was time to move his carpenter into the world mission field ... that ...Christians hear stories about ... with pigmies, cannibals, jungles, and witch doctors. It was time to go to the Ends of the Earth."

- The Carpenter Chronicles by Walter Franklin, p. 42.

19

THE END OF THE EARTH

They had crashed at a cheap motel when Dad was too tired to drive. They were somewhere in Misery, nobody knew exactly where. Dad and Mom got on the phone again and called Grandpa Franklin. There was a lot of excited talk, but Jonah was so exhausted he could barely move. He just stayed, lying where he'd gone to sleep in the back of the truck. He felt like he never wanted to move again.

When Mom and Dad came out of the hotel room, they had a plan.

Jonah let them drive to wherever they were going. He was tired. Not just physically tired, but mentally tired. He felt as if he had been through a war. Many years later, Jonah would *actually* go through a war, and the feeling afterward really was similar. He didn't want to think anymore. The knowledge that he wasn't in imminent danger every second of every day brought a flood of lethargic relief.

They drove a ways up the highway to a different part of the state. It was farther from the Arkansas border, and perhaps slightly less poor and lonely. The same muddy looking brown hills, the same wispy little trees. Now, they were at least in a part of the state that had paved roads though. Jonah and Amy commented to one another as they saw a road with streetlights somewhere.

A good drive along a highway from pretty much anywhere, there stood a slight hill, flattened at the top, with a paved road that ran up to it from the highway leading into a big parking lot. An ugly, blocky building stood there like a megalith from some ancient, long dead civilization. It was huge, with multiple wings branching off from a core area. The whole thing was built to withstand tornadoes if need be. The walls were heavy concrete slabs, like a fortress. Everything was square. It was brutalist architecture not by intent but by default, and it reminded Jonah of some kind of castle in a post-apocalyptic world.

The parking lot was empty. Two or three little vehicles huddled close to the titanic mass of the huge building, looking tiny and afraid in a parking lot built for at least 300 cars. The lot hadn't been painted in years, but the lines for parking spaces were still faintly visible. The place had no sign. It sat, looking out over empty, oddly picturesque brown hills dotted with scrub and little trees like an empty-eyed watchman staring out over a valley that hadn't needed to be guarded in hundreds of years.

Jonah was too tired to even comment at the strangeness of the place. He gingerly extracted his aching body from the truck and blearily followed the others to the door. There was a short, pudgy, almost comically excited man talking to Mom and Dad while a retired couple in matching checkered "cowboy" shirts peered like little owls from behind him. From somewhere, there was the smell of baking food … not pig slop … *real food*, still in the oven. Jonah's stomach growled.

They entered through a heavy steel door that looked like it had been built to withstand a direct hit with an RPG (rocket propelled grenade – "bazooka" in civilian slang). The door automatically closed behind them and Jonah turned to look at it. He saw that it was unlocked. They could go out freely. It seemed to only automatically lock from the *outside*, like a *normal* door. That was comforting.

Rich, the director of the organization, was explaining to Mom and Dad that this had once been a hospital building. It had been built largely with government funds, and it had always been way too much hospital for this rural area. At some point, the state and the county governments had decided to consolidate the area hospitals, and this one had been declared redundant. That was when it had been purchased by Rich's organization "for peanuts" after sitting here for sale for quite a few years.

"It was built to withstand a major tornado," Rich said as he walked through the massive, concrete floored rooms. "It has a generator, its own water source *plus* county water; basically, this place was designed to survive anything and keep on going."

The interior was very bare. The rooms were huge. High ceilings like you might find in an indoor mall, concrete floors mostly covered in industrial carpeting, huge, wide doorways designed to allow people to easily wheel a gurney through. A lot of panels in the ceiling were open, revealing massive, strange machines and bundles of wires or pipes. It looked kind of like a hangar from a sci-fi movie. The lights and lack of windows in the hallways gave the place a timeless feel. Day and night were the same inside.

There weren't many people in the vast, echoing interior. Mostly a few old, retired couples, puttering around with various tasks like termites repairing the interior of a vast mound, one little piece at a time.

They had entered next to the building's loading dock, which was currently being used as the main entrance at the moment. Next to what had once been the "back door" of the hospital was the kitchen. This was what Jonah had smelled through the open door from the parking lot. Two women who looked like grandmothers were baking something in the big, industrial kitchen. They waved and smiled as the Franklins walked past.

Rich invited them to sit down in the big hospital cafeteria which had been mostly restored and was obviously now used as a dining hall. There was a big metal container full of fresh coffee and some muffins still warm from the oven.

"Welcome to FNTM." The pudgy man seemed almost ridiculously excited. "*Friends of* New Tribes Missions!"

Jonah raised his eyebrows. That was quite a mouthful.

New Tribes Missions was one of the oldest and largest non-denominational mission organizations anywhere. They had branches, facilities, and obviously mission bases literally all over the world. Much of their work was now taking place in the Amazon Basin, Africa, and remote places like Papua New Guinea.

NTM was so big and so well known among Christians who supported missionary work that they had become something of a bureaucratic mess. Focusing exclusively on preaching the Gospel to "new tribes" that had never heard it before meant that their focus wasn't wide enough to worry about a lot of the support and logistics needs that inevitably became a problem while working in some of the most remote corners of the earth.

Rich happily explained that that was where FNTM came in. They were an *independent* organization with their own funding and their own board of directors. That meant that they weren't bogged down in the red tape and inertia that NTM was. The exclusive focus of Rich's shiny new nonprofit startup was to provide the logistics needs to support the actual missionaries. They could bring in technicians, mechanics, drivers, builders, and all the plethora of skills and resources required to sustain life in the Amazon wilderness or African bush. They could bring people in for short duration projects, and they could ramp up quickly for changing needs.

Jonah nodded and listened with no particular interest, but he could see that Walter was enraptured.

This was *exactly* what Walter had been looking for in his quest to be a "carpenter for God" or whatever they were doing.

Jonah didn't really care. He didn't really know how to judge what he was hearing anymore. He was tired and confused and honestly didn't know what was real and what was not. He was too tired to think. He was just grateful not to be eating pig slop.

There was a perfunctory "talk" with Mom and Dad which Jonah barely paid attention to. It seemed the boy's ranch had left all of them in something of a state of shock. Even Jonah's parents seemed to realize that they had made a mistake going there, and they seemed apologetic to the kids. Mom talked about what they were going to do about school for the kids. Dad favored the idea of "home school" (which obviously never materialized). They promised that everything was going to get better now, and they wouldn't have to face anything like that again. Things would become more normal. There wasn't even a question that Mom and Dad were taken up with this new place and that they were going to be working *here* now.

Jonah didn't believe a word his parents said. He had been tuning them out pretty much since they got to the boy's ranch. He was sure his Dad was full of it. His big problem was that he didn't know what *was* true. He had been down the rabbit hole so long and was so completely upside down that he didn't know *what* to believe anymore. Stay in some weird, abandoned hospital building in the middle of Misery with promises of "getting back to school" at some point? Sure, why not? Jonah's life was already a fucking train wreck and he was only just 16.

The compound was pretty isolated, but it was given a sense of activity by the volunteers who came through from all corners of the USA. Most of them were retirees who had a lot of time on their hands, had an RV, and wanted to do something to help the

Missionary effort. There were quite a few people like this across the country. They were mostly not people who could handle the physical hardships of traveling to some distant mission field themselves, but they were happy to volunteer to rebuild an old hospital, cook meals, collect supplies to be packed up and sent to the missionaries, and help plan and coordinate logistics projects.

They were good people, generally. Jonah liked quite a few of the current batch of volunteers working at the compound. They mostly seemed like kindly grandparents to the Franklin kids.

The Franklins were given rooms in the old maternity wing of the hospital. There were some pretty nice rooms there that had once been used by expectant mothers, and had since been refurbished. This was where missionaries on their way to or from the field could be put up whenever they happened to be in this part of the country.

It was kind of creepy to sleep in a room with a huge metal arm built into the wall over the bed and a strange contraption in the ceiling designed to hold all the machinery that would once have served the patients there. Jonah barely noticed the bizarre aspects of his accommodations anymore. He was kind of in the Twilight Zone, just taking everything at face value. *Of course* he now lived in a former hospital room. *Of course* there was an old, abandoned wing of the hospital down the hall from where they were staying with dark corridors and creepy medical machinery on the walls like some low budget horror movie set.

Even though the compound was in the middle of nowhere, it was not locked down the way the boys ranch had been. Jonah could have gotten out. He just wasn't sure about *anything* anymore. Escape had been a driving need in the boy's ranch because he wanted to survive. Now, survival was taken care of. The question was, what was he supposed to do with himself? What kind of future was he supposed to have? What kind of future was even possible?

Jonah had long since given up on foolish dreams of going to high school like the kids in movies did, trying out for football, having friends who went out to parties or staying out late and goofing off. Jonah was pretty sure that kind of thing only existed in Hollywood movies. Sure, maybe rich people lived like that somewhere, but it was probably a tiny minority. The world was ghetto streets and gangs, dustbowl country towns screaming in poverty, and Christian compounds, of the good *and* bad variety.

What was his goal supposed to be? Go out and go to college? He'd thought he wanted to be an aerospace engineer like Uncle Jared. That seemed to be a good goal, but now, he was somewhere in the middle of high school (theoretically), he'd probably have to get a GED at this point. How was he supposed to go to college? He'd be lucky enough to find a job where he could feed himself with basic laborer skills.

Mt. Promise was a place designed to propagandize youth who came from big, modern, secular cities, give them a great experience, and pump their heads full of Christian teaching so as to counteract the creeping secularism of where they came from. Kids from the cities were sent up to get all enthusiastic and full of faith, and then come back to the real world ready to stand up to the secular culture around them. Jonah had effectively never *left* Mt. Promise. He was starting to wonder what was actually *real*.

At Mt. Promise, Jonah had been taken aside by the youth pastor "counselors" many times. They were "concerned" that he looked unhappy. He seemed much too serious. He showed flashes of anger sometimes that scared the Christian kids. They had talked to him in a way that made Jonah understand that something was *wrong* with him. He didn't smile. He wasn't a "good Christian kid."

To Jonah, the idea that there was something wrong with him was never in doubt. He had grown up knowing for a *fact* that he was worthless, useless, and inherently bad. It was a rock-solid foundation of his life that Mom and Dad probably wouldn't have had to raise the kids the way they did except that they were basically defective people. It wasn't something Mom and Dad had ever said per se (unless Dad was in a Wrath and you couldn't take him seriously at those times), it was the way they were just ignored … sort of like an afterthought … they had learned to know that they were *not* important. Jonah had internalized the idea that he suffered because something was wrong with *him*, not his parents. Jonah didn't doubt for a moment that he was the most worthless human being on the face of the earth. It made him question his own judgement on *everything*.

Jonah didn't know it then, but he had been traumatized at some point along the line. He was only 16 now and thought he was immortal and that people who complained about "depression" were wimps, but he would find that every few years for the rest of his life, a very serious, very powerful black depression would periodically come over him like a wave, suck him down into the depths of blackness where the world was no longer recognizable, and then leave him almost gasping for air after a week or a month or sometimes even more. This was the first time he felt it for real, and looking back, it was just the first little wave in a rising tide, but it colored his perspective, drained him of initiative, and made it almost impossible to look at the world and see any reason to go on trying anything.

So, the Franklin kids hung there, like a mosquito trapped in pine sap that will one day harden into amber, sort of floating. The place was so surreal. Everything was so bizarre, everything in their *entire lives* had been so bizarre for so long that they didn't remember what was up and what was down anymore.

Jonah found himself talking to Hayden again. Mom and Dad had virtually disappeared as soon as they had arrived, leaving the kids blessedly in peace. They were theoretically "supposed" to be "working" on stuff around the compound, but the will to do anything had been sapped from them completely by the Ranch. Mostly they disappeared into the abandoned wing of the hospital and came out at meal times. The kindly old volunteers didn't say anything. In fact, they were pretty much willing to let the Franklin kids do whatever they wanted.

Jonah paced the huge, concrete floored hallway with the tentacle-like wires and tubes hanging out of the ceiling. It was always dark in "B Wing" because most of the fluorescent tubes that still worked had been scavenged for the rest of the facility long ago. He *liked* the dark, for some reason he couldn't quite explain.

"Hey, look at this!" Hayden indicated a room to their right. It had once had a glass panel to separate it from the hall, but that had broken long ago, leaving a huge, gaping frame of an opening. Inside, the entire floor was sloped toward a massive drain in the center, and there was a chair still bolted to the floor… It looked like something you might find in a dungeon in some story about the inquisition.

"Eeew!" Hayden pointed to the chair. "It has … um … *stirrups*." She shook a little bit and walked back out into the hallway.

Jonah frowned at the monstrous metal contraption, trying to imagine what had once gone on in this room. He couldn't.

"So, look, it's been a week and we have to figure out what we are going to do." Jonah, as always, had some internal drive beating against his chest, pushing him onward even when he had no clue at all what "onward" meant.

Hayden didn't. "What do you mean?"

"I mean what are *we* going to do? Not Mom and Dad and everybody … *us!*"

Hayden shook her head. "I don't know." She sounded despondent.

"Well I still think we should go somewhere…"

"Where? Grandpa and Grandma's house? What are we supposed to do when we get there? They don't even have enough room for people to stay, and everybody hates Aunt Mary…"

"Look I don't know, I just think we need to … think about our own future…" Even as he said the word "future" Jonah's voice sank. What the fuck did he mean by "future"? What kind of "future" was there? The best they could hope for was to survive, minute by minute, as they had been trained to do. What the hell did he *expect* from Hayden anyway?

Hayden shrugged with the finality of someone who had given up thinking about anything but the present a long time ago. "I think we're doing ok here." Coming from a Franklin kid, that was a glowing endorsement.

Everyone at the facility would gather periodically to watch missionary movies created by New Tribes Missions. They spent a lot of money on these movies, cranking out several new ones a year, and there was a complete collection on the compound. Each and every movie was basically the same: a brave and virtuous missionary couple overcome unspeakable difficulty and danger and either 1) are martyred (with accompanying sweet, sad music and an epitaph memorializing their awesomeness forever) or 2) overcome all resistance and bring innumerable poor savages to the Lord. In either case, the score, scripted "flashback" type scenes with stand-in actors, and overall production quality had a Hallmark Channel tearjerker beat.

Jonah would make the appropriate gesture of dutifully attending, would sit in the back of the room and roll his eyes at the "cry right… *now*" moments, then file out and go back to wherever he was lurking or (more rarely) helping with something. He learned about the missionaries still held captive in the jungles of Bolivia, the three men who had been beheaded in Central America, the heroic valor of the missionaries who had turned the most brutal, savage tribe of cannibals in Papua New Guinea into wonderful, caring people, and the tragic lost opportunity of the newly minted missionary wife and husband who had gone down in a small plane before they got to the mission field where they would doubtlessly have done amazing things.

The mission propaganda was pretty heavy handed, and Jonah shook his head at most of it, but it had definitely swept Mom and Dad up completely. The great part about that was that Mom and Dad got together with Rich and got all wrapped up in some kind of project that totally immersed them and took all their time, leaving everyone else alone. In fact, Jonah was surprised to learn that his parents were being sent to some other facility to undergo "real" missionary training in Florida, and the kids didn't miss them when they were gone.

When Dad suddenly appeared after an absence of some unknown amount of time and announced that he was flying to Papua New Guinea that week, Jonah just shrugged. He hadn't noticed that Walter had got back from Florida, to be honest. Dad and Rich disappeared like a couple of boys going out on a Boy Scout trip, all grins and excitement. Jonah felt nothing whatsoever. He was completely numb. He didn't even ask how long his dad would be on the other side of the planet.

Jonah knew that he could get out of the compound and go … somewhere. He just didn't know why he should, what he was supposed to do there, who to go to, or what kind of life he was supposed to strive to attain. He was at an age when a boy feels the drive that will take him into manhood and begins to aim at big goals, but he couldn't escape the tumbling, dizzy feeling of not knowing what was real, what was false, what was normal, what was true, what he was supposed to be aiming *for*.

So, they remained, drifting aimlessly, in an old hospital building, passing the time by reading or trying to write stories themselves since there was so little outside media available. Mom and Dad were totally caught up in some "Big Thing" and the kids hardly saw them from day to day. In fact, soon, days at a time would go by without seeing them at all.

They had come to the boy's ranch sometime in the late summer. Now Fall died away and the world began to turn cold.

As winter came, the little hills of Missouri turned dead brown, every hint of anything growing disappeared, and the sky turned slate grey. The winter in the Midwest is hard for someone from California to understand. It is brutally cold in a way that slices right through any clothing and almost burns. No sign of life could be seen out the window, and one Sunday morning, the people of the compound had to chip and hammer at the big steel door to get out to the loading dock. Two and a half inches of solid ice covered the entire world. Every blade of grass, every inch of the outside of the compound. They had to chip away the ice around the tires of the truck to free it from the parking lot.

When Christmas neared, the Franklins drove out to Branson Missouri (or "Misery" as Jonah still insisted on calling it). Branson was something of an "entertainment town" trying to follow in the footsteps of Nashville, but with a more overt Christian bent. In the darkness, miles and miles and miles of the empty, bleak, winter landscape of Misery had been turned into a wonderland by an endless light display. It took almost half an hour to drive through it all, and where all the electricity was coming from, Jonah never figured out. Every kind of Christmas light display in the world hung in the pitch blackness of the Misery night like a miracle of color.

Jonah had agreed to get out of the compound for a change. It didn't matter too much where they were going. Normally, the only time they left was to go to churches on Sundays. This had begun to morph into a major ordeal as Dad started to really get into his Big Thing with Rich. Apparently, they were now "fundraising," which meant that going to church was no longer a matter of sitting in an uncomfortable pew and staring into space. Now, the kids were dressed in matching flannels with Mom and Dad and they all had to stand up at the front of the church and smile while Walter and the pastor made a pitch and they passed offering plates around.

It was the most humiliating thing Jonah had ever experienced. At least he was left alone the rest of the time. So, a trip to Branson was a nice diversion, even if they had to hear Laura's inane Christian "rock."

Branson itself was TV perfect, with little ornate lamp posts and old-fashioned buildings. They had a "Christmas Land" set up there with everything made to look like some kind of Santa Claus movie, except with Jesus as the star of the show instead of Santa Claus.

The Franklins walked through it all with little conversation. None of them seemed to have much to say to one another. Jonah was lost in his own thoughts, spinning in an endless loop of uncertainty. He jammed his hands down into the pockets of his cheap leather jacket against the cold and trudged dutifully through the place, over little bridges, through a vast, full scale manger scene.

Dad had just gotten back from Papua New Guinea (wherever the hell that was), and had been immensely excited to talk about it to Laura. He had refrained from his usual enthusiastic pitch to the kids though. Perhaps Walter and Laura had realized that they'd made a mistake going to the boy's ranch, because they now approached the subject of "working for God" almost apologetically with their offspring. The closest thing the kids ever got to an apology from them was when they mentioned in passing that the boy's ranch had probably been a mistake.

Jonah knew he couldn't float in limbo forever. He had to do something, go somewhere, get back to school or something. He was afraid to mention it to his parents for fear of the too pat "answers" they'd probably have. He had to make a decision to walk away now, as a 16-year-old without a penny to his name and no usable skills in a place he didn't know and didn't want to get to know, or continue on the broken roller coaster. His idea of the world at large was so bad that he was truly stuck.

Mom and Dad's obsession with whatever Rich and them had been planning had been a respite, sort of a vacation, that had put off the need to face this choice. Now, that time had come to an end. Limbo was over for Jonah, now it was the elevator to heaven or hell. The problem was, the elevators weren't marked, and there were no up or down arrows.

"... FNTM represented both a worthy objective and a place of refuge from the demonology rampant Boy's Ranch. So, he moved his family into the old hospital building with the other FNTM staff and they all began assisting getting packages ... to missionaries around the world. The Director of FNTM took Walter into his office one day and challenged Walter to ... become an actual ... missionary, traveling to the ... missionary bases and conducting ... building projects for them.   ... Now Walter had to work all these questions of money raising out quickly because his little family was out of funds. ... Walter could see that the demand was large, and the need was great. ... a trip was planned for Walter and the Director of FNTM to visit ... Numonohi, Papua New Guinea to work out details and meet the other players. Walter's first trip to PNG left him with enough stories to keep children and grandchildren entertained for generations. An overnight stay in Hong Kong with an old missionary ... became an adventure. From Port Moresby to the Highlands of Papua New Guinea was an adventure. The Town of Numonohi was an adventure. A trip down the Highlands Highway to

Lea and back was an adventure in survival on one of the most dangerous roadways in the world. ... an overnight meeting where an old man sat down next to Walter ... and said, "You know, not so very long ago we used to eat nice young men like you." A week in a missionary camp where the shower was a bucket. When Walter returned to Laura in Missouri he truly felt he had become a different man."

- The Carpenter Chronicles by Walter Franklin, p. 45

20

MISSIONARIES

Grandpa Franklin bounced a little on his toes as he got out of the little Toyota sedan in the wide gravel parking lot. He looked to Jonah the same as he always had, as if years and years hadn't passed since they had seen him. Of course, years and years *hadn't* passed, it just felt like it.

Jonah turned away from the view he'd been staring at in horrified befuddlement. The entire landscape of winding little paths, manicured hills, and little toy-buildings was littered with weird little ceramic figurines. They sat in little corners, they stared up at Jonah with unseeing eyes like some kind of primitive idol. There were hundreds of them of every size and shape, all over the entire area. It was one of the most horrifying things Jonah had ever seen.

They were in Chapel, MO, in front of yet another massive complex of buildings. To Jonah, it seemed that the entire state of Misery was nothing but big compounds pumping out missionary propaganda or poor little churches. This particular propaganda compound was the "world headquarters" of Precious Moments. The weird looking little eggheaded figurines with the drip-eyes that had become a fad among churchy people. Jonah couldn't believe he was actually standing in front of an entire "theme park" (if it could be called such a thing) dedicated to *that*. For a teenage boy it was more mortifying than many other indignities had been up till now.

Dad walked up to receive ... *what*? A blessing? From Grandpa Franklin. There was something momentous in the meeting. It wasn't so much the need to *please* his father that Jonah saw in Walter's eyes though, it was more … gloating triumph. Grandpa Franklin had wanted to be a missionary more than anything in the world. He and Grandma had gotten married while attending a Christian Bible college (yet *another* big compound pumping out missionary propaganda it seemed.) The young couple had meant to go out to become missionaries in Africa immediately, but World War II had interrupted their plans. When Grandpa Franklin got back, they simultaneously started cranking out babies and went to a missionary jungle training camp in Mexico, stories of which Grandpa would eventually raise his seven children on.

What had stopped Grandpa Franklin wasn't clear to Jonah. It was possible that he had refrained from going after seeing the impact of life in such a place on his young children. That was what Jonah *wanted* to believe at least. Considering how the Franklin children had factored into Grandpa's rank of priorities from then on, it was probably not that.

In any case, Grandpa had never made it to the actual Mission Field. Now, just coming back with a fresh tan from a whirlwind trip to Papua New Guinea with Rich, Walter had.

If there was any question about the importance of the moment to the two men, it was answered by the very fact that Grandpa was here, standing in Misery, coming to see them off on this Big Thing. Grandpa and Grandma regularly drove across the country to attend Gideon Conventions- large gatherings of mostly retirees associated with the Gideons (the people who leave Bibles in hotel rooms). They spent more time on the road than in their own house. In this case, Grandpa was on the way to or from one such convention and had been able to detour through Misery to come see them off.

Jonah made himself pay attention to Walter and Grandpa. There was something there he was trying to understand. Walter felt some imperative as Grandpa's firstborn son to carry on his life's work, or so it seemed, perhaps he just wanted to one up him. Was there something in this that Jonah, the firstborn son of Walter, was supposed to remember, some kind of tradition he was supposed to continue? As a rootless nomad, Jonah paid close attention to anything he might grasp that could lead him to a sense of purpose, a history, a tradition, a home.

Jonah shook his head as Grandpa Franklin hemmed and hawed and made small talk, then began to excitedly show them around the Precious Moments garden. He pointed out this and that with the false exuberance of a lifetime of experience working as a schoolteacher and substitute pastor. No, there was nothing here that could lead Jonah to some deeper understanding of his place in the world. Grandpa Franklin had no Great Wisdom to pass on. He was muttering about how colorful the little figurines were.

They were going. Life became a rush of ever more torturous visits to churches where Jonah had begun to feel exactly like a trained monkey. He was let out of his cage, paraded in front of people by a panhandler, then put back in before they hit up the next group of suckers. Walter had gotten better at his pitch. He had never been good at public speaking, coming off as awkward and unlikeable. Strangely, Walter was very good at being charming to people on a one on one basis, if he really wanted to, but he was hopeless in front of an audience. Nevertheless, after a lot of pretty cringeworthy performances, Walter's applause lines had started to improve slightly. He had a couple of "jokes" that made Jonah want to literally tear his own ears off with pliers (created by the Walter and Laura committee to be as non-offensive as possible), but the churchgoers were easy audiences and they understood that Walter was trying, so he usually got some pity laughs.

The kids had been dressed up in flannels obtained from the "missionary barrel" in the compound. This was a vast pile of donated clothes in a crate, ready to be sorted and sent "to the missionaries." They had been each handed one of Dad's tools and stood up in front of a wall in the compound and pictures had been taken. Jonah refused to smile. He felt that he was doing his parents a favor by not vomiting. They tried to cajole him to smile for at least twenty minutes. He stared at them until they all gave up. A postcard was printed up. It looked like a bad copy of some kind of Communist propaganda flyer. This "eager team of true believers" was a "family that worked together as a team" to go "build houses for the missionaries!"

And people gave them money. Jonah had to shake his head at the absurdity of it all. People gave *money* to this traveling band of freaks…

There was a hasty discussion about Hayden. She was 18 now, and Laura wanted her to go to college, or at least she seemed to hint that was what she wanted, dancing around the issue in meek tones with Walter.

"She can go to college *anytime*!" Walter had been confident sounding and reassuring. "This is a once in a lifetime opportunity! She isn't going to get another chance to go to Papua New Guinea!"

"But she doesn't even have a diploma…" Laura had sounded like an eight-year-old feeling sad about a doll that had a ripped dress.

"Nobody gives a shit about a diploma nowadays! It's just a piece of paper! She'll get her GED and go to college when she gets back!" Walter was totally confident sounding. "She can go to any college she wants! Why not take a break from school and see the world? It'll be an adventure!"

Apparently, Hayden agreed to those terms. Jonah didn't really talk to her about it at the time.

They had to go to Florida. The main headquarters of New Tribes Missions was in Jacksonville, and despite Rich's enthusiasm, they were encountering red tape that had to be handled directly at HQ.

Apparently, to be allowed on an NTM mission base, the mother organization had to sign off that every individual had completed missionary training. There was a closed compound in Florida where new couples were sent. They had to attend something like 10 hours of classes a day and were required to sleep with the doors to their rooms open so everyone could see what everyone else was doing. It sounded psychotic to Jonah, but thankfully Rich was shepherding them through the bureaucracy. Since the Franklin family wasn't a newly married couple who wanted to be sent abroad by the mother organization and since they weren't going to be missionizing people, and worked for the spin off organization anyway, it was really a formality. Walter did get to attend some "very important meetings" going over the projects that would be built when they got to New Guinea with some old dudes who Jonah thought looked like zombies.

The highlight of the trip was when Jonah walked out to the pool next to the room the mission organization put them up in. He'd been told there would be a pool, and having spent about a year in Misery, he dearly wanted to go swimming. He'd gotten a towel and an old pair of shorts and made his way out to the pool in sunny Florida only to find the gate locked. There was nobody to call, and Walter was just annoyed by the distraction anyway and didn't want to try to get someone to open it for him. The only thing Jonah had actually looked forward to about a thousand plus mile road trip turned out to be a bust.

On the way back, they slept on the floors of farmhouses and trailers across the country. There was an entire "underground railroad" of churchy houses that would let missionaries crash for the night on their way somewhere. They would show up at these houses at odd times, sometimes be given a place to sleep on the living room floor, so the dad of the house could step over them as he went to work in the morning. Sometimes Jonah might be asked to share a bedroom with the son, who in one case was so desperately insecure and eager to be friends that Jonah could only imagine what kind of life had broken this child. Jonah hated these visits so much he would have rather just slept in the truck.

Rich was an old pro ex-missionary. He showed Walter how to arrange his travel and gave him such tips as letting him know that they could move a lot of their house supplies in a certain type of plastic tub that you could get from Wal Mart, and which the missionaries had found was the exact size of the *very* largest piece of "baggage" that airlines of the time would let someone check in on a flight. One more time, anything the Franklin kids wanted to keep had to fit in one of the tubs.

Jonah actually got static from his parents when he insisted that everything he "owned" and still actually possessed go in his. Mom and Dad had a lot of kitchen things and general household items and important Dad tools that they wanted to fit in the check-in tubs. They wanted him to take only half of one. Jonah didn't believe them when they told him that the compound in Misery would keep a storage room for them with anything they didn't bring and wanted to come back for "later." Jonah insisted. He would take *everything* he had. Anything left behind would never be seen again, he was sure.

Mom and Dad relented, and Jonah got to bring a few books and folders and things he'd managed to keep with him through all the chaos. Hayden thought he was "overreacting." Jonah thought Hayden was starting to drink the kool-aid.

So, it began. One more drive. An endless, dizzying drive back across thousands and thousands of miles of America, back in Dad's truck. Jonah stared out the back over the tailgate, watching the world recede and recede. It made everything seem unreal somehow. They had left Dad's tools in the storage room on the compound and put the plastic tubs on the trailer. This time, the journey seemed even more cramped, claustrophobic, and interminable. Jonah swore he would never ride in that truck ever again.

They broke down on the way. The truck's tailpipe was falling off and the trailer was giving out. It had been abused and overloaded and actually broke an axle on the way out to Misery the first time. Dad had traded some work for a welder's time while the kids had waited in the truck that first time. Now, the hasty weld in the trailer's axle was giving out. The truck was acting up too. They had to get a new tailpipe put on just to make it back to California. It could only take so much. At least machines were honest that way, people always found a way to take a little bit more.
They arrived at Grandpa Franklin's house. There they would leave the old truck and trailer. One of Walter's sisters drove them and their huge pile of plastic bins down to Los Angeles, from where they had managed to get the cheapest flight available to Papua New Guinea.

PNG. At the time, what Jonah knew about Papua New Guinea came mostly from the FNTM compound library. It was a remote island in the South Pacific that had been considered unexplored no-man's land even into the 20th century, long after every corner of Africa had been put on a map. Grandpa Franklin had actually been there once in WWII, he'd been on a Coast Guard cutter that was sailed all the way to Port Moresby. The allies and the Japanese both tried to use the island as a base, but even large combat units sent into the interior literally just disappeared. Cannibalism had been rampant there for millennia. In the 60s, one of the Rockefeller children had died there. People who investigated later on were able to interview local tribal people who claimed to have eaten him. Jonah had read about a brutal tribe where eating human flesh was a rite of passage. It was a missionary book, so of course the end was that they converted the tribe and they all became nice people, but the parable the missionaries used was a local tradition where the only way to make peace with another tribe was to send out a "peace child" - a child of the village, to serve as a sacrifice if need be, in order to make a truce. Jonah had read of the tribe in the lowlands that built special "cages" for their respected elders in the trees leading to their villages. When they died, the old people would be placed in these cages to mummify and remain, watching the approach to the village forever; dead people like signs nailed to the trees. Nothing Jonah had read made him really want to go see this place, but now, they were *going*.

Jonah was the boy, and he was strong. That meant that it was his responsibility to move the plastic bins from one place in the airport to the next. First, they had to unload the damn things from the car, then (telling a porter they didn't need help) they had to haul the bins from the drop off zone to the check in counter. Walter stationed one of the girls at each of the stacks of bins (the one they were carrying from and the one they were carrying to) so people wouldn't steal anything, and Jonah and Walter (mostly Jonah) arduously carried two check in bins for each of the five members of the family *plus their carry-on bags* all the way across the airport. Each one felt like it was loaded with cement.

By the fourth bin, Jonah was dripping with sweat. He looked around at the normal people walking in and out of Los Angeles International Airport, aware for the first time just how completely bizarre he and his family looked. People with headphones and portable cd players cruised past with sunglasses, businessmen walked around with briefcases, and Jonah lumbered through grunting as he manhandled a gigantic plastic tub from Wal-Mart wearing someone else's donated clothes and something that had caught his dad's eye as "necessary missionary paraphernalia": a floppy beige canvas "jungle hat" that was waterproof and would float if dropped in water (hooray!). Jonah looked, even to himself, like a castaway freakshow member or maybe a really stylish street bum who wasn't smart enough to have a shopping cart.

Mom was dealing with the tickets at the counter. The airline people looked on in growing horror as Jonah hefted bin after bin after bin into a six-foot stack next to the check in counter. They called for extra porters. The woman complained to Mom about the size. They wanted to charge an extra fee. Dad got mad and started to argue with them. Jonah shrugged and went for another load.

When he got back, Dad had his tape measure out and was demonstrating precisely how this monstrosity could be justified under their rules - technically. It looked like the airline people had backed down.

With the truckload of "baggage" finally taken care of, Jonah just sat down against a wall and closed his eyes. In a minute, it was time to jump up and run in order to get to the right terminal to be on time for the plane. It went without saying that a family of (mostly) first time flyers carrying all their earthly possessions had not dressed in a way that made it easy or quick to get through the metal detectors.

Jonah sort of faded out until they found themselves settled into the cramped confines of the 747. He remembered irrationally worrying that the load of stuff they had checked in would be too much for the plane to take off with. The cabin was massive, but the windows were tiny little portholes that Jonah could barely see out of. The seat seemed to have been designed for a petite Asian man, and he found it impossible to get comfortable. Some kid was sitting behind him using the back of his seat as a heavy bag, and Hayden's endless amount of *junk* had spilled into his feet space. Jonah fought away a rising panic. It would be better once they were airborne.

They were airborne for more than 14 hours. It was like being an astronaut in an overloaded moon capsule. Day ended, it came back, morning dawned, the light outside the tiny little windows changed until it was totally impossible to know how many days or months or years might have passed. Meals came and were served (Jonah tried to hoard anything he possibly could, even if he didn't want to eat it.) The cabin went dark and they were told to sleep. It got light again and more meals were served. Still it went on and on and on and on. Jonah would later learn that flying opposite the earth's rotation makes it seem like day and night are passing super fast. It can be really disorienting on a long flight.

The airplane bounced like a ship at sea going over a mild chop. Jonah got up to somehow fight his way down the overcrowded aisle toward the bank of fetid restrooms. The 747 was loaded to the gills, and by the eighth or ninth hour, they smelled like porta potties outside a multi-day hippy convention.

There was nowhere to go, nothing to do, just the endless loud hum of the engines and the wind. Still they went on and on and on. Nothing but ocean outside the window.

Jonah knew fun facts of geography like if you looked at Earth from this angle from space, you would see almost nothing but water. The Pacific was *that* big. Until now, he didn't understand what that actually meant.

14 hours, 50 minutes, and two lifetimes later, they landed in Hong Kong.

Some tiny mercy of the gods had allowed their check in luggage to be loaded directly from this flight to their connecting flight, so they just had to deal with carry-on. Even so, Jonah was obliged to help his sisters with their overloaded backpacks.

They were to have a layover in Hong Kong, which meant a stay in a hotel room. When the door to the airport opened and they stepped out onto the taxiway of the insanely hyperactive city sometime after midnight (local time), Jonah felt he'd been slapped in the face by the warm, humid air, even this late at night. It was so wet their clothes stuck to them like walking into a bathroom with a running shower.
The Franklins got a taxi to a hotel and crashed in soundless oblivion. The last thing Jonah heard from the floor of their single room where he had stretched out to (hopefully) die or (potentially) sleep was Mom and Dad talking in hushed, chipper tones about getting up early to go see the sights while they were here.

They awoke late, had time to walk down a couple of streets and snap a few pictures of a sprawling city that made Manhattan look "rural," and managed to get packed up and back to the airport for the next leg.

They were in luck, this flight would "only" take 7 hours.

By the time they arrived in Port Moresby, Jonah was ready to bash a stupid little porthole window open with his fist and take his chances jumping the hell out of the plane. In retrospect, maybe that was why the idea of becoming a paratrooper didn't seem that bad to him years later. At least paratroopers can *get off*.

Port Moresby is a grade A shithole. It looks like a sad, deflated, kind of falling apart cheap version of some Caribbean tourist trap. The city, being a Pacific "island nation" capital, tries for an air of cute, exotic, "tourist destination," but only manages to achieve a sad desperation, like a poverty-stricken African city trying to put flowers and "tropical decorations" everywhere and pretend to be Hawaii.

The sun beat down with an intensity Jonah had never experienced in the little open-air airport terminal. The place was concrete that looked like a gigantic concrete-eating beaver had come along and started chewing the walls to hell. There was a big tin roof, some open-air walls that were theoretically supposed to herd the different groups of incoming and outgoing passengers into different areas, and an insane amount of people pressing in on every side carrying every conceivable item from appliances to live animals - usually on women's heads. It was instantly apparent to Jonah as he jostled his way out of the plane that this country had never discovered deodorant. The smell was so overwhelming that for a moment, Jonah's vision seemed to fog up as about half a dozen people pressed in on every side.

Once your mind learned to compartmentalize the body odor, the other smells of the place began to assault you. Rotting fruit was pervasive. Everywhere in Papua New Guinea *always* had a rotting fruit smell, plus diesel exhaust and the smell of woodsmoke and human waste.

They managed to push and shove their way through the throngs of stocky, black skinned people to a sort of terminal building. There were "cops" here, standing around in shorts and open shirts (and little else) and holding AK-47s. Jonah had never seen an AK-47 outside of an action movie before.

A thin, red-faced white man came at them with an energetic bound. He was wearing a khaki shirt and shorts like something from an old movie about the British Empire (just missing the stupid looking "pith helmet"). He shouted over the bedlam loud enough for them to understand that he was a missionary sent by New Tribes Missions, and he was going to be handling their transport.

The man was there with the most sad looking Toyota van Jonah had ever seen (which matched every other car in sight). It looked like a crumpled beer can, had some cheap mud tires on it, and was painted white, like virtually every single other vehicle in the entire country. There weren't proper seats in it; just sort of plastic benches bolted to the dented steel floor, and the interior smelled like it had been used to haul cargo for a grocery chain.

Jonah, Walter and the man grabbed their stack of bins before the many eager eyes and hands of the crowd of locals could steal them and filled up the back, then they climbed onto the hard, plastic seats and started rolling in a thick plume of diesel smoke.

The van weaved and dodged potholes and oncoming cars that paid no attention to any sort of "rules of the road" with a jerky, desperation that they would become accustomed to every time they traveled on the lethal "roads." Jonah clutched a handle bolted to the bare metal wall of the van for dear life, watching with horror as they managed to escape a head on collision by inches.

"Welcome to Papua New Guinea! *What do you think?*" The missionary was beaming with happiness.

James, the missionary, let them know that they were going to stay in the NTM guest house in Port Moresby that night before catching their last flight of the trip the next day. They were going out to a different city in New Guinea called Goroka, that was much higher up in the mountainous interior of the country. Altitude was a good thing, it meant less heat, less malaria, and less (or no) crocodiles.

Jonah leaned back in his seat, letting his arm hold him upright as they jostled and dodged their way up a winding road out of the crumbling chaos of the city. He closed his eyes. *Another* flight? Seriously? He decided it might be preferable for them to just hit one of these other cars right here and now.

21

NUMINOHI

The guest house on the outskirts of Port Moresby was a classic relic of a colonial era. It stood on a gated plot with a tall concrete privacy "fence" surrounding a lush tropical garden that was slowly drifting into chaotic disrepair.

The house itself was large, but designed to have a feeling of intimacy and plenty of comfortable places to relax. It was two stories, with a big staircase going up to the second story where the entrance was, and a huge covered and screened porch wrapping almost all the way around the entire building.

In the cool shade of the banana trees, the porch was high enough and the house angled just right to catch a faint breeze from the ocean somewhere beyond the stinking, jumbled mass of the city. Ceiling fans added enough comfort to the porch that you could sit out on one of the wicker chairs even on a hot day and feel comfortable, protected (mostly) from the threat of malaria mosquitos by the screen. Many years later, Jonah would see places with similar design in the American South, where a climate that could get almost as hot and humid in the summertime had led to a lot of the same innovations. At the time, Jonah found it unlike anywhere he'd ever been before.

Even in the "city," life was everywhere in the tropical climate. Huge rhinoceros beetles the size of a child's fist crawled up the side of the guest house. Geckos and tree frogs clung to the outside of the porch screen waiting for bugs to get too close. Bats flitted among the treetops, and millipedes managed to find a way to creep up onto the porch from time to time. The "garden" looked more like a shot of the Amazon in a National Geographic magazine to Jonah than any garden he'd ever seen, but it had a paved path that meandered through it, even the stones barely able to hold the foliage at bay.

The Franklins were totally exhausted after that trip. They didn't have the strength to do much more than force themselves up the guest house stairs and flop down on the wicker chairs of the porch. Thankfully, the bins could be left in the van, since they had to be brought out to the airport tomorrow for the last flight anyway.

James showed Walter the rooms they would stay in (Jonah's ears perked up when he heard "rooms," not "room"). The missionary took the keys off of a very weathered and well used wallboard full of hooks and handed them over. Each key had a number written on tape stuck to the top. They looked strange to Jonah; not like American keys. He would learn that Europe and many other countries had door keys that looked much different from the ones he was used to.

Walter signed the guest book he was presented with without paying much attention. What the Franklins would learn about later was that that signature was very important to NTM. It authorized them to levy a full suite of charges against the account that had been created in Walter's name. Estimated kilometers traveled in the NTM van, room fees, meals, and a few odds and ends. Everywhere they went and everything they did for the rest of their time in New Guinea would involve signing such forms and being charged for things.

The Franklins had come in in the morning, PNG time, but of course their bodies thought it was the middle of the night. They were too exhausted to do anything and it was too early and busy and bright to really sleep. The flight to Goroka would leave late that night.

Jonah didn't pay too much attention to the room or the meal, except that the meal was largely rice and fruits, some of which he'd never seen or heard of before. It seemed just a minute of rest before they were up again, loading their carry-on bags, and heading back out to the van. He did have time to notice that the toilet next to the bank of guest rooms flushed the "wrong way." The water went the wrong direction … he'd never really noticed before, but every one he'd ever seen in the USA all swirled one direction, but this one went the *other way.* He would learn that it had something to do with being south of the Equator and the Coriolis effect.

Of course, it wasn't just the toilets that were "wrong." The cars were on the wrong side of the road too, which just made driving on those broken, awful roads even more frightening. Jonah's eyes kept tricking him into thinking he was about to see a car crash that somehow never happened as they wove and veered along the *left side* of the two-lane road.

The Air New Guinea jet looked normal from the outside. It was a regular mid-size jet, just like one of the big carriers in the USA might use. What he didn't know was that it had probably been bought heavily used from one of the bigger, better airlines and was now being poorly maintained in a sub-adequate maintenance hangar. All he noticed was a mid-size Airbus with a big, fancy looking, colorful bird of paradise (the national symbol of PNG) painted on the tail.

Once they were seated and the jet started to get ready to taxi, things started to get strange. Instead of taxiing under its own power, the jet was towed over to the runway by a tractor at a walking pace. The engine on the right side was going, but the one on the left kept trying to start, making a noise like the Millennium

Falcon failing to engage its Hyperdrive every few seconds. A group of airport workers walked along next to the engine on that side with big hoses and appeared to have expected this.

The Franklins looked at one another in disbelief as their jet was pulled up next to another one until the wingtips of the two airliners overlapped. Now with the non-starting engine of the one jet right next to the running engine of the other, they started hastily doing something that looked complicated with the hoses. It looked for all the world like two cars pulled up next to one another with their hoods open and a pair of jumper cables stretched across from engine to engine.

"Uh…" Jonah couldn't quite believe what he was seeing. "Can you jumpstart a *jet engine*?"

Walter was staring in fascination too. "I guess you can."

At last the engine on their jet sputtered to life and they could taxi under their own power to the runway. Jonah was pretty sure that this was going to be the most dangerous flight he'd ever been on. He thought it might be a good time for a prayer.

Walter was chipper. "What an *adventure*!"

Laura looked at him with a worried expression. "Are you sure this is okay?"

"Oh yeah, I think they did the same thing when I flew out here last time. It'll be fine."

So, they were off. The short hop to Goroka involved flying up into the rugged mountains of New Guinea. In most other places, a lot of these mountains would have been high enough to have glaciers and snow caps on them, but here, only a few degrees south of the equator, it had probably never snowed and never would. Even the rugged mountains were brilliant emerald green and covered in trees right to the top.

There was an old saying that had been going around a long time which was nevertheless very true. New Guinea has two seasons - wet season and dry season. In the wet season, it rains every day. In the dry season, it rains every *other* day. Tonight, the rain that was due to hit the interior tomorrow was making its way up the mountains in the form of thick clouds. As the plane hit them, it bounced and shuddered, undulating and wobbling back and forth in a way Jonah had never felt in a big commercial airliner before. Jonah glanced at the little porthole window, but between the clouds and the darkness, he couldn't make out anything whatsoever. He leaned back in his seat and relaxed. There was absolutely nothing he could do about anything at this moment. He might as well save his strength for the next leg of the trip.

They landed abruptly on a short runway surrounded by what looked like the palest hint of a town that just sort of dissolved into blackness. A few electric lights from buildings muddled into little fires that had been lit by the sides of roads, and then became just black nothingness all within the space of a couple blocks. This was the "city" of Goroka.

One more time unloading, one more friendly missionary man with one more beat-to-hell van. This time the airport (more like a single big runway with a couple cinder block buildings the size of public restrooms, a windsock, and a rusty chain link fence) was basically deserted. The few passengers from their plane dispersed into the quiet darkness of the city.

"We have to watch out here." The new missionary said as they climbed into the van.

"Goroka isn't safe after dark. There might be Raskols about."

"Rascals?" Jonah thought the word sounded quaint, like something Beaver Cleaver's dad might call him and his friends when they got into trouble.

"It's a pidgin word. Raskol gangs. Young men who come down to the city to find work ... there *is* no work, so they form bands, steal what they can, sell it to buy drugs and party ... they always have lots of machetes and a lot of the time they have AK-47s too. Raskol gangs are famous for their brutality. They'll kill you just to steal your shoes."

"Oh, right … *raskols*."

The missionary base was another compound. It grew up the side of a hill next to the Highlands Highway, the only major (paved) road in the Highlands of PNG, sort of crawling up the side of a hill, but just short of the summit. A carpet of electric light in the darkness broken only the reddish glow of a few campfires that invisible travelers had lit alongside the highway where they'd stopped for the night. The compound stood opposite something like the PNG equivalent of a rest stop; a gas station and marketplace that the overloaded trucks that made their way along the Highlands Highway would stop at on their way to Goroka or up the highway to Lae or even (eventually) Indonesia. Turning right on the highway would go into this tin-roofed rest stop's parking lot. A left took one to the gates of the missionary compound.

Dust billowed up in a cloud, hanging in the headlight beams as they emerged from the van into the cool night air of the Highlands. It was at least 10 degrees cooler here than it had been in Port Moresby. Sometimes in the middle of the night up there you *almost* wanted a sweater.

They were to stay in the guest house on Numinohi (the name of the mission base, which in the local Bena dialect means "rubbish land" or "cursed land") until the apartment they were to live in was ready. It would probably take a few days. In fact, they were there over a week, and at the end of it, Walter was in for a shock. He was met by one of the "Leaderships" who handled accounting for the mission base. It turned out that for every van ride, Walter had been charged for a full tank of gas. For every guest house stay, he'd been charged for meals at rates that must have included a pretty hefty profit for NTM. Every single day, every single meal, every single room, everything had been kept track of on the little paper ledgers and something deducted from Walter's account. More than a week in the guest house had bitten a nice chunk out of the funds Walter had raised for the construction projects they had back in America.

Walter was angry. He felt that he was being cheated somehow. The Numinohi leadership had told him he couldn't move into the apartment yet and they were the ones charging him high rates at the guest house. They had also told them they *had to* learn "Tok-Pisin" or Pidgin English, the local trade language of PNG, and had happily charged them a lot for books and mandatory lessons. It felt like a scam to him. He complained bitterly to Laura about it. Leadership just told them to send out more fund-raising letters to their supporters.

Something has to be understood about Leadership. In Christian missionary organizations, Leadership is not just another word for "management." Leadership does what "management" would do in a civilian organization, but in this kind of Christian organization, being in any kind of leadership position meant that a person was considered not just "in charge," but also more spiritually mature, more doctrinally correct, and more enlightened than those not in Leadership. Leadership was to live as a perfect example of proper behavior at all times, and was to be treated as spiritual authorities within the organization. If that all sounds just a bit creepy, you're on the right track.

Walter was stuck between a rock and a hard place now because he couldn't just "write another fundraising letter" to his supporters. He didn't have enough supporters.

FNTM and Walter had cut corners during the preparation for the trip. The NTM guidelines required that missionaries cover their own way completely with money raised from supporters back home. A family had to have enough supporters to cover their monthly expenses indefinitely. This was a good way to ensure that they had a good base of support that they could go back to if problems arose. Nothing drummed up the base like an "emergency" in some dark corner of the planet, and NTM was the direct beneficiary if something happened that called for a special fund-raising letter. For that reason, they were more than happy to provide all kinds of services to missionaries and charge everything to their accounts with the full knowledge that the missionaries could always just ask for more. It was kind of like having a stable full of milk cows that could be milked "so much" every couple of months. FNTM had an account in Misery where they collected and deposited the checks sent in by Walter's supporters. They turned this over to another account controlled by NTM, which was what Walter "signed against" every time they went to the general store or rented a van or spent a night in a guest house.

Unfortunately, the Franklins didn't have enough steady support to cover their monthly expenses. Walter and Rich had been so eager to get started on this Big Project here that they had had FNTM kick in their *own* funds, against normal missionary organization policy, to cover the difference between what Walter was able to raise and what the project would cost. Walter had made up a budget based on his estimate of what it would cost to build what they had come there to build and live along the way, but when it was gone, it was gone. That meant that they only had about half of the normal support network to write letters to. If the project started to cost more than projected, they would end up in trouble very quickly.

So, when NTM offered the use of a van to bring the family's bins all the way down the massive hill from the top to the very bottom, Walter demurred.

Jonah would carry them one by one across the mission base.

Numinohi was built in layers. It was a gigantic square, with dirt tracks running parallel to the Highlands Highway below, and dirt tracks running up and down the steep hill, forming a big grid. Each of the parallel "roads" sort of formed a layer, like steps going up a staircase. The lowest layer was right next to the main gate. Here, dust from supply trucks and the van fleet choked the air, and a huge "pickle pond" - the base's sewage treatment system - had been built logically enough at the lowest point on the property.

The general store was also here, and the combination of the flies from the big dumpsters behind the store, the smell from the pickle pond, and the dust from the van fleet area next to the main gate made this the least desirable area to live. As you went up the hill, things became "nicer" until you got up and all the way to the last row on the opposite corner of the huge square from the front gate where several of the Leadership and missionary families with the most support from really big and wealthy churches had built some pretty large two story houses that wouldn't be too out of place in Australia or maybe even the USA. The guest house was on the top row, about halfway to the "rich side."

The Franklins had been issued an apartment backed directly up to the pickle pond. It was the very last building wedged at the *absolute* bottom of the hill between the gate, the general store, and the sewage pond. It was also one of the very oldest buildings on the compound.

After hearing so much about malaria before coming, Jonah was a little alarmed to realize that his room didn't have a screen in the window, and the little glass window panes just turned like venetian blind and didn't actually close all the way. At least malaria was supposed to be less common up in the highlands.

In the bare, white apartment with the rickety walls through which you could hear everything people were saying at the general store across the street, the Franklins finally put down their plastic Wal-Mart bins. There was almost no furniture (most missionary families would have a container they had shipped from home that would arrive after they got there with furniture from their house). In that blank, sun-faded little apartment with the tin roof, their meager possessions looked pathetic as they tried to "unpack."

For Jonah, unpacking meant taking his books and notepads out of his bin, piling them in a stack on the bare floor, and converting the bin into a sort of grab-bucket "dresser" for clothes.

Leadership determined that Jonah and Amy were to attend the missionary school that dominated the other end of the "lower tier" of the base. Walter complained about the cost of that too, muttering something about "homeschooling," but it was charged to the account like everything else. When it came time to figure out what grade Jonah was supposed to be in now, there was a lot of back and forth. Jonah had been keeping track as best he could, and he thought that he should now be a senior in high school … at least he was pretty sure. The missionary school disagreed and since Jonah didn't have any transcripts from Blue Eye High, they were trying to place him as a sophomore (his last transcripts were from his freshman year in California).

It didn't help that Numinohi used Australian standards for academics, which made even translating grade point averages and comparing what courses were equivalent to which from an American school difficult.

In the end, after a hastily put together "placement exam" administered by one of the teachers, they all seemed to compromise and Jonah was admitted as a junior. He felt that he'd been done an injustice, and never forgave that school for it.

Amy went through a similar shuffle and ended up in the high school as a freshman. Always good with written tests, she had probably ended up a little ahead of her age group. Jonah was a little behind his.

Hayden was given a job in the print shop on base. Leadership did not agree with the idea of an able-bodied person over 18 years old living in a "family house" when they could be used elsewhere. Walter wanted to "keep the family together," and after more argument, she was allowed to stay with the Franklins and work in the Numinohi print shop for now.

The mission school was the ostensible reason for Numinohi's existence. It was a large school with a sports field and gymnasium and even a little library that had been built to accommodate the children of missionary couples that were embedded with a tribe somewhere deep in the "bush."

NTM generally paired up a missionary couple with a single small tribe, and they would remain with that tribe for years, arduously learning the totally undocumented local language, creating an alphabet for it from scratch, and translating the Bible into this new language, then teaching the tribe to read one at a time. Inevitably, kids would enter the picture, but most of these villages were not places really safe for little white kids to be living. Plus, NTM considered children a distraction that took missionary couples away from doing their mission work. When they were big enough to go to school, the missionary kids (called MKs by everyone at Numinohi) were shipped here to stay in dormitories and attend the school. They usually got to see their parents at the end of every semester or so.

Jonah was in a class full of MKs. These kids had literally grown up together in a dormitory on a little mission compound. They had been in class together since kindergarten for the most part. There were perhaps 2 or 3 kids in the class who hadn't literally done *every single grade* with the same little group of kids. It was very strange. They had their own slang, their own subculture, they understood one another almost without talking. It was like being brought into a gigantic group of siblings who had grown up in a little mountain village in a single family. By now, after Blue Eye High (which was a big city metropolis school compared to this) and everything else, Jonah was having a hard time even taking any of it seriously. The whole school seemed like some kind of cosmic joke to him.

Classes in Numinohi were small. Jonah's class only had about a dozen MKs total. These kids had been together from the time they'd been abandoned by their parents at 7 years old. They lived in dormitories that were run by "failed" missionaries. Missionary couples who had washed out, underperformed somehow, or fallen into permanent disfavor with Leadership were the ones relegated to the secondary task of looking after everyone else's children instead of going on to some remote village and fulfilling the "Great Work" that they had spent four years in missionary school preparing for. The dorms were run like a military barracks more or less, with bells indicating set times for morning prayer, homework, Bible study, free time, and bedtime for the MKs seven days a week.

If Jonah had to characterize the personality type nurtured by the MK dorms, it would be "human playdough." Inevitably, frustrated missionaries forced to stay behind on the logistics base instead of fulfilling their "Mission From God," looking after herds of broken, brainwashed kids did abuse them from time to time. Sexual and physical abuse, among other things, had already occurred in several NTM base MK dormitories by the time Jonah arrived in Numinohi. He didn't know about that at the time of course.

MKs were taken from their parents at age 7. They were expected not to cry, and they were expected to be self-sufficient as early as possible, in order to reduce the demands on the "dorm mom" and "dorm dad." Naturally, most of them carried around the psychological scars of kids growing up on a compound where their parents had long ago sacrificed them for the "mission." They were not the most stable bunch.

As a non-MK (not living in the dorms), Jonah was in the minority. The only other kids who lived with their families came from support team families who did something other than "real missionary" work (which made them second class citizens in NTM culture). Out of Jonah's entire class, only 3 of the students were not "real" MKs.

The boys in Jonah's class all lived in the boy's dorm, which was also the house of one of the richest of the missionary families. They all stayed together as a cluster at all times. At no point in the day would any of them ever be alone. They even went to the bathroom as a group. When they were relaxing between classes or sports activities, they would literally lie on one another in a pile in a way Jonah had never seen boys do before. The "hive mind" as he would take to calling them never even tried to let him make friends, not that Jonah was in any mood to make friends with anyone.

The girls all lived in the girls' dorm, and were somewhat less of a clingy collective consciousness than the boys, but on a mission base, girls and boys weren't supposed to talk to one another most of the time.

Between the massmind MKs, the constant barrage of propaganda, and the snitch culture of the mission base that encouraged everyone to turn in everyone else for suspected "backsliding," Jonah felt less like a student placed in a school whose job is to get an education than a piece of bacon placed in a skillet, whose job is to get thoroughly cooked.

That left Jonah with only one option when it came to friends. Mitch Andersen. A short, oddly proportioned kid with unusually large ears and crooked teeth, Mitch wasn't popular, but it had nothing to do with his appearance. He was not a "real" MK, because his dad worked as the chief mechanic for the small fleet of aircraft that NTM maintained to ferry missionaries back and forth to and from their remote locations back to the mission base. As a kid whose parents were actually present, Mitch was an outcast from the get go. He was treated like an afterthought by the rest of the class. Most of the MK boys acted like they didn't even notice that he existed. Mitch clung to Jonah like a drowning man clinging to a life preserver. He would literally follow Jonah around when the older boy took one of his frequent "walks" around the edge of the compound, invited or not.

Jonah and Mitch both had a similar sense of being total outcasts, and they also shared the fact that they had been exposed enough to regular secular culture to actually miss things like decent music.

Mitch, it turned out, was the ringleader of all illicit "black market" trading going on on the mission base. He specialized in cassette tapes recorded from the radio back in the USA or Australia filled with music that was "of the devil" and banned by Leadership. The first time Jonah ever heard Nirvana, he was hanging around with Mitch passing a Walkman back and forth the way normal kids his age might pass a doobie.

*Where do bad folks go when they die? They
don't go to heaven where the angels fly...
They go down to the lake of fire and fry. Won't
see 'em again till the fourth of July...*

"This is fucking *awesome*." Jonah couldn't help himself.

The younger kid was horrified. He laughed nervously. "Um... yeah..."

Jonah had just dropped the "F-bomb" in front of a kid who had spent most of his life on missionary compound.

That was where he lost Hayden.

22

RUBBISH LAND

When Leadership had come to Hayden to ask her "what can you do?" The 18-year-old had given them a steady stare and said; "I'm an artist."

The missionaries had been pretty taken aback at that. This mission base was kept running by the hard work of men (mostly local people hired for the purpose, not missionaries) who maintained the generator, fixed the well pumps, roofed the buildings, tended the injured in the clinic, and stood guard at the gate. It was like a 20th century pioneer outpost like Sutter's Fort, where Jonah had taken a school trip to in elementary school. Covered wagons and Indian attacks were much more apropos to this world than an *artist*.

Hayden was a Franklin kid though, and after living in upside-down-inside-out world for so long, she seemed to have just made peace with the fact that nothing ever made sense, nothing really mattered, and perhaps, nothing was really real anyway. She wasn't being flippant either, she had just logically replied with the set of skills she had developed the most.

Back in Oroville, Hayden had been sent to a summer program at an art college three years in a row (she kept getting full scholarships, or it would never have been an option for her). She had learned how to do illustrations, paint, draw from life, and use the kinds of tools an illustrator would be familiar with. That was the closest that *any* of the Franklin kids had come to a trade school or local college where they could get skills they could actually live on.

The missionaries pondered, and they decided that they could find a spot for her in the Numinohi print shop. "Artist" was pretty vague, and there was no particular demand for an "artist" at the moment, but they couldn't think of anyplace else to put her.

Jonah thought it was mildly funny how nobody ever mentioned the "building crew family, working as a team for God!" stuff ever again once they were done with their "donation pitch" to a church. Apparently Walter didn't want to even *try* to make Hayden work with him. Jonah had to guess that if he did, she would probably just sit down and refuse to move.

Numinohi operated somewhat like a weird colonial outpost. Missionaries, being "important spiritual leaders" and exemplars called by God for awesome and amazing Great Work, should not be burdened with the necessity of having their precious time wasted doing mundane things. Local people (undoubtedly privileged and awestruck by the *great honor* of having the missionaries among them) did all the stuff nobody else wanted to do on the base. They dug the ditches, unloaded the trucks, ran the generator, operated the pump house, and even guarded the front gates. Mundane work was considered "worldly" and not to be focused on by people committed to "spiritual things."

This, of course, caused an immediate problem for Walter with Leadership because they couldn't comprehend why someone would be sent from the USA to do the "unimportant stuff" that they just hired locals to do for pennies.

Considering the things on which all of their lives depended day in and day out "unimportant" had led to a sanitation crisis on the mission compound. The "pickle pond" behind the Franklins apartment could only handle the sewage from about half of the population of the base. The rest of the residences dumped sewage directly into a drainage ditch where it made its way into the Mat river, from which several local villages drew water for drinking.

By some kind of cosmic coincidence, the water table in the area was getting worse fast, and there had been outbreaks of dysentery and hepatitis even on the mission base, because their well water was now tainted. Such things were not a concern for "real missionaries" who concentrated on spiritual matters. If local labor wasn't good enough to solve some problem of engineering, then it was probably a luxury they didn't need anyway. As soon as Walter began to investigate the base infrastructure, he told Laura to boil every drop of water the family drank. They did this the entire time they were on the compound.

In the Print shop, there was one person who worked, and at least three who "managed" the shop and spent their time concentrating on spiritual matters. A local man named Panani ran the presses in the hot and noisy print room. Two or three missionaries manned the counter of the shop, trading mission base gossip.

None of them really wanted Hayden there.

Hayden, thinking in similar terms to Walter, considered their time on the base to be time they needed to be spending working on physical tasks, not whatever the missionaries did for most of their day. This attitude actually led to trouble with some of the locals, who, very much like a labor union in the USA, didn't like white "scabs" taking spots that could potentially be handed out to friends and relatives as a favor. In Hayden's case, this was less of an issue than Walter, since nobody could imagine a local drawing up postcards, coloring books, and letterhead for missionaries who wanted to spice up their monthly support letters.

When the "scab" situation was explained to Walter and Laura, they agreed to hire a "house Meri" - a local woman who would work as a housekeeper - in order to reduce the political tension caused by Walter's "support missionary" status.

Ironically, the Franklin family now found itself in a situation where their fundraising base was not adequate for even regular needs and they had actually hired a housekeeper to help maintain the tiny little bare apartment, just to ameliorate the pressure from the local "mafia" and missionary Leadership. As always, Laura put a happy face on and smiled through the worry, boiling up water for her family to drink every day, going with her "house Meri" to get fruits and vegetables from the local market, and scrounging whatever could be had at the general store for the family to eat.

Food was a problem that just got worse every month. The staple of anybody who was hard up for cash was "tinpis" (tin-fish, or fish from a tin) and rice. It was sort of like tuna from a can, mixed with rice with whatever anyone could scrounge for a "sauce."

Sometimes the odd, tangy type of Australian mayonnaise from the general store was all they had to give it some flavor. Fruit was cheap and extraordinarily good. New Guinea pineapples were the best fruit Jonah ever tasted in his life, and nothing at all like what you could get in the USA. The bananas were vastly better than American ones too, and there was mango and papaya in plenty.

Unfortunately, a teenage boy could not subsist on just fruit. The Franklins were starving for protein after only a few weeks. Jonah, at an age where a teenage boy is like a human eating machine under any circumstances, really suffered. For months, he desperately foraged for anything he could put in his mouth, eating sections of sugar cane local vendors would sell for a "penny" just to get some energy. It got worse after the cravings subsided and he no longer felt like he was starving. He found his body going lethargic after what used to be normal amounts of exertion. His cheekbones became prominent. His face looked hard and too sharp.

Years later, looking through old pictures at his own face on the way back from PNG, he was amazed at how little it looked like the young man who had gone over. He had to be at least 20 pounds lighter, and almost looked like he'd been in some kind of prison camp.

Jonah and Amy did their best to get used to the mission school. It was actually a fairly decent school considering the circumstances. The one thing in ready supply on that mission base in the highlands of Papua New Guinea was a lot of overeducated white people from all over the world with too much time on their hands. The high school had some advanced classes in anthropology for instance, that would be hard to find outside of a college in the USA. Obviously, academic curiosity was pretty much Jonah's lowest priority.

While kids back in the states were getting in trouble for staying out too late with their friends, Jonah was pacing the perimeter of a mission compound like a caged animal. While they were trying to get away with "buzzed driving" and going to parties, he was sitting on a folding metal chair in a concrete block "gymnasium" for mandatory church sessions. They couldn't go out because they had been grounded for doing stupid teenager stuff, he couldn't go out after dark because "Raskol" gang members patrolled the outer perimeter fence looking for opportunities and would happily kidnap a white kid for ransom. Kids in America were making out in the back of their car, Jonah was watching the bizarre activity the MKs called "coupling" and feeling like he'd landed on an alien planet.

"Coupling" was something that the MK teenagers seemed to use as a stand in for dating. Through the sibling twin-like communication that had evolved over a lifetime of growing up together in dormitories, but was too subtle for Jonah to catch, a pair of MKs would decide they wanted to "couple."

They would both move from their normal seats in the boys massmind or the girl flock, and would sit next to one another during free time. After school, during the hour and a half after "homework time" and before "Bible study" time, the "couple" would meet up at a precise time, usually somewhere near the gym, and would proceed to walk around the missionary compound holding hands. The regimented nature of dorm life left them with little time, so it was not uncommon to have a literal parade of "coupling" teenagers walking two by two up the dirt road, as they did slow laps around the compound, one after the other.

After a week or so, the couples would split up, and pretty much everybody in the tiny class would do "coupling" with someone else. Since there were only a dozen kids in total, each of the MKs had "coupled" with each of the opposite sex kids in their class probably dozens of times. There was never any crossover either, seniors never "coupled" with juniors or vice versa.

Jonah just sat there on the steps of the gym looking on in horror as the procession would line up after school, listening to his "of the devil" music on Mitch's (borrowed) Walkman. The Crash Test Dummies was his favored soundtrack to accompany the sight of parading "coupling" MKs walking in twos around and around and around the base.

> *"They shook and lurched all over the church floor… He couldn't quite explain it, they'd always just… gone there… "*

Jonah had been sure that he was a freak for a long time now. He didn't know if maybe everyone here were *also* freaks … maybe it just didn't matter.

There was no telling what might happen at any moment on the compound. The place was like a cage with way too many animals stuffed inside it. People got neurotic. They all started to get this kind of crazy, desperate look on their faces after a few months. Even old missionaries would just randomly snap at one another in public out of nowhere. People all tried to keep in their "officially sanctioned work areas" during the day and their houses at night, avoiding seeing the same faces every single day all day forever. Weird things would happen without warning, and since everyone was constantly trying to put on a demeanor of being the *most* happy and perfect Christian, the lead up to some interpersonal drama would be invisible and the result would be immediately buried.

All you would see is random arguments breaking out between otherwise totally placid looking people where they suddenly took on the rabid countenance of chickens pecking one of their own flock to death, then they would all return to work, happy as Smurfs.

That was why Jonah wasn't even surprised when Hayden's boss from the print shop came up to their apartment door one Saturday, his face a visage of inhuman rage, banging on the door like a madman and screaming for Hayden.

Apparently there had been an entire saga surrounding Hayden's art she'd been doing for the print shop. She had taken the initiative and started drawing pictures of Papuans in their ceremonial dress-up "bilas" (decorations) which usually consisted of shells, bones, feathers, and colored clay-based face paint turned into frightening or interesting looking costumes. Images of natives in "dress up" costumes were candy for National Geographic and missionary family monthly newsletters both, and everybody appreciated a new source of them.

Very quickly, when the missionaries had discovered that she could do some nice looking drawings, more and more requests had rolled in from various quarters of the mission compound for airmail envelopes, letterhead, and even a coloring book. Missionaries, focused as they were on "spiritual matters" and not the daily chores that kept everyone alive, had a lot of time on their hands at Numinohi.

Weird fads would suddenly sweep the compound, like the year one of the MKs had had a motocross style dirt bike shipped from the USA, which had *demanded* that every high school age boy have one in order to keep up. Once one of the missionary families had custom designed support letter illustrations, they all wanted them, and very quickly, Hayden found herself swamped.

Hayden, by now somewhat like an MK herself, found it impossible to say no, and so she quickly was overloaded in the inevitable result of trying to make something people actually *want* in a perfect Communist economy where you don't get paid no matter how much you work. It all became too much for her, and she had simply stopped going to work, saying that she "quit," and refusing to leave her room.

When Hayden left, she'd taken the original drawings that she had done that had sparked the entire missionary feeding frenzy. That was why the print shop "boss" was banging on the Franklins' door like a madman. He said the drawings belonged to the print shop and she had "stolen" them.

Walter told the guy something and sent him away without seeing Hayden, then he went to Hayden's room and told her that she was going to have to talk to the man and she couldn't just hide in her room forever.

Eventually, it was arranged that Hayden would take the originals back to the print shop and let them make master copies, and she would be left alone from the endless demands for tribal illustrations from the missionary families.

Of course, Hayden couldn't just stay in her room forever.

There was a guy with a lot of pull at NTM who had single handedly set up another mission base nearby. It was called ITF (short for "Interface"). This newer, smaller base was inside the exclusive territory of a tribe that had negotiated with the missionaries to host their base (which would mean a lot of money and side benefits to the tribe) in return for an agreement whereby the tribe guaranteed the security of the missionaries on the land, so they didn't need to put up a fence at all.

NTM set up a "missionary college" training course there, where people could come out to get fired up for real field work; sort of like a more elaborate version of Mt Promise. Without a fence, the mission personnel would get much more interaction with local people, and the local tribe was able to still move freely across the area. James Hartford was the man behind ITF. He was a professorial type from Canada with some significant backing both at the NTM board level and in terms of money.

James was impressed enough with Hayden's work to want her to come out and work at ITF full time. In fact, he even offered a salary (she'd been working pro-bono at the Numinohi print shop). James was in the process of a big book project, and he needed illustrations. Hayden agreed.

Jonah got a very welcome break from the surreal weirdness of the high school to go out to drop Hayden off at the nearby ITF base. He was happy just to get away from the "hivemind" for a while, even though he was leery about Hayden disappearing into no-man's land, PNG.

Walter wasn't concerned, it seemed.

They coordinated with some missionaries that were making the trip to ITF for other reasons, which cut down on the logistical challenges. They would all go up in one of the 4 door 4WD pickup trucks that were kept on hand at Numinohi for carrying supplies here and there.

The day was sunny. Unusually, there wasn't a massive rainstorm that afternoon as was typical in the highlands of PNG pretty much all year round. Jonah actually felt pretty good, just being away from the compound for a moment, even if they were traveling the roads of one of the more dangerous countries for travelers on the planet. The driver was an experienced missionary who had made the trip many times. Jonah actually felt himself relax as he sat in the bed of the 4 door Toyota pickup. He wondered why they didn't sell little 4 door pickups like this in the USA, because they seemed very practical (At the time, they didn't. It took several more years before compact 4 door pickups could be found stateside).

Gerald, their driver, was a pragmatic Aussie who demonstrated a competence with a 4WD in slippery mud that would make some rally car drivers jealous. He was keenly aware of the many dangers of the Highlands Highway, where hitting a pig that had strayed into the road may lead to a swarm of angry tribal warriors with machetes pulling passengers out of a car and taking out the price of that pig's value in terms of human limbs. It had happened before. Pigs were more valuable than people in the highlands.

Unfortunately, today was not their day. The road into ITF from the paved Highlands Highway was a switchback trail cut into the slippery clay of several hillsides, and despite the lack of rain that day, one shadowy, low point was a morass of liquid clay with a the consistency of tapioca pudding. The Toyota slowed, drifted sideways as it tried to get traction with any tire, and finally buried itself up to the underbody in the muck.

Jonah sighed. He had been in PNG long enough to have brought a change of shoes with him. There was no way he was going to jump out to help push in his new set of black Converse. He quickly undid the laces of the Converse, threw them in the bed of the truck with the cargo they were bringing in, and pulled on his older, ripped pair.

As soon as the truck got stuck, tribal people had appeared from over a ridge overlooking the road. They had probably been waiting there, knowing that any vehicle that tried to get down that road would find this particular spot impassible. They just stood up from where they had been crouching behind some bushes overlooking the road from a ridge. There was no way to see them from below until they decided to move, and they knew it. Later in life, learning small unit tactics as an infantryman, Jonah would learn how to set up an ambush. That was probably the best spot you could ever get.

The short, dark skinned, bearded men swarmed down the hill like ants. Each had a machete and a "Kilaman" spear (a spear designed to kill a man) in his hands. Jonah looked up from the bed of the truck at the ridge, not yet really having time to process what was happening. Walter was in the passenger seat, Gerald was driving, Hayden and Amy were in the back seats. These tribal guys could drop him with one of those spears at any time from their elevated position, and they were down and to the doors of the pickup before anybody else could even exit the vehicle. Technically, Jonah could have made a run for it, but he'd have little chance on territory controlled by this tribe, where they knew every hill and boulder. If the tribals wanted to harm them, they were dead.

The locals were from the friendly tribe that protected the ITF "compound." They immediately climbed down the slope and started finding corners of the truck to push on, with the air of people who had pushed a whole lot of trucks out of this particular mudhole. Jonah wasn't sure if he was expected to get out, but he saw Walter do so, so he also climbed out over the tailgate and lent his strength to the task, sinking almost to his knees in the liquefied clay. With so many hands shoving, the truck was able to get traction again and start up the slope until it got into the dryer mud, and the "road crew" smiled and waved, letting them go.

For a few moments, Jonah thought about what nice tribal guys those were, until he looked around for his Converse. They were gone. Apparently, he'd paid the "toll" for passage. Even though almost no locals ever wore shoes or could even fit normal shoes on their feet (which were very wide from a lifetime of being barefoot), shoes were worth good money in Goroka. Somebody got himself enough beer to get drunk on and enough Betelnut (a nut the locals chewed sort of like chewing tobacco that gave a pretty strong buzz and made them spit huge streams of reddish saliva that would actually stain a paved road like paint) to get a nice high on. Jonah kicked himself for leaving them where someone could just grab them out of the truck. He'd carried that pair of new shoes all the way from the USA, unworn in the box, and only started wearing them at school here. God only knew where he'd get a replacement.

ITF was actually quite lovely. Unlike Numinohi, it was not an ugly, industrial looking pile of chain link, tin roofs, and cheap concrete block walls. ITF was a combination of Western and native architecture. It was like a campground, with lots of cabins, but they were made up using some local materials, like the woven grass called "pit-pit" that was used to make local huts, surrounding more conventional wood walls and rafters. The combination made ITF look like a picturesque garden spot. It was a rolling expanse of vibrant green grass, shady trees, and a quaint looking collection of buildings.

Jonah felt a sense of foreboding. He didn't like the idea of leaving Hayden here. He had scoffed at Walter's "we have to keep the family together" sentiments when they had first arrived in PNG, but now, he felt that like a broken watch, Walter could say something "dad-like" at least *once in a while*. This was a mistake. Hayden was an 18-year-old girl. She had no useful experience with anything at all, barely any useful skills, no way of assessing what normality was, no preparation for being on her own. She was not the kind of person you could just drop somewhere and expect them to survive.

Jonah was the younger brother, but he felt a sense of protectiveness toward the only true friend he'd been able to hold on to through years and years of moves, changes, instability, and insanity. The only person in the entire world that he felt would actually understand him, who *could* possibly understand where he was coming from was now going off to some indoctrination ("training") facility. It just didn't feel right.

The 16-year-old stayed next to Hayden as she got her stuff out of the truck and started happily chatting with some missionaries. He looked like a bodyguard, escorting her around, until she got annoyed and told him to let her get her stuff set up in her cabin alone. Jonah relented. He didn't know what to say. He didn't know what he was supposed to do. He just didn't want to lose his only real friend.

Before the truck was due to pull out and head back to Numinohi, Hayden caught up with her kid brother as he sat on one of the outdoor bench tables set up around the ITF campus. He was depressed. This was all wrong somehow, and the beauty of the place and sense of peacefulness just made Jonah's danger sense spike even more. Amy had said the same thing; "Don't let Hayden go." But Amy was living in a world where Dad still had much of anything to say about their fate.

Now their lives were all in the hands of Leadership, and honestly, considering how Dad had been doing, maybe that was for the best.

"Look, Hayden, don't…" Jonah didn't know what he was going to say. "… don't … believe the crap." He meant, *"Don't drink the kool aid"*.

The thin teenager slouched forward, kicking out her own Converse. She rolled her eyes at her brother as if to say, "Me? I would *never* drink the Kool aid!" But she only said, "I'll be okay."

Jonah looked around at the peaceful tranquility of the place. He just knew something wasn't right. He was like a dog that sensed danger for his master but could not comprehend the complexity of the danger. Just as a dog has no understanding of traffic signals, Jonah didn't know how brainwashing on a cult compound worked. How isolation affects human psychology, how much his sister actually relied on *him* for strength. None of it was clear to him then. All he knew was that he had to stay with Hayden until the very last minute they had to go.

Like a guard dog, he did. He came at the last minute, jumping into the pickup truck to go back to Numinohi, feeling like he'd lost something important. Hayden and Jonah hadn't really talked much for a while now, but they had at least known that the other was *there*. Now, Jonah was completely alone.

23

JERRY'S BOYS

For most of the Missionaries and MKs on the compound, the real challenge day by day was time. Missionaries spent their time in chosen "important," "spiritual" work while leaving mundane tasks to hired "nationals." This left them with a lot of time on their hands, so they had become expert at cultivating time-consuming hobbies like growing orchids in elaborate greenhouses behind their house. For MKs, despite the regimented nature of their lives, the challenge was similar. Like inmates in a prison, one readily available outlet that was always available was sports.

Weightlifting, wrestling, basketball, baseball, rugby- they did it all. The entire school year was a cycle of sport tryouts, short "seasons", and moving on to the next one. Games were arranged against at least two other missionary schools in PNG; a very large Catholic mission base that was bigger and wealthier than Numinohi (and usually won the tournaments), and a Baptist mission school base that Numinohi could usually beat. With literally no other outlet, the boys spent almost all of their time training for the next tryout.

The ringleader of all this activity was Gerald Czernecki, a short, broad man universally known as just "Jerry." Gruffly cheerful (in a forced kind of way) in public, Jerry was rarely ever seen around the base, but was universally known. He ostensibly did something "support related" with the vehicle fleet at Numinohi, and (much more importantly) was the missionary in PNG with the single biggest support network. Whatever group of churches had sent Jerry to PNG, they were big and they were *generous*. His support letters were professional, glossy, well put together, like magazines, outlining plenty of desperate "needs," and boy did his supporters ever come through.

Jonah remembered watching in awe as Jerry supervised the installation of a satellite dish on the top of his massive, 2 story house that looked like something from an American suburb. It was the single biggest, fanciest, and best made house on the compound, situated right at the top of the hill with the best view and the greatest distance from the odoriferous "pickle pond." The satellite dish was revolutionary not only because it represented an incredible amount of effort and money in that place, but because it also flew in the face of the prevailing "TV is of the devil" sentiment. On the entire compound, there were probably only 2 or 3 TVs outside the school.

Jerry got away with it because Jerry was the wealthiest guy on the base. He was permanently wired into Leadership, and they gave him what he wanted. He had a close relationship with Mr. Lawrence, the head of Leadership itself. Everyone just pretended not to notice the six-foot-wide wire contraption on his roof.

Jerry had a son in Jonah's class. He was a big, well filled out kid showing none of the signs of malnutrition during development that Mitch and some of the other missionary kids did. Danny was a sandy-blonde kid with the soft, unintelligent eyes of a cow and almost a baby face, but he was also the son of the richest guy in "town." He was inseparable from four of the MK boys who spent more time in Jerry's house than in the MK dorm. Jerry had "his" boys up in that house a lot of the time, and he was pretty generous with them.

One week a shipping container arrived at his house and the MK boys spent all day unloading it. There were no less than four motocross bikes in there; the newest, latest, most powerful kind. Jerry's boys spent much of the rest of the year buzzing up and down and up and down the main road of the base on those things, annoying the hell out of the rest of the compound.

Jonah couldn't help being jealous of the "Jerry's boys." He had no idea about the sort of abuses that happened in some MK dormitories, but he thought he could probably understand what it might be like to effectively lose your parents at 7 years old. He could probably have handled that. All he knew now was that the MK boys were all driving around on motorcycles and he was walking in an old, torn, hopelessly dirty pair of Converse because his new ones had gone to get some enterprising villager high for a day. They were feasting on American style food that Jerry had flown in from the States or Australia while he was coming home to "tinpis and rice" and pomelo fruit dinners. He had actually seen some of Jerry's boys standing on his porch rail with *real* coke cans in their hands! Real coke cans like you saw in the *USA*, not the weird, heavy, funny-tab ones with the strange tasting local "Coke" that he might be able to afford once a week at most.

Jerry's boys were together all the time and they weren't interested in talking to a kid who lived right next to the pickle pond and had to walk everywhere because he didn't have a dirt bike. While Danny was the "ringleader," the real ace in the hole for the group (and Jerry) was a local boy named Beezo.

Beezo was the son of the tribal leader who owned the "rest stop" across the street from the missionary base. He had pull with Bena Bena tribal leaders who determined whether NTM could continue to use the side of the hill whose name translated as "Rubbish Land" in their language. This leader was the guy who "hired" the gate guards for Numinohi. That meant that he could determine which local people could go into the base to work at jobs vastly more lucrative than anything available in the rest of the Highlands, and which could not. It went without saying that a little piece of absolutely *everything* that went on around there came to him. He was the one who had been disturbed by Walter coming as a support missionary to build things, because that might mean less jobs for his tribal people (which he handed out as political favors in return for loyalty). Beezo was basically a prince. Part of the deals that had been made between the Bena Bena tribe and NTM involved letting Beezo and his sister attend the MK school all the way through graduation and get a Western education. He had basically grown up with Dave, and the two were inseparable.

Jerry knew that his son's best friend was a direct line to the most important man in the area. It gave him a lot of pull with Leadership, and that, in turn, let him set up his little castle, do virtually nothing all day, and skirt the rules everyone else had to live under.

None of that was really Jonah's concern until he decided that in the timeless pressure cooker of the missionary base, he had to do *something*, and decided to try out for the sports teams. Getting the chance to visit other missionary bases for away games was a great draw, not to mention the fact that guys who were good at sports were idolized.

The next tryout coming up was baseball. Jonah had never really liked playing baseball that much, but he was competent, and he had never encountered any sport that he couldn't be at least competitive in by applying himself. He had no reason to think he wouldn't make it through a tryout, particularly with the small number of boys in his class. He'd always been able to just pick up a sport and play it pretty well. If he didn't like it much, it was just more work.

Jonah didn't know that the team had already been determined before the tryout.

Jonah was surprised at a couple things the morning of the tryout. He didn't know that Mr. Lawrence (the head of Leadership) was actually the main coach at the high school. That made him just a bit nervous. Mr. Lawrence always had a strange, fanatic gleam in his eye and wore a carefully trimmed moustache that just made him look a bit creepy. He was basically the Lord of the Base, and Walter had already run afoul of him more than once by now, which couldn't possibly help Jonah's chances to impress him.

There had already been rain that morning. The sky had opened in the particular way it did in the tropics where one moment it would be sunny and the next, the very air would fill with heavy, massive drops of bathwater warm rain. It would come down so hard and so fast that sheets of water like waterfalls would stand at an angle out from the ends of the tin roofs of the compound buildings. The mud streets of the compound would become rivers instantly, water pouring down the main street down the hill like a flash flood, often over a foot deep even on that steep slope. There was literally no way to shed water fast enough for it not to stand on things like rooftops and streets. Walking through it (which ended up being the only option) was like trying to breathe in an aerated mass of churning surf. The idea of an umbrella was preposterous when it really came down. You just accepted that you would be soaked, but it was so warm that it didn't really matter that much.

The grass field behind the school had collected the morning's rain, and now, though the sun was coming out to turn the puddles into wisps of rising steam all over the base, at least four inches of water stood like a pond across half the field.

Mr. Lawrence was setting up the tryout. He wore mud boots. Smiling with a nasty glint in his eye, he trudged out to the part of the field where constant standing water and wear and tear had left slippery clay mud exposed like craters on a moonscape. He started dropping rubber bases, laying out a baseball diamond.

Jonah was counting the boys who had showed up for the tryout. He'd expected at least a couple more… it looked like they had exactly *one* too many for the spots for the team. He frowned. The other boys had all arrived as a group, in fact, it looked like Mr. Lawrence had driven them down here in a van with all the equipment. They were all lined up, sitting on a bench, putting on cleat shoes. Behind them, sitting on the steps of the school and watching the field were most of the girls in his class.

Jonah felt a sinking feeling. What were the chances the mission base would have cleats to share with a kid who wanted to be part of the team?

Obviously, in America, you could say, "show up with this and that equipment for the tryout" and reasonably expect high school students to do so. Even there, you might make exceptions for a student whose family was really hard up. Here, there was literally nowhere in the *country* to buy sports gear, and there had been no announcement other than "baseball tryout is this time and place."

Well, he had come here to try out and that was what he was going to do. When the whistle blew and Mr. Lawrence called the boys out to the baseball diamond, Jonah lined up with them.

Mr. Lawrence watched the line of boys standing almost to their ankles in muddy water. He stood in his mud boots, his baleful, cold stare reserved for Jonah. It was clear who was not supposed to be here.

The man with the dirty looking mustache blew the whistle one more time, then barked out; "Okay! Run the bases! Go, go, go!"

And they started running bases.

Jonah realized within a few steps that this was going to be literally impossible. He was still wearing the only shoes he had; worn out Converse sneakers. The bottoms were like two flat pieces of ice on the grease like clay. He pumped his legs, literally sliding one way then the other like a race car trying to make a turn on a dirt track, missing a base by an inch, throwing up mud and water behind him as he went. One of Jerry's boys, stable on his cleats, passed him up like he was walking.

"SLOW! Jonah! You are too slow!"

Jonah got mad. He had never met a physical challenge he could not push through with a combination of will, his physical prowess, and the boiling rage he always carried inside him every moment of every day. He was NOT going to let these guys get around him! He was *not* going to be the slowest guy here, even if he was the only one who didn't have cleats! He accelerated, pumping his legs faster and faster. He was literally skating around the grease-slick field like someone trying to sprint on ice, barely keeping himself upright, honed in on the next base like a laser beam, then the next … he slid, he slipped, he righted himself, he caught a base with his hands and scrambled to change direction…

"TOO SLOW! Jonah! You are *too slow!* YOU ARE GOING TO HAVE TO CUT THAT TIME!"

Jonah growled as he literally coasted sideways while running in a perpendicular direction toward the next base like a rally car drifting around a curve. He was totally covered in mud, more boys were passing him now. He tried to speed up even more and without warning he was on his back, the wind knocked out of his lungs, covered in mud from head to foot.

There was a laugh.

"Out of my way, Franklin!" Dave gave him a shove as he went by.

"Out of my way, Franklin!" Echoed one of Dave's sycophants.

Jonah was back on his feet. He mercilessly shouldered between two of the boys, knocking one out of his way, fighting to get back into the line to get to the next base.

"YOU. ARE. TOO. SLOW. FRANKLIN!" Mr. Lawrence bellowed. "You have 30 seconds to make time or you are getting cut!"

Jonah fought it out. He savagely grabbed the muddy shirt of one of Jerry's boys as he tried to dance past, running for everything he was worth on the slick mud. He dug his toes into the mud however he could, ran at angles to his intended direction of travel, and used twice as much effort as every other boy on the field. He was keeping up. His lungs were on fire, his legs were numb, he couldn't see because of the mud and water in his eyes, the world was reduced to a tunnel and mud covered base in the center, another tunnel and another base … but he was keeping up.

Mr. Lawrence looked mad.

"You have one more minute to cut that time or you are OUT, Franklin!" He wasn't even watching any of the other boys.

Jonah couldn't hold it. He was careening, almost out of control, barely able to stay upright, trying to use the bases themselves to help him change direction as they ran. Eventually his legs went completely out from under him as he hit home base and he slid face down across about ten feet of ice-slick muddy grass.

"THAT'S *IT*! You are *OUT*, Franklin! *Go home!*"

Jerry's boys laughed again.

It seemed that Jonah was not going to be on the baseball team.

He heard them stop running bases as he carefully got himself upright and began to stiffly move down the field. He didn't look at anyone, just pointing himself toward his little house next to the pickle pond and putting one foot in front of the other. He looked like he had been mud wrestling.

"Okay, boys, let's do some batting practice…"

Jonah worked to catch his breath as he walked down the muddy road to his house. He didn't look at anyone, and if anybody was curious about his appearance, they didn't say anything. Blessedly, he was allowed to get back to his house without having to try to talk to anyone.

Jonah ducked into the apartment, checking to see if his mom was there so he could avoid her, and finding it mercifully empty. He took off the sodden Converse on the porch, but still left a trail of mud from his socks as he went directly to the bathroom to strip and get in the shower.

At dinner that night, Laura asked if he would be going to practices now.

"Nah." The teenager shrugged noncommittally, not looking up from his plate. "I'm not really into sports right now. I don't want to play baseball." He didn't say anything else about it.

Some people might have asked their parents for the right gear. Jonah knew better. Back in 7th grade, in Fairfield, California shortly after they had moved into the house Laura grew up in, he had decided he wanted to try out for the soccer team at school. Later, Jonah would realize that he was ideally built for football, but not made well for sprint-heavy games like basketball or soccer, but he had worked so hard at the tryout that the coach had been impressed. He liked the way Jonah would find a way to give a little more no matter how hard things got, and how seriously he took the practice. The coach had let him know that to be on the team, he had to have shin guards. Passing that information on to Dad was hard at the time. The kids hid from him when he came home to avoid a Wrath. He was perpetually stressed out about his job and angry.

Eventually, Jonah had managed to do it, after a couple practices where he'd sort of skirted by without having them. The coach wanted Jonah to be on the team so much that he had even had him running the side of a field to keep up with the ball during the first game they had played as a "flag man" or something, to "show where the ball is." He simply could not put Jonah in unless he had shin guards.

Jonah began to realize he would never get them, even after reminding his parents about it and getting vague promises. He'd ended up quitting the team out of embarrassment. That had been the year his dad bought a *sailboat*. On a mission base in the middle of Papua New Guinea, there was absolutely no point in asking for anything like that.

Sports teams were now not really an option for Jonah. Mr. Lawrence was the coach for every sport, and Jerry's boys were the team for every sport. It seemed to just be the way things were there. That left him with no way to ever get off the base.

Travel in the highlands of PNG is not done lightly. Even today, one does not simply use public transport or casually drive across the country. Papua New Guinea is on US State Department warning lists even today. During the day, the Highlands Highway was a rutted, sinkhole-dotted mess of broken pavement and random pigs, dogs, and people darting out from the side of the road. If a pig or a person were hit, the villagers from nearby were very likely to suddenly form a lynch mob, pull out the driver, and machete them to death on the spot. Dogs nobody cared about. The locals thought of them like mildly more useful rats, and they even ate them when food got short.

At night, travel was worse. Heavily armed criminal "Raskol" gangs with assault rifles would set up roadblocks and stop cars. They would rape the women, kill the men, and take anything not bolted down before disappearing back into the bush. Generally, even experienced missionaries tried never to travel at night under any circumstances.

So, they remained on the compound, surrounded by the chain link fence like prisoners, smelling the sickly-sweet smell of village fires all around and looking out at the most vivid green hills imaginable beyond the fence.

Walter was caught up in one of his projects. He'd started with building some dorms in Numinhohi, fallen in with a couple other "support missionaries" who had also been tradesmen back home and gotten into a slow motion political war with Leadership over the state of the sewage and water systems on the base, and now had gotten caught up with some kind of side project involving a sawmill that saw him off-base most of the time. He'd written back home about the awful tool situation on base (Numinohi had a very limited number of power tools and actually charged by the hour to use them at rates that would quickly bankrupt most building projects) and Rich, back at FNTM had gotten together a bunch of supporters from local churches and actually managed to organize a support container to be shipped out.

Jonah was surprised to hear that they were going to receive a container. Shipping containers were typically used by missionaries to send their furniture from home, things that were too big to try to bring through check in, and lots of stuff that made life easier and more comfortable, from washing machines to flats of real canned coke. Usually, a container would come in after a lot of planning, and it would be a big affair. Neighbors would come out to watch it be unloaded, and a general air of celebration would set in at the missionary house it had come to. Since a lot of the costs of a shipping container were standard regardless of the weight (within certain weight categories) it made sense to literally pack them completely with as much stuff as would fit.

For once, Jonah felt a mild sense of hope. Rich had organized a container from the USA? Local churches had helped? His stomach rumbled at the thought of what they might have loaded in there. Even canned soup would be so much better than "tinpis and rice!" Maybe they had thought to send a new pair of shoes! Maybe some furniture for their utterly bare apartment! He fought against his rising hope when Walter called for him to come out and help like a foreman calling a laborer on a job site. Missionary-addled church people in Missouri? They were liable to put all kinds of things in a support shipment! He saw a similar hope beginning to show on Laura's face as well.

Walter ran his "crew" like a foreman, organizing the dropping of the container from a big truck the base kept on hand for the purpose. He was frustrated. Apparently, NTM was going to charge him a lot to "drop" the container, even though he had insisted that "he" (his family/crew) could do it "himself." He'd only wanted to pay for the time and gas for the truck. NTM was also going to charge for "storage" of the container, even though they were dropping it in the corner of an unused field. Caught up in these concerns, he was curt as he worked to open the big metal doors.

Jonah couldn't help himself. He leaned in behind Walter as the first lever of the metal doors was thrown. Would there be canned food in there? Did he dare hope that someone might have thought to throw a football or a basketball in on top? Books were too much to ask for. At this point, he would read a phonebook for fun. He knew better than to ever hope that some sympathetic teen supporter would record "real music" off the radio and plant a mix tape in there.

The big doors creaked open. Walter stood up, frowning. He looked troubled. Laura put a hand to her mouth, then looked down. Jonah stepped forward, stepping into the mouth of the gaping black space as if to verify by touch what his eyes told him.

The huge container gaped like a black cave under the tropical sun. A wave of grease smell emanated from it. Dust formed columns of sunlight from a couple bolt holes in the side.

It was empty.

Jonah looked down. No, it wasn't empty; Dad's tools had been hastily piled up in the center of the twenty-foot space in sort of a heap. The tools Walter had collected during his lifetime in construction were considered Holy Objects in the Franklin household. The first lesson the kids remembered was "Do not touch that!" The tools had usually lived near the entrance or the living room whenever they had lived in an apartment. They were almost a silent fourth sibling; a permanent presence they all had gotten used to.

Dad knew every inch of every tool, and he knew exactly how he had dumped them on the floor of the living room too. If you had so much as bumped a power tool, he would notice. A heavy-duty framing hammer would always be kept leaned against the wall next to the front door of wherever they lived as a brutally primitive security system.

The collection had been added to with the death of Laura's mother. Her dad's tools had joined the rest. Laura's father had been a welder and something of a handyman, and he had some antique tools including a brace-and-bit and some hand saws that went back to the 1800s. All of it had been loaded into that trailer Uncle Boone had donated and driven out to Misery, breaking the trailer's axle on the way. It had all been left in the storage room in FNTM with the worldly possessions that the Franklins could not fit into Wal-Mart bins. Now it was sitting here, piled in a heap in the middle of a massive, empty 20-foot container that could have held an entire house full of furniture on top without a problem.

Amy had come up behind them for the grand opening. "What? Why didn't they put *my* stuff in there? It was stacked right next to the tools."

Laura was peering around from behind Jonah. "Did they put any kitchen stuff in there?"

Jonah was looking around inside the container, stepping lightly over the randomly strewn tools. "Is there any *food* in here?"

"Shut up!" Walter's comment was directed at everyone generally. "Come on, let's get this unloaded!" He seemed doubly irritated that he was going to be charged to drop a basically empty container and that *his* tools were now in Papua New Guinea when he had left them safely back at home. He had wanted *tools* from Rich, not *his* tools sent to a place from which it would be extremely hard to ever get them back!

Jonah found it baffling that nobody had asked the family if they had any needs before this thing had been sent. It seemed that Walter had known about it before anyone else. Maybe he had just neglected to mention anything other than *his* immediate needs for the "Big Thing" he was working on. It seemed like a reasonable bet. As far as he knew, that container would have cost the same to ship if it had come as it did, or if half of its volume was loaded with useful supplies. They had literally paid to ship *air* across the Pacific Ocean.

So. the months rolled on. Jonah never got *used* to living in an elaborate cage, but he learned to sort of tune out the creeping cabin fever. He hung around with Mitch, he found that the school would often leave one or two old, beat up, smooth-worn basketballs in the gym for kids to play with, and he would make his way up there day after day and shoot hoops over and over and over, hour after hour, like an inmate in a prison yard.

24

HAMLET

There was a girl in Jonah's class who had always watched him as he sat alone, wearing his black t-shirts and ratty converse, looking like an outcast. Jane had very light blond hair, full lips, and a somewhat exotic look, like perhaps one of her parents or grandparents had been Asian. Jonah had definitely noticed the girl, and she definitely liked him, but he really didn't understand the protocol for initiating "coupling," nor could he bring himself to engage in the bizarre spectacle.

Eventually, they managed to meet when he found an opportunity to just sit next to her and talk as if they were just regular people who could actually make friends with the opposite sex. Jane was receptive. She didn't have a lot of people to talk to either, not being part of the popular group of girls in the dorm. Of course, she didn't really have a lot to talk *about*, since she had literally spent her entire life in an MK dorm being programmed by the machine. Still, they would sometimes manage to meet up after school and sit on the retaining wall overlooking the bottom fence of the compound. Because this wasn't really formal *coupling*, per se, another girl had to be "present" and Jane's best friend would patiently hang around within eyeshot, letting them have space to talk. How these sorts of rules worked on that base, Jonah never did figure out. All he knew was that it was all very strange.

"I mean, nothing here is *normal*, you know?" Jonah had worked himself up into a bit of a rant as he sat there watching the overloaded trucks with dozens of locals standing up in their beds, hanging on to one another for dear life as the vehicles swerved along the Highlands Highway. "It's just *wrong*! This whole place!" He stopped when he glanced over and saw no comprehension whatsoever in Jane's pretty green eyes.

"What do you mean?"

Jonah fumbled to explain himself. "I mean … I mean, like the *coupling* thing! That's just *weird*!"

Jane sat up very straight. She looked at him with genuine surprise. "You don't think *coupling* is *normal*?"

"No, I…" Jonah stopped. She was looking at him as if he had just admitted to being gay. Who knows? In MK-language he may have just done so… "Nevermind."

There was just no way to bridge that gap. She didn't know *anything* outside of an MK dorm on a missionary compound. To her, *this* was the world.

It's hard to say if Jane would have become more than a friend, but she stopped going to school about a week later. A couple days after that, word went around that she was sick. She had to be flown out to Australia to a hospital, and remained there for most of the semester. She'd contracted Hepatitis A thanks to Numinohi's inadequate sewage system and contaminated groundwater. By the time she came back to the mission base, Jonah was already gone; not physically, but every other way he could be.

Left in such isolation, Jonah was having something of a crisis.

He'd been raised to believe in the Bible and think of himself as a Christian. Grandpa Franklin had made sure that the Franklin kids had recited John 3:16 as soon as they could talk, as he had done with his own children. That formulaic utterance sealed one's soul into heaven for eternity and pretty much ended Grandpa Franklin's responsibility for caring for them. They could recite John 3:16? He'd done his part.

So Jonah had been dragged to church whenever he was staying with Grandpa and Grandma, which, considering the nomadic chaos of his parents, had been fairly regularly when he was small. He'd grown up secular, wild, basically however he could for much of his life, but he did believe that the Bible was true, and God was real, and he liked to think that in the chaos of his life, there was something absolute out there that could be counted on.

Jonah had now gone for more than two years on some kind of compound completely surrounded by people who were "working for God." He hadn't even watched TV in over a year and a half. He hadn't been able to listen to the radio or read a book other than what could be scrounged on one of these compounds. He had known for many years that he didn't lead a normal life, but he had come to doubt the existence of "normalcy," whatever the hell that meant. How did he know for sure that everyone around him, *every single person* he'd been in contact with for all this time, was all wrong? They had probably visited two dozen churches in a dozen little towns across Misery and Arkansas, and every single one of them had said the same things, repeated the same ideas, told him that "working for God" was the absolute highest, best thing one could possibly do with one's life.

The Ranch had been bad. There was no disputing that, but didn't Jesus say that his followers could expect hardship? Didn't he say not to expect an easy life? Didn't he say believers would be persecuted? Didn't he say there would be "tares" (bad people) hidden among the church, pretending to be "wheat" (good people)? Everything seemed to indicate that if you were suffering you were doing Christianity *right*.

They suffered because they were walking in the footsteps of Jesus, and he *said* his followers would suffer and be hated and rejected by a fallen world. The entire world was fallen and riddled with sin and death.

(Jonah didn't have a hard time believing that one.) Poverty was a *virtue* because money was the root of all evil. The greatest thing it was possible for a Christian to do was help to spread the Gospel to all the nations of earth. In fact, they were bringing about the return of Christ by doing so. Logically, there were Bible verses behind every single one of the precepts that undergirded this mission base.

Was Walter wrong? *Of course.* There was no doubt in Jonah's mind about that, but there were a lot of other people from all over the world who were also trying to "work for God" and a lot of them were decent people. A few bad apples didn't disprove the whole concept. But he just couldn't get past this thought that kept circling in his head like a broken record.

If these people are the very best and very brightest and very highest exemplars of Christianity in the world - and they have thousands and thousands of other Christians sending them money based on that assumption - then what does that say about Christianity? If this is how Christians are meant to live and what Christians are meant to do, why would anyone want to be a Christian?

Jonah didn't have answers. The more he thought about it, the more questions he had. The more he ran into verses in the Bible that seemed to back up every single thing the Missionaries said every Sunday, the more of a problem it became. He knew in his bones that this place was *wrong*. He believed the Bible was *right*, and if this place was established based on the Bible, then he had a problem.

Jonah felt the pressure of the missionary compound bearing down on him day by day. There was no escape. Once or twice a month, Mom and Dad would organize a "vacation" just to get the hell off that base. There was a hotel in Goroka with a restaurant called "The Bird", where some of the missionaries would go to get away sometimes. All the Franklins could afford to do was rent a van for the day, drive down to The Bird, and sit at their patio next to the pool and order a snack and drinks. They didn't trust the food there anyway, and even the drinks had to be from a bottle. They never touched the glasses or the ice.

They would sit there, watching the few white tourists or missionaries in that little town lounging around the pool for a couple hours, then head back in the van. Laura and Walter enjoyed those little trips. Jonah just couldn't stand to be on the base anymore. He felt like a goldfish in a bowl that was too small for him.

At school they had to do a report on a classic piece of literature. Jonah had thought of doing Dante's Inferno, which he'd had access to when they took a short trip to the nearby Catholic mission base library. He'd been fascinated by it, but his grand plan for writing up some philosophical comparison between the mission compound and one of the levels of Hell in the Inferno never seemed to come together.

Jonah had borrowed books from the school library for lack of anything else to do, and one that had stuck with him was a paperbound copy of Hamlet. It was just the entire play printed up and bound as a book, and Jonah hadn't been able to stop reading it.

With his report not coming together in his mind, he asked his teacher at the last minute to change his book from Inferno to Hamlet, despite that not being on the original list. The teacher agreed, and Jonah sat up all night writing.

Not understanding the irony, the teenage boy struggling with a fundamental crisis of faith found more and more that he identified with in the story of Hamlet as he wrote that paper. He knocked out something that was supposed to take two weeks in the final day before the deadline, and something about young Hamlet's futile search for his father (or the ghost of him), his disillusionment with his mother, and his questioning of whether life was really worthwhile all came together in

a way that left Jonah surprised by its force. He felt that
he was in the same position as the young man in the
story in some fundamental way that was currently
beyond his understanding.

The teacher was impressed. He gave Jonah a
very good grade and asked if he would be willing to
read it to the rest of his class. Jonah didn't mind. He
wasn't one of those people who hated to speak in front
of others. He slowed down halfway through when he
saw the eyes of everyone in the class begin to glass
over. There wasn't one person there who could *possibly*
understand what the paper was getting at.

The next morning when Jonah woke up, his face
didn't work. The left side of his face simply didn't
respond to *any* nerve signals whatsoever, it was
partially paralyzed. He didn't really notice what was
going on, just feeling slightly numb in the face until he
ate breakfast and prepared to go to school. He said
something to Amy and then laughed a little bit, and
suddenly noticed that Laura was staring at him in
horror.

When Jonah laughed, the right side of his face
would look normal, but the left side, as if a line were
drawn straight down from his nose, was dead as the
flesh of a corpse. Even his left eye was drooping ever
so slightly.

"Oh my God! Jonah! *Look in the mirror!*" Laura
stood watching him in shock.

Jonah looked in a mirror. The visage of the
monster he saw there made him laugh with black, black
humor. The laugh made the visage *more* horrible. He
laughed harder, staring at the alien face that had been
his but now reminded him of "Two Face" from a
Batman comic. He laughed until tears rolled out of his
one fully functioning eye, the sound distorted because
the left side of his mouth wouldn't open properly, like a
gurgle of some demented fiend from that book he'd
borrowed from the Catholic mission; Dante's Inferno.

"HA! HA! HA! HA! HA!" Jonah clutched the counter, wobbling on his legs as the laugh came up out of him, beyond all control. He had never seen anything so fucked up in his entire life … and it was *his own face. "HA! HA! HA! HA! HA!!"*

Looking back, it occurred to a much older Jonah that his nearly 17-year-old self was probably close to a breakdown at that time.

Laura was fluttering around the house in near-panic. She wanted to do something, but she didn't know what to do. Walter was already gone on his daily expedition to go "Do Big Things" somewhere.

Jonah waved her off. He was healthy enough to go to school. Who cared anyway? All he had to do was not smile all day and nobody would notice. *That* wasn't going to be too hard.

That day, Jonah sat in the back of the class, feeling like a visitor from a different world, watching the people around him as if they were on a microscope slide. The attempts to bait him from one of Jerry's Boys were met with an insolently blank stare. Jonah felt as if he was barely there, as if this was all happening to someone else. Who the hell cared about *any* of this shit anyway?

Laura took him to the mission base clinic that afternoon. They didn't understand what was wrong at first, then Laura told him to smile. He watched as expressions of horror came across the faces of the mission doctor and nurse. He felt a chuckle coming on… It was kind of like a superpower. All he had to do was smile and people would want to take a step back.

The doctor took a long time with his books. He said it was probably "Bell's Palsy," possibly transmitted by some kind of tropical virus. In that petri dish of a country, there was no telling how Jonah had contracted it. Laura asked about flying him out to a real hospital in Darwin (Darwin, Australia was their de-facto medical emergency location). The doctor said they could, but he didn't think that anyone there knew any more about it than he did. It was a very rare and very strange ailment and they weren't even sure how it was contracted. He said it was likely to go away on its own, and they should wait and see if it started getting better.

Jonah spent time the next day trying to move his face muscles on the left side. He felt that if he really focused on it, he could get them to twitch. He would periodically do that every now and then throughout the day, trying to condition the nerves and muscles to obey him again. The day after that, things seemed to be better. His left eye didn't look like it was drooping half lidded anymore. His mouth didn't have such a sharp delineation between the part that moved and the part that didn't.

After a week, Jonah's face was mostly normal again. It was still stiff, and wasn't completely back to normal for about two weeks, but it did go back just as mysteriously as it had all started.

***

New Tribes Mission became mired in a spiraling series of physical and sexual abuse allegations from former MKs who had lived in Missionary Kid dorms in the 1980s and 1990s. A 2010 report criticized NTM for covering up two dozen cases of child sexual abuse on a missionary base in Africa. Other victims came forward and in the next few years, allegations from former MKs who had been on missionary bases in Africa, South America, the Philippines, Papua New Guinea, and elsewhere were published. After settling multiple lawsuits, NTM changed its name to Ethnos 360. It continues to operate today.

25

HIGH PLACES OF BAAL

There was no escaping the class. They had a Junior year trip scheduled and they had all voted (without Jonah being present) to go to Lae for their big outing that year.

Lae is a big, sprawling mess of a city on the Northern coast of PNG. It is the city closest to the Indonesian side of the island, and has some fair sized port facilities and an overland connection to the Highlands Highway. As a third world shithole port right over the border from Indonesia, it was a great place for Indonesian pirates to sell stolen cargo and for smugglers to load up on marijuana, which was legal to grow in PNG, but not legal to *export*. Lae catered to these kinds of visitors with every bit of charm the odoriferous country could muster. Ladies of the night with rancid BO and nappy hair showed their round bellies on the corners of the broken streets, spitting streams of red betelnut juice on the concrete and smiling at potential customers with red stained teeth.

Lae was known for its street gangs. Raskol gangs used it as a headquarters, buying their weapons in the black market that drove the economic engine of the town. If ever any place deserved the title "hive of scum and villainy" it was Lae during those years.

Jonah didn't know why they were going to Lae, but apparently some of the MKs liked the city and *everyone* seemed to find it preferable to Port Moresby. Considering the dirty, seedy anarchy Jonah had seen of Port Moresby, he could understand that … at least until he saw Lae.

They were to be put up in the NTM guest house in the city. It wasn't as nice as the one in Port Moresby, but it was bigger, and it was fairly comfortable. The trip down the entire length of the Highlands Highway in a fleet van had exhausted all of them, and by the time they finally arrived in Lae after dark, Jonah was totally done in. It didn't help that he was only getting about *half* of the calories per day that Jerry's Boys were. He couldn't fight back the exhaustion with no fuel in his system.

Jonah managed to stumble into the room he would share with some of the boys and collapse on a bed still wearing his shoes. He was draped across his backpack, out like a light in moments.

Something tickled Jonah's face, and he awoke with a start. There was a bubble of laughter all around him. He opened his eyes to see Dave and the other Jerry's Boys standing over him giggling like idiots. There was something that felt like suds in his right hand. One of the guys quickly hid a black marker. They had been trying (and failing) to get Jonah to smack himself in the face with a hand full of shaving cream. Then, failing that, had decided to try drawing on his face with a marker, but he'd woken up too soon.

Jonah got to his feet, still confused, looking around at the idiot squad and the shaving cream filling up his hand. He started walking to the bathroom, then stopped in the middle of the room.

"Go fuck yourselves."

Jonah went to the bathroom and washed off while the missionary kids backed away in shock and horror at the kind of language that had come out of Jonah's mouth. It was as much as an open admission of being "backslidden."

The reason the MKs liked Lae was because it came closest of any PNG city to having an "expats quarter" (a section of town fairly safe for non-PNG citizens to walk around in). Safe is a relative term of course, especially in a modern-day pirate port like Lae, PNG. Drug and arms smugglers, bandits, and all manner of "service industry" workers supporting them could be found in that city. The class had been told to stay in groups, but they were allowed to move between the NTM guest house and a hotel about a block over that was considered safe. The big draw at the hotel was the indoor pool.

Late the second night, Jonah found himself standing around in the hotel, watching his classmates run around the pool room like crazy people. He had come on the trip just to get off the compound, and he'd come to the hotel just because everyone else was. He had thought he wanted to swim, but the boys were engaged in a hyper aggressive game of water polo and he just wanted to try a couple laps or something. He decided to just head back to the guest house.

Stepping out of the front doors of the hotel onto an actual sidewalk, Jonah suddenly felt a peculiar feeling come over him. He was walking out of a hotel in a city almost like a normal person … like a *free* person. There was nobody from the mission organization watching him. What if he decided to turn left instead of right?

Jonah did so, moving along the street as if he knew where he was going, paying little attention to the various seedy looking locals except out of the corners of his eyes, much as he had once learned to do in a ghetto neighborhood in California.

His choice was partly driven by the shocking realization that he actually *felt* like a cult member who was off the cult compound for a moment. Normalcy had slipped away like water heating up around a "boiling frog," but Jonah had not realized how completely controlled every moment of his life was now.

The city was dark. Very few streetlights worked. It looked like something from a post-apocalyptic movie where humanity is trying to rebuild from some kind of disaster. Except here, humanity had only barely been able to "build" in the first place. Jonah felt eyes on him from an alleyway and casually crossed the street to the other side as if he had intended to do so and knew precisely where he was going.

This is stupid, Jonah. You don't know where you are. You are going to just get yourself killed.

Up ahead, Jonah could see the port. There were a few run down looking freighters there. He could feel heat coming up the street even after dark. There was a thick smell that was impossible to describe; a combination of exotic flowers, rotting fruit, garbage and human feces.

What if I got to those ships? What if I find a freighter captain I can cut a deal with? I am sure I could be a useful crew member ... Maybe...

Jonah glanced at the area in front of the port itself. It was a huge open area dotted with campfires, large clusters of men sat around each campfire drinking beer, spitting betelnut juice, and cavorting with the local whores. They all looked pretty well armed from what Jonah could see in the darkness.

... And there are the Raskols...

Jonah had felt for a moment that he was his 10-year-old self, looking up at an airplane in the sky and wishing he could just go wherever it was going. Now, he shook his head and turned, not breaking stride, not acknowledging with body language, even to himself, that he had ever intended to walk toward the docks. He strode confidently down the sidewalk like someone who belonged there, heading back up toward the hotel, then past it… and at last to the NTM guest house.

Walking inside, Jonah saw none of his classmates anywhere. He sighed with relief and found a place to sit on the porch balcony, staring out into the humid night.

They stopped at another mission camp area on the way back to Numinohi. This wasn't much of a "base," but it did have some lovely outdoor areas overlooking a bend in a river, with some shady gum trees giving cover from the tropical sun. They had climbed a ways back up into the highlands from Lae on the coast, and the humidity had abated a little, making the kids feel as if they could actually *breathe* again. Lowlands' humidity was hard to comprehend, and it really made itself apparent in the relief of that damp air being lifted.

The boys wanted to play rugby and for a change, Jonah lined up to play with them. He didn't know rugby very well, but it was similar enough to football to pick up pretty fast. As always, the boys played rough, and as always, Jonah was acquitting himself well. Unfortunately, all of Jerry's Boys had wanted to be on one team together, which left the other team without enough good players. Jonah, as ever, was on the side that was steadily losing.

There came a moment where Dave and his Jerry's Boys sycophants were uphill from where Jonah waited. They had the ball, and they were about to rush it forward in a rugby scrum, but because most of the boys were a bit more familiar with American football, it looked a lot more like two football teams lined up before a snap. Jonah locked eyes with Dave. He was crouched, poised, ready to move. He felt like a coiled spring. In Jonah's mind, the baseball tryout was replaying itself.

"Out of the way, Franklin!" His eyes found Dave's and locked on like a missile on a target.

They were all playing this more like American football? Good. Jonah would show this backwoods jungle boy how to really *hit*.

The ball moved, it was passed to Dave. Jonah was already moving. He powered up that incline, getting as much speed as he possibly could in the few short yards between himself and his target. Jonah fed every bit of rage, every little bit of hate that he kept always inside him into the act of hurling his body, shoulder first at his target. His eyes were filled with the stupid, innocent, cow-like eyes of his enemy.

They came together hard, but Jonah knew something was wrong right away. He hadn't gotten up the hill as fast as he thought he should have. His body was just *weak*. It would not do what Jonah asked of it. Jonah had always taken for granted that his body would obey him. He had never set a challenge for it that he knew in his gut it could accomplish and had it fail. Fighting kids significantly larger than himself, scurrying to the top of a massive chain link fence as a kid, whatever.

He just wasn't getting enough food to keep up his strength. He hadn't got to Dave fast enough and he hadn't hit him hard enough. It was like he'd been betrayed by his own body. Jonah's body had always been something he could count on. Something that nobody could take away. Even at the boy's ranch, he'd known that if the ranch boys jumped him, he would give a damn good accounting of himself. At least a few of them would really, really regret doing so before he went down.

Now, even that physical competence had been taken away by a steady diet of rice and fruit. He was a nearly 17-year-old boy who was probably 15 pounds underweight.

Dave had had time to turn and deflect Jonah away. Jonah had put *everything* into the hit, and now he flew completely off his feet, spinning in the air, and landed on the gravel they had foolishly decided to play on.

Jonah felt the gravel cut into his left leg right through the jeans. He got to his feet, then winced and got his weight back off that leg. There was blood dripping down from under his pant leg and into his shoe.

The other kids came around and made a fuss of trying to help him up, but Jonah shrugged them off and hopped over to a bench. His leg was pretty ripped up, but it wasn't super serious.

Dave looked a bit shaken. There had been a blood curdling hatred in Jonah's eyes that was beyond anything the MK had ever felt or had the capacity to understand. Still, the baby-faced boy trotted over and put a hand on Jonah's shoulder.

"That was really good, man." To Dave, sports was ALL.

Jonah thanked him sourly and tried to make himself comfortable on the bench while they waited for the missionaries to get back and pick them up. There was a med kit in the van. He looked over to his left and suddenly realized that he was the only boy sitting down, the benches were nothing but a line of girls watching the game, and himself. He sighed.

He didn't actually hate Dave. Dave was just a symptom. He was too stupid and too earnest to really hate anyway, even when he acted like an asshole jock. Guys like him were in every high school in the world. Jonah's problem was Jonah. His problem was that he was slowly filling up with rage and he barely understood why. His problem was that he hated living in what he considered a prison camp. His problem was his *entire fucking life*.

Jonah would never be one of the popular kids, he would never be the quarterback, he would never go to a prom, he would never have a high school sweetheart. He would always be a freak and an outsider, and it wasn't because he *couldn't* have done those things if he'd ever been given *one single chance* in his life, it was that he had never, ever, been given *any* chances.

Jonah's 17th birthday came and went at some point. He didn't remember later whether the family did anything. Laura would sometimes try to do something special for dinner with the inadequate funds they had to live on. Jonah honestly never remembered that birthday later on. It seemed there was too much going on that too many people were caught up in. Hayden had been sucked into the activities of her "reeducation camp" of a mission base, Amy was having her own issues with being an outsider in a class full of MKs, Laura had been caught up into the drama and politics of the missionary wives who were always busy organizing and participating in group activities of one kind or another, and Walter … was being Walter. He had fought his great crusade against Leadership for an improved water supply and moved on to some project involving setting up a lumber mill at a nearby village somewhere.

PNG has no real seasons. Being so close to the Equator, summer and winter are very hypothetical constructs. It was a land of endless sun and lots and lots of rain. "Dry season" and "wet season" looked basically the same to someone who had grown up in the USA. Jonah felt no sense of time, but an ever present sense of feeling time slipping away from him, one day at a time. His strength slipping away, one day at a time. His life steadily coming to a close, at an age where it had only just begun.

Jonah didn't care about school anymore. He had considered the trials and tortures of the mission school a joke for a long time now. He was now at an age where it was legal for him to drop out of high school in the USA. He had already been old enough for a while by Australian standards, and nobody had a clear idea if there even *were* any PNG standards for that. The school ran itself by a combination of Austalian and US standards for everything, so with the US dropout age being the "strictest," they couldn't legally tell Jonah no when he told the principal that he wasn't going to be attending school anymore.

On the minus side, Jonah was now a high school dropout. On the plus side, he didn't have to have every second of every day run by a cult-like brainwashing machine, with no outlet except hyper aggressive but ultimately pointless competition with Jerry's Boys.

Walter was all for this new development. He said that diplomas are just pieces of paper anyway and Jonah didn't need them. Laura cried. She blubbered through streams of tears like a child with a broken toy; "But … but he wanted to become an *engineer*!"

Jonah stared at her in disbelief. He couldn't even wrap his head around where she was coming from. He had indeed said he wanted to be an engineer … but that was before "working for God," before the boys ranch, before PNG and mission bases, back when he saw the possibility of a normal life somewhere. Now? He would be lucky to get somewhere where he had enough *food* and he wasn't living on a prison-like *compound*. Honestly, the most useful thing he could do now for his future was probably to learn some kind of useful trade that could make money. That would come from working with his hands, not books.

Walter helped make arrangements and Jonah was quickly set up with one of Walter's co-conspirators on the water and sewage crusade, a bookish looking Canadian missionary who was nonetheless a very talented mechanic, and who could use some help on a couple projects.

Jonah knew that Walter was so supportive partly because they had to pay the mission base for Jonah to go to school, but even Walter could be right once in awhile. Would that money be better spent on food or on brainwashing? Why was Jonah going through the motions trying to pretend to have a "normal" high school experience anyway?

The first morning he walked *past* the school on the muddy main road of the mission base to an open garage beyond it carrying a lunchbox, Jonah felt a vast sense of relief. It was as if some of the intense pressure he was under had been lifted. He was now considered an "adult" on the mission base, and he would simply have to work at a job that made sense and had a concrete use. His life was no longer measured in terms of how "backslidden" the teachers thought he might be or how popular he wasn't compared to Jerry's Boys.

When he squished through the mud up to the garage area early enough that his boss wasn't there yet and saw the hulks of two massive, filthy, broken down farm tractors, Jonah actually smiled.

Jonah spent many days in that open-air shop, stripping down the farm tractors with a ratchet set and a breaker bar until there was nothing to them but an engine block, a transmission, and a rear axle. He took off every fleck of paint with a wire brush, pulled every removable part from the engines, and spread the parts out on the wooden shelf at the back of the barn-like structure. They were going to take two dead tractors and make a working one.

For Jonah, having some kind of concrete, useful work was like a breath of fresh air. No mind games, no propaganda, no cliques, just metal, tools, and time.

The kids from his class couldn't understand any of it. Jonah would find them on the side of the field toward the mechanic shop once in awhile on a break, looking his way with bewildered expressions on their faces. They knew he was unhappy here, but they couldn't understand why. They knew he wanted to do work like the local people the base hired did instead of go to school events with them, but the concept baffled them. They knew no other life, nothing other than the MK dorms, this base, and brief visits to the States for fundraising tours.

Jonah spent his time working with his hands and pondering the problem that was driving him now and would not leave him alone. If *this* is what Christianity is supposed to be, something was wrong. What his grandfather and father said they believed was now physically surrounding Jonah in concrete form.

Jonah *did* believe in God, and he did believe that God gave directions to mankind via the Bible. The Bible did say these things the missionaries always quoted, in fact, in the topsy-turvy, ever changing, nothing ever being concrete universe he lived in, it was the only thing he could count on as being actually true. When he was in a place where nobody ever said what they meant, he could count on something in the universe being true. It must be that, or there was no truth anywhere. It was just that he knew the missionaries were wrong because of everything they produced.

In the mandatory weekly church service in the big concrete block gym building, they usually heard from Mr. Lawrence (who gave sermons about as well as you would *expect* a mediocre high school coach to do). Once in awhile, they had missionaries visiting from their posts in some tribe who had come back to the main base for some reason or other. Jonah watched as a bright eyed young missionary couple fresh out of 4 years of "training" held up their infant daughter in front of the entire compound and explained with the frenzied intensity of true cult members that the beautiful little infant would "certainly" go to Hell if she died that day. This was because she was incapable of reciting the official creed of salvation- because she couldn't *talk* yet.

Jonah sat in the folding metal chairs in the stifling gym, his eyes almost boring a hole in the face of that perfect looking, blond haired missionary dad. *This*. He was telling himself. *Pay attention to this right here.*

This is what this place is. This is what it's all about.

Missionaries made it a badge of honor to stoically bear the great sacrifice of giving up their own children when they handed them over to Leadership on the mission base at seven years old. To sacrifice for the Lord's Work was the ultimate greatest thing a Christian could do, and what greater sacrifice could one possibly give than their own children?

The mission organization constantly drummed over and over that they were to sacrifice whatever was most valuable to them in order to be like Jesus.

Jonah did some studying when they gave their chapters and verses that supported what they did; why they could put their children into the hands of dorm parents where on some mission bases, at that very time, they were being molested and abused, and where they would *always* be brainwashed and left emotionally crippled by the knowledge that their own parents had abandoned them. *All* of their verses came from the New Testament. Jonah was starting to find other verses though, in the part of the Bible the missionaries never ever looked at; the Old Testament.

> *"They have built the high places of Baal to burn their children in the fire as offerings to Baal-- something I did not command or mention, nor did it enter my mind."*
> *-Jeremiah 19:5*

> *"They even sacrificed their sons and their daughters to the demons"*
> *-Psalm 106:37*

The Old Testament was making a *lot* more sense to Jonah right now.

There had been a couple of MK kids who became famous among the high school kids. The girl was the thin, blond, cute, but not too smart daughter of Mr. Lawrence, head of Leadership itself. The boy was an MK one year ahead of her in the high school. He had dark hair and eyes and a look in his eyes that was very familiar to Jonah. It was the look of a boy who had been betrayed by those closest to him. It was the look of rage boiling deep under the surface.

He had been abandoned here by his parents. She had been a tool for her father to use in support letter pictures and trot out in front of churches like a trained monkey. She liked him because he seemed like a "bad boy." He had been taught that if one wasn't perfect as defined by the mission organization, any sin was the same as any other … using a curse word or murder were equivalent, and he knew he wasn't perfect. Their story had been a naive rerun of Romeo and Juliet.

Everyone knew they were in love, nobody had said anything, her dad didn't want her anywhere near the "bad boy." It was all so predictable. They clung to one another the way kids do when they have been abandoned by their parents.

It had all come out of course, particularly after she had become pregnant. Except … except that she hadn't. That had never happened at all. What everyone knew was *never* spoken. Mr. Lawrence had gotten the MK boy kicked off the base and sent back to the States. He'd then arranged for his teenage daughter to become "ill" and need an "emergency flight" to Darwin. She'd come down with malaria or something. Everyone knew that it had not been for malaria that she had been in the hospital there. It was not malaria she recovered from in Australia. It wasn't malaria that left her with the look of hopeless depression- of someone who had lost something that could never be gotten back. Abortion was not a word on that base. It was a mortal sin to snuff out the life of an unborn child for one's own convenience. Yet Mr. Lawrence was *Leadership*. He could not have his reputation reflected upon by an unwed teen daughter's pregnancy. So, yet *another* child was sacrificed. A child sacrifice of child sacrifices.

It was as if death lived in the silence of what was never said on that base.

Jonah was able to visit ITF once in awhile. Each time he did, he met Hayden, and she seemed to be more and more remote. She was caught up in some great, shining vision that she could see and which lay elsewhere. Every time he saw her, there was more distance between them. His words echoed off of her as if she weren't really there, or as if there was a pane of glass between them.

The last time he saw her, Hayden was troubled.

"We were getting to the end of the camp…" She seemed to be looking at something far away as she talked about one of the periodic "camps" they had there with a fresh batch of youth eager to work for God every couple of months.

"Everything led up to this … The youth leaders were talking about sacrifice all that day."

Jonah sat in the little dining hall of ITF listening to the Lorrikeets chirruping in their cage nearby, smelling the scent of Frangipani flowers on the breeze.

"They made a big bonfire and we all gathered around it … we were all so excited. Then they said that we had to demonstrate our willingness to sacrifice. They told us to go back to our cabins and get our most prized possession. Whatever was most important to us in the whole world … and throw it on the fire."

Jonah nodded. Somehow, he had known that would be what they asked.

"What did you do?"

"I…" Hayden frowned, obviously still struggling within herself. "I went and got my notebook with all my drawings and my stories ... I looked at the others all throwing things in; pictures of them and their parents, their entire collections of music tapes, I saw one girl throw a really expensive stereo on the fire." She shook her head. "I just couldn't do it. I couldn't do it. I went back to my cabin and stayed there. I haven't talked to the youth leaders since then."

Jonah knew what those drawings and scribblings meant to Hayden. They had been her lifeline to sanity through everything. Jonah and Hayden (and even Amy) had often resorted to escapism during the worst times. They had made up stories, invented entirely new worlds. Jonah had immersed himself in Dungeons and Dragons for a while before Walter had told him that he couldn't bring any of his books with him while they were working for God (like rock music, they were "of the Devil", not that Walter cared, but he couldn't have that reflecting badly on *him*). Hayden clung to her notebooks as a lifeline to sanity, a secure place that she could go to in a world that was terrible. For *both* of them, their imaginary worlds they invented was their actual, real Home. She had been a moment's hesitation away from throwing Home on a fire.

"It's all fucked up." 17-year-old Jonah didn't have the words to say what he really meant about the mission organization.

Hayden nodded. "It was wrong. It was wrong." She shook her head. "I think they are wrong."

Jonah had already been through this with Hayden though, so he didn't say any more. While he was there, she would agree with him, vehemently say the same things he was saying and for the same reasons, but in her infrequent letters written when he wasn't there, she sounded more and more and more like one of *them*. It's like there was one Hayden when he was there and another one when he wasn't.

To Jonah, that conversation summed up what NTM was. They worked in a land where cannibals had sacrificed their own children in order to make peace treaties, and to do it, they sacrificed *their* own children to prove that they were holier and better than all the other Christians. Thousands and thousands of Christians all over the world supported the system, and at the very top, the high priests who did nothing else all day constructed their little altars to Baal. If Hayden had dropped her most precious thing in the world into that fire, *who* was that smoke rising up to please? It certainly wasn't the God that Jonah believed in.

Unfortunately, that left him in a metaphysical crisis, and no 17-year-old wants to have to deal with that shit.

During work time, Jonah would wrench on tractors (and when that was over, Walter started taking him out to work with him). During his own time, Jonah started looking for anything he could find on the base that had anything to do with Israel.

He needed to find pictures of Israel, because he needed to see what the country looked like. If *this* place was the logical outcome of Christianity, he needed to see the actual logical outcome of the Bible in this world. It said the land had been given to the people of Israel, it said they would be his chosen people forever, the country of Israel *had* sprung back to life in the 20th century in a manner that could only be described as a miracle. This was all Old Testament stuff, and Jonah needed to see what the outcome of it was in the *real world*, so he could know if it was just more bullshit. Luckily, Israel was one of the few topics from the outside world the mission base didn't censor.

Jonah sat back in the 4WD pickup as it lurched sideways, skating left and then right as it somehow managed to make a turn on a grease-slick clay mud trail. Walter was in the passenger seat in front, his Canadian friend (Jonah's first "boss") was driving. Outside the windows, the land looked like a solid wall of green, up the slope to their left, and down the slope to their right. Tropical plants, spiders the size of dinner plates hanging in webs that stretched 12 feet across, giant fruit bats and climbing snakes in the trees.

Jonah sat there, relaxed with the calmness of someone who absolutely, truly, and irrevocably wouldn't care one way or another if the truck made it to the village or rolled down the slope to fiery oblivion in a crash. He was still pondering his problem, but he had given up on trying to solve it on this base. There just wasn't enough material available here. No TV, very few books, no radio worth listening to … the best he could do here was survive and try to learn some skills that might actually help him later.

They were building houses in a Bena Bena village. The missionaries had a lot of building projects, and there were a ton of trees that were great for building with in PNG, but there was hardly any lumber available because there were no sawmills. Numinohi had actually been built entirely with wood shipped in containers from the USA (among other places).

So, a deal had been struck with the Bena Bena tribe. They had good lumber and were fine with selling the trees, but they wanted a couple things in return. They wanted houses like Westerners built, and they wanted to be trained to use the sawmill. If it worked out, it could become an industry that could pull the village out of Stone Age poverty.

Jonah was sure it wouldn't actually work out. It wasn't because of any lack of earnestness or effort on the part of the village either, nor their tribal leaders, nor a lack of ability to teach them from the missionaries. Whatever kind of father Walter was, he was a skilled builder who knew what he was doing. The missionary team had a real lumberjack and several other experts with good skills to teach.

It wasn't going to work because of something called the "Wantok system." In PNG, there were over 800 different local languages that were totally incomprehensible to one another. That was why they needed "Tok Pisin" or Melanesian Pidgin as the trade language. The tribes had developed a system whereby the people who spoke your own language (not the trade language) were your allies. Everyone else was an enemy. Most of the tribes had a custom where if a "Wantok" - from "One Talk" someone who naturally spoke your home language - came to you with a request of some kind, you were obligated to give it to him. If a Wantok needed somewhere to stay, you let him sleep in your hut. If he needed food, you gave it to him. If he wanted your possessions, you handed them over. Missionaries thought it was cute. Westerners romanticized it. They said things like "maybe our culture can learn something from theirs!"

In Jonah's opinion, it was the biggest reason PNG was a *permanently* hopeless shithole.

If you had to give anything you had earned to anyone in your tribe who asked for it, why would you ever strive to make money? Why would you build a business? Why would you even learn a trade? Why would you *invent* anything? The people of PNG had been practicing perfect Communism for centuries before the USSR had ever existed and they had the development to show for it.

While some ingenious Chinese guy was inventing a compound bow or a stirrup, the people of PNG were doing without spear throwers. Why would you work your butt off to invent something new if your success would be penalized by becoming the carcass upon which every one of your extended family of vultures were going to feed? Jonah had seen it several times with locals who had started some business or tried to trade and make money the way Westerners did. Every single time they got too successful, a village worth of relatives would descend upon them from the ancestral homeland and sit and eat and do nothing except make their lives miserable until they gave up. Flocks of the vultures would drift across PNG moving from one "rich" relative they wanted to mooch off of to the next.

Why learn to run a sawmill? The minute this particular Bena Bena village started making money, all the other ones would swoop in, eat them out of house and home, and leave them worse off than before. The better career path for an enterprising young PNG man was to take his machete and his "Kilaman" spear and join some group of toughs in Goroka to hunt for anything valuable on the roads, hold up the cars, take what they wanted, and drift back into the forest. That was why half the country was overrun with "Raskols."

So, they were doing something that had the potential to change the lives of a lot of villagers, but it wouldn't. Not unless they changed their culture. If Jonah knew anything, it was that changing the culture of your own family was *hard*.

He enjoyed the work. It was nice to be off the mission base. He was pretty good with a hammer and could help with framing up the houses. Unfortunately, Jonah quickly found himself fairly superfluous.

The local villagers wanted to do all the work he could do so they could learn, and he didn't have the skills the ex-lumberjack or the geologist did. Jonah kept bumping into some local guy who gave him a hard glare and tried to cut him off from nailing the board he was working on or cutting what he was trying to cut. They had *paid* for this chance to learn to build Western style, and they didn't want Jonah to take a spot from one of their men.

Walter was oblivious, of course. He serenely ran the work crews (including Jonah) as if there was no inherent conflict. At least Foreman Walter was always a much better guy to be around than Dad though. Jonah didn't have to worry about Foreman Walter flying into a rage for no reason. When he was doing this kind of work, he was logical, he made sense, and he could even show some kind of concern for the men in his crew. At least as much as a ship captain might show for a motor that kept something working on his vessel. Foreman Walter needed the men to get something done, so they were vicariously important. To Jonah, being a member of a work crew with Foreman Walter was a stand-in for father-son time, kind of like "coupling" was a stand in for dating for the kids on the mission base.

Walter had found a good use for some of Grandpa's antique tools. With electricity incredibly hard to come by, power tools were limited. They had a little generator, but it could only power a little more than one skill saw at a time. Walter had taken out the antique brace-and-bit that had once belonged to Laura's dad. It could rapidly drill a hole almost as fast as a power drill, but required nothing but muscle, which was readily available here.

Jonah watched the tribal man walking around with his grandpa's old brace-and-bit as if it were a holy instrument of some kind. The way he held the thing told him it was magic to these people. To Jonah, it was something else. The way the light gleamed from the beautifully polished red wood that had served his grandfather and his *great* grandfather going back to a real ranch in North Dakota made Jonah wonder where that wood had come from. That tool had been used by a *real cowboy*, the steel represented the industrial ingenuity of the greatest nation on earth at the time of its greatest expansion - its miraculous conquest of the West.

It was an ingenious machine, a piece of history, and it had been in Jonah's family for longer than anything else he knew about. Foreman Walter had handed it out to this guy with no more thought than a road crew foreman handing out a shovel to some illegal immigrant worker. To him it was nothing more than a temporary means to an end. To Jonah, it was a piece of Home, and he knew without a shadow of a doubt that those villagers would never, *ever* part with it.

So they worked, and so they came home, Walter talking excitedly about the Great Thing they were doing, Jonah silent in the back of the truck as always, looking out the window, human baggage, watching the little switchback trail of slick mud move under them like a snake. At least he wasn't in school.

26

BACK TO EARTH

It had to come to a head. No matter how they scrimped, how often they starved on Tinpis and Rice, even not paying for Jonah's tuition anymore, the Franklins simply didn't have enough support coming in. Walter and Rich had cut a deal, FNTM had paid the difference between what they needed and what they had raised, and they had gone, but from the first moment they landed in New Guinea, the family was sinking into a quagmire of bills owed to NTM like a deer caught in quicksand.

Jonah didn't know exactly what happened when, or which crisis precipitated what. As with the scrambling, hasty move from Fairfield when they lost their house, there was a lot of heated back and forth between Walter and Laura, a lot of panicked sounding talk, Laura crying, Walter yelling, all behind closed doors so the kids didn't know what was going on. This time it was complicated by Leadership deciding that Walter and Laura had backslidden because of their financial situation (and mostly because Walter had made enemies with Leadership) and demanding that they sit for "counseling" sessions with the Dear Leader.

Walter said that FNTM had a new board and they had new priorities, and they had suddenly stopped putting the support money that came in for them into the NTM account. Jonah had no idea, but he thought it more likely that they had been "living" off of the lump sum of project money and just going ever deeper into the hole because more went out then came in every month.

It all happened very fast. Walter came back enraged from a "counseling" session with Leadership. He said they were leaving. Jonah just raised his eyebrows and exchanged a knowing glance with Amy. This was maybe a bit behind schedule. They had been on the base over a year now, but there was no surprise on the kids' faces, just a weary understanding of the slogging grind that was to come.

This time they managed to mail some of their things ahead of them in brown paper packages so Jonah didn't have to kill himself every time they had to change planes. Laura supervised the logistics, as usual.

Walter stopped going to work, which meant Jonah did too. For the last week they were there, they lived as a hostile element, like a virus surrounded by white blood cells, the angry stares of missionaries locking onto their front door every time anyone went to or came back from the general store right next to the Franklins' apartment. They had effectively been excommunicated.

Jonah was actually surprised when he heard that Hayden wasn't coming with them. He'd just assumed that she would. Unfortunately, his parents were both in "emergency mode" and it was nearly impossible to talk to them. Jonah didn't even know if he'd be able to call Hayden to say goodbye. There was no way to know when or if he'd ever see her again. They were just told "We're leaving, Hayden is staying here."

Amy was mad. She had finally started to make some progress with her tightly knit class full of MKs. Unlike Jonah's class, they were younger and more capable of accepting newcomers into the hivemind. Now she was being pulled again, and would be moved to a new school *again*. Jonah could understand where she was coming from. Of course, he'd long since given up being mad at getting uprooted all the time.

FNTM would pay for the Franklins' ticket back to the USA (except for Hayden, who was now an adult, and was earning a salary at ITF, and who wanted to stay there). If Walter tried to convince Hayden to return to the States with him, Jonah never heard the conversation, but it seemed as if a conversation had occurred and Hayden no longer believed what Walter said. Jonah didn't like the mission organization and at the time he felt almost a frantic panic at the thought of Hayden being sucked into the "massmind" of the cult compound, but looking back later, he couldn't really blame her considering what she thought her options were. *This* was Hayden's chance to get out of Dad's truck.

In the midst of the scramble of preparations to go home, Walter made the *great and noble* sacrifice of donating his tools to the missionaries. Jonah knew it was coming, and he wasn't surprised when he heard it mentioned offhand the way you might mention passing off something that is too much trouble and work to be worthwhile to someone else. Years later, Walter would bring that up in conversation. It always stayed with him. To a builder of Walter's generation, there were carpenters who owned tools (who could work as independent contractors) and those who did not (who always had to work for someone else). To them, having a set of tools meant you could always find work. It was security. Walter had invested more concern in that set of tools than he had in anything else in his life.

Apparently, in his mind, the least he could get out of it was a little recognition by converting them into the coin of the realm of the mission organization: a Great Sacrifice.

Many years later it would occur to Jonah that perhaps God had a sense of humor after all. The missionaries sacrificed the one thing *most precious* to them on the altar of Baal; their children. Walter had now done so as well.

Jonah didn't stop to think about it too much. When he did, it just felt as if some part of his own birthright - his history, his roots was gone. It wasn't *Walter's* tools that made him feel that way, but the old antique ones Walter didn't consider practical enough to really care about. Of course, that was all of very little concern now. Now, they had to get back on an airplane and go back to earth. Back to the *real world*. Back to where everything you did and every thought you allowed yourself to have was not dictated by Leadership. Jonah had been on one compound or another for so long he couldn't really imagine what that was like.

The trip out of Numinohi, as was often the case when the Franklins fled one place or another, was a blur. They were all exhausted long before they really got going. It was a haze of details, baggage, paperwork, and schedules.

At the last minute, Jonah learned that Hayden would be there to see them off, and he thought he might be able to impart some kind of last bit of fortification against the brainwashing, maybe tell her something that would help her keep her mind her own.

In fact, when the time came, Hayden looked blank. Her eyes had a faraway look as if she wasn't really there. She remained expressionless as if this wasn't anything unusual. Perhaps she really believed that it wasn't either.

They had a few minutes to sit before the rest of the family had to board their plane at the Goroka airport. Jonah sat there on the bench in the little terminal with the glass pane showing the single landing strip, staring out at the plane that would take them to Port Moresby. He wanted Hayden to get out of the hivemind and come home, but there really was no home to come back to, and there was nobody who could take care of any of them. What was he supposed to say that hadn't already been said a long time ago?

In the end, she was lost in the haze of wherever her head was and Jonah was at a loss to try to describe why he thought it was a bad idea to stay. Hayden just smiled serenely and said she would be okay, and that was that.

She went back with the missionary who had been kind enough to drive her out to Goroka and back to ITF, and they turned and walked out to the plane, shuffling into the beginning of yet another odyssey.

Jonah was so exhausted and had been undernourished for so long that he could do little but sleep as soon as he was in a seat. He barely remembered the transfer to a different plane at Port Moresby, and only came out of his fog of exhaustion when they landed in Hong Kong again.

Jonah remembered walking out onto the streets of Kowloon, dwarfed by the vertical towers of concrete that made up the hive of a city, feeling concrete under his old sneakers, steel sign posts and beams and vehicles around him, acrid diesel smoke in the thick, muggy air, sinister looking Peking Ducks hanging, covered in dark stickiness in a shop window. He could barely breathe in the damp, thick air of the place with the smog filling the sky, but he felt a tiny pinprick of joy and hope and gratefulness at every piece of steel and every fume and every noisy motor. He couldn't see a single thing anywhere that looked natural. Not one blade of grass, not even a tree. It was more urban than Manhattan. Jonah nearly smiled. If he had not been weary in his soul almost unto death, he would have.

The 17-year-old felt like a very old man coming back from a long war.

Walter and Laura seemed to be on another planet. There wasn't a lot of talk between them all as they finally arrived in California. Each of the four seemed to be in a different place, or at least Amy and Jonah were in a different place from their parents, who were always in exactly the same place, which was not their actual location.

Walter angrily muttered about funding. Something had gone wrong with his pipeline of support, and he was still unhappy about having to come back to the States. Jonah just leaned back in the car and waited for the dizzying movement to stop. It felt like they had been moving for days and days and days, first on a van from Numinohi, then several different jets, then another long car ride.

As they made their way up the winding road to the pine covered mountains where Grandma and Grandpa Franklin lived, he just wanted the movement to stop. He just wanted *everything* to stop.

While Walter and Laura sat down with Grandma and Grandpa in the living room for serious sounding discussions, Jonah made his way down the hall in the little trailer and collapsed on the floor of Grandpa's little library room, the closest thing they had to a spare room in that place.

He felt the old carpeting under his arms, smelt the reassuring, processed smell of air from an AC unit blowing up from a floor vent, leaned his head back and just laid there with his eyes closed for as long as they would leave him be.

The darkness that would haunt the rest of Jonah's life did not leave him alone. Whenever there was a pause, some kind of peace after one of the family's "adventures," it would creep up in the absence of adrenaline and movement. It came in the dark hours, like a thick fog that soaked into Jonah's brain and left him feeling as if nothing could ever be worthwhile again. As if he were the most worthless thing, the world were nothing but darkness, and he could never hope to do or build or live or love as a man in a free world under the sunlight again.

It was a smothering, choking depression that he only knew was there when he found himself arguing with himself, fighting the words formed in his own mind that said, *"You are worthless. You will never be anything. You are pathetic. You should just end it now."*

Sometimes at night, Jonah would crawl off of the air mattress his grandparents had laid on the floor for him, roll onto the floor and put his face in that AC vent the way he had once stuck his face in the little side windows of Dad's truck trying to breathe air that didn't smell like exhaust. He would stay like that, letting the darkness wash over him, answered by the still darkness of the pine forest outside the trailer. There were times when he would look up and it would be 3 or 4 in the morning.

Walter and Laura had urgently discussed important stuff with Grandpa and Grandma and then left Amy and Jonah with them. There was very little discussion of anything, but Jonah didn't even ask. He literally did not care where Walter and Laura went or what they did. Grandma and Grandpa set them up as well as they could in the tiny trailer. Jonah slept on an air mattress in the "library" room and Amy made do with a thin mattress on the floor in Grandpa's "office" - which was a semi-partitioned part of the living room area.

The terms of staying with Grandpa and Grandma were obviously that one would attend church every Sunday no matter what, one would attend Wednesday Bible study whenever they could harass you to go, and one would join them for choir practice if they could possibly browbeat you into it. Jonah was pretty immune to pressure by now, even from his incredibly determined grandfather, and he never went to anything but the regular Sunday service.

Grandpa Franklin decided that he should do some things to try to help Jonah get a start in life. He and Grandma took him down to get his driver's license. They took him to their dentist, and for the first and last time in many years, Jonah had some of the damage that years of neglect and eating raw sugarcane for energy in

PNG had done to his teeth. He couldn't remember his parents *ever* taking him to the dentist.

Grandpa had a friend at church who owned a Carl's Jr. franchise in Chico, the big college town way down the mountains and out in the open valley below the town Grandma and Grandpa lived in. The man agreed to give Jonah a start there so he could earn some money. They let Jonah use their old car, a Toyota Camry they had taken back and forth across the country on their trips for the Gideons or one of their other organizations dozens of times, and now retired in favor of a newer Chevy Caprice. Jonah was still wracked by the darkness during the night and when he was alone, but during the day he was nothing but a constant blur of activity.

Jonah was like a coiled spring. He'd been on some compound or other for so long he felt that he had to make up time. He went down to the local community college, a dreary place where the local children of the meth and marijuana soaked trailer community of Oroville came to try to bootstrap themselves out of a life as white trash while better, richer kids who had normal backgrounds went to a real college. He sat for an SAT and a GED in the same week, not bothering to study for either of them. He passed both with excellent scores, and just like that, Jonah was finally free from the clinging ghost of mandatory school.

He enrolled in classes there. He picked up the last ambition he could remember having for himself and tried to work toward an Engineering degree. Meanwhile, he had to pay for classes, pay for gas, and pay for books, which meant working at the burger place in Chico.

Jonah got offers for credit cards almost as soon as he enrolled in the school. Grandpa told him how to use them to pay for gas, always pay that back every month, and build up his credit. Within a month, he had more offers for more cards. Before he was done, he had gotten a platinum card with a two thousand dollar limit. He used them for necessities and paid back every penny every month, and he kept working hard.

Classes were tedious. All Jonah had been able to sign up for was a lot of mandatory English and some math. None of it was specific to what he wanted to study, and he hated the classes. Still, he went, going to classes during the day and working at night. He never seemed to stop moving during that time. It was as if he were in a race with something he could not name, something that was always right behind him, which crept up in the darkness at night when he was alone in Grandpa's little study room.

He felt like a lizard running across a pond of water so fast that it stays up and doesn't sink, like those ones in Africa or wherever they were. If it slowed, even for an instant, it would sink.

Jonah would get up in the morning, drive miles outside of town in that Camry, the radio on a rock station, turned all the way up, belting out death metal, rush to classes at the college, grab something from a vending machine to eat, then drive all the way down to Chico just in time for his shift at the Carl's Jr. He would work nights, closing up the store. They started around 9PM and stayed until everything was done and ready for the morning shift. They had to serve customers until midnight (1AM on Saturdays), and also had to take apart the broilers, the fryers, the innumerable machines in the place, scrub and mop every inch of the back and the front and the bathrooms, and get everything set up and staged for the 6AM morning shift. Some nights they worked until 3 in the morning.

Jonah didn't have time to study, but he was smart, so he skated through his classes with minimal effort and some last minute scrambling when he'd forgotten about an assignment that was due. He knew that this pace of life was unsustainable, but he was afraid to stop moving. He was afraid of what followed him just behind the last curve of the highway he took at 90 miles an hour. What lay outside the bustle and activity of the burger joint, in the still, dim corners of the dreary little cafeteria at the college.

Missionary Kids were well known to face certain problems when they left the compound and tried to join real life back in the states. In most cases, the human playdough that had come out of the MK system immediately fell into partying, drinking, and inevitably drugs as they tried to fill the gap left in them by someone telling them what to do and how to think literally every second of their lives.

Catholic kids were bad, preachers' kids were worse, but Missionary Kids took the cake. Jonah had heard stories about a dozen or so graduates of Numinohi Christian Academy who were hard core alcoholics, living on the street addicted to heroin, or in some form of rehab. One kid a couple years ahead of Jonah's class had been brought back to Numinohi like a lost, shell shocked war victim, with a black, hopeless look of brokenness in his eyes. He'd been placed in ITF in the hopes that once he dried out in a place with absolutely no access to alcohol (among other things), he could be rehabilitated. Of course, everyone whispered about what he had done while he was "backslidden," and kept their kids away from him as if he were a leper. Jonah didn't know what had happened to the human car wreck of a former MK, but he didn't think it was good. As always, nobody on base spoke of such unpleasant things.

Jonah wasn't that bad, but then he hadn't lived in an MK dorm his whole life. He didn't need someone to tell him what to do, and he would never be weak enough to turn to drugs to take away his pain, but he wasn't all right either. Jonah wasn't worried about ending up as another "fucked up MK" story, but he couldn't stop long enough to think about the future either. He filled his time and his life with activity and work the way broken MKs filled theirs with parties just to have the noise, to hear people speaking so there would not be silence. He could not name what was wrong, but he felt as if a time bomb were ticking inside him and he would one day run out of fuse.

One morning, coming back from work after 3AM, no other cars in sight, the radio blaring, Jonah just stomped on the pedal of the car and held it completely to the floorboard, feeling the little motor vibrate and howl as he wound his way up into the hills, barely hanging on to the road. Corner after corner, tires screeching as he wound his way up and up and up into the steep California mountains, a yawning cliff to his left, a wall of solid rock to his right, dancing on the lip of ravines in the darkness, he kept the pedal all the way down, barely hanging on to control until he got to the streets of the little town where Grandpa's trailer was.

The boiling rage inside Jonah was always there, had always been there like an echo of his father's Wrath, and it was slowly consuming him.

"Leaving [Jonah] and [Amy] with grandparents in California Walter and Laura drove across the country to Missouri to retrieve the last of their belongings from FNTM. They were given a car and advice from former FNTM workers who told them that their support funds had been re-allocated for other uses at FNTM and hadn't been sent on to Numinohi. This explained why their monthly support had dried up ... Walter kept the hard news to himself as he collected his belongings in Missouri, packed a car to the roof and left to return to California. As they started driving out of Missouri Walter turned to Laura and said, "Let's drop in at L'Abri" "What?" "Let's take a side trip and drop in at L'Abri. We've always wanted to visit L'Abri, let's do it now. Not the L'Abri in Switzerland, but they have one here in Rochester Minnesota." So, Walter and Laura took a side trip to Minnesota to drop in at L'Abri. ... Walter felt he needed to visit in order to finalize this missionary and God's service part of his life. The books of Francis Schaeffer formed the background for a major part of his thinking and living. He had lived through the Christian Houses, he had been to the mission field, he had sought a Service Life.... Before he

closed this missionary chapter of his life, Walter needed to see L'Abri....When they dropped in only one person was home, the husband of one of Schaffer's daughters and Walter remembered his name from one of the Schaffer books. They talked for an hour or so, it wasn't important what they talked about. Walter used his ability to discern truth to learn what he came to find."

- The Carpenter Chronicles by Walter Franklin, p. 60

27

GET IN THE CAR

Walter and Laura had apparently gone to retrieve what was left of the Franklins' worldly possessions from the FNTM compound in Misery.

They returned with a beat up looking old blue car that had seen too much sun and a load of the detritus left behind by gypsies. Jonah didn't know or inquire about where they were or what they were doing.

Apparently, Walter talked with Grandpa Franklin, and Grandpa set him up with some sort of work on yet another Christian campground. Jonah didn't realize this at the time. He was so caught up with running against some kind of internal clock of his own that he didn't pay any heed. He would have had to try to listen in on one side of Grandpa's phone conversations to learn about his parents anyway and he had no interest in doing that.

It seemed that there was some tension between Walter and his father, though neither man shared much of anything with anyone else, so it was conjecture on Jonah's part. It seemed that they disagreed about what should become of Amy, and when Walter and Laura came for her, there was a scent of disapproval in the air around Grandpa.

Jonah hadn't spoken to Amy much in the last few months. Honestly, he was starting to slip. The work nights kept getting later and it kept getting harder to get to classes in the mornings. The mandatory church sessions on Sundays were utter torture, particularly since Saturday night was the latest night of the week. Jonah had finally had to feign illness more than once in order to keep his grandparents from hounding him until he went to church with them. He could not operate on 2 hours sleep.

Living as a permanent houseguest on an air mattress wasn't a long-term solution either. Jonah hadn't even been able to unpack since he'd come back from PNG. He had two of the boxes they had mailed ahead just sitting in a corner of the tiny room and nowhere to put anything. He had nowhere to work on homework, nowhere to relax, and nowhere to even put his clothes. His dresser was a corner of the floor. Grandpa and Grandma expected everything to remain ready for important church guests outside of the little study room, so Jonah couldn't leave anything anywhere. He lived in a permanent state of discomfort.

The second semester, Jonah failed to sign up for more classes. He'd done fine for one semester, but he couldn't maintain the pace of work and study, and remedial English classes were driving him insane. Without the crushing schedule imposed by both college and work, he could pick up more hours working and actually get more than 3 hours of sleep a night.

For Jonah, the isolation of the long night drive "home" with the radio all the way up was like a buzz. He could escape for awhile, not have to think about things like metaphysical crises, just forget that he even *had* parents, much less worry about what they were doing or where they were. He didn't feel free, he certainly wasn't happy, but at least he could reach a state once in awhile where he felt nothing, and that was as good as bliss.

It may have been the letter that set off Walter, or it may have been whatever tension existed between his father and him about the disposition of his children. Likely, the letter was a catalyst, but Walter had clearly been growing more and more panicked about losing control of his kids for some time. In any case, after Hayden sent home a letter describing her wish to go to a missionary organization controlled university in Florida, something clicked in his head and "keep the family together" became a mantra, pounding away at him until he was driven to frantic activity.

Jonah was unaware of any of that until his parents appeared out of nowhere one morning when Grandpa and Grandma weren't around. They looked terrified.

"We have to rescue Hayden!" Laura looked like she was about to cry.

Jonah raised his eyebrows over the coffee he had just poured. "What do you mean? *What happened?*" His mind filled with visions of a Raskol raid on the ITF campus … They had assault rifles, there was no fence … they would kill the men, rape the women.

Walter saw the look on his son's face and stepped in. "We have to get Hayden back home *quick*. She's in trouble over there. It's not safe anymore."

Jonah gave Walter a deadpan look. When had it *ever* been safe?

Laura produced a letter, waving it vaguely and starting to cry. "She's not herself! She didn't even sound like the same person!" Her voice broke.

Jonah was confused. Was this *physical* danger or was it that Hayden was becoming a cult member? The way his parents were talking didn't make it clear.

Actually, the second option was a little more pressing to Jonah. Logically, if there had been an attack on the compound, the only thing they could do was make arrangements to bring her back from the hospital in Darwin or … make arrangements concerning her body (The locals weren't *eating* white people anymore. They had finally been dissuaded from that by the Australian army in the early 1970s.) If it were a matter of Hayden being a brainwashed cultee who needed to get out, there was more they could actually do.

They never showed him the letter. Walter quickly folded it and put it away. They sounded like they were angry at the mission organization for what it had done to them all.

Jonah was trying to figure out if this was their way of apologizing. They had never seemed to be on the same page when he was openly critical of what the organization said. Maybe they had finally realized that the whole missionary thing was some kind of scam for 90% of them - a way to sit around on a compound and do nothing while having your life paid for by gullible church people.

"What do you want me to do?"

"We need your credit cards." Walter made it seem as if he was asking for a roll of toilet paper.

Jonah stopped. Something in the back of his head felt like an electric current were being run against his skin. He stared blankly at Walter. "What do you mean?"

Laura stepped in. "Oh, we just need a couple things to bring her back. We can't pay for the whole ticket and Grandpa -"

Walter interrupted. "Don't worry, we'll pay you back. We just need a little quick cash. We *have* to get Hayden back home." He had the tone of a man talking man-things with a peer, not Dad.

Jonah sighed, feeling like a fly caught in a web. He looked back and forth from Laura to Walter. If it had just been Walter asking, he would have said no, but Laura had the same look on her face as when they had said, "We have to get out of the boy's ranch tonight!"

Jonah knew that Walter and Laura had had some run-ins with scary cults, especially in Walter's "Christian House" days in the '70s. At one point he'd almost ended up with the Children of God, a cult that would later become infamous for child abuse. Walter had told the story of his "escape" many times, and Jonah knew the kinds of evil that waited in some of those dark groups. There was no way he could leave his sister in one of them.

"Okay, so, if it's a plane ticket … we can call from here…" Jonah fumbled for his wallet. He chose his student Visa, the smallest of the three cards he had. Walter's eyes locked onto it.

"No, we need some things like transportation and gas money…" Walter and Laura were heading toward the door. "Look, why don't you come and we can get what we need on the way…"

Jonah shook his head. "We can call in what we need…"

"Are you going to help or not?" There was a flash of anger in Walter's eyes.

"Well, yeah, but…"

"Look, we need to get things done here! We don't have time for this bullshit!"

Behind Walter's hard face, Laura looked at Jonah accusatorily as if he were betraying her somehow by being so mistrustful. Her eyes seemed to say, "Why do you hate your sister *and your mother?*"

Jonah shook his head. He didn't understand what was going on here. "Look, if we need to get Hayden back, then okay, let's do it."

Walter took the card from Jonah's fingers as they guided him toward the door. "It'll be quicker if I just hang on to that. Come on, let's go."

Jonah hesitated again when he saw the sun-bleached beater of a sedan that Walter had been given by some missionary in Misery.

Get in the car seemed to ring in his head.

He looked back at Grandpa's trailer.

"Come on, Jonah! What is *wrong* with you? We have to go get Hayden home!"

He got in. Walter was muttering something about "keeping the family together." His eyes had the gleam of someone who wasn't really seeing what was in front of him as he pulled out of the driveway. It was a strange light, like he had used to get back in Oroville … Jonah knew he was making a big mistake.

Jonah didn't know whether he ended up paying for the ticket itself, or just some other aspect of the trip. He did know that they were in frenzied, chaotic motion again. They went here and there, doing things, buying things. There was some kind of plan, but Jonah didn't know what it was. Walter kept talking about how everything was going to be better. Laura went on about how the family would be together again. He said he had a good job now, and he had a place for them. All they had to do was get everything together and it would all be good again.

They got the second card when they stopped for gas and Dad said there was nothing left on the first card. They were in the middle of the California valley on some backroad somewhere, hundreds of miles from anywhere. Once again, Dad "hung onto it" "just for now."

There were phone calls, some kind of activity. They picked up Amy from somewhere. Jonah must have been in shock. Looking back on it later, he couldn't understand how he had let it happen. It was like joining a cult. At no point was he ever alone. Walter and Laura were always with him, even when they went back to Grandpa's house to pick up his things. There was always the sense of fear, the being off balance, the cajoling or bullying, the lack of information about what was going on. They did *indeed* get Hayden from the airport. She actually looked happier than Jonah had seen her in a while. She seemed less than enthusiastic when she saw them all lined up next to the shitty old car, waiting for her.

Walter's attitude changed when he went up to meet Hayden and Jonah realized that he must have used a different line with her than with Jonah. He seemed to be reassuring her that he had everything taken care of; there was a place for them to go. The whole family could be together now; they could go *home*. Walter was using Jonah's credit cards to buy things to impress Hayden that they were all okay.

The old beat up car wound its way out into the countryside of Northern California, miles and miles beyond the valley, to the redwoods. Over bumpy little roads and winding highways. Jonah was crammed into the back like a sardine with Amy in the middle of the little bench seat. He couldn't help thinking what a step he had just made from driving that Camry to sitting in the back of the car yet again, crammed in with all kinds of baggage, both human and inanimate.

They turned off the highway onto a tiny little road that ran under the towering redwoods like a mouse hole in some cartoon - a tunnel of living trees.

The place was familiar. Jonah remembered it from when he was a child. He had once come here for Bible camp one summer. It was a place that was special to Walter, he had grown up working out there with Grandpa Franklin to build this place back when he was a kid. They had come to Mt. David Bible camp.

Another Christian compound.

There was a collective groan from the back of the car. Hayden looked surprised. "What's going on? What is this? I thought you said you had a house…"

"We'll have a place, we have everything all set up. Don't worry. It'll be great."

Jonah was shaking his head. This was all wrong. Everything was wrong. What the hell had he done?

Walter had gotten his dad (who was on the board of directors of the camp) to work out a paid position for him there. The camp was letting Walter and Laura stay in a fifth wheel camping trailer parked on a little dirt pad on one edge of the camp. There was literally only enough room for the two of them to sleep in that little trailer. There was absolutely nowhere for any of the rest of them to go.

"What is *this*?" Hayden looked shocked. When there was no answer, she found a place to sit down and just remained there, unmoving and mute.

Walter had taken Jonah aside with the air of someone confiding in a friend. "She's still messed up by the programming over there. Look, *we* have to do something. The family needs a place to sleep."

Jonah looked around at the dusty patch of nothing in the middle of the redwood forest, the rotting old trailer with the peeling paint, the faded blue gift car loaded to the gills with gypsy baggage. How the *fuck* had he let himself be dragged here? What the fuck was *wrong* with him?

The camp had no staff housing available for Walter's family. Whether this was due to Grandpa Franklin's dissatisfaction with Walter's decision to bring his kids there or just random luck, Jonah didn't know. All he knew was that they managed to find another trailer - the kind you might pull behind a truck to go camping with - or what you may have done that with back in the 1970s and which had spent Jonah's entire lifetime rotting and growing mildew in the forest since then. This was to house Hayden and Amy. A final, small travel trailer made of fiberglass and built sometime in the 1960s was to be Jonah's home. This had been bought by Walter with some of Jonah's money and more of Jonah's money went to repainting it.

Walter *did* have some cash on hand. It was not clear whether he had managed to continue to receive tithes from a couple of his New Guinea supporters after they had come home (which would explain how he'd managed to travel to Misery and back) either on the presumption that he was working for God in some other capacity or on the presumption that he was still in PNG. Everything was so chaotic and the things Walter said to Jonah and Hayden so ambiguous or contradictory, that nobody but Walter probably knew the real story.

In any case, Mt. David was going to start camp operations soon and they had some building efforts that they needed done. Walter's great plan to keep the family together was to work here as they had at Mt. Promise.

He had a great dream as well. As his last act working on the sense of duty that Jonah still possessed to try to take care of his family, Walter drove him out to an ATM, took out money on his biggest credit card, and promised to solve the family's homelessness once and for all. Jonah didn't understand what he was getting at until they pulled up in front of a country house a few miles away from Mt. David and Jonah saw a huge, filthy looking yellow school bus with a "for sale" sign in the window in the front yard of a farmhouse.

Walter talked the guy down to the amount of cash he had on hand. The guy didn't seem to press the issue too hard. He was clearly relieved to get the thing off his property. Jonah stood there, trying to figure out what degree of normalcy or insanity this was. He didn't know.

Walter went on and on about how great a bus was for living in, how he had converted one into a house when he and Laura had run off to Mt. Shasta to live on "Narnia," one of their Christian House experiments. Hayden had taken her first step and spoken her first words in such a hippie bus.

Jonah knew this would end badly, but he still felt caught by the sense of obligation he felt toward his kin. It took him many years to realize just *how* backwards his mind had been screwed around back then.

The minute the man smiled and took the cash and they got in the bus and started rolling, things started to go bad. Walter had sworn that he was an expert with complicated transmissions such as the ones these old busses used. He cursed again and again as he tried to shift, grinding the gears over and over. It had apparently been a long time.

They started down the winding country road, Laura following in the shitty blue car. Within the equivalent of a couple blocks, smoke started billowing out of the back of the engine compartment at the rear of the bus. Jonah was walking around inside, giving Walter periodic status updates as Walter desperately tried to coax the beast down the winding, undulating, country road.

"We're smoking now!"

"What?"

"I said, we have a lot of smoke coming out of the back! It's billowing like there is something on fire in there!"

Walter cursed again, grinding the gears badly as they started to climb a hill. "Just tell me if there's oil or anything!"

Jonah went back to the back of the bus once more, looking out. "There's a big squealing sound! It sounds like we are eating a fan belt or something! It isn't going away!"

Walter glared from the driver's seat. "Goddamn it! What the fuck are you doing back there, Jonah!"

"Hey, I'm not making it smoke! Um… hey, the smoke is getting worse now!"

Grind grind grind.

"Goddamn it, fuck, Jonah! Just *help*! Quit fucking nagging me!"

"You said to let you know if something was happening that shouldn't. That's what I'm doing."

Grind grind grind.

"SHUT THE FUCK UP!"

They finally turned onto the long road to Mt. David.

"Um… Dad...."

"I SAID SHUT THE FUCK UP!"

Grind grind grind.

"Dad … we're losing *oil* now." Jonah had his head near one of the back windows. "Holy shit! Dad, we are losing a LOT of oil!"

Gouts of black motor oil had begun to spew from the side of the engine bay like blood from a carotid artery. It was more motor oil than Jonah had ever seen at one time. It must have been gallons, spraying out behind the bus all over the drive leading up to Mt. David Campgrounds.

"Dad, the engine is going to freeze up."

"GODDAMN IT, I KNOW! SHUT UP!"

"Okay, Dad." Jonah sat down on one of the seats, waiting for the inevitable.

Somehow, they made it to the dusty cluster of moldy trailers that the gypsy family slept in. The bus gave a last, shuddering gasp and blew another gallon of hot motor oil into the powdery dirt. Walter cut the engine, and they all came out to look at the smoke-belching monstrosity that was to be their new home.

The last of Jonah's cards were burned repairing and painting it with white house paint using rollers.

The campground Leadership got mad at Walter for spewing oil all over their driveway and parking lot. Walter seemed mad that these newcomers would try to tell him anything at the campground he'd helped his dad carve out of the forest as a kid. Walter seemed to think that he was royalty in some way at Mt. David because his father had helped found the place and still served on the board of directors.

So began the last phase of "working for God."

Walter had an answer for everything, of course. He told Jonah that, as he himself had learned in his youth, that minimum wage jobs in a burger joint were pretty useless. One could make *far* more money in construction. Walter said the camp would pay Jonah more than he had been making at Carl's Jr. In a little while, he'd be able to save up and get a car and get some kind of start.

Jonah didn't believe him anymore. Somewhere in that last shuffle of chaos, something inside him had broken forever. He hadn't really trusted Walter for a long time, but now he just assumed that whatever Walter said was probably a lie unless it was proven otherwise.

Walter could see the change in his son's eyes. He grew more belligerent every day. He could see the way Jonah would narrow his eyes or pause and sift anything he said to him, as if carefully weighing it before actually accepting anything. Jonah had started to treat things his father said in the way you might treat a story on the front of a supermarket tabloid. There may certainly be grains of truth, but mostly the story is there for entertainment purposes.

Walter grew angrier by the day. He knew he was losing control of his kids. He could see that he had already lost control of Jonah's mind.

When they poured a new sidewalk area for the campground that was supposed to be exposed aggregate, and it turned out that the cement was the wrong type so it was hardening so fast they couldn't scrub the concrete off the gravel on top, Jonah worked alongside Walter as they sweated and toiled. Hour after hour, trying to save the sidewalk from being a total disaster. Jonah stood by with a hose trying to keep the cement from curing and blast off the top layer while Walter knelt and scrubbed desperately. Jonah stayed and worked, but he also asked, "Why are we doing this?" His question seemed to encompass a lot more than just a ruined sidewalk.

They were being paid to work by the camp. At least that was the theory. Walter's plan was different though. He was trying to pool the family's money in order to get first month's rent and a deposit somewhere. Jonah couldn't accept that. He was done being told after the fact what the "plan" was.

It came to a head when they took their Sunday drive one week. In every compound they had been at, Sunday church service was compulsory. One either attended the service on the compound or attended some local church service nearby. The only way to avoid being labeled as "backslidden" was to go, and the Franklins had found it easier to get in the car and drive to a church of their own choosing rather than have to face the same staffers every single day of the week.

Since they had come to Mt. David, nobody had the heart to actually attend a church anymore. Even Walter and Laura had just given up, like wind-up toys that had finally begun to slow down. So they went through the motions. The family would climb into the faded blue sedan every Sunday and they would go for a drive long enough that people would think they had been to church. It was one tiny relief. Unfortunately, it forced them to all be in the same place at the same time for far longer than *any* of them had the tolerance for any longer.

"I want my paycheck." Jonah sat, ramrod straight, staring hard at the back of Walter's head from the bench seat.

"GODDAMN IT! Laura, YOU talk to him!"

Laura turned in the passenger seat to look back at her son. "I've explained to you, Jonah, we are trying to get enough together to get a place for the whole family. We need to combine our resources to do that." She had the tone of an elementary school teacher.

Jonah hadn't looked at her. He stayed staring at the back of Walter's head.

"I. Want. My. Paycheck."

Walter exploded. "You spoiled piece of shit! Goddamn fucking useless piece of shit!" Spittle was flying from his mouth. The car swerved back and forth on the road, almost careening into a ditch. "I'LL KICK YOUR SPOILED LITTLE ASS!"

The rest of the car was dead silent. All the girls sat numb, staring ahead of them at a vacant point somewhere in front of their eyes.

Jonah stared, unflinching. He seriously doubted that Walter was capable of kicking his ass anymore. If it came to that, then it came to that.

"I want my -"

The car jerked to the right as Dad slammed on the brakes, pulling to the side of the empty country road. His eyes were pure black. A fleck of foam had appeared on the corner of his mouth. He was completely out of control. This was the kind of Wrath that none of the kids had seen in many years. This was the kind of Wrath that Jonah remembered from his childhood. Dad did not stop screaming. Inside that earsplitting scream of Wrath, it was like a heavy silence fell. Nobody heard words. Nobody heard anything.

The car came to a stop. Dad's door flew open. He was in the road, gesturing wildly as he paced next to the car.

"YOU THINK YOU'RE A *MAN* NOW? YOU THINK *YOU* ARE PAYING ALL THE BILLS?"

Walter jerked the back door of the car open, looming over Jonah, who sat, watching him with a dark, unreadable expression. He didn't flinch or even move at the violent fury of the action.

"FINE, GET THE FUCK OUT AND NEVER COME BACK! YOU *GET THE FUCK OUT OF MY CAR!*"

They remained like that in the sudden, shocking silence. Walter panting as he stared down at Jonah who was still seated in the back of the car.

In the silence, Hayden and Amy remained unseeing, unmoving, clearly hating every second, but keeping their heads down. Jonah afforded himself a glance at his mother. He was almost surprised.

Something inside him already knew what he would see, but the physical sight of it still bothered him. Laura sat in the front passenger seat, dumb, mute, blind, staring away and to the right as if none of them were there. She wasn't even present. Amy and Hayden were unseeing, Laura was worse; she was unknowing. Consciously, carefully, intentionally unknowing.

The memory of looking toward the passenger seat and Laura not meeting his eyes, just looking away to the right stayed with Jonah. He had thought she was a victim of the insanity, that she would look out for him when push really came to shove. He had believed her when she said his parents cared about him, even though she always included the obligatory phrase, "Walter really loves you, he just doesn't know how to show it," which even at 10 had seemed like bullshit to Jonah. He'd given her a pass, but now he realized that that was all she had to offer - comforting words that always rang hollow after it was too late to help.

That glance happened in a part of a second, but to Jonah time had seemed to still like water in an angry stream suddenly hitting a pool. He wanted to step out of the car and face Dad ... he wanted Dad to *try* something. His blood boiled with the molten fury of a rage which he carried inside of him every single second of every single day and which grew deeper and wider and hotter every minute. He wanted to just step out and start walking ... but he was thinking.

He had not brought his wallet that morning. He had perhaps $5 and a driver's license (plus the useless credit cards Walter was done with) in that wallet, but he didn't have so much as identification or one penny on him right now. Even the book of phone numbers he kept was in that wallet. He couldn't even call some relative without it. He also had no idea where he was. Northern California is a vast place, and on these Sunday drives, the Franklins had strayed farther and farther along the winding backwoods roads from the already remote Mt. David campground. They were *hundreds* of miles from any town he was familiar with.

Jonah never doubted Dad's seriousness. In Wraths of old, he had screamed about kicking Jonah (or one of the others) out of his house. Obviously, Walter could no longer use the phrase "as long as you are under my roof…" because he provided no roof. Still, he had meant it the same way. He would just drive away and leave Jonah in the middle of the countryside without a penny or a change of clothes, and, for the first time in his life, Jonah realized that Laura would probably say *nothing*.

Jonah wanted to just step out and walk. He could hitchhike ... somewhere … Maybe find a way to trade his basic construction skills for food, in direct competition with the flood of Mexicans standing on every corner of every town in California looking for similar work … Jonah would have done it in an instant if Walter hadn't taken every penny that could be taken out of his credit cards. As it was, he had no way to get anywhere, no way to feed himself, no idea where he was, and not even a way to get back to Grandpa Franklin's house, or even call them. He was little better off than he was trying to run away from home at ten-years-old.

Jonah felt a sick feeling in his stomach as he realized that Walter had called his bluff. He hadn't realized that it had *been* a bluff, but now it was called, and Walter had won this round. He was not ready to just live on the street as a bum … yet. One thing he would make sure of was that he never, *ever* left his wallet behind again.

The silence had stretched for a minute and a half. Jonah still openly stared right at Walter, looking him directly in the eyes. He had not moved to get out of the car. If Walter wanted to try to *make* him get out, it would end badly. He may not have been willing to become a penniless vagabond, but neither was he going to just stare at the back of a seat like the girls were doing. This was *not* over.

Walter panted, hatred written across every line of his face. He fought to bring himself under control, then jerkily stepped back to the driver's door, hands shaking from the adrenaline.

"That's what I thought."

Jonah closed his eyes for the briefest second as Walter landed heavily in the driver's seat. He felt a wave of self-loathing unlike anything he had ever known.

You are the most worthless, pathetic, piece of shit that has ever been born.

The voice wasn't Walter's, it was inside Jonah's head.

He sat in silence as the car began to move again, feeling bile in his throat. He wanted to vomit from the intensity of the loathing he felt for the entire world and especially for himself.

Well maybe so, Jonah. Maybe I am ... but next time I'll be ready. Next time it won't be a bluff.

28

COUNTDOWN

It could not continue. Walter was losing control. Jonah was a hairsbreadth away from bolting. In the aftermath of the incident on the drive that wasn't spoken of, Walter applied himself and finally found a position at a construction company in Sausalito. They made high end fancy houses for rich people in and around San Francisco. Ironically, that was basically the same thing Walter had once been doing in Beverly Hills for movie stars' houses before he had decided to drop everything and run off to Texas on the first missionary trip back when Amy was less than a year old. Now it just remained for them to get somewhere to live.

Walter and Laura were lectured by the camp director and his wife. It seemed they were backslidden. Walter had anger problems. Laura came back from her session with the director's wife shaking her head angrily at how unfairly they were being treated by Leadership.

"Do you *know* what she said to me?" Laura was speaking to Walter one of the last days they were at Mt. David. Jonah happened to be close enough to hear some of the conversation from the trailer he slept in.

"She said; 'It's awful what Walter is doing to those kids.' It's like she was trying to turn me *against* you!" Laura sounded totally affronted by the meddling.

Jonah shut his door. For some reason, that phrase stuck in his head. *It's awful what Walter is doing to those kids.*

Jonah hadn't said anything to Walter since the Sunday car ride. If he was expected to do something in the ordinary course of his duties on the camp, he did so without saying anything, asking anything, or hearing anything from him.

The next day, Jonah had just gone to the dining hall and swept up as was usual, saying nothing, going early so by the time Walter figured out where he was, he was done. If he was to be slave labor, he would do it for now, because he was out of options, but he was only here until he figured out what else he could do. Jonah made no attempt to figure out the implied meaning of tasks that needed to be done. He carried out exactly and *only* the literal meaning of what he was asked to do. If they needed to talk to him, they had to do it through Laura. He would reluctantly speak to her, though no more than absolutely necessary.

Walter and Laura got in gear. They took the money everyone had "pooled" and rented an apartment in Sausalito. It was probably twice the rent of a place farther away from San Francisco, but Walter didn't want to have to commute and anyway, he liked boats.

The move was chaotic and exhausting, but there was a palpable sense of relief in finally getting away from a "compound" of one sort or another. Jonah had watched his parents very carefully as they made the preparations. If Walter had done anything other than what he did, land a high paying job at a boutique construction firm in "Richy-Rich Ville," he would have just hitchhiked back across California one night and made the best of it. As it was, he still had the basic problem of having somewhere to live while he tried to go to college. Working and going to school had worked okay, but if he was going to work enough to pay for rent, he wasn't going to have time for school at all. He knew there were loans and scholarships out there too, but he didn't know how to start the process of even applying for them or whether he could get accepted to a real university with a GED instead of a diploma. Right now, "Walter's truck" was still the best thing available for going where he needed to get to, so he stayed silent and waited.

Walter and Laura took the living room and worked out a space with a folding couch bed, leaving the rooms to the kids. It was something of a compromise and would never have happened in the old days. It could possibly be interpreted as an apology of sorts, though Jonah didn't bother trying to interpret anything anymore, and he had never heard an actual, verbalized apology for the entire "working for God" business. He never would.

It did seem that Walter and Laura were attempting to make an effort toward the kids though. It made no impact on either Jonah or Hayden, of course. Jonah remained a boiling pit of pitch-black rage who barely gave them two words strung together, and Hayden remained a hopeless lump sunk into a seemingly permanent black depression. She barely moved, she only obediently did the very minimal thing that was necessary at a particular moment and spent the rest of the time collapsed in bed, lost in a permanent darkness. For now, the "family" consisted of Laura, Walter and Amy, with Amy herself being a bitingly sarcastic participant. Jonah and Hayden were only there in body.

Once again, Jonah began to re-start his "start in life." He registered with a community college in San Francisco and looked for work. He combed newspaper ads for a working car for cheap, and eventually found a deal on a 1964 Volkswagen Beetle that he would buy for eight hundred dollars of very hard-earned cash.

The cash would be earned working construction laborer jobs in San Francisco. Jonah found himself doing things like breaking out walls in houses that were to be remodeled and hauling plastic garbage cans full of concrete on his back down four flights of stairs in

Pacific Heights alongside a lot of illegal Mexican laborers. As always, he had no trouble working hard.

In the midst of the preparations for a real life, he couldn't avoid Walter though.

One day as Jonah returned to the damp little crowded apartment in the fog shrouded Marin Headlands, he caught Walter and Laura in the middle of one of their planning conversations. It was the sort of thing they had always done, really. Laura would bring up some problem or other with a voice that sounded like she might cry at any time, Walter would confidently declare what they would all do (unless he didn't have a pat answer, in which case, in the old days, he would fly into a Wrath). Jonah didn't pay any attention. He went to the fridge and looked for something to eat.

Suddenly he caught the gist of the conversation.

"But how are we going to pay for it? It doesn't add up."

Walter was breezily unconcerned. He sat on the couch they folded out into a bed every night, fiddling with one of his drawings of a dirigible or a tugboat or something (like Hayden, he had a collection of drawings he kept and would draw on and daydream about when he had time).

"We'll charge it to the credit cards."

"But … we already have too much on them and we can't pay it back…"

"We'll just let them go. They'll write them off. Your credit resets after ten years or something."

Jonah had slowly and silently placed the Coke can he was about to open on the counter in the tiny kitchen. He felt the blood rush into his ears. His vision narrowed to a fine point. He felt his legs and arms tingle and his stomach turn over. All the rage, all the Wrath, all of the boiling lava of anger he carried inside him every minute of every day suddenly peaked. It was like something in his head just went "click." He sucked in his breath.

Suddenly, Jonah was across the living room. He moved like a charging bear, so fast that Walter didn't have time to put down the paper he was holding. By the time Walter looked up, Jonah was over him, towering down, eyes wild. He looked like a man gone totally mad.

Jonah stuck his face a bare inch from the end of Walter's pointy nose and out of the depths of his toes, up through his body, out of his lungs came a scream of rage.

It was the sound a man might make if he were facing the very extremity of mortal terror. It was a scream of awful rage that blasted the eardrums like a train whistle. It was a voice of total, inhuman fury. It was the sound of one of Dad's Wraths … except instead of fear, there was nothing but pure anger.

"THOSE. ARE. *MY*. FUCKING. CREDIT. CARDS!"

Walter fell back in the couch, a look of stunned shock on his face. He'd gone pale.

Jonah was actually seeing stars. He was shaking. Every limb trembling with an overload of adrenaline. His eyes didn't leave Walter's face, but he stopped, saying nothing more, just standing there in the middle of the living room.

Like a cornered rat, Walter suddenly flung himself off the couch. He was trying something he'd learned in high school wrestling and had to re-learn while helping "take down" boys at the boy's ranch. The momentum of his drive forced Jonah back into the tiny hallway of the little apartment, but Jonah kept his feet without any trouble.

Walter growled and tried to grab Jonah's legs. He managed to get one, but Jonah just clenched the muscles in his legs and broke his grip. These were legs that carried cans full of concrete up and down stairs all day, every day. They were like steel.

Jonah wasn't trying to fight. He didn't want to *hurt* Walter, but he didn't want his stinking breath in his face either, so he shoved him back with enough force to throw him back into the living room. If Jonah had wanted to take him down, he could have done so right then.

Walter came back. It was like a pug desperately hanging on to the neck of a bulldog. Jonah shook him off. He was bigger, stronger, and in better shape. Jonah also had something Walter never had. He had learned Wrath from his father, but he *controlled* it. He could reach down inside and pull it out whenever he wanted, and vent just a little of the rage. He could have kept on shaking Walter off all day.

Walter threw himself at his son one last time, desperately trying anything. He tried to wear him down, trip him, pull him down. Jonah was finally getting mad enough to try to hurt him now, and he slammed them both into the wall, with Walter caught between the wall and Jonah's shoulder. Jonah grunted like a bull and shoved his father away again.

Walter was done. He collapsed on the couch, gasping for air. He looked like a guy who had just tried to wrestle two stages above his weight class. He had nothing left. He bent over and stayed there.

Jonah walked back into the living room and stood there one more time, looking at Walter and Laura. She didn't look at him, she was bending over Walter in concern. Jonah shook his head, turned, and went to go get that Coke. He was shaking.

That was when Dad died.

Jonah never heard another word from him ever again. After that, Walter's attitude toward him changed completely. Amazingly, he became polite, solicitous, and even made an effort to try to clumsily demonstrate some approximation of affection. He was like a completely different person whenever Jonah was there.

It didn't stop Jonah from leaving, but it certainly made his preparations easier.

The Pacific Ocean runs up against the land on California's Coastal Range. It is like a sea wall that holds back the largest and most powerful ocean in the world. The mountains are green and grey, covered to the top in springy turf and scrubby looking little bushes. Sea and wind and salt and clouds race in from the Pacific and shred themselves against those mountains, and it can be sunny one second, foggy the next, and pouring freezing rain from the Alaskan current in an hour. The Marin Headlands are a peninsula of rock that runs with the Pacific battering against one side in a glory of twenty foot waves and hundred foot cliffs, and the San Francisco Bay roiling on the other, pushing or pulling in or out of the Golden Gate - the gap between San Francisco and Marin through which millions and millions of gallons of water from the entire Bay Area must rush at every change of the tide.

From the top of the Marin Headlands trail, you can look down on the Golden Gate Bridge as if you stood in a small airplane, the city of San Francisco laid out behind it like a glittering jewel of towers and streets. It is truly one of the most beautiful spots on the entire earth, and Jonah loved to take long hikes up into the Headlands from the trail that started behind the damp little apartment.

He was working hard. He was going to classes at the community college and driving back and forth over the Golden Gate Bridge every day in his little Volkswagen. He still had no "home" per se. He used Walter's apartment as a place to sleep, never staying a minute longer than he had to, barely acknowledging his parents if he happened to pass them while they were there. Since Walter and Laura had always been workaholics and Jonah was busy with work and school, he barely saw them, which was fine with him.

Jonah spent what little time he did have walking the trails of the Marin Headlands in the sun and the wind and the foggy rain, reading Tolstoy and Hemingway, and even writing again, as he had not done in years. He actually wrote a 300-page book in one month, printed the entire novel, then looked through it with a growing realization that it was complete and utter crap. He put it in a drawer and left it there.

Hayden came with Jonah to the community college for classes of her own, catching a ride with him in his Beetle. It seemed that when Jonah was doing something, she had motivation enough to try as well, but when he wasn't around, she just stayed shut up in a little closet she had taken over in the apartment, scribbling in her notebooks, sipping tea, and increasingly seeming to talk to people who weren't there.

Jonah was preoccupied with the problem of escape now. He had been steadily digging himself out of the debt his father had left him, paying off the cards one paycheck at a time, until he would once again have the ability to go … somewhere. Walter never offered to pay him back and he never asked. It didn't matter anymore.

The somewhere was the problem for Jonah now. The engineering classes he had been taking at the college had begun to teach him something valuable; he was never going to be an engineer. Jonah loved physics, geometry, trigonometry, and building things, but the "real" maths like algebra and calculus made him want to kill himself. Walter had been born with a natural inclination for that kind of math, but to Jonah it would remain a foreign language. Unfortunately, Jonah now started to realize just how much time most engineers spent doing math, and he knew he had to rethink his choice of profession.

The thing Jonah was probably best at was writing, but even at that age, he wasn't stupid enough to think anyone could actually make a living as a writer.

Jonah liked the idea of going into the military. He was driven as always and wanted to be the best, get into the best, most elite thing he possibly could. If he was going to go for the military, he wanted to be a Navy SEAL. He felt that his stubborn drive and physical competence would get him through. He was the kind of person who just never, ever gave up once he had set his sights on something.

The only thing that was stopping Jonah was Judaism. Ever since Numinohi, he had been trying to work through a problem he couldn't get around. He believed the Bible, he believed in God, but after everything he'd seen and every compound he had lived on, he no longer believed in "Christianity." Jesus had said, "by their fruits, you shall know them."

If the fruits of Christianity were pig slop, terror, and child sacrifice, then he wanted nothing to do with it. Unfortunately, he just couldn't leave it alone. This problem of what part of the Bible he had grown up with was really real and what part must be bullshit just stuck with him like a sore in his mouth that he couldn't leave alone.

Realistically, Jonah should have thrown up his hands, said, "fuck it all," and joined the US Military, probably as a career soldier as his mother's sister had done. In fact, virtually *everyone* in his mother's family had been in uniform at various times. Escaping a horrible home life to the military was a long family tradition. It would be the most *practical* thing to do, and God knew Jonah was hungry for practicality after the years of being blown around by whatever wind blew Walter across the face of the earth.

Still, in the time since he'd had his own car, Jonah had started showing up at a conservative synagogue for Shabbat (Sabbath) services. He had borrowed a line-by-line Greek-English literal translation New Testament from Grandpa Franklin, and spent hours trying to work out whether, or how, the NTM Missionaries were misinterpreting it, or whether there was just stuff in there that really shouldn't have been. He'd bought a scholarly translation of the Mishna, the core of the Jewish Oral Tradition and second most important book after the Torah (Old Testament). In the comparison, he'd been shocked. Here was Paul telling you to sacrifice and suffer and be happy about it, and there was a book that had taken the time to record two different Rabbis completely opposite opinions about how to interpret the Old Testament because it was *that* important to them, and because they respected the intelligence of the reader to think for themselves. There were whole lists of "do this, do that" in Paul's letters, but in the supposedly "legalistic" Jewish tradition, there was debate, not bowing to absolute authority. No kissing the ring of a pope or stand in local pope like "Leadership."

People were *disagreeing with one another* in their most holy literature that they *all* had to study to be good Jews. It was like oxygen on Mt. Everest for Jonah after years of sucking up and obeying the mandates of whoever was the stand-in for God on the compound they were on. None of the greatest, most revered Rabbis had *ever* been a "pope" as far as Jonah could tell.

So he went to the synagogue every week, watched people genuinely happy to be there. They had ancient traditions going back five thousand years. Their culture was to make a guest welcome, and to always bring *food*, not cheap dishes of casserole like Grandma Franklin brought to church, they brought wonderful things as good as you might find in a store, but cooked up with profound love and competence by people following generations of passed down knowledge. They didn't sit on folding chairs over a rotting, moldy carpet in a building that looked like it should be condemned like the churches in Misery. They made that synagogue the most beautiful place they could. They built an ark for their Torah scroll that was a piece of art. Unlike a Catholic church, it wasn't just a cookie-cutter fancy church exactly like every other one either, and it didn't have creepy niches where you could burn candles to idols (saints). The things decorating the walls and windows were the words of God written out in the oldest still living language on earth - Hebrew.

To Jonah, Judaism seemed to be saying, "Judge me by what you see in front of your eyes. If we are God's chosen people and blessed, it should be obvious." Christianity, to Jonah always seemed to have said, "Don't trust your eyes, trust your heart. Don't listen to your heart, listen to Leadership. Don't think, just obey."

While Christianity went to the farthest corner of the earth to find one more soul, Judaism had a tradition of turning away would be converts at *least* three times before even letting them start to study. It was almost as if they *knew* they had something valuable. They weren't trying to give out free samples like a crack dealer on a street corner or trying to browbeat people into coming to their services.

The crisis of faith in Jonah's mind was solidifying into a laser like intensity on Israel. If he was going to judge things by their fruits - what they actually *did* and created in the real world instead of a lot of rhetoric, he wanted to see the physical result of God's prophecy regarding his people.

Was it like Numinohi? A neurotic glorified cult compound where everyone pretended to be perfect while they did the opposite of what they claimed to believe? Would it show the Old Testament to be hollow in practice as (to Jonah) all the Christian compounds had shown the New Testament hollow? He wanted to see it. No matter how much he read about it, studied about it, or how many pictures he came across, he could not find any trace of the self-deceiving phoniness he had seen on every one of the Christian compounds he'd lived on.

Jonah was not his father. He was far more practical than Walter, though it would take more years and some hard lessons to fully realize that potential. If he did something, he was going to think it through and he would have a plan.

So the choice seemed clear enough. Jonah could not stand to continue to live in Walter's apartment. Every second in that place was like hot ash on his skin. He *must* escape. He knew he was not going to become an engineer, so getting a massive loan to go to some college and learn what the hell he actually *could* do seemed like an extraordinary waste of more money than he'd ever seen in one place in his life. His best bet was the military. That would get him out, get him a practical education in useful things and teach him what he could do, and leave him with a GI bill that could get him started in college. It was a no-brainer.

Until Jonah learned that the Israel Defense Forces also had their *own* version of a "GI bill." There was a Hebrew study program at Tel Aviv University that lasted six weeks and would give Jonah the chance to see Israel. Maybe from there, he might find his way to the IDF ... Maybe he could escape *and* resolve his crisis of faith at the same time.

Jonah decided he had to go to Israel.

Should he have stayed and just gone to college like a normal person? Probably. Was he jumping from a forced "adventure" in PNG into another one in the Middle East? Certainly. This time though, Jonah was doing so on his own, with his own money, and for his *own* reasons, and that made all the difference.

At a little over 18-years-old, Jonah was by no means done with doing possibly stupid things in his life (as he would later learn), but he was certainly done with doing *other people's* stupid things.

29

THE HOLY LAND

Out of at least the *hundreds* of times that Jonah had waited in a terminal and boarded an airplane in his life, the first flight out from San Francisco that would deposit him in Tel Aviv was actually not very memorable. Looking back, he always remembered arriving in Israel, but he barely remembered that first flight away from "home."

Walter and Laura had been on their best behavior for some time by then, making every appearance of being part of a nice, loving family. They had convinced a reluctant Jonah to sit for a phony looking, staged, studio photo with his siblings before he left, so they would have a picture to keep. Jonah barely remembered it later, it was so inconsequential to him.

They all came out to see him off at the airport. Jonah had signed up for a six-week program at Tel Aviv University, but nobody was even pretending that this wasn't permanent. Laura had clearly been crying, but for once, she had done it in private and tried to smile at the airport. Walter looked slightly lost. He also looked like he had aged about ten years in the last six months or so. The beginnings of an "old man" could be seen in his posture.

Jonah was shocked when Walter came up to Jonah, mumbled something about always travelling with cash in your pocket, and handed him a couple hundred dollars. Jonah had paid for his ticket and trip himself, and he had his now paid off credit cards as backup. He hadn't expected a penny out of Walter. It seemed that there may have been some apology in

Walter's eyes and those folded up bills. Jonah couldn't be sure.

Hayden looked sort of lost. Amy looked sort of bored. They all stood at the terminal and nodded to one another but didn't have a lot to say. Jonah got the feeling that some part of his sisters resented him for flying away to some extent. Surely Amy was just biding her time until she too was old enough. She would join the Coast Guard as soon as she could (carrying on the long tradition in Laura's family of joining the military to escape a troubled home life).

Jonah was worried about Hayden. She hadn't really recovered from her black depression and had never seemed quite the same since she'd come back from PNG. She had lately spent sometimes a week at a time in her little closet never coming out. Jonah had overheard Walter complaining to Laura that, "We're going to come home someday and find her with her wrists slit in the bathtub." Not that they were going to do anything about it.

Jonah wanted to do something, but he couldn't. The best he could do was get away himself. He had no way to carry someone else. He had tried everything he knew to get Hayden to do things for herself. She had even had a retail job at an art store for a while and bought an old beater of a car that was at least something to get around in. It hadn't lasted and now she had receded into herself again. Jonah felt as if his own internal clock had just run out. He couldn't stay here one more minute. It was like that moment when someone on a sinking ship just stops trying to convince the reluctant passenger to get out of their stateroom and get to the lifeboats and just goes. No more time, Jonah just had to get out now. It was that simple.

At least Hayden looked cheerful now. She had said that Jonah getting out gave her hope, and that was good. Maybe it would inspire her to action.

The flight was a blur. Compared to the flights to and from PNG, it was downright boring, which was absolutely perfect as far as Jonah was concerned. He had packed as light as he could, not wanting to repeat the torture of the Wal-Mart bins. Despite having almost no possessions to his name *again*, he actually felt almost wealthy in a funny way as he looked at the tickets printed out with his name on them that had been paid for with his sweat.

There was a stopover in Paris. It was hot and nasty compared to San Francisco's year-round natural air conditioning from the Alaskan current. Diesel smoke choked the air and stung Jonah's eyes. He had time to get to downtown Paris and see it before he had to get back to the airport. It was pretty nice, but (to him) seemed way overhyped. Paris was nothing compared to Las Vegas or Beverly Hills.

Getting onto the plane for the last leg, it occurred to Jonah that going to PNG, he had been traveling to the very end of the earth in more ways than one. He was now traveling right to the middle of it. Ancient maps had once literally placed Jerusalem as the center point of the map and drawn Europe and Asia and everything else they knew about out from that central place. Something about the trip felt like it too. He was going to older places that had been built up by man far longer. From the American West to the East. From there to Europe, and finally from Europe to the Middle East, where Europe's castles and cathedrals were like the boomtowns of the West compared to the ruins of Babylon and Assyria. With every stop, he could feel the weight of years of human tragedy and achievement piling up.

Israelis sometimes consider all that history and all those ruins oppressive. They worry about having it all hanging over their heads. To Jonah, it was like the physical manifestation of the roots he had never had.

They came in at night, banking in through the clouds over the Mediterranean. Tel Aviv glowed up in the soft light of the seashore like a thousand neon signs. It looked somehow more modern than even Hong Kong. This was definitely no Papua New Guinea.

As they came down for a landing, Jonah looked out over the fields in the Jezreel Valley that looked eerily like a smaller version of California's agricultural San Joaquin Valley. He saw the rows of orchards and the blazing lights of the Jerusalem-Tel Aviv highway and he suddenly had a weird feeling. This place felt like Home. There was something here that felt more "home" to him than San Francisco ever had. It was a feeling he couldn't shake for the next several weeks.

The air outside the terminal building was soft and carried a hint of the Mediterranean. The concrete of the sidewalk was warm from the sun of the day before. The air was dry, much like California, and date palms rustled in the slight breeze. Everything was light. The airport was lit almost like a stadium, the highway was lit with huge streetlights, and there were dozens of taxis cutting what was left of the darkness to ribbons with their headlights.

The course he'd signed up for was in Tel Aviv, but it didn't start for three days, and the one thing Jonah wanted to see more than anything was Jerusalem. He'd given himself time before the start of the course, so he could see the city that ancient cartographers had called the center of the world, the place where the Second Temple had once stood.

Jonah shouldered his bag and made his way over to a line where several passengers had lined up for a shared taxi (called a "sherut" which meant "service") to Jerusalem. He'd read a lot about Israel already and understood the "sherutim" to be the cheapest way to get around when the busses weren't running. In a few minutes, a European vehicle like a cross between a small bus and a van pulled up and they all climbed aboard. Everyone passed money up to the driver in the front, and they were off, flying along the Jerusalem highway with virtually no traffic.

Jonah was impressed by the fact that the roads were as smooth as an airport runway. There were no potholes. The entire highway had huge, fifty-foot-tall lamps over it. The money spent on infrastructure had clearly been significant. California freeways were nowhere near as nice as this. Even the overpasses had decorative stonework on the sides, not the bare concrete he took for granted. Everything was clearly marked, the roads were wide, and the driver knew exactly what he was doing. It was in all ways the opposite of Jonah's first drive through Port Moresby.

Not really having a clear destination in mind beyond a hotel in Jerusalem, Jonah waited until they got into the city and just said "the old city" in English when the guy asked him where he wanted to stop.

When Jews return to Israel (it's called "returning" even if they had never been there before) the term for it in Hebrew is "Aliyah," which means "going up." The same term is used when someone in a synagogue "goes up" to the central podium to read out of the Torah scroll (considered an honor). One is said to "go up" to the Holy Land. In a very physical way, the road from Tel Aviv to Jerusalem is such an "Aliyah." The road climbs the entire way until it tops out after a very steep series of grades that force all but the most powerful cars into low gear. The whole way up, rocky hills hem the highway in on either side. They are littered with the remains of the deadly battle to hold that road and desperately bring supplies into the starving Jewish side of Jerusalem in 1948. Improvised armored cars that had been destroyed by enemy fire or just broke down have been painted and permanently mounted where they stopped in that desperate fight all along the road; commemorating the battle for Jerusalem and the birth of modern Israel.

Suddenly, the road levels off at the top of a rise and then dips, and for the first time, the city itself can be seen. In the day, the towers of the city shine with a light reflected from the sun that gleams almost with a rose color from the yellowish limestone of the buildings that grow out of limestone hills like new shoots from an old tree stump. In the night, the lights of the city reflect from the dust brought in from the deserts to the East, softening the glow of the city's yellow lights. The first glimpse after coming up the mountain was like a shock to Jonah as he suddenly came down into the city on the mountain. It was ancient. Not the new city itself, but everything about the place as a whole. The line of "Jaffa Street" ("Yafo" in Hebrew) runs the same way as the old Roman road that went all the way from the gate of the Old City to the port on the coast near modern Tel Aviv. That Roman road was almost certainly built on top of a far more ancient one that ran the same way. To think of Roman ruins as *new*, built over the top of the *really* old ones, gives you some idea of how long people have inhabited that place.

They arrived at the Old City itself sometime around 1AM. Despite the city being the most populous in Israel, Jonah was surprised to hear almost a dead silence in the streets. No sirens, no car horns, no dogs barking, no music from late night parties somewhere.

Jonah looked up at the medieval castle-like gate of Jaffa Gate and felt an incredible sense of peace and silence in this place. He set foot on the more than two-thousand-year-old stone of the old city street and walked through the darkness of the gate and into a city that looked unchanged from one built a thousand years ago. Tiny little alleys between flat roofed multiple story stone buildings that had been literally worn by time like a bar of soap in water.

There was an old man sitting on a traffic bollard in the open area behind the gate. He looked like he was patiently waiting for someone. He rose to his feet when

Jonah walked under the arch into the Old City and nodded to him.

"Hello!" The old Arab man said with an Israeli accent. "Welcome to Jerusalem! I am David" (He said it like "Dah-veed") "Do you need some place to sleep?"

Jonah was kind of shocked. He would later learn that the guy was probably a taxi dispatcher on a night shift, coordinating his little fleet of taxis via walkie-talkie. Jaffa Gate was a hub for all things related to moving tourists around. Still, it was kind of extraordinary to have such a simple, personal, and polite greeting when entering a major world city.

David's cousin ran one of the hostels in the Christian Quarter (undoubtedly he sent tourists that way whenever possible). They had a room available for cheap rates, and Jonah gladly paid cash for a bed and a shower and a place to crash after his long trip. Despite being in a foreign land surrounded by Arabs (at least in the Christian Quarter), Jonah had rarely felt so safe. There was an inexplicable and overwhelming sense of peace in the air over that ancient place.

He spent two days just walking every inch of Jerusalem and seeing everything. Jonah walked from the Western Wall (called the "Kotel" by Jews) to the Israeli Knesset (parliament) building way out in the new city. He visited the open-air market off Yafo Street where the new city residents came to buy and sell almost anything imaginable, and he visited the open-air markets in the old city near Damascus Gate where the Arabs did the same. He saw the trendy rich-American-tourist section of Ben Yehuda Street and the filthy, poor, but somehow not desperate or *hopelessly* poor neighborhoods of Mea Shearim, where nobody but Orthodox Jews lived in a huge modern, self-enforced Shtetl. In every book about Israel or trip there he'd heard of on one of the Christian compounds he'd lived on, the Garden Tomb and the Church of the Holy Sepulchre were always prominently mentioned and pictured. Jonah didn't visit them until much later. He was fascinated by the Jewish Quarter and the yeshivot (Jewish "seminary" type schools) there.

Jonah was drawn like a magnet to the Jewish Quarter of the old city where he found other American boys who had grown up in "assimilated" Jewish households (non-religious, just normal Americans) and were in "JTown" seeking some kind of connection to their roots. Most of them were about Jonah's age, some had come to "JTown" instead of college, or had taken a semester off in order to study a little bit of Torah and make their families happy. There were programs in the Old City that catered to them, funneling them into one of the big Yeshiva schools that crowded that part of the city. As a fellow young American seeking "roots" with big theological questions on his mind, Jonah fit right in. To him, the opportunity to study the Torah in Hebrew from Rabbis was too good to pass up.

After a quick visit to Tel Aviv University which convinced Jonah that TAU was *very* similar to one of the hyper-political universities back home in California, he decided that he was going to follow all the rootless American Jewish kids and go back to "JTown". Instead of a six-week Hebrew language course in Tel Aviv, he ended up doing a six-month immersive dive into Hebrew, Orthodox Judaism, Israeli culture and politics, and Jewish History in the super Orthodox Jerusalem neighborhood of Mea-Shearim.

Like most of the American boys, he started using the Hebrew version of his name; Jonah became "Yonah," and for the first time in his life, Yonah found himself with a very common name. Instead of having to explain "Jonah" to a lot of "John"s and "Steve"s, he found himself having one of the most popular names in the country. Nobody said anything about "Yonah" when they heard it in Israel.

There was no doubt in Jonah's mind now that he was going to join the Israel Defense Forces. It was a long and arduous battle of paperwork that was facilitated by a letter of conversion from a friendly Rabbi in California. In the end, Yonah had acquired legal citizenship in Israel and was on a schedule for mandatory induction into the IDF (which had been his intention from the beginning). Jonah had no interest in the many "volunteer to help the IDF" programs out there. He didn't want to have a glorified two-month camping trip, help to repair some tanks, and go home. He wanted to get into the *most* elite unit and do the very best he possibly could. If he had been back in America, he would have tried for the SEALs. In Israel, his goal was special forces ("Shayetet" units).

The land was hot. The air was like what came out of a hair dryer, but it was so dry that Jonah hardly noticed the temperature. Jonah almost wondered what was travelling over his head as he came out of the shade of a building; some kind of gigantic, invisible magnifying glass boiling his brains like an ant, or just the sun? He walked through the dusty streets of Jerusalem, a vibrant place, bustling with life and energy from every pore at the end of the old Millennium. It was an ancient city that felt as though it were a young child... all was eagerness, waiting for the millennium to happen. Nobody knew that in less than six months, these streets would feel deserted, empty, lifeless. Today they were packed, it was like moving against a human current to try to walk down the hill from the Western town to the Old City as he did almost every day. What nobody knew was that war was right around the corner. By the time Jonah was ready to be inducted into the IDF, the streets of Jerusalem would be like a ghost town, and terror attacks would be happening on a weekly basis.

After a government-sponsored Ulpan (Hebrew language course) for immigrants, Jonah finally received the letter that requested his presence at the IDF recruitment center in Teverya (Tiberias). By this time, he was living in a tiny apartment in the northern city of Tzfat, which was much cheaper to live in than the big city of Jerusalem, but also had Jewish religious learning readily available.

Jonah spent his time when he wasn't at the language course in training. He ate hard boiled eggs for the protein (and because they were cheap), got up every morning and did a calisthenics workout, and then jogged down the steep mountainside upon which the city of Tzfat was built. Past the ancient Jewish graveyard below the city, overlooking the rugged, green, poppy dotted hills of the upper Galilee, he would catch the head of a trail that zig zagged like a snake down into a huge "wadi" (basically a ravine). With the surefootedness of a mountain goat, Jonah would jog down this trail all the way to the floor of the ravine, down the stream and to the limestone caves which may have been some of the "clefts in the rocks" mentioned in the Bible that the Israelites would disappear into during really hard times.

The way back up was obviously the killer, and he would never stop jogging, even on the steepest part of the grade back up the snake trail where he could easily reach out with a hand and touch the ground in front of him as he powered up the grade. Every day, sometimes even twice a day, Jonah would run the ravine, preparing for his enlistment date.

Jonah enlisted with the IDF in early Summer of 2001.

In Tiberias, he took a Hebrew test in the army recruitment center that determined that he needed further language training before he could be put into a combat unit.

Jonah told them that he wanted to undergo the tryout to get into the special forces' units. They told him that those who hadn't gone to high school in Israel couldn't do it. The best he could shoot for was the Paratroopers. They didn't want foreign nationals in the special forces anyway; they said that if the identity of a special forces soldier got out, their family could be captured by the enemy and used against them. If his family wasn't in Israel, they couldn't guarantee their safety.

Jonah thought this was a bit ridiculous since his family was in America. "Come on, this is 2001, what can happen in *America*?"

Walking away from the dusty concrete structure, down the streets of Tiberias, the asphalt radiating warmth up through his shoes with the reflected heat of a summer day, Jonah gingerly avoided the discarded ice cream bar wrappers and soda cans that littered the sidewalks of any Israeli city. He walked down toward the water, catching a glimpse of red, purple and orange brilliance glittering in the oily flatness of the Kinneret (Sea of Galilee). He bought himself a soda and found his way to the rail overlooking the water, just away from the bustling main street with the park where the Russian prostitutes stood, even in the middle of the day.

The Middle East was a wild land. Here, Arab gangs and terrorist groups smuggled drugs and explosives across the long borders between Syria, Iraq, and Jordan. They got into Israel too; any hard drugs in the country were probably brought in by groups like Hamas. Here, the Russian mafia had moved in with force, carving up sections of Tel Aviv, Netanya and Haifa; people went missing, especially fellow Russian immigrants who crossed them. Here countries stood poised, always ready to move at a moment's notice. You could feel the tension in the air like smog. At any moment, war could break out. At any moment, a gang could suddenly form in an Arab village, as had happened to the two IDF reservists a year before. No warning, two men in Israeli uniform made a wrong turn into the outskirts of Ramallah. The angry mob, furious in seconds. The men dragged from their car, beaten to death, their bodies dragged into a police station and literally torn to pieces. The happy man appearing at the second story window displaying blood stained hands to the seething mob. It was Israeli blood. They had cheered.

That had been a year before. The start of the new war. Some called it Intifada War, others Al Aqsa Intifada. It didn't matter; it was a *war*. Busses and restaurants and schools were being detonated about every other week. Bodies in the streets; pieces of people smoking and sizzling in the aftermath. Children were a great target for the Palestinians, because they were easy, and because the media made a big deal out of it.

Still, in that evening, with the last of the heavy, humid breeze flowing past his face in that sweet-smelling evening on the Sea of Galilee, Jonah couldn't really imagine people in America being at risk. Those army recruitment people were just ridiculous. It seemed like the USA was doing a damn sight better at protecting its civilians than Israel was at that moment. At least Americans weren't scraping them off the main streets of their cities with shovels every other week.

Jonah (or as he would start to think even of himself as "Yonah") selected the next most elite unit on the list from the special forces. The holy trinity of elite units in the IDF went pilots (literally *every* single Israeli boy's wet dream), then special forces, then Paratroopers. If they wouldn't let him even *try* for the first two, he would become a Paratrooper or die trying.

The first day was confusing. Jonah got a ride in a van the army recruitment center in Tiberias had set up. The ride was comfortable in the air-conditioned van, but quiet, as he and about almost a dozen, sullen, brooding Russians made the hour and a half trip, staring out the windows at the bright colors of the Israeli landscape in the magical Middle Eastern sunlight.

The van had left Tiberias in the early morning, so they got to Tel Aviv in good time. They were ushered through the huge, swinging gates of a massive, crowded base by two sets of guards, small, wiry, little olive-skinned Israelis standing cockily with mirrored shades and short M-16 carbines.

They went down a street, and Jonah noticed with interest that this base seemed to actually have a McDonalds inside the base itself, along with a half-dozen shops. Not that different from Travis Air Force Base, the giant USAF base near where Jonah grew up in Fairfield California ... except, like the rest of Israel, the base was awash in litter; the sidewalks stained by dropped bits of food, sunflower seeds spat out on the sidewalks. Israelis swarmed back and forth in surging tides of 18-year-old youths carrying huge, heavy camping backpacks.

The van made a turn and they were let into a fenced-off area with its own set of guards. Here, they were let off with few words exchanged. The Russians looked like they were being sent to an execution. The barbed wire on the top of the fenced area didn't help, it was clearly designed to keep people in.

The recruits were ignored for quite a while. Jonah began to feel very alone. He had become pretty good at getting on with the Israelis in Hebrew, but was at a loss surrounded by about a hundred people speaking Russian. After his experience with Russians from the language course, he wasn't in a friend-making mood, but he needed to get some information about what they were expected to do. He wished there were some Israelis here, but it seemed to be exclusively immigrants.

There was a huge pile of canvass army sacks. Massive, green duffel bags with a zip down the center and two handles. Some of the more clued-in guys were picking up sacks. Jonah found a Russian who had lived in Israel long enough to speak a little Hebrew and become somewhat less surly, and asked him what that was all about. He explained that the Israeli soldiers had dropped those off that morning and the recruits were supposed to get a sack and put their names on it. This Jonah proceeded to do as they waited for another half an hour for something to happen.

Periodically, other vans or busses would arrive until a couple hundred immigrants filled up the courtyard.

Tall, heavy boned Russians slouched on the curbs, smoking like chimneys, spitting none-too carefully onto the sidewalks and cursing steadily. They regarded Jonah with the guarded eyes of a beat dog. He just shrugged. Nothing new there. He had discovered the strange problem of Americans and Russians not getting along in his language course. The strange relationship seems to go from an immediate liking inevitably toward a deep, unreasoning hatred. In Jonah's case, it was exacerbated by his falling for a popular, charismatic Russian girl in the language course, which had elicited a lot of resentment from the Russian guys.

Jonah found himself somewhere to sit where he wouldn't be spat upon and, ignoring the billowing clouds of acrid cigarette smoke all around him, pondered what it was that made Americans and Russians so incompatible. It was as if they understood each other too well somehow. Their culture seemed less alien than that of Central or Western Continental Europe. Americans and Russians seemed to be able to see all of their own societies' bad qualities clearly in the other culture and didn't like the view.

Of course, the fact that morality had been utterly ground out of the people under Soviet domination didn't help any. Drugs, prostitutes, free sex, whatever you wanted; there was no sense of right and wrong whatsoever. Need to raise money? Rent your wife out as a whore for cash. They didn't even blink at the idea. Jonah leaned back against a concrete wall and waited. He had grown fatalistic about Russians. They didn't suddenly snap into vicious attack as Arab crowds might. You could see them coming with all the posturing they did, so he wasn't worried, even if most of them were about three inches taller than him and twenty pounds heavier.

More and more immigrants streamed in, most former Soviet types looking as if they were being herded to a death camp. Jonah came from a nation with a volunteer military. He was *proud* to be given a uniform. They came from a place where service in the Soviet army meant a dangerous, disease-ridden, desperate period of interminable duration forced on you at gunpoint, and to which Russian jails were favorably compared. That was just where these guys were from.

Like new prisoners, Jonah could see them forming into gangs and cliques, sizing one another up and establishing a pecking order. He ignored them. He wasn't worried. This was the Israeli army after all, not the old Soviet Union.

After some time, short, imperious Israelis swaggered out of the low, beat-up looking concrete blockhouses forming two walls of the courtyard. They were all told to line up, which they did with exactly the attitude Jonah had seen a hundred times in TV news clips of inmates lining up in their orange jumpsuits. The soldiers herded everyone into the building in single file, and for the first time, Jonah was conscious of the fact that he was dressed in jeans and a polo shirt, while the rest of the base around him was a uniform sea of green.

They walked down the line with their bags out and open. As they passed various stations, they received strange looking items. Some kind of unidentifiable object he would later learn was a medical pack to keep in his "A" (dress) uniform. A belt which didn't seem to have any buckle on it. A pair of boots, a zipped bag like thing. It went on.

The blockhouses were all connected inside, so they snaked down through the long, U-shaped complex being given something at various stations, finally getting to a large room and being told to change; Jonah was embarrassed to have to ask how the belt worked, and was told that he couldn't lace the boots up the way he would a pair of work boots. They re-formed into the shuffling line after the changing room and, stuffing their civilian clothes into the bag and trying to figure out how the get the laces to stay the way the Israelis said to lace them, they found themselves faced with a series of booths, each equipped with a digital camera.

Here, the worst pictures any of them would ever take in their entire lives were taken, they were asked how they spelled their names in Hebrew (which has a different alphabet from English), and were given a number which they thankfully wouldn't have to remember too long since the last station deposited in their hands a pair of flat, metal tags, perforated through the center, with their Hebrew names and a number on each one twice. They came with the cheapest looking metal bead chain imaginable, and Jonah vaguely wondered where the Israelis got those nifty looking olive nylon jobs he could barely see around their necks. He also thought the dog tags ought to have a rubber edging around them like on Top Gun, but apparently not.

They all emerged, blinking in the afternoon sun, back in the courtyard, sloppily uniformed and burdened with strange articles. Each was handed an ID card and that was that; they were now soldiers.

Jonah sat down to re-tie the boots. He still hadn't gotten it right yet. The Israelis made a knot at one end of the long bootlace, putting it underneath the flap of the lowest eyelet of the boot, they strung the lace through the eyes going up once, over once, and repeating until you had a long end coming out the top, with nothing at all to tie it to. Then, you had to pull it tight, wrap it around a finger until it was a neat bundle, and stuff it down the inside of the boot top. This actually became quite easy and convenient with time.

You could loosen the laces, pull your feet out, and then be able to get your feet in, pull once with the top of the lace, wrap it, stuff it, and be booted up in about a second flat with practice. That was the idea-speed.

The part with the yelling drill sergeants that Jonah had expected from American TV only started once the convoy of busses full of newly-minted recruits arrived all the way back up at the north of the country very close to where his journey had started that morning. By the time they got there, it was dark, but that didn't matter. Boot camp was officially underway the very second the bus wheels stopped turning.

Like a well-oiled machine, an Israeli trainer in a ball cap carrying a "Galil" assault rifle stood ready to move the second the long line of busses stopped. Even before they stopped rolling, the drivers opened the doors, and the little Israeli men bounded up the stairs into the big tour busses with a bellow.

"Up, up, up, up, up! Yallla! You have twenty seconds to line up outside the bus!" This was all in Hebrew of course, but the message was pretty clear to Jonah as the little man charged down the aisle of the bus amid the scramble of thirty recruits desperately trying to get their gear and force their way down the narrow aisle to the doors. "Yalla" was Arabic for "move your ass" and was the favorite word of every trainer on the base. Everything they did was done with a man with a stopwatch yelling at them. If they took too long to complete whatever was requested, they had to ask for more time before the time ran out or they would be penalized. Being penalized was not fun.

"That's it! You are too slow! On your faces, give me fifty push-ups!"

Jonah had just tumbled out of the bus and onto the giant asphalt square at the center of the base and had to look around at the other recruits because he didn't know "push-ups" in Hebrew. It was "matsav shtiem" which literally means "position 2." He saw what people were doing and bounced to his hands, rapidly complying.

"UP, UP, UP, UP, UP! You have 20 seconds to line up on the other side of the square!"

Jonah glanced across the vast open square of the base, sucked in his breath, and charged across the square as fast as his legs would carry him.

"TOO LATE! DOWN! DOWN! DOWN! Give me twenty!" The great trampling herd of recruits went to their faces wherever they happened to be and did another set of push-ups.

And so it went, late into the night, until the recruits understood how to form a "Het" formation, how to line up in less than twenty seconds in a perfect "square" (a "het formation looks like a squared off letter 'U' like you would see on an old fashioned alarm clock display) and how to properly salute a superior (which was basically everyone other than them) as a unit.

They were eventually allowed to grab their rucksacks and drag themselves to the concrete bunkhouses they had been assigned. Jonah was one of six non-Russians in a bunkhouse built for 200 soldiers.

The reason Israel was flooded with Russians in 2001 was because when the Soviet Union broke up, Russians were suddenly free to leave the disaster area created by a hundred years of utopian experimentation. A lot of Jews remained in Russia, and the Israelis saw an opportunity. They needed citizens who were not Arab, because they were surrounded by a hostile sea of them and Israel was barely holding on, demographically speaking. They decided to informally loosen the standards of what they required in order to make "Aliyah" (immigrate) by allowing thousands of Russians with the most tenuous (in many cases totally fabricated) connection to the Jewish people to come into the country en masse. The tail end of this wave of immigration that would nearly double Israel's population was still going on when Jonah entered the military. As an immigrant with poor Hebrew, he was placed right in the middle of it.

Unfortunately for the Israelis, anti-Semitism is still deeply rooted in Russian culture, and just because a person was willing to escape the desperate poverty of Russia didn't mean they liked Jews any better. Among the social problems the Russians brought with them like high rates of drug addiction and constant alcohol abuse, the Russian mafia, human sex slave smuggling, and forms of crime the little country had never seen before, there came problems the Israelis had never anticipated- such as when one of the instructors found a swastika drawn on the wall of the bathroom of Jonah's bunkhouse.

The Israelis went totally ballistic, and as every single soldier scrubbed the walls with toothbrushes for the next several hours, they were treated to accounts from their drill instructors of their parents and grandparents surviving the Holocaust. It was *inconceivable* that someone would *ever* even see a swastika in Israel. Jonah couldn't believe it. The Russians just snickered and rolled their eyes.

Jonah came to learn that Mikve Alon, the basic training base he was on, was something of the "trashcan" of the Israeli military. Immigrants with bad Hebrew were not expected to get into combat units, much less *elite* combat units like the Paratroopers. Most of the recruits in the immersive Hebrew training boot camp had missed out on the "gibush" (tryout) system by not attending high school in Israel. Like Americans taking SATs for college, Israeli students usually attend a gibush while still in high school. These tryouts determine which unit that student would later be eligible to join. Obviously most of the immigrant recruits on that base had gone to high school in Russia. In Jonah's case, he'd gone to high school basically everywhere *but* Israel.

The commander of the base knew that in this huge mass of sloppy, scowling, spitting Russian immigrants there were a few soldiers who genuinely did want to get into an elite unit and were not treating their IDF service like a prison term. He had worked out a special deal with his old unit (the Paratroopers) to create a special, one-time gibush tryout just for his soldiers. Old Paratroopers stuck together, and they complied despite bending a lot of rules (Israelis have no qualms about bending rules, as Jonah would learn).

Out of a base with over 3,000 recruits, *eight hundred men* told their instructors that they wanted a chance at that tryout. They soon learned that there would be only 80 spots.

Jonah was not a man who ever gave less than everything. He knew that every second of his life, every moment he was here, was at the mercy of those who allowed it. He had sought service in the IDF and he did whatever was required of him with pride. He put one thousand percent into every exercise, every drill, every training rotation. He acted like the one man on the base with the most to prove, and in many ways, he was.

Over the next three months, every single thing Jonah did, he did with the intention of fighting for one of those 80 spots. If they had to line up, he would be there first. If they had to do training, he would be the best. On cross country hikes, he was first, at the range, he was in the top. Only in Hebrew was he average. Some of the Russians had been in Israel longer than Jonah, and he didn't have the sort of mind that made picking up a foreign language easy. Hebrew not only had a totally different syntax than English, it had a completely different alphabet too. There was basically nothing in common between the languages except words that modern Hebrew had borrowed from English like "banana." The recruits had all been divided into three groups - low level, intermediate level, and high level classes. After all the studying Jonah had done at the government ulpan before his enlistment, he barely managed to make "intermediate."

The other soldiers knew that something very deep drove Jonah forward. They all noticed the way he threw himself at every single thing they did. The Russians started calling him "Terminator" after the killer cyborg from the movies. Jonah's few friends on the base, the handful of fellow Americans in the unit, actually came to him once to ask him to stop trying quite so hard. It was toward the end of the three-month basic training and everyone assumed that Jonah had probably earned himself a shot at becoming a Paratrooper by then.

"But you're making the rest of us look bad, you know?" The somewhat pudgy blond American Jew who everyone called Benji had pulled Jonah aside during one of their rare moments of "free time" after dinner.

"What do you mean?" Jonah had never even considered doing anything less than his absolute best on any challenge or assignment.

"I mean everybody *knows* you are going to get to the Paratrooper tryout okay? Why don't you just … dial it back a little so the rest of us can keep up?"

Jonah shook his head. "You want me to act like the Russians?" The Russians had tactics they used, sort of a mass-passive resistance that they immediately applied as soon as they came together in a military unit. They would intentionally slow down to whatever speed the lazier soldiers were comfortable with and stick together out of solidarity. Punishing them just made them slow down even more. Trying to get Russians to look like real soldiers was like trying to take a bunch of cats on a walk with leashes.

"No, not like that … just, ease off some."

Jonah shook his head again. "I can't Benji. I'm on or not. If I am not doing my best, to me it's the same thing as the bullshit the Russians do. I came here because I wanted to serve in the IDF and I am going to do the best I can."

Benji was right. Jonah was selected as one of the recruits who would have the opportunity to attend the special tryout that the base commander had arranged just for them. Before he left the base, the Romanian Israeli instructor who had overseen the scrubbing of the bathrooms with toothbrushes after the swastika incident found "Yonah" and pulled him aside.

Unclipping the M-16 that was always slung across the back of every Israeli soldier whether they were in uniform or not, the young, blond Romanian undid the custom made sling support that allowed him to sling the M-16 Israeli style instead of the American way (Israeli style allowed you to swing the weapon around to the front from behind you in one smooth motion and have the trigger in hand immediately).

Traditionally, soldiers would make their own sling supports out of carefully tied and melted parachute cord, and there was definitely an art form to this.

Jonah looked on in growing shock as the instructor removed his front sling supports and handed them over to him.

"These were made by my brother when he went into the Golani Brigade. He saw combat. I never made it into a combat unit myself. My brother would want them to be used by a combat soldier." The fierce glint in his pale blue eyes told the whole story. This was the guy who had told of the horrors his family had experienced in the Holocaust. After that, they had been turned into slaves by the Communists. To him, "never again" meant if you were an enemy of the Jewish people, he would be *happy* to put a bullet between your eyes.

Jonah nodded solemnly. "Thank you." He didn't know what to say. He felt that he were carrying on something; entrusted with something far more important than just a pair of paracord sling supports.

"You'll use them *in combat*?"

Jonah knew that he had only earned the right to *try out* for the Paratroopers, he was nowhere near actually being one yet. He nodded anyway. "I will."

The hard-faced young man slapped him on the shoulder and walked away, having passed on, in some indefinable way, the defense of his people and the vengeance of their dead to a new generation of warriors.

30

PARATROOPER

The busses took them back to the first base Yonah had seen in the IDF. It was a sprawling near-metropolis of its own in Tel Aviv. A holding tank for incoming and outgoing soldiers, storage for the millions of articles of supply kept on hand by the military, and hamster wheel where the very worst of the draftee soldiers who were no good for anything else would be kept busy sweeping floors for the minimum two-year mandatory service they had to perform as Israeli citizens.

By the time they got from the north of the country to "Bakum" (pronounced back-koom) base, it was late, and they were hastily filtered through a chow line at a nearby dining hall and told to set up tents for the try out that would commence at "0800" the next morning.

Yonah didn't believe the "0800" business for a second. He'd heard plenty about these tryouts and knew that from the moment you arrived, they would be trying to screw with your head. With three months of basic under his belt, he kept his uniform on and slept in his boots over the top of his perfectly made rack, ready to be on his feet the second the instructors woke them.

It came sometime after midnight. The instructors had waited until the entire group of recruits seemed to be in a deep sleep, the better to disorient them. Suddenly, they had attacked the tents, firing blank rounds right outside the canvass next to the heads of the recruits, shouting, and randomly yanking guys off their bunks and throwing them to the ground.

"YAAALLLA!" Yelled the Paratrooper instructors. They had twenty seconds to stand for inspection, fully dressed and with boots polished in front of their tents.

In Yonah's tent, the other guys had noticed the way he had ever so carefully made the bed, tucked in his uniform, and laid down still in his boots on top of the blanket. Several others had done something similar. As they lined up, all dressed, boots on, in a perfect "Het" formation yelling "ACHSHEV!" ("attention" to recognize the superior officer and notify him they were ready to be inspected) within the twenty-second time limit, Yonah saw a look of surprise on the face of the instructor. He was used to high school boys, not the very best 5% out of a three-month boot camp.

There was something different in the demeanor of the Paratrooper instructors. They were all bigger, taller, and meaner than their counterparts had been at the language training base (still not big by American or Russian standards, but big for Israelis). They had the hard, wiry look of extreme sports enthusiasts or outdoor survivalists. They moved with an economy of movement like a timber wolf pacing a caribou across the tundra, like they could move fast but keep it up for days at a time if need be. There was a hard, merciless gleam in their eyes. Yonah decided he liked them.

"There are 80 of you here!" The leader of the Gibush wasn't especially big or loud, but his voice carried across the entire base. "80! I want you to know something right now! I *don't* want you. I *don't* need you. I have ALL of my Paratroopers already! This gibush has been set up as a personal favor, and I think it's bullshit! I want you all to know that there are exactly 8 spots in my Brigade. There is *no* time limit on this tryout; I will run you, I will wear you down, and I will *hurt* you until there are only eight of you left! If I have to run you up and down the beach for a week, I will do so. Now … MOVE!"

And they did.

They had to fold up and put away the US military surplus tents in twenty second increments, then they had to equip themselves with gear, also in twenty second increments, scrambling to strap filthy, sweat soaked, sandy combat vests on, grab canteens, fill them, and load up the stretchers which would carry several hundred pounds of sand bags to the beach.

They were to carry water and full canteens, but they were not to drink. The instructor gleefully explained that if they wanted a drink at any time, they were welcome to quit: there would be a refreshment table full of nice things set up in the center of the obstacle course that they were welcome to go to at any time - obviously at the cost of quitting. If they collapsed in the Middle Eastern heat from dehydration, he was okay with that too, they had an ambulance on standby.

They crawled across a newly-plowed field to get warmed up, instructors firing blanks over them just to get them in the right mood. Paratrooper instructors walked among the crawling soldiers shoving their butts down with a boot and firing next to their heads if they got more than an inch off the ground.

Yonah found himself glancing desperately at his canteen as the first rays of a very hot sun began to reflect from the Mediterranean just beyond the field. He noticed that one of the other guys from the Hebrew training base was glancing at him. It was Boaz. The dark-skinned man grinned, glanced around, and took a rapid swig from his canteen in direct contravention of orders. He winked at Yonah.

Boaz was from Florida. Despite his exotic name, he looked very American. His dad had been African American, and his mom was an Israeli resident of the USA. Boaz had grown up in a ghetto city somewhere near Miami without a father, joined the US Marine Corps to help get a green card, and gotten in trouble with the authorities mostly because of the hot Puerto-Rican girl he had married, had a kid with, had a violent divorce from, and planted an "8 ball" of cocaine in her car in order to get custody of his kid after she had cheated on him. In every way possible, Boaz was a colorful character.

He was a flamboyantly friendly, energetic man exactly Yonah's age, who had had a life just as crazy as his own, but in very different ways. Despite the sense that Boaz was basically amoral, Yonah liked him a lot. As a guy who had served in the Marines, he also looked to him for guidance in military matters.

Yonah quickly imitated crazy Boaz, pulling out a canteen when the instructors weren't looking, taking a long pull that included a good helping of freshly tilled soil in the water, and shoving it back in his belt before anyone caught him. Israelis actually regarded highly people with enough chutzpah (bravado) to break rules and get away with it in the pursuit of the mission.

Yonah knew it was part of the culture, though as an American, he would always have a hard time understanding when the Israelis expected people to break the rules and when they would have absolutely no humor about such things. It was people who weren't clever enough to get away with it that would be punished. To Yonah, it reminded him of what he'd read about ancient Sparta, where young warriors in training weren't given enough food to eat so they would learn to steal and get away with it in order to become a better warrior.

Now warmed up from the field, they headed to the beach. First, they had to group up around the stretchers piled with several hundred pounds of sand bags, carry them up and down the beach through the surf for a while, and bring them over to where the Israelis had made several massive artificial sand dune mountains with tractors.

"Get those up the hill!" The instructor snapped. "YALLA!"

The men began grabbing a sand bag, scrambling up the incredibly steep sand dunes, sometimes sinking up to their waists in the loose sand, and arduously piling the sand bags, one by one on top of the dunes. When all the sandbags were on the tops of the dunes, they were ordered to load them back onto the stretchers at the bottoms of the dunes once more.

Yonah was panting in the heat, sweat pouring off him. He had lost track of time, but it must have been mid-morning sometime. They were completely covered in sand, unable to even see in the haze of grit and salt crystals in their eyes. He charged up the hill with a burst of power, grabbed the last sandbag, and jumped down, tossing it on the stretcher with a satisfying thud. The instructors frowned. They didn't like this. These recruits weren't being challenged enough.

"Back to the top! Back to the top! YALLA!" Yonah started to pick up a sandbag, but this time the instructor stopped him. "TWO! Take two! Come on, move!"

With one huge sandbag on each shoulder, Yonah charged at the mountain of loose sand. Without hands to steady him, it was a war to even make uphill progress. In seconds, he was gasping for air, flailing for some kind of traction in the shifting sand, feeling himself start to run out of oxygen as he battled his way up the mound.

"COME ON! MOVE IT! YALLA!" The instructors were claiming scalps now. Some of the big, powerful, ox-like Russians were complaining that it was just too hard. The chief instructor was gleefully describing the cold Coke, juice, and even sweets they had on the refreshment table if they would just quit.

Jonah stumbled blindly down the slope in an avalanche of loose sand, gasping for air. His mouth was open as he gasped, trying to get oxygen back into his lungs. Every movement was pain, every part of his body was screaming for rest. He was seeing stars. He clumsily grabbed at the sandbags, trying and failing to throw another pair of them on his shoulders.

For the first and last time in his career in the IDF, the words crept out of Yonah's mouth.

"I ... can't..."

The instructor was moving toward Yonah like a wolf smelling weakness in a deer. "You can quit anytime." He said in English. "Just head over to the table and get yourself something to drink!"

Beside Yonah, Boaz had suddenly appeared, gasping for air as he was.

"Yonah! You big, stupid bastard! Get those fucking bags on your big, wide-ass shoulders and get up the fucking hill before I kick your ass!" The shorter man was gasping so much as he said it that it barely came out, but he bounced with the typical energy of crazy Boaz, his dark eyes looking wild, grasping Yonah by the shoulders as he did.

Yonah would have laughed if he hadn't felt as if he were about to pass out. The best he could do was a silent chuckle, then a quick grab of the bags, a wrenching heft to get them up on his shoulders, and he was moving again, pushing up the hill like a bull.

Boaz stayed with him, yelling encouragement. "Come on! You can do it! Get up! You got this!"

Yonah noticed that he'd only grabbed one bag himself and immediately suspected something. Boaz would later thank him for that little show, telling Yonah that if he hadn't paused there to "talk his friend up the hill" he wouldn't have made it through the tryout.

For Yonah, that push up the hill required a herculean effort. He glanced up at the top, feeling his legs sinking into the soft sand, feeling his lungs compressed by the heavy sandbags, hearing the instructor telling him to quit, to just give up ... like a loser ... a loser ... like what *Dad* had once called him.

Yonah felt inside of himself and knew that the rage was still there. The boiling fury he had carried his whole life. The Wrath. He grunted, gritting his teeth, and charged up the hill on pure adrenaline, growling in rage the whole way. His Wrath carried him to the top.

Now that they were properly "warmed up," they were to do a 5K run in full gear. By now, the sun was at full intensity and Yonah realized with a shock that it must be after noon. The run was to be up the soft sand of the beach of course. He noticed another couple of guys peel off, shaking their heads. There was no way to know how many of them were still out there. All he had energy to do was try to keep himself upright.

They ran through the surf in their boots, then up the dunes and over the hilly terrain just inland from the beach. Now the Middle Eastern heat was at full cook, like an oven that had finally gotten warmed up. Jonah looked around with bleary eyes, sneaking another slug from his filthy plastic canteens when he hoped the instructors didn't notice. He had to keep going. Just one more step, one more step…

Behind Yonah, several of the instructors had converged on one guy who was lagging way behind. Like jackals moving in on a weakened herd animal. There were three of them yelling at the guy now as he made his incredibly slow way around the course they had just run. Yonah realized that it was Attila, a small, short, Hungarian Jew who had been with his group of non-Russians in the base. Yonah couldn't understand why he was so far behind until he saw the small shape hopping along, barely able to put weight on one of his feet. Attila must have sprained his ankle on the sand dunes. He was now so far behind the pack that he would never catch up. Yonah shook his head sadly. He had liked the little guy - he had a warrior's spirit. He was a fighter. It would be sad if he was knocked out by an injury.

Now they had a series of obstacles to cross. Once again, the instructors tried to distract them, firing blanks, yelling, and basically harassing them every step of the way. They managed to scramble over a ten-foot wall, over the tops of a series of logs stuck in the ground, across a rope strung between two posts, and finally to a series of overhead metal bars where the instructors collected them back into a group.

Yonah looked around. He was surprised to realize that their group was now down to only about twenty soldiers. Somewhere along the line, most of the big, powerful Russians had dropped out. They had muscles, but they didn't have heart.

"Now you are going to do something very simple." The instructor had an evil gleam in his eye. "You are going to jump up, grab the bars, and hold on until I tell you that you can drop!"

Yonah glanced at the bar. That sounded far too simple. It was probably a lot harder than it sounded.

The instructor clicked his stopwatch and they all jumped up and grabbed the bars, hanging like monkeys from the steel. Within a minute, Yonah realized what the problem was. His arms were strong, his legs were strong, but his fingers were only as strong as fingers could get. They were tiny little muscles that were no good for keeping 230 pounds of man suspended just on grip strength alone. Within another minute, his hands were loosening of their own accord and he was desperately rocking where he hung, trying to get some angle that worked. Inevitably, Yonah's grip failed him and he landed in the dust. Not the first one to drop, but not the last either.

"Pathetic! You didn't even make it three minutes! What is wrong with you?" The instructor was addressing everyone in general. Nobody in the group had managed to hang on much longer than Yonah. They were desperately tired, covered in sand and sweat, and barely able to stand, much less hang from the bars.

"Okay, okay, up, up, up! AGAIN!"

This time, Yonah thought it through. He didn't have the strength, but what if he could find some kind of leverage? He shifted where he stood before jumping, then jumped with his hands on opposite sides of the bar. When he grabbed it, he laced his fingers through one another from opposite sides of the bar, all his weight falling on his knuckles, which interlocked over the top. Now he wasn't relying on muscles to keep himself up, but the bones in his fingers.

Yonah hung there, fingers laced together over the bar, diaphragm unable to completely exhale the CO_2 he was pumping out, each and every breath getting shallower as he hung by his arms. He kept his feet up just enough to be off the ground but relaxed his legs and every other muscle in his body, trying to keep his head down, breathing as well as he could with his arms stretched over his head. He could feel his breath catching more and more with each cycle of his lungs.

One by one the others dropped. They couldn't hang on. Still, Yonah hung there, unwilling to give up. He looked up and was surprised to see that every single other soldier was on the ground. They were all watching him as he hung there, too stubborn to let go until the instructor told him to. He glanced at the instructor, unable to breathe, unwilling to let go.

The instructor turned to the men on the ground.

"Do you see THAT?" He moved among the men, pointing at Yonah. "DO YOU SEE THAT?" The little Israeli bent to yell in the face of an exhausted soldier who was dropping to sit down in the dust. "*THAT* is a Paratrooper! That, right there! That is a Paratrooper! What the fuck are you? Are you tired? Are you hungry? Are you having a bad fucking day? Do you want to go home? STAND UP! STAND THE FUCK UP! LOOK AT THAT! THAT RIGHT THERE IS A PARATROOPER! You are *shit*!"

Yonah hung there, watching the men, keeping himself focused on not passing out. He couldn't take breaths anymore. His breaths were coming as fast as a panting dog, and he felt like he couldn't get any air. He was on the edge of blacking out. He had read that when Jesus was crucified, he would have died because hanging from his arms, he couldn't properly exhale. His lungs would eventually fill up with carbon dioxide and he would basically drown, even though he wasn't underwater. Hanging like that, watching as if it were some remote drama taking place on a TV screen but unreal to him as the instructors harangued the poor schmucks who hadn't managed to hang as long as him, he felt as if he had some inkling of what that might have been like.

What do you think now? He was thinking to the voice in his head that always told him he was a worthless piece of shit. *What do you think now? Silent, huh? Well fuck you. Fuck you, Walter. Fuck all of you. I will never give up, I don't care if I die trying. I will never, ever give up!*

The instructor finally told Yonah to drop. His reward for hanging on longest was that he didn't get any rest before they were run through the obstacle course.

It finally wrapped up sometime after dark. The rate of dropouts had increased after the bars until, by twilight, there were only eight of them left. Yonah noted that many of the biggest and strongest Russians had dropped out pretty early. The guys who made it were not the musclebound hulks. They were usually the medium sized guys with good athleticism and a *lot* of determination. In fact, the Israelis were so impressed by sheer willpower that they suddenly announced that they were going to take 9 guys instead of 8. The last one was Attila, the short, brown haired Hungarian who had been hopping around on a sprained ankle all day unwilling to stop or give up. The instructors would have had to carry him off that field. He had insisted on completing every part of the course, coming in half an hour after everyone else.

So out of the 800 who had wanted this shot, 9 of them were to become Israeli Paratroopers. At that moment, Yonah was too exhausted, hungry and thirsty to really grasp it, but the fact that he was to become a Paratrooper at last finally began to sink in as he collapsed on an old metal cot in a tent that night. Whatever internal critic he would always carry with him, whatever he may think about himself during those dark times when the blackness came over him, he had set out to do this and had actually done it. Nobody would be able to take that away.

2003

31

SANUR

Yonah had ducked under the overhang of a building, staring out into the black, chilly night for signs of movement. On his back, his M-16 bounced as he stealthily moved, unloaded now, but a clip ready at hand. He checked the night, listening carefully for enemy movement, and was rewarded by nothing but an eerily empty army base. With a sudden burst of speed, he sprinted across the wide truck lane, moving fast to lower the chances of a sniper getting a bead. Finally, breathing hard, he tried to kick the mud off his flip flops as he ducked into the concrete blockhouse where they slept.

As he rearranged the towel on his shoulder, Yonah heard a soft call from the darkened bunker. "Hey Yonah, you find hot water?"

He nodded. "Yeah, on the other side of the base, where the Officers used to be."

"Of course," the other Paratrooper growled, scowling out into the night. Like Yonah, he was clad in boxers and a t-shirt, towel and soap in hand along with his assault rifle. "Have they gotten that sniper yet?"

Yonah shook his head, toweling his hair as dry as possible. "No, he's still out there."

"Shit." The other soldier ducked out into the muddy night, jogging across the open space. Yonah made for his bunk.

Sanur (sah-noor) base was a crumbling, muddy shithole that crept up the side of a hill but for some inexplicable reason, did not include the *top* of the hill inside its perimeter. It had begun probably as one of the hastily built "police" stations during the British Mandate before the 1948 war. At that time, the base would have just been a blockhouse or two and a place for some vehicles for the small garrison of British or Australian soldiers charged with keeping the peace in the general area.

After many wars and many changes in fortune, the place now found itself as a large (for Israel) IDF base nestled pretty close to Jenin and surrounded by hostile Palestinian towns. The location made it a natural target for Palestinians looking to take out a few Israeli soldiers, which in turn made it an ideal place for the Paratroopers to hold basic training.

Paratroopers were considered the most mobile unit in the regular IDF infantry, and they were also considered the most elite non-special forces unit. Like American Marines, the idea was that the Paratroopers could be quickly deployed with a large, powerful force anywhere needed on a moment's notice. During the Six Day War, the Paratroopers had been hastily pulled away from another operation, loaded into trucks, and sent to take Jerusalem in a lightning urban battle the Jordanians didn't expect. That was the kind of thing they were designed for. Sanur was the kind of place they trained, because the IDF believed in training as realistically as possible, and it was hard to beat a basic training base which regularly came under sniper fire for realism.

You wouldn't take a bunch of 18-year-olds from South Carolina or Kansas who hadn't spent a single day in uniform in their lives and conduct basic training on a base that also served as a real frontline post and came under fire like that, but the boys at Sanur were Israelis. Their elder brothers had been in combat, their uncles, their fathers, their grandfathers. They did not expect to get through their mandatory service without getting shot at, especially the ones who had volunteered for the Paratroopers.

The first time Yonah had seen the base, he had felt an uncontrollable excitement at the air of buzzing activity. Sanur, in those days, had been an active front line post right in the middle of the West Bank. In fact, to get to the base, the IDF mandated that only armored vehicles be used and they must come in a convoy. No "soft skin" jeeps or Hummers that weren't armored were allowed by IDF regulations.

The first thing the commanders had done with the new "class" of Paratroopers to arrive at Sanur (after the mandatory scraping bare of a hillside with entrenching shovels and painting rocks to make a suitably perfect Paratrooper logo on a hill overlooking the road) had been to call all the new boys into the largest of the blockhouses, wheel out a TV, and play the beginning of "Saving Private Ryan" where the Americans were storming the beach at Normandy.

A wiry, energetic looking Israeli with bars and a "falafel" (slang for a rank insignia) on his sleeve strode out, paused the movie near the end of the scene of carnage, and said; "*This* ... this is *bad war*. Sometimes you *have* to make bad war. Sometimes there's no way around it. Paratroopers had to make *bad war* at Ammunition Hill."

The room was silent. The vision of men charging into the fire of machine gun positions was still dancing in front of everyone's eyes.

"I don't *like* bad war. I want *good war!* Good war is when you bring home your boys ... alive. Now, you all know we are at war now. It will be good war or bad war depending on how well you listen, how well you learn. We are here to make you into *Paratroopers*. We can't do that unless you learn. Now I want you to all understand something. War is out there right now. I don't need to tell you, everyone *knows*. I think some of you are not going to finish your service and go home. Some of you will *die* in this war. I want to bring back every single one of you, but I know I probably won't. I promise I will do everything I can so we don't fight a bad war, but fight a good war, and you promise that you will learn, and you will instantly obey what you are told to do. There is no room for error here."

The men yelled, "Yes, commander-sergeant," in unison. He smiled with a malevolent smile, and suddenly the doors behind the men burst open and their trainers rushed in, yelling for the men to get to their emergency stations immediately.

"YALLA, YALLA, YALLA!"

So it had begun.

The pace had been faster, tougher, much harsher than the first basic training Yonah had gone through.

Everything was ramped up. No tolerance for errors was ever made. Paratroopers understood that something done sloppily or incorrectly meant a friend who was relying on you being dead. So they trained hard every day and most of every night, learning the ancient trade of killing better than their enemies so that they might preserve life.

The IDF didn't have time for things that weren't strictly necessary. They trained in fieldcraft, but spent little time learning to march properly. They spent hours and hours on the range until every single man in the Brigade was a damn good shot. They didn't put a lot of effort into perfect looking uniforms (though they did have to have polished boots at the *start* of the day), but they made sure the men knew how to work together as a smoothly operating machine, a hunting pack, and that they knew what to do under fire instantly.

Israel had less than half the amount of money per soldier as the USA. That meant that they focused on what was essential for the mission. Paratroopers had to move and kill when they got where they were going. So they had great boots, the latest, state of the art weapons with "invisible" lasers and reflex sights and night vision scopes, and precious little else. Their uniforms sometimes had holes in them, their tents were falling down from overuse, they didn't quite ever get enough to eat, and they regularly ran out of toilet paper, but they sure as hell were fantastic at moving and killing. American soldiers might have looked askance at their uniforms or their idea of a parade march, but nobody would *ever* laugh at Israeli Paratroopers in combat.

The tryout wasn't technically over until the three-month training ended. Washing out was always a possibility, and the men were tested in ways that were physical and ways that were not. At one point, Yonah remembered the sheer torture of being brought in late one night after a physically grueling day and made to sit at little desks, be handed a paper and a pencil, and have to try to do a written test like you might do at school. The instructors dimmed the lights of the room, and after a few minutes of silence, the need to sleep was so overpowering that the trainees sat there, nodding in their chairs like bobbleheads, trying to keep their heads up and their eyes open.

They trained a lot on an obstacle course. In order to graduate basic training, every man had to beat the 12-minute mark on a nasty obstacle course that the IDF maintained north of Herzliya on the coast.

They started the "hikes" that would culminate with their 90 kilometer (almost 60 mile) "beret march" after which they would be entitled to wear the famous red beret. The first ones were pretty short; they started at 8 kilometers (about 5 miles) and worked their way up every week. The pace was intense though. These were not really "hikes" or "marches" as much as something between speed walking and a jog in full combat gear, always carrying one of their number on a stretcher just to make things interesting. Every year, the graduating class of Paratroopers tried to beat the time of last year's class on the same final march into Jerusalem, so from the very beginning they learned to move extremely fast across country.

The first real "Masa" hike, Yonah remembered the cold blackness of the night, the battle to keep his breath as they charged up hillsides and over boulders behind their commander. They had ended on the top of a hill somewhere in the rolling hills near Jenin. There, the unit had set up a sign written in wire that said "November '01" which was their "class" of paratroopers. They lit the sign on fire so the words were spelled in living flame against the pitch blackness of the night, and their commander stepped forward, welcoming them to the elite brotherhood of that fraternity. In the dark hills around them, they knew Palestinian terrorists crept toward the cities on the coast, carrying suicide vests, guns, knives, and anything they could find to kill the Jews.

Yonah had asked a guy, who considered himself a "peacenik" and wanted a peace deal with the Palestinians why he had volunteered for the Paratroopers if he was such a "peaceful" dude. He pointed to the lights of the city, clearly visible from that hilltop deep inside the West Bank and said; "That's why. Because my family lives *right there.*"

32

YERUSHALAYIM

Yonah's eyes snapped open and without any hesitation his body shot straight up in bed.

For a second, he wasn't sure where he was. He had been deep in the soft warmth of the deepest sleep imaginable. He was now sitting bolt upright in his boxer shorts in a small room with little curtains over the windows through which light from a streetlamp shone with an orange glare. There was a little bar fridge humming next to a tiny sink and a TV opposite his bed, which also folded into a couch.

Yonah had his M-16 in his hands. He'd snatched it out from under his pillow as his body propelled him upright in bed of its own volition. Somewhere in his subconscious, he knew there was danger.

Making no sound, Yonah's bare feet came down and he eased himself out of the bed without a creak. He grabbed the double magazine he always carried with his weapon and gently eased one of the magazines into the M-16, giving it a shove to make it "click" home with only the faintest sound.

Yonah was "home." At least, it was off-base. The IDF had arranged for a Kibbutz (originally a Jewish "commune." nowadays more like a village) to give him a special rate on housing in one of their buildings since he was a "lone soldier," someone who had no family in the state of Israel. This little room was his "apartment," and it was pretty comfortable, though Yonah barely ever saw it. He did get leave now and then, catching a bus from where the IDF dropped him off so he could get back here for a weekend.

Something was wrong. Yonah had heard it, he knew it. There was an enemy out there…

Suddenly he heard it again.

"K'tchink." "Tat-tat-tat." Gunshots.

Yonah carefully looked out the sides of the curtained windows without disturbing the curtains in case anyone outside was looking. These walls were flimsy; this room was nothing but a box to trap him in. The safest place was out in the night, hunting, not being hunted.

Yonah knew by the sound exactly what type of gun had made those shots. He'd been listening to gunshots out in the West Bank far too long now. He could tell an M-16 by the sound from a mile away, or a 7.62 mm machinegun. This was neither. Yonah had just heard a "Kalatch," a Russian "AK" family assault rifle. The *only* people around here who used those were *not* friendly.

He was out the door, past the streetlamp, and into the depths of the shadows beside the parking lot in a second. He made no more noise in his bare feet than a hare in a glade foraging for food at night.

Yonah's eyes were wide, his mouth just slightly open to minimize the sound of his breathing. Every muscle in his body was controlled. He prowled through the darkest shadows listening, looking, patiently stalking. In the buildings of the little village outside Jerusalem, the residents slept. It must have been after 1AM.

"Tat-tat-tat." Controlled shots, but several of them … what the fuck were they shooting at? They had been close.

Yonah moved through the bushes and across the little lawns, stalking across the darkest places of the Kibbutz grounds. He was homing in on the sound.

In Israel, soldiers were required to carry their weapons with them even off-duty. In fact, the Israelis considered it especially useful for off-duty soldiers to be armed. At any given moment there were hundreds of soldiers using every type of public transportation in the country, coming from or going to some base, all carrying fully automatic assault rifles on their backs. With terror attacks an almost weekly occurrence now, these off-duty soldiers were considered a semi-official backup emergency response system. A police officer had come up to Yonah on a bus in Jerusalem, put a hand on his shoulder, and said, "I'm sure glad *you're* on the bus!" as they heard the news of yet another terror attack on the radio. The Paratrooper had been surprised and asked why. Surely a trained cop was better at dealing with the complexities of urban terror than an infantryman. The cop had said; "If I shoot a terrorist ... so much paperwork! If *you* shoot him..." He snapped his fingers. "No problem." The grizzled man had winked at Yonah in that over-familiar Middle Eastern way Israelis had, then suddenly turned dead serious. "If you see a terrorist *shoot him in the fucking head.*"

Yonah prowled toward the edge of the Kibbutz grounds, systematically checking between buildings, sweeping around corners, checking rooflines. He moved with the liquid precision of a machine, totally unconcerned about the fact that he was wearing nothing but boxer shorts. It wasn't like clothes were some kind of protection anyway. The only protection he had was to remain unseen; to shoot them before they shot him. He had every intention of doing so.

There was one more shot. Loud now. He was close. Yonah suddenly realized that the shots were coming from just outside the Kibbutz perimeter.

He passed the last line of little buildings in the village and turned a corner, making his way downhill.

Suddenly, in front of him, Yonah saw blazing lights. He heard loud Arab music blasting from somewhere nearby. There was movement, voices … some kind of party.

Yonah frowned in shock as he came to a chain link fence beyond which a lot of tuxedo-wearing Arabs were dancing in a circle. A live band was playing Arab music. He could smell the food laid out on the tables.

It was the Arab village that had always been friendly to this particular Kibbutz. The two were back to back, almost running right into one another. These were Israeli-Arabs, not Palestinians. They had been loyal to Israel for a very long time and were given a lot of leeway as a result.

Yonah heard another shot from the AK about the same time a couple of kids on the edge of the wedding party saw the strange man in boxer shorts standing in the darkness just beyond the fence holding an M-16. He began to back up, realizing what was going on.

Arabs traditionally fired off guns at wedding parties. Weddings usually went on until way past midnight. Apparently, the Israeli government had let these guys retain an old AK-47 because they were friendly, and they were shooting off rounds in celebration.

Yonah saw one of the kids pointing at him and laughing. He glanced down, suddenly conscious that he had nothing on but boxers.

"Shit!" Yonah rapidly backtracked up the hill, moving fast to avoid any locals who might come out of their houses because of the noise the Arabs were making.

At least it wasn't a terror attack...

A man may be *in* the Paratroopers, but he isn't actually a Paratrooper until he has the right to wear the red beret. Yonah had earned his distinct, red-brown IDF paratrooper boots at the tryout, but he would not earn a beret without completing the 90K (almost 60 mile) "Beret hike."

Generations of IDF soldiers had completed these hikes. Most of them ended at Masada, the ancient fortress in the Judean Desert where thousands of Zealots (ancient Jewish rebels) had killed themselves rather than submit to slavery under the Romans. The Paratroopers had the longest such "hike" outside the special forces, and they ended theirs in Jerusalem. They would swear in in front of the Kotel (the "Wailing Wall") in the Old City, which the Paratroopers had captured in 1967.

For Yonah, it would be a return to the first place he'd come when he came to Israel. This time, his unit would climb the mountain on which Jerusalem rested on foot, making their way from the base near the coast where they had conducted jump training. Since the hike got faster every year, what had begun as a hike now resembled a nearly 60-mile marathon in full combat gear carrying a stretcher with a man on it the whole way. To go that distance on foot, they would start in the late afternoon, go all night, and end up in Jerusalem sometime by mid-morning.

The night was cold, a deep, humid chill that settled into the bones. Their uniforms were thin, designed for the desert. The IDF lost a lot more men to heat stroke than hypothermia, so they had extremely thin material for uniforms. Somewhere close to 0300, drizzle coming and going in sporadic bursts, the soldiers were soaked through and cold, even though they were moving fast.

Yonah kept his eyes on the men in front of him, strung out along the endless pavement of the road. He thanked God for the yellow stripe of paint that marked this dark nowhere as a *real* road, since they had started out across the rough hills surrounding their base, literally jumping from rock to rock down the steep, stony hillsides, a badly broken leg just one little slip away. They had been on the flat for an hour or so after that, the road a gentle incline through the Jezreel valley, and had kept up a fast jogging pace, their gear bouncing on their backs until they didn't feel it anymore, the four men carrying the stretcher changing out like clockwork, again and again as each grew exhausted in his turn, hour after hour after hour.

After the flat had come the climb. They had charged up the hills toward Jerusalem at something not quite a flat out run and way more than a march. After the briefest of hesitations, their platoon commander had just plunged straight into the first stream they came across, instantly sinking up to mid chest in the icy water. He charged across, not slowing a bit, and the unit went right after him. They had gone through the drainage tunnels under the new highway around Jerusalem, charging through endless, pitch dark tunnels up to their waists in freezing water. The rain had barely broken for their "beret march," and the runoff was still flowing in rivers down the steep hillsides around Jerusalem.

Now they had gotten back to something like a real road again and Yonah was just grateful that he didn't have to push his numb feet through water and silt any more.

Everything from the waist down was numb, and he wished desperately that everything from the waist up was too. He reached for his canteen, pulling it out and realizing immediately by the weight that he'd already drained it. He picked up his pace, moving toward the stretcher carriers. In addition to one of their guys (the lightest man in the unit), that stretcher had been used to stow a jerrycan of water, and Yonah needed some. As he jogged forward, he could see the empty jerrycan bouncing a bit in the grip of their unit lightweight, the plastic top dangling by its cord. So much for that.

Even if they hadn't gone right through a couple rivers of drainage water back there, Yonah would still have been soaked. He was sweating out liters of water every half hour, and desperately needed more. He knew perfectly well by now why these "marches" were usually done at night. In the Middle East, you jog a unit of guys more than 55 miles in the daytime and you will *kill* some of them. It had happened before. There had been a special-forces unit a couple of years earlier that had timed their start wrong, ended up doing too much of their march during the day, and had three men die from heatstroke.

Before the "march" they had spent the entire day hydrating. They'd had to line up every fifteen minutes and drain off an entire canteen of water in front of their commander.

Yonah had been extremely glad that they had been able to set out directly from the base where they had completed their jump course, since for the 60K "march" (the last of the "training" hikes before the big 90), they had been transported to the starting point by bus, which turned out to be a major logistical problem.

Imagine 80 ultra-hydrated men crammed into a bus in full combat gear, each of whom was so full of water that he had to urinate every ten minutes or less. Guys *had* to piss, they asked the commander to stop, he was having none of it, they drove on. The soldiers got creative. A large plastic water bottle was discovered and passed around in the back of the bus. Guys got in trouble, but they finally pulled over and lined up in a huge line of soldiers, shoulder to shoulder, literally filling a roadside ditch with a river of urine like a gigantic yellow stream.

Luckily, before the 90, they had *not* had a bus ride beforehand. Apparently, the commanders had learned their lesson.

Once Yonah settled into one of these things, his body seemed to absorb all that water, sweating it out through his skin and he didn't have the bus ride problem any more. In fact, after three or four hours of jogging in full gear, he got very, very thirsty again.

Yonah was relieved to see a few glow sticks on the side of the road. A couple of army trucks were parked under a streetlamp, and they had set out eight or so jerrycans of water, spaced about twenty feet apart, down one side of the road. The men gave a collective groan, it was the closest thing they could muster to a happy sound at the sight. Yonah heard a very hoarse squad leader doing his best to yell "five minutes! Get water! Five minutes!" in a voice that sounded like he had strep throat.

They stumbled to a jerky halt, bodies unwilling to stop their perpetual movement, clustering around the jerrycans. In seconds the areas around each had become sodden and muddy as water was spilled by men lined up to fill canteens.

Yonah gratefully filled his canteen, drained it, and filled it again, then did the same with the other one. He reached into his combat vest and dug around for the candies he had stowed under his ammunition clips. It was a trick they had picked up from each other after the first or second of these hikes. Your body would crash without some kind of blood sugar, but your digestive system was in "shutdown mode" and anything solid would make you puke, so Yonah carried little candies under his ammo.

He sucked down a couple of candies, putting them in his mouth and drinking water around them. It masked the overwhelming taste of plastic that all jerrycan water had, along with the taste of the mud and grit that inevitably got into army canteens. In minutes the exhausted squad leaders were herding the bleary, semi-conscious mass of men back into formation and onto the road again.

Jerusalem doesn't make any sense if you think about it in American or European terms. Just as cities in

Europe are older than those of America, so those of the Middle East are older than those of Europe. Paris was built on a river, because commerce was important and the technology existed to fortify a city almost anywhere, but Jerusalem was built thousands of years before that. Any city on the coastal plain was destroyed by endless waves of invaders until it disappeared or became a "tell", a man-made mountain of the rubble of hundreds of destroyed cities with the new one built on top.

Jerusalem was built *away* from the main trade route, in the middle of the high ground. It was built on the top of a mountain high enough to get snow some winters. It was a natural fortress, not built for commerce, but for war. Now they had to challenge that mountain like ancient invading Philistines charging up from the coastal plain on foot.

Another hour. They had settled into it now. They were perhaps dimly aware of the fact that they tread in the footsteps of the Israeli Paratroopers who had come this way in 1967, fighting a hellish, zero-range trench battle through machine gun nests and a maze of wire to take Ammunition Hill, and then proceeded into the Old City of Jerusalem, fighting their way to the Temple Mount. They were in their footsteps, but they were barely aware of it; focusing merely on putting feet in front of each other and keeping up their pace.

Yonah kept finding men struggling, slowing down and even starting to walk, and as they had been trained in the IDF, he shoved them and urged them on until they rejoined the group. They had been trained to grab any stragglers and pull them forward. The group advanced as a unit or not at all. As an American, he always found this communal mindset difficult, since it punished the merit of being the guy in front, but he did what he was supposed to do, pulling and shoving other guys as they neared the walls of the Old City.

The dawn was on them, and as soon as the sun rays hit, the heat started to build. As always, Yonah was a little surprised at the sudden intensity of the Middle Eastern sun.

As they came to the main highway between Ammunition Hill and the Old City, the commanders tried to revive their men from their stupor.

"At a run!" One of them yelled. "Come on! Yalla! *AT A RUN!*"

They started a Paratrooper chant, picking up the pace as they came into the city proper. Compared to their typical chanting during advanced training, it was weak, but they put what they could into it.

The Paratroopers charged up the winding road to the top of Ammunition Hill, belting out "Matayim ve Shtayim!" ("202" they were the 202nd Airborne) like fans at a football game. "Matayim ve SHTAIM, MATAYIM ve SHTAYIM!"

The presence of parents, girlfriends, and various relatives standing in the park to see them come in added to the energy, the young men didn't want to be seen as weak by all their families. Israelis knew the Paratroopers finished their beret march here, and dads, moms, and all sorts of assorted people had arrived to cheer on their boys, standing in the park under the monument built to honor the sacrifice of the Paratroopers who had once captured that place.

At last it ended. There was no more hill to climb. The trailing parts of the formation piled in as the earlier one started to circle, forming a clot of jerkily moving, sweat soaked, panting soldiers.

They got formed up into lines and came to attention. Their commanding officer walked up and down in front of them and said some words that for the life of him, Yonah wouldn't be able to remember later. He was trying not to wobble over too far and fall on his ass. Standing in a line seemed more challenging than usual.

They were dismissed, and the unit broke into a burst of filthy green uniforms. Soldiers found benches, the edges of the old trenches, or the ground, and finally came to a halt, looking a bit like battle casualties.

They'd run from evening of the day before to mid-morning, Jonah later learned that they had made record time. The march was over at last. They had earned the right to wear the red beret.

Blearily sitting on the ground with his back to a retaining wall, Yonah looked out at the boys in his unit. Moms and dads had come out in their cars, some of them bringing picnic lunches for their sons. Siblings and girlfriends had managed to be there, in that park at this particular time, because they knew their boys would end their march here - where Paratroopers had ended their marches since the fighting stopped in 1967.

For a second, Yonah imagined Walter and Laura, maybe with Hayden and Amy, walking up the hill, smiling the way the Israeli families were smiling.

The vision died. He couldn't imagine it. He couldn't imagine them smiling at this, at what he'd accomplished. He couldn't imagine them sitting there, happy, like the families with their little picnic baskets proudly hugging their sons.

Yonah shook his head. *Whatever*. It didn't matter now anyway.

He did end up calling his Mom long distance on his big, chunky Nokia cellphone to tell her that the Paratroopers would be lining up to do their swearing in ceremony at the Western Wall that night. He told her about a webcam that one of the Yeshiva schools kept focused on the wall all the time. He figured they might be able to see. As it turned out, they couldn't. Yonah was never sure who resented what more - she about the fact that he had barely even bothered to tell them about his graduation ceremony, or he that they hadn't asked about it and certainly never would have been there.

Yonah served through three of the most violent years of the Second Intifada War. The senior NCO (non-commissioned officer) at Sanur Base turned out to be right, some of those boys in that room didn't come home, except to an IDF military graveyard. In those days, there was no "separation wall" between the West Bank and Israel, so Yonah and his friends *became* that wall. They served in Operation Defensive Shield, and captured the city of Ramallah almost a dozen times during the course of the war. By the end of it, Hamas was permanently destroyed in the West Bank and the Palestinians were exhausted. Their campaign of terror against Israeli civilians was stopped in its tracks, and their attempts to join the Iraqi insurgents fighting the Americans right on the other side of Jordan were thwarted.

Jonah was changed forever by what he did and what happened. There were so many things that happened in so short a time, that they would take decades to sort out in his head. In the aftermath of his own little war, he signed up to go help the USA, working for a security contractor that was sending men to Iraq, and in the aftermath of that, all the bright, rapid years of adrenaline and movement and no time for thought finally came crashing down and Jonah faced a suicidal depression that was the blackest of his entire life.
He went back to Israel, cashed in his IDF "GI Bill" for a degree at an Israeli university, and, for the first time in his life, had a *damn good time.*

In the end, Jonah spent about ten years in Israel. Once in awhile, maybe once a month or so, there would be a call back to his family in the USA, an awkward conversation, and silence.

33

GOD'S COUNTRY

The evening was thick and muggy in the soft way that seemed particular to the South Carolina coast. The warm air from the highway blasted in through the open sides of the Jeep Wrangler as it buzzed along the straight country road between nowhere and somewhere.

Jonah leaned back in the passenger side of the Jeep. He didn't mind Miranda driving because it was her Jeep, plus he'd just spent several years in Israel without a car, as many Israelis did in the tiny country with European style public transportation. She said she had "control issues" in a sort of apologetic way. Jonah just smiled. His idea of "strange" and hers were completely different.

The countryside reminded Jonah just a bit of Papua New Guinea. It was vibrant green, but not quite *tropical* the way New Guinea had been. The air would sometimes carry the scent of magnolias and the dense brush seemed to hide mysteries like fireflies dancing in the summer night air.

Jonah was enchanted. The place was nothing at all like California, about as far from the Middle East as you could get. He had spent years and years in the Holy Land, now, on a very different sort of quest, he had arrived in God's Country. He liked the change.

Miranda's blond hair blew back in the wind as she stared at the long stretch of highway ahead of them. Jonah liked calling her "Randi Lee" even though she was too proper to approve of the nickname. She was a child of the South; a product of the idyllic town of old Mt. Pleasant right across the bridge and a little bit back present which was unlike any memory of his long, long past.

Jonah suddenly realized that he had spent so much of his life so keyed up, waiting for the next emergency, or watching for danger, that he literally could not remember the last time he had just sat back and relaxed. Sure he would take a moment at the beach in Tel Aviv to drop his things where the city ends and swim out into the warm Mediterranean, feeling as if he were alone in the silence of the water, but even there, he'd always have an eye on the beach in case someone tried to steal his stuff. Nobody in the Middle East ever completely relaxed, ever. Maybe that was why he'd survived there so long. He'd learned to be on edge and ready for disaster at any moment from the time he was a child.

Fighting against decades of subconscious training, Jonah forced himself to lean back in the seat, pick up the big beer can full of awful tasting cheap beer, and take a long pull. He listened to the music, watched the countryside … not as baggage, as a man on vacation from his demons. He looked over at Randi Lee. Her hair gleamed golden in the South Carolina twilight. She sat with the poise and certainty of a woman who had grown up knowing what the absolutes in life were; knowing without having to question or work it out, what was real, what was fake, what was right and wrong. Jonah felt a sense of pride that *this* woman loved *him*. Like the slope of a hill suddenly giving way; what had appeared to be solid hillside becoming a liquefied torrent of moving earth all in one instant, he felt something let go inside him. Jonah felt himself actually *relax* for the first time in many years.

As they came back to the little town with the flowering crepe myrtles and magnolia trees along the sides of the road and the little houses surrounded by Southern pines, Jonah suddenly felt that he had really, finally come *home*.

He had come around the world, back to the USA, when he realized that Miranda and he were in love. They had kept up a long-distance relationship over email and text and Skype calls for quite a while before she surprised him by suggesting he come to South Carolina and he surprised her by actually *doing* it.

Some of her family had wondered at the possibility of a man who had spent half his adult life in the Middle East being content in the sleepy town of Summerville, South Carolina. Jonah had smiled and explained that he was absolutely, completely, and in all ways done with having "adventures." Growing inside him for many years had been a longing for everything those quiet little suburban streets represented. He was finally home.

Jonah made the turn onto his street, noticing the way the front yard of their little house looked with the white picket fence. He and Miranda had spent hours building it by hand and painting it, but it had been worthwhile. The little house looked like something from a magazine, and more importantly to Jonah, he knew every drop of sweat and curse of frustration that had gone into all the work they had put into it. It was the kind of place that was perfect to raise a child.

He turned his truck, pulling into the driveway, noticing that his mother-in-law was sitting on the porch steps.

Jan (short for Janet) was a tall, graceful woman with an old-fashioned civility about her and a country sense of practicality. She could talk about the people who, more than the geography, made up the history of old Mount Pleasant before the flood of "Yankees" had irrevocably changed the town. Jan was the kind of person that anyone who met her would immediately recognize as truly kind. Jonah had liked her the minute he met her.

Undoubtedly, she was here to help Miranda watch Jase.

When Jonah had been living in Israel, he had had a lot of time to think through the idea of having a family. He had always wanted to have kids. It wasn't just a sense of wanting some sense of immortality, or loneliness like some people seemed to have as the sole reason for bringing a child into the world. Jonah had always wanted to take care of a child, to raise them, teach them, protect them. He had been scared for a long time that people become their parents when they have children. He had sworn to himself that no matter what, if he was going to be like his Dad, then he would never, *ever* have children.

That fear had faded when he and Miranda talked it over, and they both realized that they really wanted to have children. They had planned it, prepared for it, and consciously thought through everything from what kind of formula to get to what kind of names would *not* sound weird to all the other kids in school. Around their second anniversary, they had pulled the trigger and brought Jase into the world.

The wide shouldered man with the dark beard stepped out of the truck, smiling as he opened the gate. A little one-year-old was charging around the front yard. He was as blonde as his mom, as strong as his dad, and as stubborn as both of them put together.

Jason (who everyone called Jase) turned from where he was playing with one of his balls. He spotted his Dad walking into the front yard and dropped the ball, his dark eyes lighting up and his mouth going open with a wide grin.

"Daddy!" He said as clear as a bell. "Daddy-Daddy-Daddy!" Arms up, he charged faster than anyone would credit a one-year-old, with an extraordinary agility that spoke of future athletic greatness.

Jonah dropped his briefcase and reached down as the little blond bolt of lightning made for his leg like an incoming train. He ran with his forehead just a touch down, like a bull charging at life, enjoying every step.

In one swift motion, Jonah lifted his son into the air, tossing him, then catching him and holding him against his chest. Jase was laughing.

"Love you, buddy." Jonah said as he let the little rocket back down so he could continue running off his crazy energy.

Jonah never got tired of that greeting coming home from work.

34

CARPENTER CHRONICLES

Late that night, with Jase asleep in his crib, Jonah frowned at his computer screen. There was an email from Laura.

He sighed, feeling the heaviness of years of unspoken things that always weighed on him when he got something from his parents. The Franklin family never talked about anything. Things that were unpleasant just "went away" … except they *didn't* really.

Everyone talked in lots of happy sounding half-truths and it was always hard to know what was real and what wasn't when you heard from one of the many Franklin relatives. Everyone's lives were "so awesome" but they seemed so miserable. Jonah had ignored most of his family for years now.

He'd made an effort when he married Miranda. He had wanted, for once, to have a real family event. He'd paid for the wedding with his own money of course, spending a lot on good food and good drinks so that every guest would feel comfortable and have a good time. He'd been diplomatic, and coaxed Walter, Laura, Hayden, and Amy along with an aunt and an uncle to South Carolina where he had gotten married on the beach.

Jonah had wanted something normal, something proper. He had wanted the acknowledgement of the start of his life with Miranda to be recognized, witnessed, and celebrated. To that end, he had made a great effort to rebuild bridges with his family. Now, he wanted his son to have grandparents, so he maintained them.

It seemed that Walter and Laura were opening up to him.

He clicked on the email from his mom. As always, it was impossible to say what was from her and what was from Walter. He usually sat right behind her when she was on the phone or typing a letter and interjected his own commentary. Jonah had come to accept communication as being from "them."

Laura was asking him to look at a manuscript that Walter had written. They seemed eager for his feedback.

Jonah frowned as he opened the attachment, knowing that any "Big Thing" Walter might be working on had a less than zero-percent chance of ever being completed. Still, why not?

"The Carpenter Chronicles
By Walter Franklin
The life of a Carpenter. The Destiny of a World. The God of the Universe Chooses a People."

Jonah raised his eyebrows. "The *destiny of a world*?" It looked like Walter was as self-aware as ever.

The book seemed to be some sort of attempt to coalesce Walter's life story into a theological book, except it never quite got to the theology. Sort of like a "coming to Jesus" story without the "Jesus."

It hinted at "great truths" that would undoubtedly be revealed, but ended just before it had to actually enumerate them. It was typical of Walter. Jonah brushed past some of the hyperbole in the early chapters without paying much attention.

"God in his wisdom asks for a carpenter to be born. Not the Carpenter from Nazareth, born in Bethlehem. The Nazarene's task isn't complete yet ... A simple son of a poor minister will do."

Yeah, yeah yeah, you are like Jesus somehow… Jonah shook his head and scrolled...

"Walter could remember a time before he was formed, a time when he floated in the stars and communicated with God about the plan on Earth."

Uh huh ... talked to God about the earth before you were born ... gotcha...

The early chapters started to get interesting. Walter was telling a story of his life. How he had grown up. The challenges of living with a father that was more focused on his "Great Mission" than his kids. Walter had things in there that Jonah hadn't known or remembered about Walter and Laura's life before the kids had been born.

In Walter's memory, life before the burden of children seemed to have been sort of idyllic. He and Laura had been free to roam where they would and "search for truth." Some of the details of exactly how Jonah had come to live in some of the many places where he remembered being as a young child were interesting. He was surprised to realize that Walter had turned his back on a promising career making super expensive houses in Beverly Hills for rich people in order to run away on the First Missionary Trip when Jonah was only about four-years-old. They had lived in a travel trailer at an RV camp in Texas, hunting lizards and scorpions while Walter built some dormitories for missionaries.

Jonah shook his head in disbelief. As a father, it all struck him in a totally different way. *"How the hell do you decide to do that with three children?"*

Suddenly he came to the parts of his own life that he did remember. Things that Jonah had seen, places he had been, faint echoes of the vivid film reels with sights and sounds and colors and tastes that he carried in his head. Jonah felt anger rising within him.

It seemed that Walter had basically written the kids totally out of his life. They were mentioned … as baggage. They were mute, two dimensional cutouts that smiled in the background as The Carpenter went about his merry adventures like a cross between Indiana Jones and Jesus. He traveled out to permanently change the life of poor little savages in New Guinea, and the happy family smiled at the privilege of supporting such a "Great Man."

Jonah scrolled more, coming to the end of the book. It had taken a turn. It seemed that The Carpenter had now decided to reconcile his "growing doubts" by studying Judaism … The great insights of his amazing epiphany were soon to come. It ended there.

Jonah closed his eyes for a second, suddenly understanding the nature of what he'd been asked in Laura's email. They were eager for his "feedback" … it seemed they needed Jonah to fill in what he had learned in his odyssey from a mission base to a Yeshiva school in Jerusalem so that Walter's book would have some "meat" (or an actual point).

The thought of why he had made that journey, what it had cost him, what it meant, and how it had begun started a trickle of memory in Jonah, flooding back up from where it had been kept buried all these years. In an uncontrollable leak, the drops of colors and sounds and words began to unravel into live mental "video clips." It drummed from the inside of his skull, beating out an inescapable conclusion.

He stole your childhood. He made sure you started life in the hardest way possible, never living for anything but his whim of the moment. You were worthless baggage your whole life, and now, he wants, on the whim of the moment, to steal what you made out of that wreckage?

Jonah was being asked not just to sign off on a vastly edited version of his life, an act of self-immolation in itself, he was being asked to hand over the things he had learned as a result of his rejection of everything he'd seen, felt, experienced, and survived.

Jonah heard the voice of Laura on the phone, crying as usual, after an argument he'd had with them when he told them never to promise something to Jase and not come through. It had been a small thing, but it had bothered Jonah how Walter and Laura brushed off a promise to come to Jase's first birthday at the last moment. It had made him tell them not to make promises they weren't going to keep. He could still hear the wounded, self-righteous voice of Laura crying in an accusatory tone: "You've been done with us since you were 18-years-old!" He heard the response he'd given. "Have you ever stopped to think about why that is?"

Jonah leaned back in his chair, drinking in the peace and silence of his little study across the hall from Jase's nursery. Out the window a vine that South Carolina natives all considered a "weed" crept up the outside of the window. He actually liked it, and had "forgotten" to trim it on purpose. The rustling of the leaves in the nighttime breeze was comforting.

He had written after the army. He had written several books in fact. Action thrillers or fantasy stories, but he had stayed well away from his own life. How could you even begin to tell such a thing? How could you ever explain how the fuck you had ended up living in Papua New Guinea for more than a year? Where would you even start? Why even open up those in time from Charleston. She'd come from comfortable upper-middle class in a place where that still meant what it had back in the heyday of America. A place where guys played football and high school kids had "woods parties." It all tickled something in Jonah's mind that brought back a vision of life he'd once had on a freeway in Los Angeles, dreaming about having a *normal* life.

Randi Lee reached down and pulled the tab on a beer can. Jonah grimaced.

"Look, be careful! We don't want to get pulled over!" He'd spent so many years being on edge, watching for the next disaster, waiting for the inevitable catastrophe, or keeping on the lookout in case of a terror attack that he couldn't stop glancing at every bush along the side of the road expecting to see a police cruiser.

She smiled, laughing at the ridiculous contradiction of "Mr. Macho Paratrooper Guy" being a worry wart about an open beer can. "Oh for God's sake, would you *relax*? There is nobody out here! Nobody is going to care! Just listen to the music and chill already!"

She cranked up the radio and Jonah sat back in the seat, frowning for a second. Seriously, why was he constantly waiting for and expecting disaster at every moment?

He looked around. The South Carolina highway was completely empty except for them. It was like they were alone in the universe; a stretch of country highway, the fireflies in the woods, the buzzing of the Wrangler's exhaust, and the bro-country coming over the old speakers. It was the kind of music that puzzled Jonah. Nostalgia for hanging out with friends and drinking? Woods parties? None of it made any sense to him, but he liked it, not as a connection to nostalgia for some happy former time, but as a connection to a wounds? Why incite the reaction from his family? He still wanted Jase to have grandparents…

Jonah remembered the way the sun glinted off the waves as the morning dawned in the Pacific Ocean off the coast near Santa Catalina Island. The morning after the storm on the sea and the storm in his soul. He remembered how grateful they had all been to still be alive.

The Puker had slowed its sideways bobbing enough for Walter to finally climb up from the lower berth and navigate their way to the harbor at Santa Catalina. Jonah had rowed the dinghy to the island in search of help. Eventually, like survivors of some kind of natural disaster, the family had extracted themselves from the old wooden hulk and arranged passage to Long Beach on a ferry.

Hours from San Diego but still at least eight hours by freeway from the apartment north of San Francisco, they had gone to a car rental desk at a municipal airport to find some kind of transportation "home."

Walter and Laura took the lead, asking for a decent rental car, negotiating with the rental desk. Jonah and the girls had just stood by with incredulous looks on their faces. They should have *known* that this would be the end of a "fun family vacation."

Suddenly, Walter had turned to Jonah and reached out a hand. As if he were asking for a light from a fellow smoker, he asked Jonah to hand over his credit cards.

21-year-old Jonah, fresh off the plane from Israel, had stared at Walter as if he had just asked him to commit suicide with a fish in Klingon.

"You want me to…" His hand gripped his leather wallet where the credit cards that had started off the infamous hallway wrestling match were kept.

"Well we don't have any credit cards, we need to use yours!" Walter was impatient, annoyed. He didn't seem to understand how loaded his request had been.

Jonah had shaken his head. Of course they didn't. They had talked and talked and convinced their offspring to go on "one last family vacation" with them and now they needed Jonah to pay for the rental car which they had just *upgraded* with the salesman so they would be comfortable. His alternative was being stranded hundreds of miles from "home."

"I'll pay you back, Jonah." Walter had been fighting back his annoyance at the way Jonah was dragging his feet.

Jonah had swallowed a feeling of physical nausea. It was a lie and they both knew it.

"Uh huh." He'd handed over the cards ... *again*.

Walter had actually wanted to drive and Jonah had barely been able to restrain himself from punching him in the face. He'd just said; "No. *I'll* drive!" So he had, with no sleep from the night before, driven them straight through the night one more time, from Long Beach to Sausalito. One more night, kicking himself at what a fool he was to ever listen to his parents.

That had been just before he went back to Israel to be inducted into the IDF.

Jonah closed his eyes, opened them again, flipped open the aluminum lid of his old, dirty Mac laptop, and started to type...

"From things that have happened and from things as they exist and from all things that you know and all those you cannot know, you make something through your invention that is not a representation but a whole new thing truer than anything true and alive, and you make it alive, and if you make it well enough, you give it immortality."

-Ernest Hemingway